IG636804

Editor: Adie Hart

Cover Artist: Etheric Designs

ASIN: B0F8TYSF9H

ISBN: 978-1-961972-07-0 (Paperback)

Cosmic Captain

Cosmic Romance 4

Mars Quinn

Content Notes

The following is a list of what you can expect in my book. Some of these are triggers that may bother certain readers, and some may also be spoilers. If you have no triggers, please feel free to continue. If any of the following bother you, please skip this book. Your mental health is of the utmost importance.

**Please note that I am human. I tried to list everything, but if you're concerned about a particular topic or trigger, please DM me.

- Explicit sexual content

- Past sexual assault (not shown, but alluded to and discussed)

- PTSD

- Flashbacks

- Slavery

- Forced prostitution

- Co-dependency

- Depression (no SI or attempt)

- Self-harm

- Disordered eating

- Discussions of weight gain

- STI

- Immolation

- References to fights to the death

- Past domestic violence (side character)

- Swearing

- Alcohol use

- Minor references to alcoholism

- Praise Kink

Chapter 1

IS THIS A RESCUE OR SOMETHING ELSE?

Vince

I sat in my cell, hugging my legs, and pushed my face into my knees while trying to get lost in my thoughts, but it didn't work. The chill seeped into my bones and froze me in place, and the lumpy cot only had one scratchy blanket to keep me warm. The cold clung to the rough metal walls, not releasing its hold even when the sun was high and shining through the yellow smog of Xome.

Two years had passed since I'd been abducted by aliens. One night I'd gone to sleep, then woken up in a cramped cargo bay packed with humans. There had been no water, no food, and no escape. I'd spent that short journey pretending everything was a dream, which of course collapsed around me the second the ship landed and people rammed into me, sending me to the floor. Teddy had picked me up, and I'd clung to him for dear life. In the end, we'd been bought together to clean up after a fighting ring and dispose of the corpses in the incinerator.

It had been a rough life, but Teddy had been there. Quiet. Steady. Sure. Offering a hand or a hug when I needed it. That had changed a few weeks ago. He'd vanished one day without a single explanation. Someone had probably stolen him, or Agk, our owner, had killed or sold him and hadn't bothered to tell me.

Why would he? I was nothing but his property.

A single night later, I was sold.

Holding my knees even tighter, I shivered, exhausted, but I was terrified to close my eyes. Not that it would change what I saw. Everything was pitch black. There wasn't even a stream of light peeking through the cracks in the door. Tryk, my new owner, left me in darkness and only allowed me to see the light when he came for me.

Still, the moment I went to sleep... I shook my head. I had to remain aware.

The metal door creaked open, and I jolted, sweat sliding down my spine. My pulse ratcheted up as the light slowly spread across the dirty floor to my single cot against the far wall. As it brushed me, I pressed against the frigid wall, as if that would somehow stop what was about to happen. But it wouldn't. Nothing would.

Someone had bought my time. That was the only reason my door ever opened. If I performed well, I would be fed. If I fought, I would be punished.

With a deep breath, I lifted my head. I fisted the thin material of my jumpsuit to still the trembling. I would go somewhere else in my mind; I would be with someone else. Seth. My childhood best friend. My first love. My everything.

His deep brown eyes. His soft brown hair. His round face that was usually tinged with red. I missed him.

Regret was hard and cold in my stomach. I hadn't seen him for years, even before being abducted.

My new owner, Tryk, stood in the doorway, light illuminating his thin figure. "Get up."

I didn't fight, slipping into the fuzzy place in my brain that no one but I could touch. I'd put up a meager fight in the beginning, but I'd quickly learned it was pointless. Any damage I did was repaid tenfold. Inside, I wanted to rip Tryk apart. If I ever got the chance, I would kill him. I would slit his throat and grin at his dying face before pissing on his grave. That, after Seth holding me, was my favorite daydream.

"I sold you," Tryk growled, his skeletal fingers digging into my arm.

For being rather small, xoi were surprisingly strong. Their pencil bodies and watermelon heads topped with conical horns certainly didn't suggest it. Of course, Tryk and Agk both frequently employed batons that crackled with green electricity coming out of one end. That was without even talking about the towering garganlic aliens they both hired to guard them and their assets.

My stomach dropped when his words finally pierced the dark cloud in my head. To whom? Where was I going now? What was I going to be expected to do? My shoulders sagged, and my thoughts retreated behind the fog. This was my life. Being sold to whoever wanted me.

We stepped into another room with customers meandering around and other... workers moving through the space with blank expressions. Tryk threw me forward. My forearm burned from his tight grasp, and I staggered forward, crashing into a solid frame. Gentle hands caught me and directed me away from the warm heat that radiated from the wall in front of me. I looked up and up and *up*.

Man, this alien was huge. He wasn't only tall, he was broad as well. His pure black scales glimmered in the artificial lights, and red and gold glimpses of skin peeked behind the thick scales. His wavy purple hair framed his broad shoulders, falling down his back, while his deep green eyes, with slit pupils, took up a good portion of his face, giving me almost doll-like vibes. His chin was strong, though, and his nose was long as well as perfectly straight.

He was a drakcol. I'd seen a few on the screens around the city but never in person. This was who had bought me. Why? I'd never seen him before. Maybe he wanted me because of that drakcol prince who'd married a human, and now he had to have one.

Keep up with the current trends and whatnot.

Fucker, I thought. I would kill this one if given the chance, just like Agk and Tryk.

The large hand that held my bicep tightened slightly.

I shivered at the touch, bile rolling in my stomach. Seth. His perfect face appeared in my thoughts. His blushing cheeks. His soft voice. His kind heart. Why couldn't I have had him?

The drakcol's forehead crinkled as his head tilted. "Vince?"

How did he know my name? I didn't even think Tryk knew it. I was his property; he didn't need to know, let alone care, what I was called.

"I'm Captain Dontilvynsan. I am here for you."

Well, that was ominous.

"Do you have everything you need?"

What? Did he think that I had luggage? Like this was a resort and he was my chauffeur?

His lips quirked up at the corner. "I will take that as a yes."

The drakcol gestured to the door. Tryk watched us with a sneer before turning back to his waiting client, dismissing my existence.

The sunlight, while meager, blinded me. The yellow smog was thick, softening the rough metal buildings that crowded the street, which was lined with trash, puddles of piss, and aliens of all kinds. People called out their services from windows, doors, and from where they roamed the streets. Many of these "services" weren't what I would call reputable; they were everything from pleasure houses to stolen goods to taxi services. Shuttles zoomed overhead, making me flinch and crane my neck to watch them rush by. Foul odors of sewage, sweat, and an acrid chemical scent punched me in the face with every inhale.

But all I could truly focus on was the drakcol beside me, who breathed in an even rhythm while heat emanated from him and sank into my very bones.

As we took our first steps away from the pleasure house, I glanced around. Maybe I could make a run for it. Life on the street had to be better than whatever this alien wanted with me. Didn't it? Or would

another Tryk snatch me up? Could I even get away? Probably not. I
did have a tracker in my arm.

The drakcol's long fingers curled around my bicep, easily meeting.
"Please do not run. I will not hurt you, but I assure you, I will chase
you."

I recoiled from his burning touch. I hated the feel of his smooth
scales on my skin; I hated the feel of *any* skin on my skin.

A scoff built in my throat at his words. Not hurt me? Unlikely.
That's all aliens did to me.

He released me. "A human named Bartholomew asked me to
retrieve you."

I staggered. "Teddy?"

"I believe that's his endearment."

"You have Teddy?" I asked, my voice dropping. "What the fuck
are you doing to him? Where is he? If you hurt him, I will kill you.
I swear it."

"He's safe."

"Where. Is. He?" I demanded. I probably shouldn't shout. This
muscular alien could beat me to a pulp and not break a sweat,
but this was about Teddy. He'd been my sole comfort, my sole
companion. I would protect him no matter the cost.

"You are protective. Interesting." The alien led me through the
crowd with ease, not touching me as he gestured where he wished
me to go. "Bartholomew is safe on my ship. I will take you to him."

My hands fisted, shaking. I wanted to fight, because this was
clearly a lie, but I wouldn't make it far. He owned me. There was
no escape. There was *never* any escape.

When we reached the bustling port, the drakcol gestured to a sleek shuttle that stood out like a sore thumb. All of the other ships were boxy heaps of junk that appeared unable to fly, or at least not safely, but his shuttle was elegant with a pointed nose and perfectly painted markings on the sleek silver metal that I couldn't read. At least he had money. I would probably be able to eat most nights—as long as he wasn't an ass who enjoyed starving people. That was always a possibility. Fun times.

The alien glanced at me, forehead crinkled, and I couldn't say why. I hadn't spoken.

Stepping into the back of the shuttle, he led me into a room lined with stools on the sides and nothing else. Well, nothing besides four other human men that sat in there, huddling together near the back wall.

"What's going on?" I asked.

"I'm here for you. All of you," he said in an even voice. "I cannot retrieve all of the humans who have been stolen from Earth, but I can save all of you who remain on this planet."

The alien helped me sit down when my knees buckled, though I yanked out of his grasp as soon as physically possible. Either he was the kindest alien in existence, or he was planning something truly horrific. I assumed the latter. If being taken by aliens had taught me anything, it was that the universe was a hard place and the worst always happened.

He lingered in front of me, hands behind his back. "You are safe here."

I sincerely doubted that.

Dontilvynsan

The crowd teemed around me, shouting at me to come spend my money for whatever disreputable service they offered. I kept an eye peeled for trouble as the thoughts and emotions of those surrounding me crashed like an unending tide through me. Most of the time, I could keep a barrier between my thoughts and others' to calm the noise, though it was impossible to completely silence it. That human, Vince, had unnerved me.

His pale-pinkish skin, brown eyes so dark they appeared black, and straight black hair didn't set him apart from any of the other humans I'd seen, though he was smaller. Thin and delicate, too. His sharp features made his aspect pleasing to the eye as well.

None of that had distracted me, though. It was the dark swirl of despair, like a black hole in his mind, that had made me wish to pull away from him. Every time I'd touched him, my awareness had intensified. My inner fire was inconvenient most of the time, for I stole the thoughts and emotions of others, but physical touch made it far worse. And this human... When I touched him, the anguish had been far too much to bear. Then the human had thought of Seth. My youngest brother Kalvoxrencol's mate, Seth.

How did they know each other? Seth hadn't indicated knowing him; he hadn't even thought about it. Bartholomew knew Vince and wanted to retrieve him. They'd been bought together. Serlotminden, my immediate younger brother, had taken Bartholomew as his mate, and he would never let his mate be upset.

And we drakcol couldn't leave any human in captivity. It was our fault they were here. We were honor-bound to save and return them to Earth if they so desired.

Humans within Coalition space would be easier to free, as slavery was illegal; it would be a matter of finding them. But this planet, Xome, and many others, weren't a part of the Coalition of Planets. We couldn't force them to follow our laws or to free the humans, which was why I was purchasing all of the humans who remained on Xome.

I pushed Vince's unnerving presence out of my mind. The answers wouldn't be found as I roamed the streets. I had to claim two more humans. My second in command, Bimwoxcol, was finding the other three. She would bring them to the ship when she'd retrieved them.

We'd located the humans while aboard my ship, and I had them on my sensors. One was in another brothel, like Vince had been, and the other was owned by a family. Neither would be difficult to purchase, as before landing, I'd entered negotiations for all of the humans and reached an agreement with their current owners.

I went to the brothel first. This one was much more upscale than the one that had owned Vince, and it was in a far richer part of Xome, with cleaner streets and a lack of people offering their services at every moment. This human, too, was Vince's opposite, with a muscular frame, shining golden hair, and tall stature. He was... wary when I purchased him, but he was far less suspicious than Vince had been.

"What's your name?" I asked after I introduced myself and led the human outside.

"Camden," he replied, not saying anything else, and I didn't force him to.

What he and the others had suffered here were wounds that wouldn't easily heal. Securing the second human, Roman, whose skin was far darker than any human I'd seen before and who was completely bald, with facial hair, was far easier to retrieve because of Camden's presence. They stayed right next to each other, eyeing me and the aliens that swarmed around us.

I didn't blame them for their suspicion. Their lives had been at the whim of others, and this seemed the same.

It was not. They were free.

Once all the humans were gathered on my ship orbiting Xome, Seth would explain the situation. He was the leader of what Caleb, my second to youngest brother Zoltilvoxfyn's mate, called Team Human.

I ushered the two humans into the shuttle. All of them huddled in the back corner, watching me with narrowed eyes. Vince was in the front. His knees were drawn to his chest, and his thin arms were wrapped around them. The swirling emotions of his mind sucked me in as if it had its own gravitational pull. He was pain and anger and sadness and fear and numbness and hatred and longing.

I'd spent my life perfecting the static shield around my thoughts to protect my calm—I'd had to. But this human cut through it like a well-sharpened blade. The people that called to me most were my family. I felt them no matter how hard I tried not to. This human was worse, and it made no sense. He shouldn't affect me.

Caution would be needed when I interacted with him. If I felt anything too strongly, he might feel it to some extent. When I was angry or experienced a deep emotion, my inner fire sometimes shared it with those closest to me. On more than one occasion, my brothers had all inexplicably experienced the same emotion and known it was mine, not theirs.

As hard as I tried to contain it, I gave as well as stole. My calm and control had to be absolute.

My eyes moved to Vince as his thoughts bounced. He was frightened of me, and of what I wanted with him specifically. He'd spoken to the other humans and learned that I hadn't called them by name.

Vince was different, and he knew it.

I met all ten sets of eyes with their odd round pupils. All the humans who'd remained on Xome were now in my cargo hold.

I said, "I am Captain Dontilvynsan, second prince of the Drakcol Empire."

A few gasps sounded, but my focus was on the small human. Vince simply stared at me, eyes hard. He thought I wanted him because my younger brother had mated a human. He knew Seth, but he clearly didn't know that Seth was Kalvoxrencol's mate. Kalvoxrencol had done his best to keep Seth away from any news coverage. It appeared he'd been successful.

"The Drakcol Empire has recently become aware of the human trafficking problem, and we are taking steps to correct the situation," I continued.

Politicians, Vince thought, his voice as loud and clear in my thoughts as my own. Why? It made no sense. The word was familiar; I believed it referred to their leaders. I understood English, mostly, but occasionally there was a word or phrase that I didn't know. Vince also thought of wrinkled men with pale skin and even paler hair. What that signified and how it was attached to his snarky thought was a mystery.

The other humans still had an edge of wariness, but relief was also there as well. So was hope. Bright and burning.

"When we arrive on my ship, I have someone who will explain everything." It was better to let Seth say what the humans needed to hear. He would understand his own species better, and they would trust what he said for the simple fact that they were of the same species.

I headed toward the door, but at the last moment, I glanced back at Vince. His fear was a needle puncturing my calm. I wanted to reassure him and soothe the tension in his coiled muscles, but that wasn't my place. And from the way he drew away from every human and flinched at every touch, he wouldn't want it anyway.

As the door closed, Vince's thoughts crashed into mine. Once again Seth's face appeared, as well as a deep ravine of longing. What was Seth to Vince? And how was Kalvoxrencol going to react? My youngest brother was exceedingly protective of everyone he loved, and Seth was the dearest to his soul.

It would be interesting, to say the least. I would have to monitor the situation closely to protect Kalvoxrencol.

Chapter 2

SETH? IS THAT YOU?

Vince

The huge drakcol, Dontilvynsan—what a fucking name—left us behind in this... waiting room. The other humans clung to each other, basically piling into a heap in the corner. Security in numbers, as the saying goes. I sat away from them, on the same side of the room, but not touching.

I'd spoken to a few of the ten humans. Eight of us were men and the other two were women. The youngest was twenty-one and the oldest was forty-two. All but three of us were white. One woman was Black, as was one man, and one man was Latino. Everyone gave their names, and I nodded along, speaking up only when I had to.

Very quickly, I discovered that I hadn't been the only sex worker among the group, which wasn't shocking, I guessed. Camden, a blonde Adonis in his mid-twenties, had mentioned it first, and then Pierce, a red-haired woman in her thirties. I couldn't get my voice to work to spit out the words of what I was or had been, but I caught their gaze. We all shared the same hollow-eyed expression.

Soft conversation filled the room, but I didn't pay attention to it. I should have. We were literally all in this together. However, my thoughts remained on the drakcol. The man was massive. I'd never seen someone so large before. And those eyes. Fuck me. Why had they been so large and looked so innocent?

He couldn't be, obviously.

He'd known my name. How? Why? Dontilvynsan hadn't known the others' names, but he'd known mine. He'd said he had Teddy. Had Teddy told him? I gripped my legs tighter as I pushed my face into my knees. I didn't want to be taken. I'd had enough of that.

Seth.

I missed him. Though if I was honest with myself, I missed what he represented. Home. Earth. A time before this hellish nightmare had happened. I wanted to go back, but the past couldn't be overwritten.

One second I was thinking about Seth, and the next the engines had shut off and the shuttle was utterly still. I blinked, looking around. I had no idea what had happened between point A and point B. It was like time had jumped. Which was stupid. And it didn't matter. Survival. That was what mattered. I looked at the other humans. All of us were tired and scared. We'd been ripped from home, taken from people we loved. No one wanted to be here.

I stood. "We all need to stick together."

Camden nodded, arms crossed, making his muscles bulge. "These drakcol don't seem bad."

The older man, Brad, scoffed, his already harsh features looking even more so. "We've all thought that before."

Pierce said, "True. But we won't know until we go, and it's not like we have a choice."

That made all of us fall silent.

Choice. None of us had been able to make a single choice in the last two years. Many of us who'd been taken had been sold to restaurants and eaten as exotic tastes. Others had been sold to fighting rings and had died at the hands of far larger aliens. More to brothels. More to the homes of the rich. And even more had been sold off-world.

Our choices had been stolen time and time again, and here we were with no choice once more.

The door opened, and Dontilvynsan and another drakcol stepped inside. The second one appeared female. She wasn't as tall as Dontilvynsan nor as muscular, though she was still a sight bigger than me at probably the mid-six-foot range. Her dusty red scales had pink and orange skin around them, and her black hair was cut short on the sides and much longer on top.

Dontilvynsan introduced her as Commander Bimwoxcol, then said, "This way. Someone is waiting to explain everything to you."

Someone. Perfect. Nothing like a mystery when you'd been abducted by aliens and sold into slavery. It wasn't like our whole lives were a giant fucking mystery.

Dontilvynsan paused and stared at me, head cocked. For the first time, I noticed his pierced ears. They looked like elf ears—not Tolkien, they were longer than that, but not quite *World of Warcraft* elves either.

A small green stone hung from the golden ring at the pierced tip, and studs trailed down the length to his lobe, which had long chains that also ended with rough green stones. A golden cuff accented the length of his ear.

His tail flicked, and my gaze widened. He had a tail. Interesting. I'd never seen any drakcol with one on a screen. The dark purple tuft on the end was like a lion's, and the entire appendage was covered in scales like the rest of him.

"It's a human," he said, looking directly at me.

"What?"

"The person waiting to speak to you. He's a human. My youngest brother Prince Kalvoxrencol's mate."

Well, that was something. I would rather speak to another human. A single glance at the group assured me they agreed as well. Another human would understand more than an alien ever would.

He motioned for me to exit.

My hands curled into fists as I shuffled past him, but he didn't touch me, which made me relax. The bay door opened, and I stepped out. I spotted not one, but two humans. Both were familiar. My eyes skittered over the tall human with short black curls. Teddy. He called my name, but my gaze was riveted to the other human, a husky, average man standing next to a gray-blue drakcol.

My heart thumped so loud that it reverberated in my ears. Every dream I'd conjured hadn't done justice to my childhood friend or my first love. His soft brown hair brushed his forehead. His round face was covered with a shocked expression, his deep brown eyes wide. He was wearing a hoodie, like he always did.

"Seth," I cried.

A choked sob escaped from my lips. I was running across the sprawling room before I'd even thought about it. Seth met me halfway. We crashed into each other. I cried as I wrapped my arms around his solid frame, burying my face in his chest.

He gripped my back. "Vince, what are you doing here?"

"I could ask you that."

Seth chuckled. "It's a long story."

I leaned back to look at him. He was here. Seth was right in front of me. Every dream I'd had was possible. I couldn't go home, but I sure as hell could have the man I'd loved since I knew what love was.

"I'm so glad you're here." I went up on my toes and pressed my lips to his.

He started, but didn't pull away. I'd kissed him many times over the years, all friendly in his thoughts, though I wanted more. Seth cupped my cheeks and kissed me back for the barest moment before pulling away.

Suddenly, light flooded the cargo bay. Seth was yanked away and was replaced by the gray-blue drakcol, snarling. Silvery-blue hair hung around his muscular frame. His amethyst eyes practically shot sparks as light pooled under his scales, nearly blinding me. Massive dragon wings sprawled, completely shielding Seth from me, and his tail thrashed.

Teddy appeared by my side and said, "I'm here too."

I barely spared him a glance. I glared at the drakcol, refusing to back down. "Seth, come here."

The drakcol clasped Seth's arm, and I stepped forward. I'd let Seth be hurt once before by that asshole Travis, and I wasn't going to let it happen again.

"Let him go," I said.

"Do not kiss my mate, human."

"Mate?" Seriously, Seth? Again. Again, you were with some asshole.

Seth glared at the drakcol. "Kal, calm down."

The drakcol took a deep breath and stepped back, though his tail coiled around Seth's ankle in a possessive move that had me glaring.

Seth grabbed the drakcol's arm and smiled. "Vince, this is my husband, Prince Kalvoxrencol. You can call him Kal."

Seth was the human mate to the drakcol prince who'd abducted him. My heart shattered into a thousand pieces as I stared at them, wrapped in each other's embrace. Then I shook my head. No. I'd loved Seth first. I was a better option than this angry alien. I refused to give him up.

"Vince is my childhood friend. Remember, Kal? I told you about him."

"I do." Kal's expression softened as he looked at Seth, but it hardened the moment he turned toward me.

I crossed my arms. I wasn't going to give Seth up again, not after the last time when Travis had separated us.

Teddy draped a bony arm over my shoulders. In a small voice, he said, "I'm here too, Vince."

I shrugged him off, fighting the curling unease. "Hey, you didn't vanish or die."

"Nope." He pointed to another hulking drakcol with royal-purple scales and white hair and a lot of gold jewelry at his side. "He's Kal's older brother, and he wanted to rescue me, but we crash landed on an ice planet. Took me a bit to get back to you. Serlotminden, this is Vince. Vince, this is Serlotminden or Mindy."

"We are also husbands," Serlotminden announced.

My eyebrows rose. Jealous, much? "Well, you two move quick."

"He's cute and has a nice ass," Teddy commented.

I forced a chuckle, but my eyes went back to Seth, who grinned. Seth disentangled from Kal and pulled me into another hug. "Let me talk to everyone, then we can catch up. It's been years."

Since Travis, but I wasn't sure if we were talking about that or not.

"Everyone," Seth said, "if you can come this way, I'll explain everything."

Dontilvynsan

People were confusing and rather annoying. I watched the situation unfolding in front of me closely. Vince was in love with Seth. Kalvoxrencol had realized as much, sensing the threat, and Serlotminden and his human mate, Bartholomew, headed toward them, also guessing Vince's feelings. The only person who didn't know was Seth. He was simply overjoyed to see his oldest friend.

I moved toward Vince as Bartholomew introduced Serlotminden, who promptly declared he and Bartholomew were also husbands—the human term for mates, I believed. Serlotminden didn't want competition for his mate, and Vince was perfectly happy to oblige. He had no feelings but platonic for Bartholomew that I sensed.

Vince joked with them, but his eyes stayed on Seth. A strong sense of longing ripped through him. He wouldn't relinquish Seth, and he was willing to fight Kalvoxrencol for him, which wouldn't end well. Kalvoxrencol loved his mate desperately. He wouldn't have surrendered him, even if it had been possible for drakcol to mate more than once.

What a mess. A mess I would have to watch to ensure Kalvoxrencol wasn't pushed too far. He didn't cope with such things well, and I didn't want him to lash out in anger or fear.

When Seth moved across the room to the other humans, Vince and Bartholomew remained where they were. That would not do.

"Go, Vince," I said. "You should hear what Seth has to say as well."

He rolled his eyes and strode across the room. Bartholomew sidled up to him, leaving me and Serlotminden alone.

"This is not good."

"No," I replied. "He loves Seth."

Serlotminden scrubbed a hand through his hair. "Pest will not survive Seth abandoning him. Humans don't mate only once like we do."

I glanced at Seth. Nerves churned in his gut as he spoke. He hated talking. He disliked being the center of attention, but he was the best choice to speak to the humans, because Caleb didn't look human anymore and Bartholomew was as new as the rest of them.

Kalvoxrencol grabbed his mate's hand, and Seth relaxed. Love bloomed in his thoughts. Seth didn't care for Vince romantically.

Vince could desire romance all he wanted, Kalvoxrencol could worry all he wanted about humans being able to have several mates mate in their lifetimes, but both were a moot point. Seth loved Kalvoxrencol, and that wouldn't change.

"Seth will not leave him," I said.

"He doesn't like Vince?"

"Not romantically." Normally, I didn't divulge the thoughts and emotions I overheard, because people were entitled to their privacy, but Kalvoxrencol was different. He was our youngest brother who'd caused so much trouble because he hated himself. Seth had saved him. We would do anything to keep Kalvoxrencol safe and content.

"Vince will be disappointed," I said.

"Should you warn Pest?" he asked, looking at our little brother.

I clapped his shoulder. "Pest should trust his mate, Speedy. As should you."

He frowned.

"You don't need to claim Bartholomew. You know how he feels about you."

"They were close."

"So? He's allowed to have friends."

Serlotminden glanced toward his mate, who stood next to Vince and Seth. Another addition to Team Human—Caleb would be pleased. Of course, all of the humans, including Vince, might choose to go home.

The thought of Vince leaving made my soul clench and my tail flick. I did not like it, which made no logical sense. I didn't know this human. But... but I sensed his emotions and thoughts like no other.

That was more of a curse than a blessing. When he realized what I could do, he would despise it. Everyone did, even my brothers, though they felt guilty about it.

I should want him to return to Earth to ease Kalvoxrencol's stress and mitigate the inevitable drama, not to mention the hurt Vince's anger would cause me. But I didn't. Why? What was it about this slip of a human? I didn't know, but I needed to bury it deep within me. I had to be in complete control at all times.

Chapter 3

YOU CAN DO WHAT?

Vince

I stood next to Seth, unable to take my eyes off him. His hands trembled in the pockets of his hoodie, but he was pressed against Kal, and the drakcol had his tail wrapped around Seth's ankle. While Seth shivered with nerves, his deep voice was steady.

"The drakcol have offered to take each of you home, should you want to go. The choice is yours. We first have to go to their planet, Tamkolvanloknol." At the wide-eyed expressions, Seth laughed, and I closed my eyes to savor the throaty noise. "I know. Believe me I know. This," he said, gesturing, "isn't a long-haul ship. Unlike the xoi who abducted you, it'll take the drakcol six months to reach Earth. They need a different ship."

"And if we want to stay?" Brad asked, gripping his tattooed biceps.

"You can," Seth replied. "Anyone who wishes to remain is welcome to. Emperor Kontolmakqilnen will extend citizenship to anybody that decides to stay. It'll be your decision completely, but if you want to go home, you're going to have to be patient. It'll take time to arrange transportation, but I promise you will be able to get home."

Several people sagged in relief.

Before people could ask questions, Seth continued, "You do need to be aware of the fact that if you choose to go home, your memory will be erased."

"What?" I asked, heart pounding. I could forget all of it. Everything that had happened could be taken away. The blood, the burning bodies, the dead, the abuse, the... I couldn't even finish that thought.

Time could be unwritten.

Seth said, "The Coalition of Planets doesn't allow undeveloped species to retain their memories if they go home. Either you become citizens or you're categorized as samples taken for science and your memories of being off Earth will be wiped."

That ignited rounds of questions that Seth did his best to answer. For me, the words went in one ear and out the other. All I focused on was the fact the memories haunting me would be taken. Freedom. I would be free.

Seth lifted his hands and ordered people to let him finish.

I'd have to leave him. I wouldn't remember seeing Seth again. That gave me pause. Yes, I had a family on Earth—my parents and my siblings, namely—but I'd been gone for years. They would think I was dead at this point, and if I was honest, we'd never been that close. But Seth... I'd regretted leaving Seth the first time, what about this time?

Teddy grabbed my arm, and I shuffled away, stomach lurching from the contact. He frowned at me, but I ignored the look and hugged myself.

The captain, Dontilvynsan, came closer while Teddy's husband, Serlotminden, snagged Teddy's hand. Teddy gave him a small smile.

My focus returned to Seth. Could I leave him, to be free of the memories of the past? My breath stuttered at the memory of someone screaming at me. The snap of my finger. The drip of sweat as a man panted above me. Bile burned my throat as I struggled to breathe.

"Vince?" Seth asked.

I couldn't answer; the past was strangling me. Dontilvynsan appeared in my line of sight. He took a deep breath as his eyes met mine. I struggled to copy, so he repeated it. I managed to suck in one breath, then another and smile at Seth. My Seth.

"I'm good. I don't suppose there is food somewhere on this rust bucket? I'm starving."

"My ship does not have rust," Dontilvynsan said in a bland voice.

"He's joking, Don," Seth said. He draped an arm over my shoulders, and I stiffened. My first instinct was to yank away, but I forced myself to remain calm, though my pulse pounded and sweat gathered on my temples.

This was Seth. He would never hurt me. Ever.

I slung an arm around his waist, pulling him close. I buried my face against his shoulder, breathing him in. He smelled the same. Citrus. I'd always associated him with that fragrance. "I missed you."

He kissed my head. "I missed you too."

We settled in a mess hall. A couple of other humans, Brad and Camden, had decided to eat with us, while the rest had retreated to their rooms. Don had tried to place us in separate rooms, but everyone, besides me, decided to double or triple up. They didn't want to be separated, which I didn't blame them for. Personally, I was looking forward to some space. Besides, when the nightmares came, I wouldn't wake anyone.

Seth and, to my dismay, Kal sat down across from me. I glared at Kal, and he returned my cold look. His tail coiled around Seth's wrist in a possessive gesture that I refused to get used to. I wanted to rip the prehensile appendage away. Seth wasn't a possession, and I wouldn't let him remain with another abuser. Never again. I wouldn't watch my best friend lie about bruises or excuse his boyfriend's temper.

I should've fought harder to get him away from Travis, and I wouldn't abandon him a second time. Fate, the universe, or whatever had given me a second chance and I wasn't going to squander it.

Oblivious to my silent stand off with Kal, Seth asked, "How did you get here?"

"I could ask you the same thing, but I've heard of the drakcol prince who abducted and mated a human. You. I guess."

He grinned, blush staining his round cheeks. "Yeah. Kal came and got me."

"Stole you."

Kal crossed his arms.

Seth laughed. "Yeah, he abducted me and my cat."

"You got a pet? You always wanted one, but..." I trailed off, stopping before I actually said Travis's name.

But it was enough. Seth turned a pale green.

Kal pulled Seth close, hand buried in his hair, and whispered in a low voice, "I'm right here, Husband. You are safe." He glared at me, but he continued to snuggle Seth.

Longing shot through me. I should be the one to comfort him. I shouldn't have upset Seth in the first place. My stupid mouth had gotten me in trouble again. Shocker.

After a minute, Seth drew away and gave me a shaky smile, though he stayed pressed against Kal's side, holding his hand in a tight grip. "Anyway, Kal and I got married, basically." He gave Kal a sappy look. "We fell in love."

I grunted. Sure. Fall in love with the dude that kidnapped you. That was healthy.

"And you?" he asked.

"Got taken in my sleep. Woke up on a ship. Was sold to a fighting ring for a couple years with Teddy." At the thought of Teddy, I shot a glance around the crowded cafeteria. He was nowhere to be seen. A stab of... longing, hurt, I wasn't even sure went through me. We'd been inseparable, and he'd left me without a word. Perhaps that husband of his had made Teddy leave? I would have to make sure Teddy was safe too.

"Did you...?"

"I didn't have to fight," I replied. "We cleaned up after the fights and burned the bodies. Not pleasant, but we survived." That was putting it mildly. I shook off a blood-curdling scream and the thud of desperate hands against metal. The "dead" fighters weren't always dead when Teddy and I had to dispose of them. I would never forget it, not for as long as I live.

Seth grabbed my hand, and I entwined our fingers, all the while fighting the urge to yank away and hug myself. The feel of our palms touching... I forced the sensation to the back of my mind, lest I remember other times skin rubbed against mine.

Seth said, "We're together now."

"We are."

I forced a smile to my lips, staring into his deep brown eyes. I'd spent years looking into these eyes, then spent years missing these eyes, and now I never wanted to look away. After everything we'd been through, here we were again. I was never going to release him.

Dontiluynsan

Kalvoxrencol was two soulbeats away from launching across the table or dragging Seth away. He couldn't decide on which choice was better. Both would make Seth mad. I hated interfering with such things, but Kalvoxrencol was more fragile than most.

Unfortunately, I couldn't rely on my next younger brother. Serlotminden and Bartholomew had made only a token appearance in the canteen before disappearing with fucking on their minds.

Thank the Crystal, Zoltilvoxfyn recognized our younger brother's plight. He and his mate Caleb walked toward them. Caleb was trying to socialize with the other humans, but he was struggling. He didn't look human anymore, because he wasn't.

He'd been a wayward human spirit who had died many cycles ago. Zoltilvoxfyn, because of his inner fire, could see him. They fell in love, and the Crystal ended up forcing Caleb's soul into an empty drakcol body.

Caleb sat next to Vince and smiled and leaned his cane against the table. "I'm Caleb. Nice to meet you," he said in garbled human speech.

He struggled to speak his native language, and the ship's NAID—Network of Artificial Intelligence for Drakcol—couldn't translate him when he did. Edith, a sentient NAID, did better, but she was linked to Kalvoxrencol's system back on Tamkolvanloknol. Caleb's Drakconese was near fluent, but he liked to speak in human speech. It made him feel human while the mirror told him he was not.

Caleb held out a hand, and Vince recoiled as fear and disgust washed through his mind. He didn't want to touch anyone—this seemed to be the same response he had when someone attempted to touch him. Only Seth and Teddy were acceptable, and even their physical affection wasn't highly desired.

Zoltilvoxfyn held his mate close when Caleb's expression fell.

Seth explained, "Caleb's human. It's really complicated."

Shock followed by disbelief rolled through Vince.

"It's not so complicated," Caleb said as he launched into the story.

Vince listened, but his thoughts returned to Seth.

The emotions and thoughts bouncing around the canteen were a lot, but between my uncanny ability to sense Vince perfectly and my brothers' and their mates' sweeping emotions, it was enough for me to want to crawl into bed and seek sleep to simply have a break.

Seth glanced at his screen for what must have been the thousandth time, and I suppressed a laugh. He couldn't stop checking on his and Kalvoxrencol's unborn child. It was an obsession. His anxiety—I believed that was the human word for the medical condition he had—made it difficult for him to be away from their kit.

"What?" Vince asked.

Seth grinned. "Kal and I are having a baby."

"What?" Vince's voice was laced with pain as the agony that whirled through him nearly sent me to my knees.

He turned the screen around to show the growing fetus in a tube of green liquid. "Drakcol technology allows for same-sex couples to have kids. As well as inter-species ones," he added, cheeks pinking. "This one is mine and Kal's. The doctors don't know how long our baby will gestate, because humans are pregnant for forty weeks and drakcol are pregnant for eighty-two, roughly. Our rotations are not exact."

Drawn in by Vince's spiraling emotions, I walked in his direction to... I was unsure, and yet, I couldn't help but close the distance between us. He needed someone. He needed protection.

Vince swallowed. "You're having a child? I never thought you wanted one."

"I didn't, because I was afraid of being my grandparents," he said, looking down.

"You are not them," Vince barked.

"I know." Seth grinned at Kal.

"Congratulations," Vince said, drawing Seth's attention back to him.

"Thank you." Seth beamed, stroking the image of their baby as Kal snuggled him close. "We're really happy."

"I can see that," Vince whispered.

"Perhaps you would like me to show you to your room," I offered, coming up behind him.

Fear spiked in Vince, making my hands fist. Images of me forcing myself on him wafted through his mind as he ordered himself to stay still. "I'm good."

"Of course. I merely hoped to offer assistance. Nothing more."

Seth smiled shyly at me. "That's so nice of you, Don."

Kalvoxrencol looked directly at me and thought, *Take him away, Captain. Please. I need a moment, and I don't want to hurt my mate's feelings.*

Zoltilvoxfyn caught on to what was happening, though he couldn't hear our younger brother. "It's late. We should retire as well. Seth, you will have a busy day starting early. The humans will have questions. You are the leader of Team Human."

Seth groaned, and Caleb laughed, bouncing in his seat before he stilled, grimacing in pain. He often forgot the differences in this body versus his old one. He was taller, broader, and stronger, but this body had been in a severe shuttle accident, which left him in constant pain, with scarred skin on one side of his head that was free of light gray scales and reddish-brown hair. His condition was managed, but even our technology couldn't heal him.

Standing, Seth grabbed Kalvoxrencol's hand. "We should go to bed." Seth faced Vince and asked, "Did you want me to take you to your room?"

Only if you join me, he thought. "No. The captain here will show me the way."

I led Vince out of the canteen. He stayed as far away from me as possible, nearly hugging the vine-covered wall. I watched him closely for an allergic reaction—something Bartholomew suffered from—but nothing. It appeared he was fine with the multi-colored flowering vines creeping over the ceiling that draped down the walls, the potted plants, and the blue moss flooring.

His thoughts bounced around from the plants to me to what the future held and to Seth. Always Seth. He never left Vince's thoughts for long.

We stopped in front of his quarters, and I said, "Here you are."

He crossed his arms. "Now you want to demand payment for saving me."

"No." I'd expected as much from his thoughts. "While you seem perfectly attractive and I don't have a preference of gender in who I'm sexually attracted to, I have no interest nor would I force or blackmail you into such an arrangement."

"Then why were you trying to get me alone?"

"I was attempting to remove you from Kalvoxrencol's presence. He knows of your affection for Seth. He feels threatened. I wish to protect my younger brother."

"If Seth truly loves him, he wouldn't worry. And he has a fucking bad temper. I won't leave Seth with someone like that again."

I almost asked him to clarify when a fuzzy memory surfaced of a blonde-haired man slapping Seth across the face. My hands fisted. I'd known that Seth had been hurt in the past, but seeing my mate-brother abused made me furious. I wanted to hurt that human. Badly. I would protect Seth. He was my brother as much as the ones who shared my blood.

"Kalvoxrencol would never hurt Seth. Not physically or emotionally. He loves Seth, and Seth loves him."

Vince scoffed.

"He does." I didn't like divulging private thoughts, but Vince had been hurt badly enough that he needed to be told. I'd seen his thoughts, and I'd had a glimpse of what he'd endured. "I do not say this to hurt you. In fact, it's the opposite. Seth loves Kalvoxrencol. He doesn't think of you romantically."

"And you're an impartial person to ask? You want me to go away for your brother's sake."

"No. Seth is ignorant of your infatuation, and he will not leave his mate."

"I don't believe you."

"You don't have to, but I'm right."

"How do you know?" he questioned. "I can't imagine Seth confiding in you."

I disliked telling people of my gift even more than speaking of private thoughts. Everyone, and I did mean everyone, reacted poorly. Maybe I didn't have to tell him? I wasn't obligated to. I could keep it hidden for one more night, though not for much longer. Vince would hear about it from someone else eventually.

I hesitated, but in the end, Vince had been harmed and he needed someone to protect him.

I carefully said, "I don't know how much you know of drakcol, but we each have gifts called inner fires. They vary from person to person."

"So?"

I couldn't tell from his thoughts if he knew or not. "I have a rare inner fire."

"How special for you. I'm sure you're proud. Let me throw you a parade."

"I can steal thoughts, or read minds is the more common way of thinking of it."

This dude is full of shit, he thought.

I didn't understand all of the words, but I understood the gist. Human speak, specifically English, had been fairly easy to learn. Both Seth and Caleb thought in it constantly. I could understand it, but I couldn't speak it. Some things I didn't know, but most people also thought in emotions and images, which assisted me in understanding the context.

"I'm not insane. I can hear your thoughts."

Vince stared straight at me and thought, *Then let's play a game.*

"Sure."

He blinked. *Repeat after me. Elephant. Pink. Detective. Diamond.*

I tried to the best of my ability to repeat the words he thought at me. I had no idea what the first one or the last one was. The second was a color, and the third was a word Seth thought of often regarding his human entertainment.

"Well. Fuck," he breathed.

Humans. They used that word for many reasons. Drakcol used it for a single reason—copulation.

"You know... everything." He bobbed his head, which startled me. Why would he be conceding to my dominance? I shook my head. Humans used this bob or nod as an acknowledgement. So many differences I'd had to learn over the years.

"Only what you have thought." Here was the part where he hated me. Everyone did. They despised my inner fire, and most of the time, I tried not to agree, but it was difficult. My life would be much simpler if I hadn't been given this curse.

Vince smiled. "God, this makes it so much easier."

He... wasn't upset. At all. He was happy. I stared at him, mouth hanging open. Even relaxed Caleb and sweet Seth disliked my inner fire. Even my brothers detested it at times. Even my parents despised it when my inner fire revealed itself.

Vince leaned against his door frame with a cocky grin, which rang false in his mind, but the expression did... something to me. He said, "I'm not giving Seth up. I don't give a fuck about what Kal wants. I gave Seth up once before, and I regretted it. Kal is not the best person for him. I am. And you can feel my sincerity."

"I can, but it doesn't make it the truth."

He laughed, and I swallowed at the light sound. It was lovely. So very lovely.

"True, but let's see." Vince turned toward his quarters, then paused. "I would prefer if Seth didn't learn of my feelings from you or about what happened to me."

"I'm not in the habit of sharing people's private thoughts."

"Thanks."

Vince disappeared, but I lingered, unsure of why. Eventually, I wandered to my own room.

Vince

I scrubbed my arms, shaking. The warm water sluiced over me and the lights were on as high as possible, illuminating every nook and cranny. I could see everything: the large soaking tub and toilet on the other side of the bathroom. The shower was formed of rocks, and the water escaped from what appeared to be a waterfall. Not even the bathroom was free of the plants that grew all over the ship. Moss grew on the rocks and small plants grew along the edges.

Sitting on the wide stone bench, I vigorously rubbed my skin with a washcloth until it was bright red, and even then, I kept going. I swore I saw the hands from the various aliens holding me.

At least it was a water shower. The only "shower" I'd had access to when Tryk bought me was a vibration one that knocked off the dirt and disinfected me. But it never felt clean. Something about water was cleansing and freeing. Sort of.

A chime sounded, and I looked up from where I was tucked against my knees. I shut off the hot water and tugged on clothes. The apartment I was in was nice enough, with a bedroom, bathroom, closet, and a living room that had a small table in the corner, though there wasn't a single chair with a back anywhere in the apartment. The table had woven mats around it, and the living room had a single backless couch.

I glanced at the door. I had no idea who was on the other side. Perhaps it was Don. He'd said he wouldn't force himself on me, but I didn't believe him. Though it could be Seth or Teddy. That made me smile, a bit. Though it was super late, not that you could tell, because we were in fucking space and the only thing outside the window was distant stars.

Wrapping an arm around my waist, I opened the door. I practically sagged when I saw Teddy standing on the other side. Bartholomew was his given name, but he went by Teddy, though I had no idea why. His black hair was short, barely curling near the nape of his neck. He was so much taller than me, over six feet, but he was thin as a whip. His long face aided in the general stretched look he had about him. His bones were poking out of his tan skin, like he hadn't been eating well.

"Hey," he said.

"Teddy, come in." I hugged my middle, and my shoulders curled in tight as tension wracked me. I sat on the backless couch, pressing into the tall arms that easily reached my shoulders.

He took a seat on the other end, peering around at all the bright lights, and asked, "How are you?"

"Fine, Teddy. Though you look thin. Has your husband not been feeding you? Punishing you for some obscure reason?" Was his bastard husband starving him? Did I need to protect Seth *and* Teddy from their shitty husbands? Probably. Teddy had been forced to leave the cafeteria without saying goodbye to me.

"Mindy's extremely paranoid about feeding me, so yeah, I've been eating. I'm on nutritional supplements as well. I imagine Klars—that's the doctor in charge of humans—will start you on some."

All of us humans had had a basic scan and our trackers removed, but we would be required to have a more comprehensive exam, or so Seth had said. "Are you happy? With him?"

"Yes," he said. "I love him. I love him a lot, and I'm happy."

"So you're staying?" I asked. Teddy was close with his mothers and sisters. I couldn't imagine him leaving them. As little as he talked, Teddy had mentioned them a handful of times on Xome, which told me exactly how important they were.

"Yeah."

I fought the urge to say something. How could he leave them? Teddy must really love this alien husband of his, though I wasn't convinced this Serlotminden was actually taking care of Teddy.

Teddy took a deep breath. "I didn't mean to leave you. I would have never intentionally abandoned you."

"I know," I lied, tugging my knees to my chest. Maybe he would have, after all? I would've never guessed that he'd pick some guy over his family. My thoughts kept spiraling as I constantly searched the room. For what? I had no idea, but my body wouldn't relax.

He frowned. "What happened after I was gone?"

"Agk sold me," I said as nonchalantly as possible.

"I'm sorry. Are you alright?"

I smirked. "Of course, I am. I'm alive, aren't I?"

Though I couldn't say if that was a good thing or not.

We lapsed into silence, which wasn't odd for us. Teddy wasn't much of a talker. Back on Xome, I'd dominated the conversation, usually lying on him or snuggling. But this time, I couldn't get my voice to work. Besides, if I did somehow manage to speak, what would I even say? Words wondering if Teddy had abandoned me? No, that was too assholeish for even me to contemplate. We'd been everything to each other. I would've killed or died for him and I had to believe that Teddy felt the same for me. But what else was there to talk about? What had happened when I was sold? Not likely.

When the silence continued to prevail, Teddy finally stood. He stretched toward me like he intended to hug me, and I flinched back, panting.

With a deep frown, Teddy asked, "Are you sure you're okay?"

"Sure," I forced out. "Why? Do you need to tell me how horrible your husband has been? He hasn't been, right? He looks like an asshole."

"Seriously?" Teddy asked, crossing his arms. "Mindy loves me. I just wanted to check on you."

"Well, you did," I snapped.

Teddy shook his head. "I'll see you tomorrow."

The second the door closed, I sighed, hugging myself. I simultaneously felt safer and terrified that I was alone.

Chapter 4

LET ME HELP.

Dontilvynsan

A shriek of agony made me jolt up straight in bed, sheet tangling around my waist. I was on my feet, wings sprawling and tail lashing, before I even had a chance to think. My quarters were empty. The cry had to have been a mental one. The only people who I could sense this closely were my brothers and cousin; I was tied to them.

Another mental cry pierced my thoughts and made me wince. A snap followed by yelling raced through my thoughts. Fire. The stench of death. Desperate screams. Bartholomew sliding a bolt home on an incinerator.

I shook my head. It was a jumble.

Vince. His name hit me squarely. He called to my inner fire in a way I did not understand.

I moved toward the door and froze. Vince wouldn't want my help. I *could* help him, though. I swallowed as his screams echoed in my mind. His pain and fear reached through the halls and clawed me open.

Jaw tight, I strode out of my quarters.

Vince

"You are safe," a deep voice said.

My eyes shot open. Sweat drenched the sheets surrounding me, and a hulking form hovered over me. I screamed, sliding away from the hand stretching toward me.

No more. Please, god. No more.

"Vince. Vince, it's me," the shape said. "It's Dontilvynsan."

"Donny?" I asked, panting. I finally looked at him in the bright light of the bedroom. "What the fuck?"

"I can help you. Please let me help you." His hand moved in my direction.

I jerked away. I didn't want to be touched. Why couldn't people stop touching me?

His hand fell, and he crouched right beside the bed. His hair was falling over his bare shoulders. Wings were behind him. He had wings. No, I knew that. I'd seen that fucker Kal's wings. Why was I seeing Don's? Don was half-naked in my room. Why was he here? I couldn't think. The dreams had come and flayed me raw.

"I am not going to hurt you. I heard you crying," he said, tapping a clawed finger to his temple. "I can help. If you let me."

"How?"

"I would have to touch your face."

I jerked back and smacked into the headboard.

"I won't if you don't want me to," Dontilvynsan said, "but I can help you sleep."

"Just my face? Nothing else? You won't hurt me?"

"I promise."

That meant literally nothing.

"I will never touch you without permission, except for if you are in danger. I swear it."

That still meant nothing, but I nodded.

"Lie down."

Shaking, I stretched out, my eyes never leaving his face as my muscles tensed. My mind was already starting to slip into that safe space that no one could touch.

"I'm not going to hurt you, Vince. I'll never hurt you."

I didn't believe him. I only trusted Seth and Teddy. Everyone else could take their promises and shove them up their asses.

Don's lips quirked. "I shall keep my promises to myself, then."

God. It was so convenient I didn't have to speak. He heard my silent threats.

His hand slowly stretched toward me, and I tensed, containing a whimper. I fisted my hands around the sheets. I was a fucking coward. Scared of a damn hand. Pathetic. Still, I trembled when memories began to surface. I tried to shove them down, but they kept rising like the tide.

A low hum reverberated in the back of Don's throat. I didn't recognize the melody, but it was soothing. My fingers released their stranglehold, and my shoulders loosened. His voice deepened pleasingly as he started to sing without words, following the tune.

He cupped my cheek, the smooth scales of his palm warm against me. I whimpered, wanting to pull away, though hating myself for it.

"I have you, Vince. You are safe," he said, his luminous green eyes on mine. "No one will ever hurt you again. You will never be touched against your will ever again."

Don couldn't promise that.

He smiled; it was the slightest quirk of his lips, but I liked it. He said, "I can and will."

Gentle, warm waves crashed over me like the sea. I groaned. Calm. I felt inexplicably peaceful. Don continued to hold my face as he stared into my eyes. A weight started to pull me away.

"What are you doing?" I asked, my voice slurring.

"Giving you my peace." His scales had an unusual sheen to them, and his breath had turned harsh.

"I'm hurting you."

"No, Vince. Sleep," he said; his voice had taken on a cadence that was oddly soothing. "Just sleep like you want. I have you. I will keep you safe."

A gentle roll of sincerity washed over me. He meant it. I closed my eyes as my fingers found his. "Thank you."

"Just sleep."

Warmth laced with music drew me away.

Dontiluynsan

I kept my hand on Vince's cheek and pushed peace into him. In exchange, I took his fear, his pain, his nightmares, and his worry.

I swallowed, fighting the unease. Sweat gathered on my scales as I struggled to remain in control. I'd never done this with someone I was so strongly connected to, except for my brothers, and even then, it had hurt. Badly.

Pulling my hand away, I continued to breathe through the unease while I monitored his sleep. Part of me wanted to curl up beside him and guard his sleep the rest of the night, but that wasn't acceptable. Vince didn't want me to touch him aside from helping him, and I wouldn't betray his trust. Enough people had done that—I was fairly certain.

But he might wake up again from another nightmare. I couldn't keep them away indefinitely, even if I did take up residence in his room, which wasn't an option. This was a bandage, not a cure. I wished I possessed the ability to remove the nightmares permanently, but they stemmed from his trauma.

I brushed his short black hair away from his forehead, then jerked back. No. Vince hadn't consented to that. My misstep had gone unnoticed, though. He lay on his stomach, mouth open and light snores escaping his lips.

"Sleep well, Vince," I whispered.

I hoped his sleep would remain undisturbed, and that he wouldn't wake again, but only time would tell.

I slipped out of his quarters and stopped. Zoltilvoxfyn leaned against the opposite wall. His scales were the same pure black as mine, though his mottled skin was silver and white, and while we had the same green eyes, straight noses, and strong jaws, my features were far rougher than his and I was far taller and broader.

"Bloom," I said.

"Have you taken the human as a lover? Already?"

"No. You know as well as I do where his affections lie. Why are you here?"

"I felt your terror. It woke me up. NAID said you were here."

I paused. "I won't say what happened besides the fact it wasn't my terror and I was assisting him."

"I see." Zoltilvoxfyn flicked his white hair over his shoulder and moved in step with me, his tail grabbing mine for a second before flicking away. "Are you well?"

I ran a hand through my hair. It was easier to speak to Hallonnixmin, my elder brother, and Monqilcolnen, my sole cousin, than my younger brothers. They were both only a cycle older than I was and we shared a tight friendship that transcended our blood relationship, but I loved and was close with all of my siblings.

"People's emotions can be hard," I said.

He grabbed my tail with his own again. "I know."

I closed my eyes.

Zoltilvoxfyn stayed by my side, silent, as he followed me to my quarters. "Do you want me to stay? Caleb won't mind. I can even rouse our other brothers and we can make a night of it."

Part of me wanted to accept. I liked the idea of all of them being curled around me, safe, but I said, "I'm fine. Go back to your mate."

I watched him disappear to his own quarters down the hall from mine. I stepped inside and ran a hand through my hair yet again. I'd been so out of it, I hadn't put on a shirt or shoes. I was lucky none of my crew had caught me wandering around in my state of undress.

That would hardly bestow confidence in my crew.

I plopped down on the couch and blankly stared at the wall in front of me. What was it about this human? It made no sense. He shouldn't affect me so. Seth's trauma didn't. Caleb's readjustment to living flesh hadn't. Bartholomew barely registered on my senses. I assumed as I grew to care about him that would change, but still, he didn't bother me.

Vince did.

I wouldn't find any answers here, and there were possibly none to be had. I needed sleep. I was due on Command first thing in the morning. I sprawled on my bed, but my thoughts returned to Vince. I couldn't perceive him now, which was a good thing. I took a deep breath and thickened my static shield so as not to disturb him or my brothers, then tried to sleep.

Chapter 5

A GATHERING OF HUMANS, TIMES TWO.

Vince

I sat in Seth's apartment with Caleb and Teddy. It was identical to mine, except there were a few personal items, such as a hoodie thrown over the arm of the couch, a small bookshelf that had several figurines on it, and several pieces of artwork around the room. An easel with a half-done painting of Seth was near the eating area, and I was having a hard time pulling my gaze off it. Seth's broad back was the main focus, with him peeking over his shoulder. The artist—Kal, I assumed—had perfectly captured him, and love was in every stroke.

Kal, that fucker, actually cared about Seth.

I ripped my gaze from the painting and turned it to Seth. He'd met with the other humans earlier to answer questions and give them a tour, explaining how to use everything, including NAID, which was the artificial intelligence that was always listening. The dispensers that could literally make anything that you could think of. They, plus the computer, were going to be interesting to play with, and I planned to explore exactly what I could do later when I was alone.

During the tour, Seth had been more at ease than I'd ever seen him. Oh, I'd been able to detect his nervousness, but I'd also spotted a calmness that I'd never perceived before. He seemed at peace, which was new, but oh, so welcome.

Now, we were all hanging out in his room. Caleb was chatting about nothing, changing conversation topics quickly, Teddy was silent, not that I expected different, and Seth was staring at the TV-sized monitor in front of his couch that showed his and Kal's child. I wanted to be mad about the little fetus growing in green liquid, but Seth's obvious joy when he looked at the baby had stolen any anger. I wanted him to be happy, and clearly his kid made him happy.

"So, you and Mindy?" I asked Teddy, leaning against the couch. None of them had backs. They were tall, too. I was short, and my feet didn't touch the floor when I sat back, so I'd chosen the floor.

Teddy nodded. "Yep."

"How?" I demanded, trying to pry details out of my silent friend. I needed proper material to tease him with and "yep" didn't tell me anything besides that he and Mindy were easy. Also, I needed to know if Mindy was actually a good husband. I was worried. Teddy was acting distant, though at the same time, I felt awkward with him. Now that we weren't in a life-or-death situation, I wasn't sure how to act.

"Serlotminden was trying to rescue me. He cut out my tracker and kidnapped me."

"So you were abducted twice?" I asked with a laugh, relaxing further. While I didn't know Caleb well, there was something perfect about being with Seth and Teddy, even with the awkwardness. I felt safe... or as safe as was possible on an alien ship.

"Three times if you count the alien on the planet who tried to take me," he said with a slight grin. "They kept patting my ass. Apparently, I'm popular among aliens."

Sweat immediately gathered on my temples, and a sick feeling churned in my stomach. Teddy appeared perfectly fine. But I couldn't help but remember strange hands on my butt.

I shook it off and forced a laugh to match everyone else. I said, "Well, your flat ass, Teddy, has never inspired much interest from me."

He flipped me off, and I felt a modicum of normalness return between the two of us. I softly smiled at Teddy. Teasing aside, I saw why others would find him attractive. There was an ease about him that provided comfort and stability. He was solid, and there was something super hot about his calmness.

Seth said, "I was abducted twice too."

"What?" I snapped, whipping back to him. I reached for him, then yanked my hand back at the last second, tucking it beneath me and against the spongy floor.

Teddy frowned at the movement, a deep divot forming between his eyebrows.

I averted my gaze and kept it locked on Seth.

"We went to a planet, and I was wearing, well, this necklace," he said, fingering the silver chain. "I lost my touchstone, so I didn't understand them, but they tried to take me."

"Touchstone?" I asked.

Teddy said, holding out a perfectly round stone that pulsed in a low blue light, "You should've gotten one. It connects to NAID. It translates and lets you speak to anyone else who has one if you say their full name."

"I did. I forgot." So much had happened so quickly yesterday and this morning. I couldn't believe I'd let Don touch me, or that he'd been able to help me sleep. I couldn't remember the last time that I'd slept so well or so deeply. It had been miraculous and so unexpected. "What happened?" I asked, pushing away thoughts of the odd drakcol. "Kal, I suppose."

He shook his head. "I fought them off. Got beat up, but I fought them and returned to the port where Kal was amassing a search party for me."

Seth never fought. Ever. I'd seen Travis hit him, and Seth just let him. Of course, I was no better. I'd stopped fighting Tryk and the aliens who... Nope. Not thinking about it. I asked Seth. "You fought?"

"Yeah." He looked at Teddy. "You?"

"Mindy and I fought the alien. They were huge and had four arms."

Caleb bounced, then stopped suddenly, wings hugging his shoulders. "I was kidnapped too. Sort of. I went on this ship because I was a ghost, and they tried to keep me."

"Tatas," Seth said, chuckling.

"What?" Teddy asked.

"That was their name," Caleb said. "The leader's name was Tatas of the Boobaas. No one got it when we laughed."

"Don did, probably, because he could read my thoughts," Seth said.

"That's real?" Teddy asked, expression as blank as ever.

"Yep," Caleb said. "He can hear everything you think and feel when you're in range. It's his inner fire. Every drakcol has one. Even me."

"What is it?" I asked.

Caleb's face twisted up, and I pressed further away from him. Teddy placed a hand on my shoulder, which made me yank away, though I did give him a tight smile. None of us spoke, but when a figurine on the bookshelf lifted into the air, my mouth dropped open. The black cat statue hovered for a moment before lowering again.

Panting, Caleb said, "Telekinesis. I'm not very strong or skilled. Also, it's not an impressive inner fire. Not like Fyn or Don, or, well, any of Fyn's brothers, except Mindy."

Teddy crossed his arms. "Mindy can create fire with his mind. It saved our lives. It is amazing."

While Caleb and Teddy argued, my thoughts returned once again to Don and last night. I hadn't had such a peaceful night in a long time. The nightmares had started right after Teddy and I were bought by the fighting ring. They happened almost every night. But after Don had come and sent me to sleep, I hadn't had another one for the rest of the night.

I'd felt his sincerity when Don said he wouldn't hurt me. I didn't trust anyone. Seth and Teddy, yes. Other people? No. But Don had kept his word. He hadn't hurt me. He hadn't touched me beyond sending me to sleep.

The fact he heard my thoughts was nice. I didn't have to try and phrase things right or explain what I was feeling. He knew it all. It was... I honestly wasn't sure, but it was nice and I liked it. There was no struggle; Don just knew.

"Wyn," Seth said, yanking me out of my thoughts. A drakcol with lavender scales with gold and magenta peeks of skin appeared on the screen. His long bubblegum-colored hair was plaited in a single braid down his scalp. He smiled at Seth, and I was struck by how attractive he was.

This man was, like, model hot. His heart-shaped face was lovely. His eyes were crystal blue and his lips were full. Hands down, he was the most gorgeous man I'd seen. If it had been three years ago and this drakcol had been here, I would have tried to fuck him.

"Seth, I was coming to read to your child," he said in a velvety smooth voice.

"I always appreciate you checking on them," Seth said. "Wyn, this is Bartholomew, or rather Teddy. He's Serlotminden's mate now. And this is Vince. He's my childhood friend."

"Greetings," he said. "You were all rescued from Xome?"

"Yeah," Teddy answered. "I crash landed with Mindy."

"I wish you and Prince Serlotminden every happiness."

"Thanks."

Wyn turned toward me. "Seth has told me about you. While I wish you hadn't been taken, it's nice to meet you."

"Any friend of Seth is a friend of mine," I commented, more to be polite than anything.

He smiled again, and Seth beamed.

A disembodied head popped up on the screen, and I jolted, my pulse jump-starting, at the sudden appearance. She was an old human woman with a tower of curls and heavy jowls.

I blinked. "Edith Smith."

"No," she replied, bouncing in a way that made me nauseous and brought unpleasant memories of picking up a head of an alien and chucking it into a furnace. "I go by Edith, but I'm a NAID who has become sentient. I'm friends with Seth."

"Edith," he said, pointing at us, "meet Vince and Teddy."

"Hello."

"Hi," I said slowly. I'd followed Edith Smith on a couple of platforms. It was weird to see her face here, and to see it so blue.

"You know my grandma?" Caleb asked.

"Your grandmother was a computer?" Teddy asked. "I thought you were a ghost?"

Caleb laughed. "No. Edith Smith."

My mouth opened. "You were *that* Caleb? She mentioned her grandson who died a couple of times."

"Yep," he said.

"I followed her on social media before..." I trailed off. I really didn't need to talk about that part.

Edith bounced on the screen as she began to relate the newest information to Seth about his child, the emperor and empress, the eldest prince, and anything else she thought he would like to know. Seth asked questions, and Wyn contributed as he sat beside the tube with the fetus.

I watched the interaction closely. Seth had made friends. He'd made a life. Something inside me relaxed. He was happy. That was all I'd ever wanted. Maybe I *could* go home? I didn't want to leave Seth, but if I went back to Earth, I could be free from my memories. I wouldn't have nightmares, because I wouldn't remember any of it. It would be like going back in time before all this shit happened. A quick and easy fix.

If Seth and Teddy were safe, then maybe I could go home to lose what I'd experienced.

⬬

I sat in the cafeteria with Camden and Brad. We'd invited Pierce and the rest, but they begged off. Pierce had been comforting Shannon, the other woman who'd been rescued from Xome. When she'd been taken from Earth, she'd left her children and wife behind. Now, she was desperate to get back.

Brad and Camden had both already decided to stay. It had taken them no time to come to that decision. Shannon and one of the other men, Randall, had decided to go home. The rest were undecided, which made sense to me. I was still bouncing back and forth, so why wouldn't everyone else?

Brad and Camden, who were rooming together, seemed to get along well enough, despite their vast age difference.

"So what are you going to do on the drakcol planet?" I asked, leaning as far away from them as possible while I kept glancing around the room.

Brad shrugged. "No idea, but it's better than whatever I left behind on Earth."

"I'm thinking something with science. Once I'm a citizen, I can attend school. It would be fun to wander the stars," Camden remarked, leaning back effortlessly in a model-like fashion. "I like the idea of working on a ship. I mean, it will probably take years."

"Probably, but if that's what you want," I said, "then you'll like it."

"Yeah. I think it will be nice. Figuring out how everything works."

I nodded, but that didn't sound particularly interesting to me. If I did stay, which I really wasn't sure if I wanted to, I'd have to find something to do. What that was, I had no idea. I had interests, but none that translated into the work field. Tarot and fashion didn't scream a job to me, and I didn't really want to have to turn my hobbies to something for profit. But I would have to find a job. There was no way I was trusting this government to help me.

"I don't ever want to set foot in space again," Brad grunted, crossing his arms. He, like all of us, had been forced to adopt Drakcon fashion, which was plain trousers, boots, and high-collared, sleeveless tunics. Brad wasn't particularly muscular, but he was toned enough and his arms were decorated with Classic American style tattoos. I spotted a ship and anchor on one bicep, an entwined mermaid and merman on the same arm, and a dagger on the other, but he was covered in them.

"It's not so bad," Camden replied.

I wanted to scoff as he struck another pose with his chin in his hand. While I looked utterly ridiculous in these clothes, he looked hot. Then again, Camden had the whole Grecian god physique and would've looked lovely in anything.

"It's fine." I didn't like or hate it. It just was.

"Well, I like it," Camden claimed.

"Good for you," I replied, taking a drink.

Brad cocked an eyebrow at my tone, and I met his stare. I didn't give a rat's ass if he liked me or my tone. He frowned, and I simply smirked.

The door opened, and I looked toward it, hoping for Seth. It wasn't Seth, but I did recognize the person. Don. He was speaking to his second in command, Bimwoxcol. He pointed to something on his tablet, hair falling around his face.

I'd had nightmares last night. I'd woken up a couple of times, hoping Don would come through my door once again. He didn't. I'd even asked NAID if he could override the locks, and it had given me an affirmative; Don had an override as the captain. He and the head of security weren't supposed to enter my room without permission unless I was in danger, but Don could. Yet last night, he hadn't.

He possibly hadn't heard my terror like he had the first night. I'd been given a touchstone, but I hadn't wanted to bother him.

Don looked in my direction, and I sent him a silent hello plus an invitation to join us. Lunch would be far more interesting with him, not that I disliked Camden or Brad—both of them seemed perfectly fine—but I was intrigued by Don and his wide green eyes, though my sudden interest confused me. I knew nothing about the drakcol, but I wanted to. Like yesterday, I'd seen nothing of him, and I'd kept thinking about him and where he was and what he was doing.

"Oh," Camden said, "look who came in?"

Brad looked at the door and grunted.

Camden took a deep breath. "Time to think about the food."

I didn't quite get what their problem was. My eyes flicked to Don, but he inclined his head and walked toward a table near the long window on the back of the mess hall.

I frowned. He'd heard me and had chosen to ignore me. *Asshole.*

His shoulders twitched, and I smirked.

"I'll be right back," I said, not waiting for their responses. I darted across the room, avoiding the people and the square metal tables. I slid into the metal stool across from him, chin in my hand. "Hello."

"Greetings, Vince."

"Why didn't you come say hi?"

"I didn't want to disturb your lunch with your fellow humans."

"I invited you, which I know you fucking heard, by the way. You can just say no. You don't need to make a big deal about it," I replied. He should've at least said hi. We were... something. It didn't matter what we were or not. He shouldn't ignore me. I didn't like it. Why? Who knew or cared. I didn't like it, and I felt safe enough surrounded by people to play with Don.

"I bother them, Vince. They learned of my ability and it disturbs them."

"What?" I asked with a growl, glancing at them.

Both Brad and Camden were staring at me. I shot them a glare. Camden got busy looking elsewhere, but Brad lifted his eyebrows in clear challenge or question, who knew. Those fuckers; that's what Camden had meant. Why the hell were they judging Don?

"It upsets everyone," he commented. "I'm used to it."

He shouldn't have to be used to it. It wasn't Don's fault. Besides, I didn't care. Why did anyone else?

Don smiled and the left side of his mouth quirked up higher, making his smile crooked in the most adorable way. "You're the first. Thank you."

I shrugged. It was what it was. I couldn't help but wonder if he'd heard my earlier thoughts about the touchstone.

"I did, and yes, you could have pinged me. I would've come and assisted you. I apologize I didn't hear you. If I had, I would've come."

"I know." I believed him. It was an odd feeling for me after everything, but I believed him. I didn't trust him, but I sure as hell believed he would've come, to at least be able to sleep without me bothering him.

"You're not a bother," he said, scrolling on his tablet.

"Nice to know. Now come eat with us," I demanded. I had no idea why I wanted him to, but I did; that was enough of a reason.

"My presence will upset them."

"So? Let it," I said. *Fuck them*. "Doesn't mean you can't have friends or fun. They'll get over it or they won't. I want to eat with you. Do you want to eat with me?"

"I do."

I stood. "Then come on. I'll tell them to fuck off."

He got to his feet and tucked the tablet under his arm. "Will you eat well if I come?"

"Are you worried about how much I eat?"

"Yes."

I shook my head. "Come on."

Chapter 6

MEDICAL EXAM. YAY...

Vince

I sat in the plain gray room, the only one without plants that I'd seen on the ship. Lights shone from every corner, which comforted me as much as someone sitting on an examination table in a fucking alien ship could be comfortable.

A female drakcol with golden hair and light brown scales bustled around the room, not paying me the slightest bit of attention, all while a man tutted over me. Physician Klars was his name, and he wasn't human, not that you would know by looking at him. The only thing that set him apart was a series of dot tattoos that went in a V shape from his temples to his nose, then the reverse from his nose down to his jaw. Otherwise, his short black hair flecked with gray, his paunch, his white skin, and his large nose all passed for human.

Teddy was leaning against the bed I was sitting on, arms crossed and expression blank. He wasn't nervous about the proceedings. Of course, he had no reason to be—he wasn't getting examined. But I couldn't do more than force myself to glance at him every few minutes. I knew he was there, though, as I played with the silky blue blanket beneath me.

My time for a comprehensive medical exam had come, an appointment that I couldn't refuse and I'd tried. I'd kept putting it off for days, insisting everyone else went first. Neither Seth nor Teddy had made me go, but when I was the last one left, they both had offered to come. In the end, Seth had to meet with the drakcol government, the Cohort, so Teddy had come with me. It had been easy for Teddy to come with me anyway; he'd been hanging out in my room with me. Every day for the last week or so, he'd visited me, not leaving me alone. We were still awkward, but I hoped we were finding our way back to each other.

Klars pressed a clear tube to my neck, and I jolted from the sharp sting. He said in a cheery voice, "Don't mind me, just taking some blood."

I fisted the blanket, breathing through the cold feeling that swept through me. Thankfully, none of the tests had been invasive—mostly scans. I hadn't even gotten undressed, which was a relief. If I'd had to... I took a deep breath. I didn't want this doctor to touch me, even for health reasons.

The doctor stepped away to place my blood in a hole in the wall.

A light touch on my hand made me leap and skitter away. I slid off the bed, heart pounding as I screamed in my head, *No!*

"Vince," Teddy said in his even voice. "It's just me."

I closed my eyes, head thudding against the metal frame of the bed. Fuck, that sucked. No, I sucked. Overreact much?

"Are you alright?" he asked in a soothing tone.

My eyes popped open, and Teddy was crouched in front of me, his expression blank as a board, but that was normal. He wasn't an expressive person. Even during the entire two years of captivity with Agk, I'd rarely seen him react to any of the horrors around us.

"I'm fine. Why are you asking that?"

He gestured to my cowered position on the ground.

I glared at him and returned to my place on the examination table.

Teddy picked at his tunic, eyes anywhere but me. "You know it's not your fault, right?"

What did he know and how did he know it? Had Don told Teddy about what he'd seen *after* Agk had sold me? I didn't want anyone to know my shame, the dirt that covered me, or what I'd been. No one needed to know. Hell, even I was better off forgetting about it, which was the plan. Push the memories where the sun didn't shine and never think about it again.

"I was the one who locked that bolt. It was me," Teddy said, practically strangling the hem of his tunic. "Not you. You aren't at fault."

What in the hell was he talking about? My mouth fell open. "No, Teddy," I said. Oh my god, he blamed himself for what happened at Agk's? "It wasn't your fault."

His jaw tightened.

"Agk made us. We had no choice," I said.

When we'd cleaned up the fighting ring, disposing of the bodies, not everyone had been dead when we'd put them in the incinerator. I didn't know if the screams would ever leave me for as long as I lived, but I didn't feel guilty about it per se. I felt horrible those people had died and we'd had a hand in it, but in the end, it had been us or them. If we said no, Agk would've killed us. Each time, Teddy had insisted on closing the bolt to the furnace, locking them inside.

I took his hand, swallowing at the feel of his skin on mine. Every instinct in me screamed to let him go and hide, but I held on. Teddy needed this. Needed me. I had to protect him.

"It was not your fault," I said. Teddy refused to look at me, so I tugged on him. "But thanks for protecting me. You're my big, brave hero." I batted my eyelashes at him. "Oh what, oh what would I do without this strong man to protect me?"

"Asshole," he breathed, then laughed.

Pulling him closer, I ignored the unease that settled in my stomach and the sweat that gathered in between my shoulder blades—Teddy needed this. I whispered, "It wasn't your fault. Alright?"

He nodded.

"Let it go. Let all the shit go," I said. "It's the only way we're going to survive."

Teddy slid away from me slightly, staring at me with drawn eyebrows.

Klars returned, interrupting us with a kind smile plastered on his face. "Bartholomew, would you allow me to speak to Vince alone?"

Teddy glanced at me, and I said, "Go. We both know your husband is outside."

He flushed, shrugging.

"I'll be fine," I said. There was no way in hell I wanted Teddy to overhear whatever Klars had found. It couldn't be good.

After the door had closed with a low whoosh, Klars sat down on the other side of the bed. "You were forced to work in a brothel."

I crossed my arms and looked across the medbay, but there was no one around. Klars had dispersed the staff without me noticing. Unease coiled in my stomach, and I shifted further away from the man.

"You're safe," he said in a soft voice. "I noticed some issues in your blood work."

"Which were?"

"Diseases that are transmitted sexually. That plus the finger breaks, starvation, and the anal fissures... I made an educated guess."

I fought the urge to vomit or curl into a ball. Life would be so much easier if I never had to move again. "I don't want anyone to know."

"You have nothing to be ashamed of," Klars said.

My jaw clenched. What the fuck did he know?

"I can treat you. There will be no issues in the future, and you don't have to worry about passing anything on once the treatment is complete."

Who would fuck me right now, anyway? I swallowed a sudden rush of bile at the thought.

"You also need to start a high calorie diet as well as nutrition supplements."

Teddy had mentioned that possibility. Who cared if I was skin and bones?

He stood. "I want you to know, what happens here is completely private. No one will know."

I stiffly nodded.

Klars disappeared for a few moments, then returned with a series of injections. As he administered one after another, I stared blankly at the wall, flinching with each injection. None of this mattered. None of it. All of it was going to disappear. I would force it down and pretend that nothing happened.

Once he was done, he told me to come back in a few days for another round.

I bolted out the door and didn't look back.

Dontilvynsan

I leaned against the wall outside of the medbay. Serlotminden and Bartholomew had been there only a few moments ago, but once they'd realized I was staying, they darted off with a plan to walk their nightmare of a pet Pookie, though Teddy had lingered and interrogated me on whether I would be kind to Vince before he was satisfied enough to leave. I had no idea what the rest of the humans would think of the animal when they finally caught sight of her running on the walls. Seth was terrified of her. She resembled an Earthen spider and a mammal fused together, with a snout, floppy ears, and a curly tail. She was an odd thing, but harmless.

My eyes closed as I took a deep breath, strengthening my static shield. However, it didn't help. Vince's discomfort prodded me like a hot needle. It was nothing compared to the sheer terror that had stabbed me and had me racing out of Command without thought.

Something about this human wouldn't leave me alone. I felt him all the way across the ship. I couldn't even do that with my brothers. I would be able to locate them anywhere on my ship with my inner fire, certainly, but feel distinct emotions? No. Vince was different.

Vince rushed out of the medbay, but froze when he didn't see Bartholomew or Serlotminden.

"I'm here," I commented.

He started, then turned to me with a tense smile, not meeting my eye. "You heard all that, didn't you?"

"Just what you thought about."

A long gust of air rushed out of his lips, and he shoved a hand through his black hair. My soul throbbed at the sight of his pale fingers playing with the silky strands. Vince said, drawing me out of my random thoughts, "Why are you even here?"

"You were afraid."

"You felt that?" His eyebrows went up. "All the way from wherever you were?"

"Yes."

"I have no idea how you get any work done," he commented.

"Practice," I teased, and Vince laughed, making me smile.

We started walking in the general direction to his quarters. He asked, "So you know?"

"Yes."

I'd heard what he didn't want me to—he'd contracted something from the people who'd assaulted him. A growl rumbled low in my throat. It was very good for those people that I would never set eyes on them, because if I did, I wouldn't hesitate to shred them to pieces.

Vince crossed his arms, shoulders curling inward.

"There is no shame, Vince."

"Like hell there isn't."

Hell was a human swear, but NAID pointlessly supplied: oath, fiery afterlife, punishment. I paused in my step to face him. "There is none."

He scoffed.

"Prostitution is a valid job."

Vince cocked his eyebrow. "Are you fucking serious?"

"I mean, there is no shame in sex work." I shook my head. "No, I mean, there is no shame in what happened to you. You had no choice. You were abducted, then sold to a brothel to work in. You were hurt. There's no reason for you to feel even the slightest amount of shame in regards to what happened to you. It wasn't your fault. At all."

"Are you serious? Work? Working?" Vince snarled. "I didn't work there."

"No," I said quickly. "That isn't... I didn't mean—"

"Just shut up, Don."

My mouth snapped shut. I wasn't explaining my thoughts well. Besides, I couldn't convince Vince that it didn't matter, because he cared and he was perfectly right to do so. It wasn't my place to question his feelings or tell him how he should or should not feel or react to what had happened.

"What are your plans for the day?" I asked, inexplicably curious. I wanted—no, needed to know what he did with his time.

"Don't you know?"

"Unless you think about it, no."

Vince smirked and walked backward, facing me. Even though I felt the shame and pain from his visit to the medbay as well as my blunder circling in his thoughts, I swallowed at the arrogant confidence that was easily displayed on his features and in his wide stride. My tail flicked, and I longed to coil the appendage around him, pulling him flush to my chest.

"You and me are going to eat lunch together."

"Are we?" I asked, though I had no intention of refusing him.

"You need a friend, Donny, and Klars said I need to eat a high calorie diet."

"I shall accompany you, then."

He grinned. "I figured you would. Come on, I'm hungry."

Chapter 7

NEW CLOTHES. NEW MAN.

Vince

I stared at my bed; a dark cloud filled every cell of my body, making me numb. I was clean, after what had to have been a two-hour shower, and ready for bed, theoretically. Every light was on full blast, banishing the shadows, but it wasn't enough. The very thought of lying down sent tension to my muscles. Nightmares would come—they always did—but Don would come with them.

Nonetheless, I wasn't ready yet.

The day had gone by so much faster than I'd liked. I had a pleasant and long lunch with Don. He was humorous in an understated way. When he'd gone back to his duties, I'd hung out with Camden and Brad, then we all met up with Roman, who was quiet, but not in a surly way like Brad, but in a he-just-didn't-have-anything-to-say way.

Roman was in his late thirties with a shaved head and mustache and goatee. He was taller than Brad and Camden, and well me, but that wasn't shocking. His skin was a deep brown, and he was well-built with broad shoulders and a narrow waist. His deep-set brown eyes always roved the area, like he was scanning for danger.

The thing that made me instantly like Roman was the fandom tattoos on his arms: a sonic screwdriver, a Star Trek emblem, the village symbols from Naruto, the four elements from Avatar: the Last Airbender, and more.

But hanging out with them had bled to chilling with Seth—and fucking Kal—who spent the entire time glaring at me. Seth hadn't noticed, or had ignored us, as we watched a baking show he liked while we chatted. But all too soon, they were calling it a night. I'd then gone to look for Teddy, but he was already sleeping.

So then I showered until my skin burned.

Sighing, I went back to the living room and paced. There wasn't much to do. Yes, I had access to the full breadth of the human databases, or well, up to the point Seth had been abducted by his fucker husband. I could binge watch whatever I wanted. I loved anime, and I could easily watch one I'd seen a million times, but I didn't feel like it. I could also read. I was a huge reader and loved a multitude of genres... and yet, I didn't want to.

In truth, I didn't feel like doing anything. I was rudderless. I could go home; I should go home to be free of these encroaching dreams and memories, but that meant leaving Seth and Teddy. Though both of them were happy with their alien spouses. They probably wouldn't care if I left.

No. That wasn't fair. They would care; they were my friends. In reality, they would be fine, though. Neither of them needed me, and I needed peace. I needed to shove these memories down into a little box, then maybe I wouldn't have these nightmares. If I could finally rest, I was positive I'd be able to figure out what to do.

I wish I had my cards.

I'd often gotten teased about believing in tarot, but more than once tarot cards had directed me, helping make decisions or illuminating what I needed most.

My eyes flicked to the dispenser. Seth had said NAID could make anything. Not anything *anything*. It wouldn't make a gun for me to shoot Kal in the ass, but it would make more non-lethal things.

"NAID?" I asked. It was supposedly listening all the time, which was sort of stalkerish.

"Yes, Vince Lyford," a disembodied, monotone voice said.

Yeah, not creepy at all.

I shook it off and asked, "Do you know what tarot cards are?"

"Yes. Do you wish me to define it?"

"No. Can you make a set in the dispenser?"

"Yes. Please select which one you would like," it said.

I picked up my tablet and blinked. There were thousands upon thousands of tarot card sets. The computer had compiled all of the versions in its databanks and spat them out. I wasn't going to search through all of them—that would take a lifetime—so I selected the first ones I liked.

"They are in the dispenser," NAID said. "Do you need anything else?"

I was about to say no when I paused. "Can you make clothes?"

"Yes."

Drakcon fashion wasn't for me, and now, I didn't have to stick with it. I flicked through the different clothes on the tablet, making my choices, and they all appeared in the dispenser. The clothes didn't feel the same as the ones on Earth, or at least how I remembered them—probably because drakcol didn't use the same fibers—but they were more familiar than what I was currently wearing.

Shuffling out of my clothes, I yanked on a pair of gray joggers and a black tank top. Better.

Now, I was determined to see what else my dispenser could make. The more I played, the more limitations I found. It wasn't that NAID couldn't make certain things, like a comfortable chair or couch, it was that those items were too big for my dispenser. However, I found plenty of things it could make, and it passed the time as I ignored the need to go to bed and my new tarot cards lying on the table.

But as my eyes grew more and more tired, I had to face the matter head on. Sleep would be impossible to hold off forever. Unfortunately.

"NAID, can you make a candle?"

"Fire is prohibited."

I frowned. I preferred to start a reading with a flame to concentrate on to center myself, but it made sense why it wasn't allowed. I guessed the drakcol didn't want someone to burn their shiny ship down. Shocker.

Electric candles were a thing, and I was positive that NAID could make one, but it wasn't the same as an open flame.

Forgoing the candle, I sat down at the table and took several even breaths to center myself. Then with my left hand, I touched each and every card to establish a physical link. All that remained was to shuffle and fan out the cards.

I stared at the fanned deck, deciding to do a simple three card draw of the past, present, and future, instead of my usual Celtic cross. It had been a while since I'd done this, and while NAID had also created the instruction booklet, I didn't feel confident. In fact, as I stared at the cards, I felt shaken.

Normally, I formed my question and drew, but this time, all I felt was terror. My past was bad, my present was manageable, and my future had the potential to be either. I was terrified of what I would or wouldn't see if I picked the cards. Also, for the life of me, I couldn't think of a single question.

"This shouldn't be this hard," I snapped, smacking the table with the flat of my hand. This was nothing. It probably wasn't even real... However, I believed.

With a loud sigh, I pushed the cards into a neat stack and set them aside. Next time.

Getting to my feet, I headed to bed. Might as well get it over with.

I rubbed my tired eyes as I waited outside of Teddy's room. Three fucking nightmares last night. Don had come the first time, and I'd leaned into his warm touch to soothe the terror coursing through me. The second and third time, he hadn't. He had to have not heard me. I believed Don when he'd said that he would come if he heard me. I could've called him with my touchstone thing, but I didn't.

Now I was dead tired, but I'd promised to meet Seth, Teddy, and Caleb for breakfast. I didn't want to. I wanted to hole up in my room and curl into a ball and never move again. God, that sounded so much nicer.

The door opened, and Teddy blinked. "Where did you get the new clothes?"

I stepped around him, not answering, and was met with the same stunned looks.

"You look nice," Seth said.

"He means where the hell did you get the clothes," Caleb demanded, standing with a grunt and leaning heavily on his cane.

I glanced between them. "Do you mean to tell me that *none* of you thought to make clothes with the dispenser?"

I smoothed a hand down my crop top band tee, ripped skinny jeans, and flowy cardigan—all black. I'd even painted my nails pink. From their gaping mouths, I realized I was right.

"I can make more hoodies," Seth shouted, standing, then he immediately glanced over his shoulder with a nervous expression at an empty pile of blankets, pillows, and ripped up stuffed animals.

"Don't worry," Teddy said. "Mindy has Pookie."

"Who is Pookie?" I asked.

"His pet," Caleb whined, sitting back down. "I want a pet, but I'm so allergic to everything."

"Not to the plants," Teddy commented.

"I'd take the daily injections to be able to snuggle a cat," Caleb remarked.

"We should eat," Seth said, taking my arm.

I flinched, ripping away.

"Vince?" he asked.

Forcing a smile, I slipped my arm around his and leaned into him, closing my eyes and breathing in his citrus scent. My Seth. Everything would be better with him beside me.

"I want french fries so bad," Caleb said, moving toward the dispenser. "But with my drakcol tastebuds, they probably wouldn't be as good anymore."

"Why don't you try?" I asked.

"Because there's not a fast food drive-thru," he replied with a laugh.

I shook my head. "You all really lack imagination. NAID, do you have a recipe for french fries?"

"Yes," it replied.

"Can you make them with the closest substitutes?"

"Yes."

French fries appeared in the dispenser. I took one and ate it. The fry didn't taste quite right, but fuck, it was heaven. I faced the other humans and smirked at their shocked faces. "You're really lucky I'm here."

"Mine," Caleb squealed, taking a handful. Teddy and Seth weren't far behind him, making me chuckle, but I pulled away, hugging my middle. We shouldn't be as desperate for french fries as we were. None of us should be here. None of this should've happened.

Time might not be able to be unwritten, but maybe I could just forget it all. That's what going home meant, right?

Chapter 8

A BONDING EXPERIENCE.

Vince

"Why are we doing this?" I asked, my voice almost at a whine, as Seth put what looked like a vest with wires and nodes and techno shit on me. He tightened it, and I shivered from the slight touches of his fingers. It wasn't all fear or disgust either; it was need, want, attraction. Also, just bone-deep longing. It had been far too long since someone had touched me pleasantly, and I was starved for it. For Seth especially.

How did he not understand what he did to me?

Seth grunted, tightening the straps. "Because I love experiences. It's a kind of immersive shooter game that Kal and I play. It'll be fun for all of us. Team Human, I guess."

"Aren't all the humans on Team Human? That's what Caleb says." He'd inducted Camden and Brad into Team Human almost instantly, because they'd decided to stay. I hadn't. I was waffling. Leave or stay? Seth and Teddy or unwriting the past? Nightmares or peace?

"Fine. Because I want you and Kal to get along," Seth said, his hands slipping into his hoodie pockets. When I opened my mouth to lie, he said, "Don't pretend. I noticed. It was fairly obvious."

That he noticed. Fuck Kal.

"He's not Travis, Vince. I promise. Kal has never hurt me and he won't. Not ever. I know you're worried. You wouldn't be you if you weren't worried, but he's not him."

"I'm trying to protect you. He has a temper."

"He does," Seth said. "So do you, if I remember correctly."

"I won't hurt you."

"Neither will Kal." Seth tugged me into a hug, and after the initial flinch, I settled into his embrace, burying my face against his shoulder to inhale his citrus scent.

I rubbed my cheek on the soft hoodie, so unbelievably pleased he was wearing one. At the height of Travis being the ass that he was, he'd controlled everything Seth wore, which meant no hoodies. Seth had reclaimed that part of himself, and I was so damn proud.

Seth whispered, "Please get to know him."

I wanted to throw Kal over a cliff and watch him splat on the ground, though that probably wouldn't work. He had wings. Annoying fucker. I squeezed Seth tight. I kissed his cheek and pulled back, my tense shoulders instantly relaxing once Seth was no longer touching me.

"Fine," I conceded. "I will try. But if he ever raises a hand to you, I'm figuring out how to open an airlock."

Seth frowned. "I love him, and he won't hurt me. Besides, I can take care of myself."

He never had in the past.

"Are we going to do this?" Caleb asked, gripping his cane as Fyn got him suited with the same techy vest.

All of the brothers had joined. We were working in teams, and I was paired with Don. I would've liked to be with Seth or Teddy, but I much preferred Don over Kal.

As Seth went to Kal's side, Don came to mine. I smiled in welcome; he returned it, keeping his distance from me.

"Why are we paired up?" I asked.

"Because the mates want to play together."

I figured as much. "Why am I here?"

"You're Seth's and Bartholomew's friend. Seth wanted you, and Kalvoxrencol won't deny him anything."

I grunted.

"As we start, watch out for Seth and Kalvoxrencol. Both are skilled at blasters, Seth more so."

"Truly?"

"Yes. Also watch out for Caleb and Zoltilvoxfyn."

"Are they our other main competitors?"

"No," he said, lips twitching. "Caleb is an—" He broke off into a snarling growl. "I believe that is the correct word."

That garbled nonsense meant nothing to me.

"They both like having sex where others might find them. Zoltilvoxfyn won't start anything here, but Caleb might if he is feeling aroused."

I laughed, turning toward him. "They will seriously fuck during our game?"

"No. They don't have our consent, but they might become distracted. But when we get back to Tamkolvanloknol, do not approach Zoltilvoxfyn's greenhouse after dark. You might find them there, though Zoltilvoxfyn does try to prevent people from seeing them in the greenhouse. He simply finds the possibility arousing."

I wasn't going back. Maybe. Probably not. I wasn't sure. Besides, I wouldn't be in the palace, even if Seth and Teddy were there.

He paused in adjusting his vest. "You're returning to Earth."

I glanced at Seth; he was talking to Kal, who had his tail coiled around Seth's ankle, then my eyes flicked to Teddy who was flushed as Mindy chattered on. I whispered. "I don't want to talk about it right now."

"You haven't told Seth or Bartholomew."

"No, and I'm still deciding."

"I will not say anything."

"Thanks."

Dontilvynsan

We crept around the jutting red rock formations filled with nooks and rough holes. This experience was based on a canyon on Barus. A good friend of our family, Urgg, was from Barus and had helped craft this experience for our family, though others besides us enjoyed it.

As far as experiences went, this one was rather simple and lacked any and all story. The goal was to shoot the other teams and be the last one standing. It was merely a way for my family, including my parents, to play together.

Normally, I'd have my entire mental focus on the game, but I kept staring at Vince's narrow back and the way the light danced on his shiny black hair. He was concentrating on the game, unlike me. He was solely focused on finding and shooting our competitors, but I kept returning to his thoughts from earlier. He wasn't planning on staying, in all likelihood. I'd assumed, much as Seth had, that his and Bartholomew's presences would be enough to hold Vince here, even though Vince had given no indication of wanting to stay.

I wanted him to, and I didn't know why.

Vince's acceptance of my gift was intriguing. His humor enjoyable. I wanted to chuckle at his thoughts of throwing Kalvoxrencol off a cliff, only to have him fly up. The way he trusted me to hold his face and ease his mind so he could sleep. Last night, his fingers had touched mine as he grinned sleepily at me. I had wanted to trace that smile, but I didn't, because he hadn't given me permission to do so.

An orange blast went over my head, and I instinctively crouched while reaching for Vince to pull him down. The instant my hand gripped his arm, terror flashed in his mind followed by scattering memories of someone holding him down as he cried. I ripped away, but his fear didn't quiet. He held the front of the black leathers simulated by the techplate. He'd gone even paler than usual as sweat dotted his brow.

"Vince," I said in a low voice. "I didn't mean to. I'm sorry."

He didn't respond. His mind stuck in eddies of memories, ripping him around.

We were crouched behind a sizable rock, lending us a bit of privacy. None of the other teams had found us, but they would soon. Vince wouldn't want anyone to see him like this. He hadn't told Seth or Bartholomew, and I didn't know if he intended to or not. Regardless, Vince should be allowed to reveal his past however wanted and only if he chose to do so.

Slowly, I reached toward him, and Vince scuttled back, making divots in the red sand. I paused, hand still extended. "I will not harm you," I whispered. "Let me help."

Vince pushed his cheek into my hand, and I fought the urge to draw away. The fear and pain were overwhelming. My jaw clenched, grinding my teeth together, as I struggled to find my inner calm. I could not give what I didn't possess. I had to be centered and calm to provide it to others.

I breathed in his crisp floral scent, and it soothed my soul. This was Vince, and he needed me. I pushed my own calm into him while stealing his fear. The panic slid through my veins as the memories rushed over me. My muscles tightened as my soul pounded in time with the terror I was stealing. As I was taught, I released the memories.

They were still there, but I didn't allow them to touch me. I could easily be traumatized by what I stole, but I'd been taught to let them go by another who shared the same inner fire.

Vince sagged toward me.

I gently held his arm, comforting him as best I could. Vince scooted closer until his head rested against my chest. My soul sped from the small contact. I wanted to draw him into my embrace, but I didn't. I kept cradling his cheek while I held his arm in a loose grip.

Vince rubbed his forehead against me, breathing deeply.

"You are safe," I said in a quiet voice. "I will allow no one to harm you."

Vince took a shuddering breath.

The memories of the past had disappeared under the gentle waves of calm. I'd supplied him with one of my own favorite memories. Standing on the beach. The green-blue water lapping against the purple sand. The double moons of Tamkolvanloknol hung in the night sky while a warm breeze ruffled my hair. The stars winking in the distance. The trees shivering in the wind. I was alone, but content in the peace of the night sky.

"You're down, Mindy," Seth shouted.

Vince jolted out of my embrace, looking around. He backed away with a flush on his pale cheeks and embarrassment ringing in his mind. "Sorry."

"It's I who should apologize. I shouldn't have touched you. It was instinct to protect my comrade in arms."

"It's fine," Vince said.

But it wasn't. I had frightened him; something I never wanted to do. Vince was usually much calmer when Seth and Bartholomew touched him. I wasn't the same. The thought, while painful, made sense. He'd known Seth since they were children, and Bartholomew and he were exceedingly close because of their shared experience on Xome. I was new, however much I was helping him.

Kalvoxrencol cheered when he shot Bartholomew in the shoulder. Seth grinned and took his mate's hand before they disappeared around an outcropping of rocks.

Vince smiled tensely before he began creeping forward. I longed to pull him back against me, as I had immensely enjoyed the feeling of his face pressed against my chest. It had been right—his small form tucked against my larger one. I wished to experience it once again. No, I needed more than that. I needed... I needed to feel his slight form beside me at all times.

I shook the random thoughts away and followed Vince. We rounded the different jagged rocks, searching. Seth and Kalvoxrencol had turned quiet. I heard Kalvoxrencol's thoughts, but I tuned them out to keep the battle fair.

In front of me, Vince froze, and I stopped behind him. Caleb and Zoltilvoxfyn were in front of us, but they were otherwise occupied. Caleb was braced against a rock, and Zoltilvoxfyn stood in between his legs, wings out and tail wrapped around his mate's leg. They were in the middle of a frantic kissing session. Caleb had his hands buried in Zoltilvoxfyn's hair and he rocked against him in steady movements.

Ridiculous. They could barely go an hour without inhaling each other.

Vince covered his mouth as he smothered a laugh. "You were right."

I laughed, head lowering near his shoulder.

His shock at my laughter, followed by a warm, pleased feeling, went through him and sparked awareness within my own body. I ignored it. Vince was allowed his privacy, even if I sensed him better than others.

"They are insatiable," I commented. "At least Seth and Kalvoxrencol have the sense to only copulate in their room. I'm not sure about Serlotminden and Bartholomew yet."

Vince's hands fisted, and it was because of the thought of Seth and Kalvoxrencol together. I wouldn't apologize for it. My brother and his mate were allowed to fuck, and they did so frequently.

"Shall we interrupt them?" I asked, lifting my blaster.

He smirked as mischief gleamed in his dark eyes. "I'll take Fyn."

I inclined my head before using his shoulder as a level and aiming at Caleb who was half-hidden behind Zoltilvoxfyn's broad frame. Vince took aim and thought clearly, *One, two, and three!*

While I'd never used such a counting measure, I understood his desire and squeezed the trigger on three. An orange beam burst out of the tip of my blaster at the same moment as Vince's did—the two of us perfectly in sync. We both hit, and the couple jerked.

Zoltilvoxfyn snarled while Caleb burst into fits of laughter. Vince recoiled from Zoltilvoxfyn, pressing against me. I didn't react to the feel of his cooler body against my chest, though my soul beat faster, and said to my brother, "You're out."

Caleb kept laughing as he snagged Zoltilvoxfyn. "We are. You found us."

"It wasn't hard," Vince remarked. "You were sucking each other's faces off, so that helped."

Zoltilvoxfyn glared, arms crossing, but embarrassment mixed with arousal curled in his mind. His thoughts were of stealing his mate away and stripping him bare before fucking him.

This was one of the worst downsides of my inner fire. I was witness to each of my brothers', parents', and many others' private thoughts that I would much rather not know. I didn't want or need to know how my different siblings enjoyed their mates, or how my parents desired each other. I couldn't shut it off. My static shield could block the general thoughts of others at a distance, but physical proximity or emotional closeness eliminated its effectiveness.

"Come on," Caleb said in a husky voice that made both Vince and I roll our eyes. Zoltilvoxfyn glared at me, but his thoughts had already turned to his mate and their shower.

Vince lifted an eyebrow at me, and I chuckled, head dipping toward his, but I didn't touch him.

Zoltilvoxfyn paused, looking at me with an open mouth. His gaze flicked between me and Vince while a clear question formed in his thoughts. My expression cooled as I stared at my younger brother. He didn't say anything, but he thought of Kalvoxrencol, and I knew I'd have at least two brothers asking unnecessary questions. Where they led, Serlotminden, Hallonnixmin, and our cousin Monqilcolnen would follow.

Just because three of my four brothers had chosen to mate with humans and I enjoyed this human's presence did not mean anything. Besides, he was in love with Seth and not planning on staying. No future existed.

"One more couple," Vince said.

"Let's find them."

We crept around the different outcroppings, searching. We couldn't go far. The program only extended to the length and width of the suite, and unlike other programs, it wouldn't follow us, slowly transitioning to new places, because this experience was intended for group play.

Muzzles sweeping, we searched but didn't find our prey. They were proving to be elusive, which didn't surprise me. Both were skilled in experiences, and Kalvoxrencol was a crafty warrior and a master at evading people when he so chose. Seth was his equal in many ways. He'd taken to strategy and war with surprising ease. Though perhaps not too surprising, given he was the purest warrior soul ever recorded in written Drakcon history.

The slightest flap was my only warning before two shots in quick succession hit me and Vince. Seth laughed loudly as we turned. Kalvoxrencol was flying with Seth trapped in his arms. Seth lowered his gun with a smirk. "We win."

Kalvoxrencol flew up higher with a laughing Seth. He kissed his mate's neck, and they whirled through the sky.

Vince stared at them with sadness like a dark cloud gathering inside of him, blocking out all light and hope. "He's happy."

"He is." The truth could not be denied.

"Hmm," was all he said.

I didn't know what that indeterminate noise meant, and I chose to remain silent. Vince didn't need a reminder that Seth's affection lay somewhere else.

Chapter 9

THE FUTURE IS NOT CONCRETE.

Vince

After yesterday's game, I'd stayed quiet, unable to get my voice out from wherever it was locked deep inside of me. I'd eaten with the other humans. Everyone now felt brave enough to exit their rooms, but most moved in a herd, like they were afraid to be picked off. Pierce, though, had separated from the group rather easily. She was either spending time with Shannon, comforting her, or with Commander Bimwoxcol. I spotted them wandering around, talking low with soft smiles on their faces. There was something between the two of them. What? Who knew. I wasn't even sure if I cared.

I wanted to care—I did—but I couldn't muster the will to do so. I was too tired.

Seth had tried to speak to me, multiple times, and I would talk, but my thoughts had kept going back to his smiling face in Kal's arms. I'd never seen Seth so at ease. Not when we were kids. Not when he lived with my family after his grandparents kicked him out.

Not when we were adults. Never. He'd always hunched and shied away or stayed quiet, eyes wary.

He was still the Seth I knew and loved, but it was like he was finally comfortable in his own skin. Unfortunately, I knew Kal was probably part of that reason, if not the whole damn reason. I wanted to chuck the blue alien into a ravine with an anchor tied around his ankles, but at the same time, I could begrudgingly admit that Kal had been good for Seth. In some way, at least. Some very small insignificant way.

That night after the experience, I hadn't asked for Don's help, embarrassed at the way I'd snuggled against him, attracted to the burning heat coming off him and the soothing way it comforted me, and had paid the price. Nightmares had assaulted me all night long, making me start awake until I finally gave up sleeping and washed the sweat-drenched terror off of me.

Now, I was sitting in an atrium full of weird-colored plants. Everywhere I looked I found a different color from the vines to flowers to trees. There was no break from it. Trees that had deep red with gold striations in their trunks. Purple trees with wisteria-esque flowers. Green ferns. Red Ferns. Pink ferns. Blue. Yellow. Orange.

The atrium was truly lovely, and there was a reverent peace to it that calmed my soul in a way I didn't understand.

Seth was seated against a wall covered in dark green vines with tiny light blue flowers, staring at me.

I smiled, leaning back on my elbows. "What? I'm suddenly so gorgeous you can't look away? I will admit I do look rather nice today." My crop top and skinny jeans looked like all the others I'd worn.

"You and Don have been spending a lot of time together."

I groaned, flopping back and covering my face. "Do not try to set me up with your alien brother-in-law." God, that was the last thing either of us needed. Don was nice, and that was why he was helping me, but I was in love with my idiot friend.

There was nothing between Don and me.

Seth laughed. "Fine. I thought I'd ask."

I looked over at him and a smile tugged at my own lips. "You look good."

He flushed. "I am good. Did I like how I got here? No, but I'm glad I'm with Kal. I like Tamkolvanloknol, and I can even say its name now. It did take a minute, though."

I sat up and grabbed my knees as nerves plucked at me like an over-taut string. "I don't want to upset you, but..." I licked my lips. "What happened with Travis all those years ago?"

His face instantly paled, and I wanted to smack myself. Why couldn't I leave well enough alone? But... I needed to know. The last time I saw Seth was at a party that I'd thrown. Travis had been an ass as usual, but when he'd backhanded Seth, sending him to the ground, I'd lost it. I'd punched him. I'd told Seth to stay with me and Travis to get the hell out, but Seth had gotten up and followed Travis, head down, shoulders hunched, making apologies.

Seth had refused to leave him and kept making excuses, then he started bailing on seeing me until he stopped talking to me at all.

Travis had made him choose, and Seth had chosen his boyfriend over me.

I'd never gotten over it.

Yes, logically, I knew there was more to it and Seth was a victim, but it had hurt worse than a punch to the dick. When Seth tried to restart our friendship after Travis dumped him, I'd told him no. I'd had to keep myself safe, and I'd refused to wait around for some other person to make Seth give me up.

With a sigh, Seth leaned his head back against the vines, his brown hair brushing a flower, which released a light scent. "Long story short, Travis isolated me. I couldn't go anywhere without him, do anything without his permission, or wear clothes that he hadn't approved of. Every little mistake was my fault and he would take it out on me, and I just took it." He shrugged, meeting my gaze. "I felt like that's all I was worth."

"You're not," I said, rushing to his side and gripping his hands before I'd even thought about it. "You're worth everything."

Didn't he see that?

"Kal says the same thing." Seth squeezed my hand. "In the end, Travis made me pay for the move to Washington, then dumped me. Best thing that ever happened to me."

I swallowed, releasing his hands. "Do you have nightmares?"

"Sometimes, yeah. More panic attacks with my anxiety, or freaking out when people suddenly touch me. Or yelling. I can't handle yelling." Seth stared at me and shifted to his knees. "Vince, are you okay?"

I hadn't told him or Teddy anything. Both of them would listen; I knew that, and Seth was here and waiting. He wouldn't judge or blame. He would let me say what I needed. Or at least, I thought he would. But I felt... dirty. I felt used. I felt like what happened must somehow be my fault, though I'd been taken. But I could've fought more. I could've resisted. I'd made a token effort, then just gave up. Hadn't I?

Seth simply stared at me, and I wanted to say something, but I couldn't get the words out. I trusted him. I did. But saying what happened would make it real, and all I wanted was for it to disappear. I needed to forget. I needed to push it away, bury it. Thinking about what happened was pointless. I needed to move on and let it go.

"Yeah, of course. I mean, for being abducted by aliens, I'm doing fantastic," I teased.

He touched my arm, and I flinched, hugging myself.

"You can tell me anything," he said in a soft voice. "Whenever you want. I'm always available. I love you, Vinnie. You know that, right?"

"Yeah," I said, voice barely audible. He loved me, but not like I loved him.

I shook and shivered as I sat on the bed, looking at all of the corners of my room. Not a single shadow remained from the blinding bright light. No one was hiding, but every time I turned,

I saw things in the corner of my eyes. Logically, I knew there was no one, but my brain and my body were having a war.

With a deep breath, I stood and trudged out to the living room to mindlessly scroll through the multitude of offerings on my tablet. I lay on my back, leg swinging off the edge of the couch, and absentmindedly stared at the tablet, not truly seeing anything. I wasn't even thinking about anything, just existing. I didn't want to think. I didn't want to feel.

There was a guaranteed way to do that.

With a frown, I glanced at the dispenser. I could drink myself to oblivion. No nightmares. No thinking. No feeling. Nothing.

A chime sounded, and I ripped my gaze from the dispenser to shift it to the door. I stood, my toes curling on the mossy floor. "Come in," I called out, voice shaking and hands fisting the thighs of my sweatpants.

The door slid open with a low whoosh, and Don stood on the other side.

I sagged, releasing a huge breath. "Donny, you scared me."

He cocked his head, sending his purple hair tumbling. "Why?"

"You should know that."

"I only know if you think about it, Vince."

My eyes ran over his plain red shirt and black trousers. "Why are you here? I didn't have a nightmare."

Don tapped his temple with one of his claws. "I can feel you panicking, though I'm not sure what about."

I waved him in. Tension ramped up in my gut and made my spine straighten, but I forced it away. I truly didn't think Don would harm me. He'd already had ample chance if he'd wanted to attack me.

"I will not," he said in response to my thoughts, and I grinned. I had no idea why I liked his ability as much as I did, but I didn't bother to question it. I liked it. His mind reading was convenient, to say the least.

He wandered around my room, taking in all the shit I had synthesized, from blankets to books to beaded pillows to pretty shit that made me feel better. Don glanced at my deck of tarot cards. I hadn't touched them since I'd made them. They sat there on the table taunting me.

"I was curious about the power usage for your quarters, and now I know," he commented.

Guilt curled cold and hard in my gut, but I crossed my arms and snapped, "Here to punish me? Can't spare a little bit of energy?"

Don glanced over his shoulder. "Hardly, Vince."

I looked away from his intense green eyes, running my tongue over my teeth. Why did his fucking eyes have to be so expressive and lovely?

"Thank you," he whispered before continuing his evaluation of my room. He paused near the table and looked at the cards. "What are these?"

"Tarot cards."

"What do they do?"

"Provide insight into the past, present, and future."

His brow furrowed as he looked up at me. "You can do this?"

I shrugged. "Some people don't believe, but I've always found them helpful."

"Would you do this for me?"

I bit my lip, then nodded. "Why the hell not?"

Taking a seat on one side of the table, I gestured to the opposite for Don. I shuffled the cards. "Take a deep breath."

He did with the utmost seriousness, which made me smile.

"Again." When I couldn't find any tension in his body, I fanned out the cards. "I'm going to do a three card draw. Think of a question, or even say it out loud if you desire."

Don closed his eyes.

"Look at the cards and point to the three that speak to you the most, all while concentrating on your question."

He carefully indicated three cards with a claw.

With my left hand, I flipped over the first card. "So the first card represents your past, and it's the Hierophant. Basically, it's saying in the past you've clung to traditional paths in career and love. You like to stay within the conventional, whether that is in love, money, or your career path. None of that is bad."

His expression didn't give anything away.

I flipped the next card over. "This second card is your present, and it's the Ace of Cups, which is good. It signifies a new beginning is coming right around the corner. You need to let go of everything that's holding you back and embrace what's happening now. That can mean several things. Like in romance, this can be new feelings. Or if you are looking for a new career, an opportunity might present itself."

The last card flipped over, and I said, "And lastly, this is your future. The reversed Queen of Cups." I licked my lips. "Reversals tend not to be good in my experience. The card is saying that in the future, you and your emotions won't be in sync. This might mean that you struggle to communicate, which can lead to an inability to cope, or you might let your imagination run away from you. So like, in love, it might feel turbulent and like you have no safe place. Career-wise, you become exhausted and like you're not doing what you want. Both might lead you to compulsively spend money."

Don stared down at the cards, tail wiggling.

"It wasn't a great way to end," I said, putting all the cards in a pile. "But the future is always changing, and most people think this is nonsense. It might mean nothing."

"You believe," he said with utter certainty.

"I do, but that doesn't mean bad things are coming for you, Donny."

"Why do you call me that?"

"Donny?" I asked.

He tilted his head to the side, and I blinked. Don said, "When I offer you my throat, it means I'm agreeing with you. It can also mean I'm conceding to your dominance."

So they were like those werewolves from the smutty shifter romances I liked. Good to know. "It's a nickname," I said with a shrug. "I like it. Do you hate it?"

"Not when you say it."

I grinned, smug as fuck, even though I shouldn't be.

"Do you wish me to help you sleep tonight?"

Nodding, I bit my lip. "Do you mind?"

"Not at all."

Getting up, I headed to the bedroom, and he followed me, not close enough to freak me out. Much. I lay down, body stiff, and looked away from Don. He crouched next to my bed, not touching, merely looking at me.

"Peace, Vince. I will never harm you or touch you without permission."

I nodded, gripping the sheets, but I couldn't get my body to relax. All I could think about was how much bigger he was than me. Right on the heel of that thought was utter disgust with myself. This, all of this, shouldn't bother me as much as it did. I just needed to suck it up and ignore everything. Who fucking care what happened to me? Was I going to sob about it or get over it?

Don shook his head. "Life does not always work like that, Little Warrior."

My forehead wrinkled.

"If you give me an endearment, it's only fair that I give you one in return. And no matter what soul type you have, you're a warrior, Vince."

"Soul type? What the fuck does that mean?"

He sat back, folding his legs and resting his elbows on his knees. "Drakcol believe in four types of souls. Warriors, like myself, are red in color. They are the most venerated in our culture, probably due to our warring origin. Then are the spiritual souls. They are the rarest. They have a connection to the Crystal. Their souls are white. Then come the seekers, who are blue. And finally, the creators, who are green in color. Warrior and seeker souls grow darker the purer they are, and spiritual and creator souls grow lighter the more pure they are."

"How do you know what type of soul you have?" I asked, rolling onto my stomach and pulling the pillow closer.

"A spiritual soul, usually one of the Ranks, must test you," he said, and my breath began to deepen at the calm, smoothness of his voice. "You touch a piece of crystal that connects to the true Crystal."

"What's that?" I asked, eyes closing.

"It's a giant Crystal that is the center of our culture. It's guarded and understood only by the Ranks, who are its priests and priestesses. It's our religion."

"Hmm," I moaned, curling around the pillow. The sheets covered me, and a smooth palm with a subtle scritch cupped my cheek. Peace flowed over me like a wave of warm water.

I pressed my hand over Don's and smiled at him. "You're pretty wonderful."

"Thank you, Little Warrior. So are you."

Chapter 10

A DIFFERENT WAY TO BE TOGETHER, MAYBE?

Vince

Seth was pressed against Kal's side while he stared at his tablet that showed the feed of their baby as we sat in their room. He'd invited me over before they went to their hand-to-hand combat class; I imagined Seth only went there to drool over his husband. Kal and I were making no effort to speak, and we silently glared at each other. Seth either didn't notice the strain or he'd decided not to comment on it. I assumed the latter, honestly. He wasn't unaware of our mutual hatred, though he was clueless as to the reason why.

Part of me wanted to get to know Kal because Seth wished for it, and I had a hard time denying him anything, especially after so long. Besides, being friends, or at least on speaking terms, with his husband would make my friendship with Seth easier. I didn't want to give him up this time, but as far as romance went, I was fighting an uphill battle that I was pretty sure I would lose, for all my bluster and confidence.

My gaze ran over Kal, trying to find what Seth liked about him so much. He was attractive. I was a strong enough person to admit it. His silvery-blue hair was long and silky. His scales were steel-blue with purple and neon blue glimpses of skin around them. He was broad and tall, but not humongous like some of the other drakcol—Don and Caleb mainly. His full lips, wide forehead, and tapered ears were all lovely. He wore a ridiculous amount of jewelry in my opinion, but it worked on him. All of it was silver, except for a gold chain with a raw amethyst that matched his eyes and the slim gold band on his left ring finger.

So he was hot. Seth liked attractive guys. Who didn't? I enjoyed a pretty face and a nice ass as much as the next person, but that didn't constitute a relationship.

"The baby's doing well," Seth said, putting the tablet down on the backless couch next to him.

"How much longer?" I asked.

He shrugged. "No idea. The doctors at the nesting facility don't know either. This is the first drakcol/human baby."

"Well, they will get more with Mindy and Teddy if they want kids."

"Yeah. Mindy strikes me as someone who wants kids, but I don't know. Have you talked to Teddy much?"

"About kids? No," I replied. The thought of asking if he wanted kids hadn't even crossed my mind—it probably should have—but we were still in some awkward dance after Xome. It's like neither of us knew exactly where we stood anymore. "We talk every day, though," I continued, defending him and crossing my arms. "It's not like he's too busy for me or something. He's a good friend."

"I wasn't saying that, Vinnie," Seth said, reaching for me, but I shifted away. He gave me a slight smile. "When we get back, there will be plenty of time for all of us to hang out. I need to get to know Teddy better."

My heart was like ice in my chest. I was almost positive I wanted to go back to Earth. Not for my family, which made me sound like an ass, but for me. I wanted to forget, and that was a way to do it.

Maybe they would take my memories without me going home, then I could stay.

"We should go," Kal said, standing. His tail coiled around Seth's ankle as he held out a hand. Seth interlocked their fingers, and I wanted to growl, but I forced a smug smile to my face while quirking my eyebrow at Kal. I smirked when his expression darkened and a low growl rumbled in his chest.

Oh, he would probably win this confrontation between us, but I wouldn't make it painless for him. No, there would be poking and prodding until Kal snapped and snarled.

I followed them as we headed to a training room. I guessed the drakcol took physical fitness seriously, which wasn't surprising, because they all looked like they lived in the gym. I was expecting weights and exercise machines, but that wasn't what I saw.

On the far wall were targets with bright blue lines, and people fired blasters at them. In the center were several mats where most of the people were in loose workout clothes. Seth was dressed similarly to Kal—both in black sweats and loose tunics. Kal's were much tighter, letting me see his strong muscles.

"Where do we sit?" I asked Seth, annoyed. Kal was too attractive. I'd never been muscular. No desire to work out in a gym or hike. I preferred to look pretty rather than sweat. I accomplished that easily enough, thank you very much.

"You can sit over there. I have class. You can participate too if you want. Learn to fight. Protect yourself."

"Wait," I said, taking a step after him, hand up. "You fight?"

"Yeah. I'm not great at it, but I'm getting better. Wyn and Monty are teaching me. Kal can't."

"Not a good fighter?" I asked, smirking. Something, finally, the asshole wasn't perfect at.

"No, he's great. He just freaks out when he thinks I'm in trouble. This class will be interesting, to say the least." Seth laughed and walked over to his husband, slinging an arm around his waist.

Someone sidled up next to me, and I glanced toward them. Don watched Kal and Seth, obviously reading my jealousy. I practically dared him to call me out on it, crossing my arms and cocking an eyebrow, and while his lips quirked, he didn't remark.

"If you would like to learn to fight," he eventually said, "I'll teach you."

"I bet you're the best because of the mind-reading thing."

"It can be helpful, but it's not perfect."

"You beat everyone, don't you?" I asked, imagining him pummeling Kal.

"I would never hurt my younger brother, even for you, Little Warrior," he said as he faced me, leaning against the wall. His long purple hair was tied in a messy knot, and I had to say I dug it. I liked dudes with long hair. Sue me. He smiled again. "I cannot beat Kalvoxrencol. I haven't been able to in years."

"Really?"

"Yes. He's the best fighter. No one who has tried has beaten him. When we fight, his brain shuts off and it's all instinct. Something he taught himself, to beat me. Creative soul he might be, but Kalvoxrencol forged himself into a weapon."

"Why?" I asked before I could stop myself.

"He has troubles as anyone does." He pushed away from the wall and left me to stew.

Ass, I thought at his back.

His tail twitched, and he flashed me the barest grin.

As people paired off, I sat against the wall. Caleb joined me and stared unabashedly at his husband with basically hearts in his eyes. Teddy also came, but he was a little less obvious in his ogling, simply following Mindy's movements with a bland expression. Teddy tried to talk to me, and I managed a few words here and there, but I couldn't tear my eyes from Seth.

He wasn't anyone's equal here—they all beat him time and time again—but he would get back up and square off. Against taller and stronger foes, Seth could hold his own. It was amazing, and my heart warmed as I watched him fight and laugh. No one would ever hurt him again, or if they did, they wouldn't come away unscathed.

Kal, though. God, he was fury on two legs. The dude moved faster than anyone. He knocked everyone who challenged him to the floor. His only weakness was when Seth was in a bout, he couldn't fight. He stared and growled at Seth's opponents, then fussed over Seth afterward.

I watched as Kal straightened Seth's clothes and tutted over him. Kal was a mother hen. Who would've guessed? I lingered on his long fingers and claws before running my eyes over his form, then looking back at Seth, who blushed profusely but didn't move away from his husband. Seth wasn't going to leave Kal, especially with their baby on the way.

But perhaps we could be together still?

Polyamory had never been something that was for me. I was too possessive. I would even say I was unhealthy in how possessive I was, but I could share Seth, couldn't I? I would rather have part of him, then none of him. If Seth was the hinge, I could bear it. But what if they wanted an equal relationship?

My gaze returned to Kal. Could I let him fuck me if it meant having Seth?

A slam went through the room, and I jolted, pulse spiking.

Don landed on the mat with a low groan. Caleb was half up, whereas Fyn, Mindy, and Kal rushed toward their fallen brother, Seth two steps behind them.

Don was holding his stomach, and the other drakcol said, "I thought he saw the kick."

"It was my mistake," Don said with a pained grimace.

Fury ripped through me. I wanted to rip the other drakcol with golden scales apart. I took a step toward Don to comfort him, but Caleb rested his hand on my arm, stopping me. I yanked away, heart pounding, and fear slid like ice through my veins.

Don growled, and I looked at him. He was staring at Caleb, snarling, but he quickly averted his gaze.

Caleb appeared nonplussed. "Don doesn't usually get knocked down, except when he and Kal fight. Weird."

Teddy grunted. His usual reply. My Teddy wasn't much of a talker, at least that hadn't changed.

Don waved off his brothers and walked toward the door, leaving without even sparing a glance toward me.

Chapter 11

UTTER DISTRACTION.

Dontilvynsan

I stepped into my room, sore even though Doctor Muznim had helped promote healing and fixed my cracked ribs. I couldn't believe I let Ensign Gogvon kick me in the stomach, but I'd been distracted. Vince's thoughts wouldn't leave mine. It didn't matter if he'd been across the room or not. It had been as if he was whispering in my ear.

He'd been distracted by Seth and his ability to fight, as well as tinged with jealousy. Vince wanted to ensure by his own two hands that no one would ever hurt him again. Then he'd begun to think of the three of them being in a triad. While many species had multiple partners, drakcol did not. Our single mate bond made such a thing difficult. Before a drakcol formed a mate bond, it wasn't uncommon to have multiple partners. But as far as mate bonds went, either a drakcol sought the Crystal for their soulmate and was bound to someone, or they fell in love and the bond formed naturally—bound or chosen mates were the only ones in existence for us.

On Tamkolvanloknol, a single triad existed who were all mated to each other, but they were the first in our recorded history.

I knew my brother well enough to know Kalvoxrencol would never wish for such an arrangement. He would never be alright with Seth fucking someone else—it would break his soul—nor would he desire another person besides Seth.

Once we formed a mated bond, it was impossible for us to want or desire anyone other than our mate. Seth was it for Kalvoxrencol; there would be no others.

But none of that was what had caused my distraction to the point I'd allowed an ensign to send me to the floor. I growled as I ripped a hand through my hair, my tail lashing and my wings flaring. Vince was actually considering offering himself to Kalvoxrencol. He'd allow my brother to fuck him to have Seth.

If I thought for even a moment that Kalvoxrencol would accept him, I wouldn't have been able to leave the training room, to leave Vince with a competitor.

I sat abruptly when my knees trembled, losing the ability to support my weight. Why? Why did it bother me? Vince didn't mean anything to me. He was a human that we'd rescued and would escort home. Nothing more. Him contemplating a physical relationship with my brother shouldn't bother me. There was no competition. I wasn't and never had been jealous of nor bothered by Kalvoxrencol's relationships before.

Why did the mere possibility of this one upset me?

I feared I didn't want to know the answer.

My eyes closed as I took a steadying breath to try and regain my calm, but it didn't want to come. Giving up, I limped to the shower and washed off the sweat and frustration. Once clean, I donned my uniform and headed back to Command.

When I entered Command, Bimwoxcol said, "Captain entering." Everyone faced me.

"Return," I ordered, and everyone went back to their duties. "Report."

Bimwoxcol started to update me on a few new problems with the ship. Nothing too alarming, though our long-range communications and sensors were fluctuating a bit more than usual. It was possible we needed to replace some parts or a few nodes. I made a note of it, then continued to my seat at the front of Command, wincing when my ribs compressed.

Hopefully, I wouldn't be sore for more than a few days.

I flicked through the reports that had been submitted from the different departments. I flagged the important ones to review and respond when I went back to my office, then I started working on system functions while keeping an eye on the long-range sensors. They were still functional, but without them we'd be flying blind; also I needed to be aware of what was around my ship. It didn't matter that we were in Coalition Space, which was relatively safe; I refused to take that assumption as law.

Besides, staying focused on my duties kept my mind from Vince, which I desperately needed. The small human was taking up more and more of my focus, and it unnerved me to say the least, but more importantly, he was stealing my attention from where it needed to be. I took a deep breath, then shoved Vince from my thoughts.

———

An agonized scream made me leap out of bed. I was on my feet and out the door before I'd consciously thought about it. My bare feet dug into the soft moss and my hair hung around my broad shoulders as I panted, chest heaving. I forced myself to stop and search my mind for the origin, though deep down I knew where it came from.

Vince's terror spiked as fuzzy memories raced across my mind. It was another nightmare.

I hesitated. He hadn't asked for my help tonight. If he didn't want it, I shouldn't impose it on him simply because it disturbed my sleep. Of course, I hadn't suggested it, still oddly hurt by Vince contemplating offering himself to Kalvoxrencol. I started to turn around, shoving a hand in my hair, when another sharp jolt of terror washed through me.

My hands fisted as I fought the instinct to protect Vince for a single beat of my soul, then I was racing down the hall toward him. I overrode the lock on his door and slipped inside.

He was in the center of the bed, thrashing. The sheets were twisted around his thin waist and sweat covered his bare chest. I was across the room in two steps and beside him. I wanted to crawl onto the bed and draw him close, but that would be a mistake.

Instead, I gently brushed his cheek.

Vince struck my hand away and his eyes snapped open, wide and unseeing. "No. No!" he screamed, trying to get away from me.

"It's me. It's me," I repeated over his cries. I caught his face in my hands so he would look at me. His deep brown eyes landed on me as he panted, writhing. I repeated, "It's me, Little Warrior."

His breathing began to slow.

"No one will ever touch you again without your permission. Not ever."

"Promise," he demanded, voice breaking.

"I promise." If he stayed, I'd protect him for the rest of his life. If he went home, I would ensure he was placed in a safe situation on Earth. Nothing would ever happen to Vince that he didn't want if it was within my power to prevent.

Vince grabbed my hand. I almost drew away from the alluring softness of his skin, but he pulled me closer and took several deep breaths. "I woke you."

My thumb slid across his silky cheek without permission. Vince released a long gust of air that swirled over my scales. Trembling, I continued to stroke his face as Vince simply breathed. His thoughts were calming, and I hadn't used my inner fire once. He didn't mind me holding him, and I believed he wished me to continue, though it was difficult for me to ascertain with his muddled thoughts.

An instinct tugged at me to lie on the bed and hold him against my chest, but I forced myself to remain crouched where I was. My tail did not listen. It slithered across the blanket and coiled around his slim wrist. I was about to uncurl it from him, but Vince grabbed it.

A jolt went up my spine from the contact, sending the most wondrous shocks of electricity through me. Drakcol tails were extremely sensitive, and I loved mine being touched. Vince kept a firm grip on it as his eyes fell closed. He started to settle, and I hummed gently in the back of my throat and smoothed my thumb over his pale cheek.

He continued to calm until he was limp on the bed and waves of sleep began to draw him under.

Vince hadn't needed my gift. He'd simply needed me.

"Stay," he ordered in a firm voice despite the tiredness clouding his mind. "Please," he added belatedly. The request was soft and hesitant. He thought I would abandon him.

My soul pounded against my ribs, and my eyes never left him. "I will stay as long as you want me to."

Vince

Fuck, I'm tired, was my first thought as I opened my eyes. My room was as light as usual, without a single shadow to mar it, just how I liked. The window over my bed depicted nothing but black space and distant stars. I looked away from that small glimpse. That never-ending darkness bothered me.

The nightmares had plagued me badly last night. Endless stretches of darkness. People hurting me, pushing me down. My stomach eating itself. The fiery burn of the incinerator as Teddy and me had chucked a body into it.

I dragged a hand down my face. Sleep had been impossible.

Of course, I could've asked Don for help, but I hadn't, because he'd been injured and I didn't want to bother him.

I blinked as a blurry memory surfaced. Had he come last night? I almost remembered him being there. Hovering over me. Holding me. Humming to me. Soothing me. Was that real or a dream?

I shifted and something warm slid from my face and landed onto my chest. With my pulse elevating and a cold sweat gathering between my shoulder blades, I looked at the massive hand covered in black scales. I followed the muscular arm to the broad shoulder to Don, who was sitting next to my bed, head against the mattress. He was completely passed out.

I tensed in preparation for the panic or fear or disgust, and nothing happened. Don was still there, and I wasn't freaking out. His royal purple hair hung around him in soft waves. His broad shoulders and his wide face were relaxed as his eyes flicked behind their lids.

Had he come to help me and fallen asleep? It was possible.

His presence wasn't freaking me out. Why wasn't it bothering me? I should be screaming, shoving him, swearing up a storm as a panic attack threatened to overtake me.

I smothered a laugh when I realized why I wasn't doing any of those things. I trusted him. I trusted he wouldn't hurt me. God, I was fucking stupid. Don could change in a second. People did that.

But while I wasn't panicking and he was unconscious, I could try and work through some issues, maybe. If I was even going to try to be a third to Kal and Seth, I was going to have to get over... everything.

Fuck, I was a man. I just needed to sock myself in the dick and move on. Why was I letting this shit bother me so much? I could've fought harder, and I hadn't. I needed to push through it and sideline these issues.

Though working out said issues on Kalvoxrencol's older brother was weird and creepy as hell—and he hadn't consented for me to touch him. I didn't want to be that person. No, I refused to be that person. I would never take advantage or hurt someone like... I shook my head. I simply wouldn't. I was an asshole, but I wasn't a dick.

Besides, Don was nice. Truly nice. He deserved the best. He deserved everything. Not someone who screamed at the ghosts in his head or the nightmares that wouldn't stop.

Forcing everything away, I grabbed his hand and pulled it over my heart, and scooted closer. His breathing didn't change, but the closer I got, the harsher mine became. My body screamed at me to move away, but at the same time, I wanted to move closer. I wanted to feel his scales beneath my fingers. I wanted to see his deep green eyes as my name fell from his lips.

What was it about this man?

When I reached the edge of the bed, less than a handbreadth from him, I lifted his hand to my face and pressed his wide palm against my cheek. I should be afraid of his claws nicking me or him smacking me, but I wasn't. I just wanted to keep him beside me.

Some part of me was convinced that if Don stayed right next to my side, everything would work out.

I snuggled closer until my head bumped his and kept his hand on my cheek. I closed my eyes and breathed.

I had never felt safer in my entire life.

Chapter 12

TEDDY, I MISS YOU.

Vince

"You're not hanging out with Seth today?" Teddy asked, sitting on the opposite side of my ridiculous backless couch.

Seriously, these couches sucked so much. They were way too fucking tall, and I couldn't find a comfortable spot to snuggle into. Yeah, they had tall arms like a chaise or a divan or some shit, but they were hard under my ass, even with the pink blankets I'd spread over the seat. I missed big plush couches that basically ate you when you sat down. I yanked my oversized hoodie closer and pulled my legs up to sit cross-legged.

Nope, still annoying. My ass was going to be numb eventually.

"Not sucking Mindy's face today?" I rejoined, picking at my peeling pink nail polish, and Teddy grunted with the slightest flush on his cheeks.

I hadn't felt like leaving my room today, and with the food dispensers, I didn't have to. Honestly, I hadn't felt like doing anything besides holding a pillow to my oddly hollow chest and drinking as much booze as I could to drown whatever these pesky emotions were. But I didn't want that. I'd seen friends give into the bottle, and I refused to be that person, yet the temptation to forget was so damn strong. So I called Teddy on the glowing, touchstone thing. I'd had to say his full name. Bartholomew Reginald Lucian Cavendish-Wallingford. How ridiculous was that? Like the good friend that he was, Teddy had immediately agreed to come and hang out.

We sat there in awkward silence. I didn't know why things were so strained between us. Teddy and I had been through literal hell together, and I was closer to him than almost anyone. Why were we fumbling to find our rhythm?

Trying to be a functioning adult, I asked, "Are you mad at me?"

Teddy cocked his head. "Why would you think that?"

I motioned between us.

"I'm always quiet."

"That's not what I meant," I replied.

He sighed, then chewed on his bottom lip for a moment. "I was... hurt when you ran toward Seth, not caring I was there."

"Fuck, I didn't mean to hurt you." I'd just been overwhelmed with seeing Seth.

"I know that," Teddy said, reaching for me but stopped when I flinched from his sudden movement. "I also don't know where we stand. Everything feels different."

I nodded. "I want us to be close still."

His serious eyes ran over my huddled form. "I do too."

I was keeping things from Teddy, but I couldn't get the words out about what happened. It was too real. Besides, what was the point? I was going to forget it all eventually.

Teddy said, motioning to me, "I see you are finally embracing your style again."

Chuckling, I smoothed my skirt over my legs and the rest of the tension in my body slid away. "How many times did I complain about the jumpsuits on Xome?"

"Too many times to count."

"Fair, but fuck, they were the ugliest brown and so thin and unflattering."

"Yep."

"Now," I said, "I can finally wear everything that I want to."

He nodded.

Something inside of me uncoiled. It was like the past. I would talk—rant, more accurately—and Teddy would listen while nodding along.

"Mindy is good to you, right?" I asked. I hadn't been as good a friend as Teddy had been; I'd been more focused on Seth and his stupid husband. However, I was concerned about Teddy.

"He is. Mindy loves me."

"He feeds you and doesn't hurt you?" I pressed, unable to stop the protective urges coursing through me.

"Vince, Serlotminden is obsessed with making sure I eat and that I'm happy. I promise I'm doing okay."

"Good," I said, though part of me wanted to keep bugging him for the details. Instead, I demanded, "So tell me how he stole your heart so I can tease you."

Teddy laughed, but didn't deny me. His smooth, even voice soothed me further as he told me about him and Mindy crash landing on an ice planet and Mindy courting Teddy with a caveman routine that seemed to work for my friend.

"Hmm, I'm sure I can find multiple things to tease you with," I said.

"True."

We fell silent again, but it wasn't as oppressive. It might take time, but I was positive we'd be close again eventually.

Right in time for me to leave, my brain unhelpfully supplied.

"So you have a thing for Seth?" he asked bluntly, and I burst into a fit of laughter as warmth filled my aching chest.

"God, Teddy, I missed you."

Our friendship was different from the one I had with Seth, as Teddy and I had been forced together, and our relationship had been forged in fire, literally, but it was no less special. He was so important to me, and I loved him dearly, even if I could never get the words out. Admitting I cared about people, even platonically, was a no-go for me. Of course, admitting romantic feelings was worse. I didn't do that, and I didn't do long term. I had Seth. Why would I ever need anyone else?

"I missed you too. I kept trying to get back to you when I was on that frozen planet. I didn't want you to think I'd abandoned you or died."

"As you said. It's alright, Teddy. I'm not mad at you and I don't blame you. I blame your kidnapping husband," I teased.

Teddy rolled his eyes.

"Seth," I said with a sigh, going back to his earlier question.

"I don't even remember you mentioning Seth when we were on Xome, but you clearly have a thing for him," he said.

That was my Teddy. He wasn't the most expressive person, but he shot straight to the heart of the problem. I played with the ripped part of the black jeans that were under my equally black skirt and said, "He was my childhood best friend, my first and only love, and he meant—*means* everything to me."

Teddy nodded. "He was abducted. You were abducted. Now you're both here."

"And he's married to an alien and has a baby on the way." I finished, grinning at the ridiculousness of my situation.

"Yep."

"Just my luck."

Teddy smiled, but it was tense. "You know... they mate for life, right?"

"I do. And from the way you and Caleb can't seem to breathe without your alien husbands attached to your faces, I'm going to assume you both like it."

He flushed again.

I leaned back against the tall couch arm, head falling back. "Seth. God. I've loved him forever and now he's with someone. Permanently."

"How are you?"

I ignored his question and said, "I had the insane idea of asking to be their third."

"I know we never discussed it, but you don't strike me as someone who, well, shares." Teddy and I had known each other for over two years, and he knew I was a possessive bastard.

"You're not wrong."

"From what little I've seen of drakcol, I don't think polyamory is a practice for them, but maybe they'd be interested?"

Kal's fierce glare and the way he held Seth so tight said something very different. Kal share? I had a feeling he was more similar to me in that regard. Kal aside, Seth didn't like me, not romantically. He never had, as much as that hurt to think.

"I'm gonna say no," I said.

"Yeah, Kal doesn't seem the type to be alright with Seth having another relationship, and I doubt you want to sleep with Kal."

I shook my head, hugging my knees to my chest. I'd thought about it for one second, and it made my stomach churn. Fucking Seth didn't bother me as much because I completely trusted him, but at the same time, my muscles tightened at the thought of his fingers on my bare skin. Of him pushing inside of me. Of him on top of me. Of his low noises. Of his warm breath on my face.

Sweat gathered on my forehead, and I shivered. I didn't think I wanted that even with Seth. I could force myself to, if it was him, but panic wouldn't be far from my thoughts if we had sex. And it shouldn't be like that.

Hell, I'd loved casual sex before all this. I loved kissing, touching, and everything that came with it. I needed to go back to who I was. Not this terrified weakling, but the confident man who had fun.

"So are you still going to keep pursuing Seth?" Teddy asked, and I had no answer.

Was I? I loved him. I did, but I didn't want to make him sad, which I would if I kept this up. Even if I had Seth, I didn't think I wanted to stay, because I wanted to get rid of these memories. And Earth was how I would do it. Earth was the only way to be free, and I needed it like I needed to breathe. I *had* to be myself again.

I wouldn't remember Teddy, though. I wouldn't remember seeing Seth again. They would be gone along with the bad.

"Are you happy?" I asked him.

"This again." Teddy said slowly, "Ridiculously happy. I don't think I've ever been this happy in my life."

While his voice was even and his face betrayed none of those feelings, I nodded. "I think Seth is happy too."

"He seems happy to me. He's always staring at his baby."

I wouldn't remember them. Well, that wasn't strictly true. I'd remember Seth from before, but not that he was married to an alien prince. But me not knowing Teddy or that Seth was safe wouldn't matter. They would be happy. I didn't have to remember that for it to be true. They would be living their lives content, and I could be free from everything; I'd return to who I was.

Was it selfish to leave them? Probably. But I deserved to be a tad selfish. I deserved to be happy, didn't I? Maybe I didn't. I sighed. I had no fucking clue. Why was everything so tangled up?

"What's going through your head?" Teddy asked.

"I'm thinking about going home."

"You are?" Teddy sat up straight. "You're not close to your family. I assumed you would stay."

I shrugged. "Why wouldn't I want to go home?"

"Me. Seth."

I gave him a sad smile. "I would miss you."

"No, you wouldn't," he said. "You wouldn't remember me. You wouldn't remember us. You wouldn't remember anything that happened to us."

Teddy got to his feet and stalked toward the door, and I didn't blame him. I was basically telling him that he and Seth weren't enough, which was a fucking slap in the face, especially after everything that we'd been through together.

"Please don't tell Seth."

He grunted and left.

My head fell back against the arm of the couch. I should've told him the truth about... everything. If I explained why I wanted to go home, he would've understood. Wouldn't he? The words refused to come. I didn't want him to look at me like I was broken or weak. I should've fought more, but after the beatings and punishments, the lack of food, and the never-ending darkness, I stopped. Letting customers fuck me seemed easier.

I couldn't live with these memories. I couldn't live with myself. I couldn't.

First things first. I had to find out if I could stay and have my memories removed. Who would know that? Immediately, I thought of Don and his sleeping face next to mine.

Dontilvynsan

Thoughts of this morning wouldn't leave my mind, no matter how much I tried to banish them. I'd woken up to my hand on Vince's face and his forehead pressed against mine. He'd been asleep and curled up against me. I'd been surrounded by his crisp scent and his warm presence. I hadn't wanted to leave. I'd wanted to stay there forever.

When he woke up, I'd braced for his terror, but he grinned and stretched, leaving me to follow the movement and the tantalizing glimpses of his bare skin. I'd wondered for all of one moment about him not being upset by my close presence, then he'd thought about snuggling against me. Not only that. He'd felt safe. *I* had made him feel safe.

I was a captain in the Planetary Navy. I was a soldier. An older brother. I'd protected a lot of people over my life, but none had felt as satisfying as making Vince feel safe.

My arms had ached to pull him close, but I'd resisted. His sleepy smile had made it far harder than it should've been.

Sitting in Command, reading scans and notes on my screen, should've kept my thoughts from Vince, but it didn't. I had to actively stop my inner fire from seeking him out across the ship. I doubted I'd be able to hear his thoughts at this distance, but I could probably feel the ebb and flow of his mind, which I was desperate for.

Forcing my thoughts away from Vince yet again, I focused on finishing my shift. When we were in Coalition space, I didn't remain in Command the entire time. I usually sat in Command and made sure everything was running correctly before retreating to my office to go over reports. Soon, I would have the privacy to allow my thoughts to wander more than when my senior officers were right beside me.

Warmth grew in my pocket as the voice I wanted to hear most in this universe whispered in my ear, "Dontilvynsan."

I stood, and Bimwoxcol said, "Captain departing."

Everyone turned toward me, standing straight.

When I reached the door, I ordered, "Return."

All of my officers went back to their duties.

The second the door blocked me from sight, I fumbled for my touchstone and yanked it out of my pocket, dropping my screen in my haste. "Vince," I said breathlessly, making the connection.

"Where are you?"

"Outside my office. How can I assist you?" Instinctively, I reached for his mind among the many on my ship. I felt him, but no distinctive thoughts came to me. However, the lure of his warm mind and the gentle flow of his emotions that I couldn't quite perceive intoxicated me.

"Can we talk?"

"In person?"

"If you're not too busy, then yeah."

"I will never be too busy for you," I replied without thought, then paused. What had I just said?

I heard the smile in his voice as he said, "Come to my room. I'll even get food from the dispenser."

"I look forward to it."

My smile didn't want to dim, but I forced it away and strode to his room. I didn't know why Vince wanted to speak to me, and I didn't care. I wanted to see him, and I blatantly refused to contemplate why. I was allowed to become friends with this human. Friends liked to see each other. That was all.

I pushed the chime on his door, and it rang loudly.

"Just come in, Don," Vince shouted, making me smile again.

Vince was sitting on the couch with a plate of food in the middle. It was a mix of fruit, meat, and flat bread—a typical drakcol meal—but there were other things I didn't recognize. Long, crunchy-looking tubes, a meat circle in between two pieces of fluffy bread, and square brown things that appeared to be soft and chewy. Taking a seat, I focused on the swirling anxiety in his mind and not the stretch of pale skin of his belly, which was harder than it should've been.

"What's wrong?"

"Can you erase my memories?"

My soul stalled before leaping into a dizzying speed. "Repeat that."

He swallowed, meeting my gaze. "Can you erase my memories?"

"Why?"

"That's why I want to go back to Earth. If your scientists can get rid of them, then I won't have to."

I relaxed, practically sagging backwards. He didn't want me to *personally* take his memories. I'd never tried to wipe someone's mind clean, but my mentor had assured me that I could do so if I ever had to. I hated the thought of basically killing someone by stealing all that they were and leaving nothing but a mindless husk behind.

"You want to forget what happened," I stated. It was unsurprising. I'd caught glimpses of what Vince had endured, and it had been horrific.

Hands tight on his thighs, he bobbed his head. "I could stay here with you. I mean, Seth and Teddy. Not just you. Not only you. You understand."

His mind swirled in many emotions, which tugged on my soul but made it difficult for me to follow exactly what was bothering him. Nonetheless, I wanted to soothe all of his tension.

"Please," he begged.

How I wished I could say yes, but it wasn't my decision. "You would have to appeal to the Council of Seekers for them to erase your memories for psychological trauma, and I don't think they are likely to approve."

"Why? Why wouldn't they help me?"

I set the plate on the floor to sit closer to him. When he didn't move away, I felt honored with the show of trust. "It's not helping you. Erasing your memories is a bandage to the true underlying issue. It's like when I assist you into falling asleep. You wouldn't have conscious memory of what happened, but your body will remember. You will tense and panic and not understand why. You will fear people like those who harmed you, and you will not know why. The technicians will do it when they return you to Earth, but the seeker in charge of your wipe would probably recommend you not to go."

"Who are you to say what is best for me?" he snapped, standing. "You have no idea. None. You do not get to make my choices for me."

"It's not my decision, and I cannot say what's better. I've never been hurt like you have. I have no idea what or if there is a better option. I cannot speak on it, Vince. I can only tell you the likely outcome. But you can petition the board of seekers for a memory wipe. I will assist you if you want to walk down this path. The council may require you to seek treatment with a professional first."

"I don't want treatment," he yelled. "I want to forget. I want this to be over. Do you understand? I need this whole fucking thing to be over! I want to go back to who I actually am!"

I didn't say anything, because I didn't know what to say. I couldn't promise Vince the council would give him what he desired, nor could I say any comforting words. This wound wouldn't disappear easily. It would take work to heal what had been done to him, and there was no guarantee that everything would return to how it used to be.

His thoughts bounced, never remaining in one place. Anger. Fear. Longing. Despair. That brightness I'd sometimes glimpsed in him was swallowed whole by a void that was drawing him in, crushing him. Losing his memories wasn't the cure he'd hoped it was. Vince had counted on that cure. He'd needed it more than anything.

While our technology was superior to that of the humans, we couldn't fix everything. Much like humans, we possessed psychological doctors to help people heal from the mental wounds inflicted upon them or brain disorders like Zoltilvoxfyn's deep moroseness and Seth's anxiety.

Vince reached for me, eyes shining, and I moved toward him without thought. He pressed my hand to his face and dropped his head against my chest. "Help me."

I pushed gentle waves of calm into his mind to steal the dark pit of emotions. As he sagged in my embrace, I couldn't help but wonder if I was doing more damage to him, but it was Vince's choice and I wouldn't refuse him.

Chapter 13

WELL, THAT'S INTERESTING.

Vince

I sat beside Seth in the near-empty cafeteria as he spoke to the other humans about their options. I hadn't wanted to leave my room this morning after learning what I had from Don yesterday. All of my slight hope at staying with my friends had come crashing down, leaving nothing but rubble. I'd curled up into a ball on my bed and refused to move. My mind had been utterly numb. That had been the entirety of my plan: never leave my bed unless Don was close by to calm me down.

Seth had ruined that rather morose and dramatic plan when he invited me to participate in this "Team Human" meeting. I hadn't been able to refuse him, and I'd tried in every way feasible, short of actually telling him to fuck off. Of course, if I'd managed to beg off, Teddy would've probably shown up, as long as he wasn't mad at me still. So I'd left my room.

Sure, I *should* connect with the other humans here. Camden and Pierce had both been in brothels like me; they would understand my issues. Roman seemed nice, as did some of the others. I mean, Brad was a surly dick, but I could ignore him or prod him into snapping, depending on my mood. And yet... I didn't want to do any of that. I wanted to be in my room, lying on my bed and pretending to not exist.

Seth vibrated with nerves, drawing me out of my bleak thoughts, and I held his hand to calm him, ignoring the initial flash of disgust from the skin to skin contact. Seth gripped my fingers in his sweaty grasp, but I couldn't pay any attention to him or his words. My mind zipped straight back to what I'd learned from Don. Most likely, my memories would remain intact if I stayed. And even if I went to Earth, I would have the same physical reactions and no idea why.

Of course, having been missing for two-plus years would make me guess about what happened, but I wouldn't remember.

Camden, Brad, and Pierce, the newest members of Team Human, paid rapt attention to Seth. Caleb was also answering questions, but most of the humans moved away from him. In soul, he was human. In body, not so much. Also, he was fucking huge. It was taking a moment for everyone to get used to the drakcol proportions. Teddy didn't speak, as he was brand new too, but he paid attention.

A few drakcol wandered by our table, but they gave us a wide berth, respecting our privacy.

Seth handled the questions about citizenship, school opportunities, and work fairly well despite the fact he'd had very little time to prepare, but his words drifted in one ear and out the other. I didn't want to be here. I wanted to be anywhere else but here. Alone preferably. In bed. Squishy pillow pressed against me.

The door whooshed open, and Don walked in, talking to another officer. A grin spread over my face at his sudden appearance, and my gaze ran over him. He looked good in his dark blue uniform with its high collar. I caught sight of several gold pips on his neck that probably meant something. The gold made my eyes flick to his earrings. He didn't wear as much jewelry as his brothers, but what he had on was lovely. I liked the rings that pierced the tips of his ears—the green stones winking in the light—and the long chains in his lobes that nearly brushed his broad shoulders.

I sent him a greeting in my mind. He glanced in my direction in acknowledgment, but he didn't do anything more.

Ah, fuck no. That wouldn't do.

Smirking, I thought about when I'd tweaked his tail last night. Don had helped me sleep again, but his tail kept edging closer and closer to me on the bed, so I snagged it, making him jump near to the ceiling.

He stumbled over his words, the tail in question wriggling, and glared at me, which made me smirk harder. *Don't like that, Donny?* I teased, burning with the urge to poke and prod him into reaction.

Don shook his head as his lips quirked.

My pulse spiked, and I warmed at the sight of that small, little, tiny quirk. I loved it. So much. I wanted to be the one to pull it from him for... well, for the rest of my damn life. It was so satisfying.

He turned toward me, eyes widening. He'd obviously heard me, but I didn't care. Don was more than welcome to creep on my thoughts, and it wasn't like I was trying very hard to hide them.

"Captain," the drakcol said multiple times before Don shifted toward him to finish the conversation.

I leaned toward Seth. "I'll be right back. Are you alright?"

"Yeah," he said, waving me off as he continued to answer questions that I hadn't heard.

I rushed over to Don, who glared at me, but I knew he didn't mean it. Of course he didn't mean it. He liked seeing me. Why wouldn't he like seeing me? Besides, I looked rather fine today. I was wearing my usual crop top and oversized hoodie, but I had a short skirt on, leaving my legs bare.

At said thought of my legs, Don glanced down and his tail moved even faster.

I smirked.

"You distracted me," he said gravely, like I'd committed some horrid crime rather than a simple teasing.

I scoffed. "My prerogative." He shook his head, but I continued, "Why are you here? It's too early for your lunch."

Don crossed his arms as a slight smile tugged on his lips. "You know my schedule?"

Did I notice him coming and going? Sure. Was that memorizing his schedule like an obsessive stalker? No. Don always had lunch at the same time. It wasn't hard.

He moved closer, leaning toward me. "You're annoyed."

"At you? No. At everything you told me? Yeah, pretty much." His response wasn't great, but I got it. It wasn't *his* fault, but yeah, I was pissed off. At everyone. At everything. Fuck, I was even mad at Teddy for walking out of my room and not giving me a second. I was mad at Seth for marrying that fucker Kal. I was mad at Kal for being alive. I mean, the list went on and on. I was pissed at everyone, except Don. He was too nice. It would be like being mad at a puppy.

"You told Bartholomew about Earth." His voice had turned grave.

"Yeah," I said, even though it wasn't a question. Don hadn't moved away, but his expression was closed, as if he was fearing my reaction, which was stupid. None of this was his problem or fault. I poked him in the chest, and he jolted. "You didn't tell me why you're here, Donny."

"You were distracting me."

"How?" I was across the ship. If I was distracting him among everyone that was closer to him, then how did he work or function for that matter?

"You were upset, though oddly… vacant. I couldn't catch more besides the turmoil in your thoughts, but it was enough I decided an early lunch was in order."

"I shouldn't have bothered you." Fuck, was this going to be a daytime issue too?

"No," Don said forcefully. "There's no issue, Little Warrior." He glanced toward where Seth was. "Did you want to rejoin Seth and the human huddle?"

I laughed at the term, which made him smile. "No, I would rather stay with you."

"I would like that."

We moved toward a table in the corner, near the long window that framed one wall—which I refused to look at—and took a seat on the round stools. Every seat or stool was backless. It drove me bonkers. I couldn't get comfortable. Drakcol had to have abs of steel or something.

Don chuckled. "They are backless because of our wings. When we relax, we often let our wings out."

"Why aren't they always out?"

"Besides the inconvenience of space and tight corridors, we consider it an aggressive act. Back when we were warring clans, we would spread our wings to make ourselves larger. Also, the talons are sharp enough to cut through our scales. They are weapons, our freedom to fly, and in some cases, shields for those we love."

"Hmm. Interesting. When did you stop in-fighting? Or are you like Earth and have many nations?"

"We are unified," he said, taking a bite of a bright red berry. "We unified under a single empress after the Crystal elected her. The legend says she was a great warrior who had the gift of light and life."

Don had talked about the Crystal, though I'd been half-asleep, but I didn't really get it.

"I can explain in more detail," he said.

I grinned. God, it was convenient having him hear my thoughts. I got why people didn't like it, but at the same time, I didn't mind. He couldn't help it, and he didn't go around spouting people's secrets.

Don placed his hand on the table next to me, not touching but close. I spanned the distance and grabbed his hand without thought, enjoying the feel of his warm scales against my skin.

I froze, tension making my muscles creak with strain.

Don paused as well.

I enjoyed the feel of his hand in mine. I liked the feel of *him*. That hadn't happened since... I refused to take that thought any further. Instead, I interlaced our fingers. Don's were so much thicker and longer than mine, not to mention tipped with those deadly-looking claws. I wasn't afraid, though. He wouldn't hurt me.

I pressed my palm flat to his and smiled softly at our two hands. His was so large next to mine, and his scales were so dark next to my deathly pale skin. I liked it. Our hands looked good together. And hell, he was warm. I swore I was always cold now, and he was so hot.

"So the Crystal?" I asked, restarting the conversation.

He cleared his throat and began eating again as he spoke, but his hand remained in mine. "As far as we can determine, it's an entity or thought. It came from space long ago before we were a space-faring culture. A religion was built around it. It identifies our soul types and finds soulmates."

"Soul types? Right, I remember. Scientist, fighter, and something or other."

Chuckling, he said, "Warrior, spiritual, seeker, and creator. I'm a warrior soul type, as are all my brothers, except Kalvoxrencol, who is a creator."

My eyebrows raised in disbelief.

"He makes lovely paintings," Don said. "Seth is also a warrior soul."

If my eyebrows lifted any higher, they would join my hair.

"Seth has the purest warrior soul ever tested, and the Crystal called him chosen."

"What?"

"While spiritual souls have a sense of the Crystal, we drakcol cannot hear it. Humans can. I don't know why."

"And Seth being this great warrior matters?"

"Indeed," he said. "We record all soul tests. The four purest souls in history are: Seth Harris as the warrior soul, Monqilcolnen, my cousin, as the spiritual soul, Lexvonqyn, who was a research scientist, as the seeker soul, and Min, who was a gardener, as the creator soul. These things matter to us because we believe in the Crystal."

"Hmm," I said, snagging some of his food. Don prodded the plate closer to me, and I took another piece of purple fruit that was crisp and tangy like an apple. "So is your cousin like a priest or something?"

"No. It was quite the scandal when he joined the Planetary Navy. The Ranks wanted to keep him close because sometimes he simply understands the Crystal in ways no one else does. He has a deep link to it, though perhaps not as deep as you humans. When we arrive on Tamkolvanloknol, you will be tested for soul type. The Ranks are trying to force all humans to touch the Crystal, but we only do that in adulthood when seeking our soulmates so it will probably not be a requirement."

"Soulmates? You mentioned that earlier."

"Drakcol only mate once. Usually, we fall in love and the bond will naturally form. Some appeal to the Crystal for their perfect soulmate. Not everyone has one, or your soulmate could be dead or not born yet. Once your soulmate is identified, a link is formed between the two of you. That's it for you. No other mate or person will ever happen. Your last chance for romantic love. You find, court, and affirm your bond by creating a genetic link. To break it or reaffirm it, you touch the Crystal again. If rejected, no matter whether bound or chosen, the other drakcol doesn't often survive. We mate for life, and living without your mate is near impossible."

"Interesting," I said as my thoughts whirled. That was hella romantic and sad all at the same time. Naturally, I loved it.

"Crystal-bound mates can speak mind-to-mind and cannot be more than a certain distance from each other. It's quite special to have a soulmate, but not all desire it."

I frowned. "You're talking around something."

"Kalvoxrencol appealed to the Crystal, who gave him Seth."

My mouth opened. That was how Kal got Seth. It wasn't a random chance. Also why they quietly stared at each other made sense—they were talking.

His fingers tightened on mine—I'd forgotten we were holding hands—and he asked, "Are you alright?"

I wasn't sure. That some rock thought Kal and Seth were perfect soulmates didn't mean anything, or at least I tried to tell myself that. I forced a smile. "I'm fine."

Dontilvynsan

I had no sooner taken off my uniform when the door chimed. My soul leaped as I searched for Vince with my inner fire, desperate for some reason to see him again and maybe feel his much smaller fingers slot between mine. Disappointment flared. He wasn't outside my room. In fact, he was with Seth, Caleb, Bartholomew, and a handful of other humans in the canteen. It was my brothers who stood in front of me, and their thoughts were similar. They wanted to know what I thought of Vince.

Zoltilvoxfyn had witnessed me laughing, a rarity. I'd growled at Caleb for touching Vince without permission. Both Kalvoxrencol and Serlotminden had seen encounters between Vince and I that they had questions about.

"Come in." There was no escaping this. If Hallonnixmin and Monqilcolnen were on my ship, they would've joined in. As a family, we were united, but sometimes the closeness was irritating when I was forced to answer questions that I had no response to.

"You know why we're here," Kalvoxrencol said.

He was the youngest of us, but he often charged in front of us all so as not to be outdone. A habit he hadn't outgrown. I didn't mind in most circumstances, yet in this situation, it annoyed me to no end. They acted as if me befriending someone was odd.

Maybe it was. I had no friends outside of my family. Vince was special. Very special.

I motioned for them to sit while I took a seat on the floor, my wings slipping out of the slits in the back of my shirt. I kept them at a relaxed position, but the fact I couldn't retract them alerted me to how upset I was.

"I'm allowed to make friends," I said in a preemptive strike.

Serlotminden scoffed. "You are, but you don't."

"What is Vince to you?" Zoltilvoxfyn asked, the calmest of this horde—unlike my youngest brother.

Kalvoxrencol vibrated in excitement, his thoughts and emotions practically stabbing my brain. He wanted me to be interested in Vince partly for me, but mostly because he wanted Vince to stop pursuing Seth.

"A person who needs help. He is amusing. Nothing more, nothing less."

"Are you sure?" Kalvoxrencol asked, his tail wagging to the point that Zoltilvoxfyn caught and held it with his own so it wouldn't smack him in the face. "You never smile or laugh like that. You seek him out, Captain. All the time."

I leveled each of them with a glare. "Just because you each have decided to take a human mate, does not mean I will. Vince is not interested in me. I'm not interested in Vince. We are nothing but two people who enjoy time together."

"If you say so," Kalvoxrencol said.

"Yes," I said, though I wasn't sure. Vince was special. What that meant to me or the future, I wasn't sure. Nonetheless, I wasn't going to admit anything to this rabble.

Chapter 14

WHAT ARE YOU LOOKING AT?

Vince

"You have an appointment with Physician Klars today," NAID announced not long after I'd woken up. I'd actually slept, with Don's help, and for the first time in I don't know how long, I felt rested. However, I didn't want to leave my room. I found as time passed that I wanted to do nothing more than curl into a ball and sleep or pretend I didn't exist.

So NAID's proclamation about my appointment was met with deep loathing. I had to get more treatment for the disease that... that I'd gotten. I swallowed the sudden bile that was climbing my throat in a burning wave. I stood and went straight to the bathroom. Mechanically, I stripped out of my sweats and climbed into the shower and turned the pouring water up to the highest temperature I could stand.

The burning water made my pale skin redden, but I didn't care. I scrubbed and scrubbed and scrubbed with a cloth like it could rid me of the imaginary fingers grasping my arms or erase the filth that had clung to me.

Dropping the cloth, I sank to the stone floor of the shower and hugged my knees to my chest. I simply breathed under the scalding hot waterfall. The rocks in the shower had little plants and moss growing on them and the rough, jutting stone bench on one end of the shower both added to the outdoors feel. It was almost like I wasn't shoved into a metal box hurtling through foreign space but was rather on a vacation somewhere on Earth.

I could pretend, even for a moment, that I was home, that nothing had happened, that I was safe.

My head pressed against my knees, and I pretended. Fuck, how I pretended.

But there was only so long I could sit under the burning water before I had to move forward. Actually, I would've sat there all day, but NAID reminded me once again of my appointment and stirred me into action. My every movement was precise as a numbness filled me. I yanked on ripped black leggings, then pulled on a short pleated black skirt, another band crop top, and finished the outfit with a fishnet shrug.

I glanced at my reflection, and my bruised eyes were the first thing I noticed. My eyes had always been so dark brown that they appeared black, but now, they looked bleak, wounded, broken.

A growl built in my chest, and I lashed out, punching the glass. It shattered; my image fractured and the screen shorted in lines of color. Panting, I stared at my destroyed reflection and hatred swelled in my chest like a balloon, pushing everything else out.

Screaming, I punched the screen again and again and again. Images flashed before my eyes. My burnt hands helping Teddy throw groaning people into the flames of the incinerator; their screams rang in my ears. The stinging thwack of Agk hitting me with a baton. My nose bleeding. Agk selling me to Tryk and being pushed into a small dark cell. My stomach eating itself. The snap of my finger after I'd smacked someone. A person on top of me. My tears dripping down my cheeks. Dark. So much darkness. It never ended. There was no light. I would never see the light.

"Stop," a deep voice said.

I couldn't, though. There were still fragments of my face covered in red. The screams kept escaping my lips as my fists connected with the broken, winking screen. It was mocking me.

Bands of iron surrounded me and drew me into a soothing warmth. My breath sawed in and out as I trembled. Head bowed, I sobbed. The tears wouldn't stop pouring down my cheeks.

"I am here," Don whispered, his forehead resting on the back of my head. "I am here. You are not alone, Little Warrior."

More tears slid down my cheeks, and my blurry gaze refused to move from my broken reflection. "Please."

"What?"

"I don't want to see."

A hand covered my eyes while his other arm supported my weight. Don whispered, "You don't have to look."

My feet left the ground and my breath whooshed out of my lungs. I was moving, but I couldn't see anything. Oddly, I didn't care. Don had me.

Gently, Don set me down on the couch and crouched in front of me. His eyebrows were drawn together, and his mouth was a hard line. Not thinking about it, I brushed my fingertips over his forehead to ease the tension. With a deep inhale, he closed his eyes. I traced his face and left red streaks behind. Numb, I studied my hands. The knuckles were split and bleeding while my fingers were swollen.

"You hurt yourself," Don said.

I had. I didn't feel it, though. My body was distant and my thoughts were deep in a mire that I couldn't escape.

"Vince."

I stared at my damaged hands. My broken hands.

"Vince," Don repeated, voice harsh.

My eyes shot to his. Don stared at me with those huge green eyes of his. I rested my palm over them. Right now, I couldn't handle the pity that must be there.

"There is no pity," he replied to my thoughts. "Only concern. You harmed yourself."

"I'm fine," I said, voice light.

"You are not."

"I am."

Carefully, he pulled my hand away from his eyes and grabbed my other, so both were trapped in his much larger ones. I felt him. I felt the warmth of him seeping into my cold digits.

"I must apologize for touching you without permission," Don said, and I tightened my hold on him, afraid he would pull away. I had missed this—touching with no expectation of more. I was starved for it, yet terrified of it. Pathetic. "No." Don drew closer, his head near mine. "No, Little Warrior. Not pathetic. Never that. You're fighting a battle right now. A battle of the mind."

A tear slid down my cheek, and I looked away.

He brushed it away before snagging my hand again. "Please don't harm yourself."

"It's not a big deal," I snapped. "I'm fine."

His eyes narrowed, but he didn't contradict me.

I kept tight hold of his hands, leaning closer so I could breathe in the comforting sweetness of his scent. It was similar to vanilla, and yet... softer, lighter somehow. I closed my eyes and breathed. I needed to let what happened go. It didn't matter.

Don started to hum a low tune, and I relaxed even further until my forehead rested against his.

Slowly, awareness crept back into my body, and with it, a deep throbbing stab from my damaged hands. I was fairly certain I'd broken something, but the bleeding had finally stopped.

"I got blood on you," I whispered.

Don lifted my damaged hand to his mouth and pressed it against his lips. "It's fine."

I swallowed.

His eyes flashed up to mine, lips brushing my skin and setting it ablaze. "I would lick these clean if you allowed me to."

"W-what?" I forced out, pulse in my throat.

"Drakcol have an instinct to clean wounds. I will clean yours, Vince, if you allow me."

Never in my life had I nodded so fast. The thought of his tongue on my skin… Shudders went down my spine and settled somewhere in the region of my dick.

Gently, Don dragged his black-scaled tongue over my first split knuckle, and I whimpered. Eyes moving to me, he continued to bathe the injuries so softly. Under his ministrations my body came alive and tingles, like little shocks of electricity, flitted through my veins and made my heart stumble in my chest.

There was no rush or impatience in his steady movements as Don thoroughly cleaned each wound with painstakingly slow movements. His tongue dragged over me and stole all rational thought until I was panting and whining under his delicate touch.

"Donny," I whispered, my voice one millimeter away from begging.

"What?" he asked.

"Don't stop."

The slightest quirk pulled at the corner of his lips, and I moaned. Fuck, I loved that small smile. Don dragged his tongue over my middle knuckle. "I wasn't planning to, not until you're clean."

I would never be clean.

He growled, no more than a rumble in his chest. "You are perfect."

I scoffed. "I'm an asshole."

Don kissed my damaged knuckle and repeated, "You are perfect."

When he said it, I almost believed him.

Dontilvynsan

The metal taste of Vince's blood was still on my tongue as I escorted him to the medbay. He hadn't wanted to go for his hands, though they did need treatment, but to finish his round of injections for the disease he'd contracted during his enslavement. Vince had asked me to accompany him, his eyes down and body stiff. I'd accepted, of course; nothing in the universe would've pulled me from his side.

Vince walked beside me, so small compared to me, but there was an unbreakable will inside of him that was alluring. He was strong, yet fragile. The dichotomy was interesting to watch and sense. His mind was focused on his aching hands, though beneath it was a void of darkness that was slowly consuming him. It was eating away at Vince, and I wished to rid him of it, but that wasn't within my power.

People offered me their throats as we strode through the corridors of my ship. I acknowledged each of my subordinates, all while keeping a wary eye out for my brothers. They were already seeing more into my and Vince's friendship, and I didn't want to give them more weapons against me.

I swallowed, savoring Vince's taste on my tongue. I liked it, more than I would have thought. More concerning, my instincts demanded that I check his hands and clean them once more, even though *I knew* I'd been thorough. Vince needed medical assistance, not me, and yet, my instincts rebelled against such notions. He needed me. His wounds needed my tongue upon them.

When the medbay door appeared, I paused in my step. "I will remain here."

He rolled his eyes. "You're going to hear anyway."

"Yes, but..." Didn't he desire privacy?

"Come on, Donny," Vince ordered, and I followed him without question. My soul sped up. I would follow Vince anywhere.

Klars saw us almost instantly, his gray eyes locking onto Vince's damaged hands before moving toward us. He demanded, "What happened?"

"Nothing," Vince replied, brushing off the whole incident of me finding him incoherently beating his reflection to pieces.

"This," the physician said, unexpectedly serious for once, "is not nothing."

Vince glared at him. "I punched the mirror. It's not a big deal."

Klars released a long breath. "I am concerned about your mental health."

"I'm fine," Vince snapped, voice harsh. "It was a fucking mirror. It's not a huge deal. I got pissed and I hit it. End of story."

I pressed my lips together to remain silent. Vince had been utterly distraught, but it wasn't my place to contradict him. So many choices had been ripped from him over the last two years, and he needed to make his own, even if I didn't agree with them.

"I'm going to recommend you speak to someone."

"No," Vince replied, looking straight forward. "Can we get on with this?"

For the first time, Klars looked at me, but I didn't react, though internally, I agreed—Vince needed help. This wound would fester until it was dealt with, but he was the only one who could choose to move forward. If Vince didn't get better, Klars would report it to the Council of Seekers, but I wasn't sure what they'd do. They might force Vince to do things he didn't want, or they might respect his decision.

When I didn't respond, Physician Klars moved toward the console to prepare what he needed to treat Vince.

The second he disappeared, Vince reached for me, and I moved to his side. He was so cold, abnormally so. Humans ran cooler than us drakcol, but he was ice against my scales. I sat beside him, and Vince dropped his head against my arm. I swallowed, wishing I wasn't in my uniform so I could feel his skin against me.

Vince rubbed his forehead on me. "Why is it so much easier with you?"

"What?" I asked, because his thoughts were unclear.

"Everything."

My soul burned, thrashing against my ribs.

Klars returned, interrupting us.

I swallowed a growl; whatever was occurring between us, I was enjoying and wishing for it to continue. The physician was clueless, though. For once, he wasn't smiling or cheerful. Instead, he watched Vince closely, but Vince had his face turned toward my arm as he pressed close to me.

His thoughts were nothing but a numb cloud that dulled everything. It was like Vince was truly not here, but rather, somewhere far away. Where? I didn't know, because I was unable to see or sense more without forming a connection, which was not needed, nor did I have his permission to do so.

Klars worked quickly, disinfecting Vince's split knuckles before sealing the skin. Once the cuts vanished, he ran a sensor, then a wand over Vince's swollen hands. Klars said, "You have fractured several bones in your hands. I can fix them, but it will take time for them to be completely healed. I'm going to put a nanite plaster on your hands to assist in healing them faster."

"Fine," Vince bit out.

"Try not to move them too much," Klars said.

"That should be easy. They're only my hands," Vince muttered.

I cupped the back of his head, burying my fingers in his impossibly smooth black hair, even though I didn't have his permission to do so. I would've thought from his lack of nutrition that his hair would have suffered, but it hadn't. Vince groaned and pushed his face tighter against my arm.

"I have you," I whispered, soul throbbing.

"I know, Donny," he replied, and I burned for him.

Klars slid yellow tubes over Vince's fingers, like gloves, and stuck a square to the back of his hand. "There. Now just an injection."

Vince tensed, and I held him tighter. We truly needed to have a conversation regarding permissions, but I sensed his need for me and his utter hate that he even needed this injection.

It only took a moment to administer, then Klars said, "In three days, you should no longer be infectious."

"Oh, joy, oh, bliss, I'm the luckiest boy in fucking Toyland," Vince replied, making Klars blink, but I caught the sarcasm in his tone and in his thoughts.

"Now we need to discuss your weight," Klars said. "You have lost weight since your first exam. You're not eating enough."

"I can't stomach that nutritional supplement."

"I understand that it doesn't taste good," Klars said, his voice growing almost sing-song like he was speaking to a kit, "but if you do not eat it, I will be forced to hook you up to a support machine."

Vince launched to his feet and snapped, "Just try it. I will rip it out of me."

Klar's nostrils flared. "Now, Vince—"

"No," Vince yelled. "No one is forcing me to do jack shit. Do you hear me? Not one single damn thing!"

Shaking and breath harsh, Vince blinked away tears and stared at Klars, not relenting.

I stepped in and stood right beside Vince. "No one will force you," I promised. Vince couldn't lose his choices again. "Perhaps we should leave?"

He bobbed his head.

Together, we stepped out of the medbay. The instant we rounded the corner, Vince glanced at me with a shaky smile. "What should we do?"

I needed to return to my duties, but I couldn't deny him. "I think we should eat."

Vince frowned.

"I'm hungry."

His brow furrowed and concern lit up his thoughts. "Are you?"

"I am."

"Come on, then." Vince dashed forward, heading toward the canteen, and I fought a smile at his protective thoughts. I liked him protecting and taking care of me, though I refused to think about why.

Chapter 15

I HAVE A PROPOSITION.

Vince

I lay in the bed, staring at Don. It had been almost a week and half since the whole bashing-my-reflection-in incident, but whatever. It was fine. I was fine. The stupid glove-plaster things were gone, but Klars still hounded me about talking to someone, which I didn't need, and my weight loss, though that had slowed. What I needed was for everyone to leave me alone. Well, everyone except Don.

We'd spent every day together, and I loved it. It was easy to leave my room when Don was outside. He never pestered me or gave me searching looks like Teddy. I didn't have to pretend like when I was with Seth. Don was there, beside me, simply letting me decide what I wanted to do and when I wanted to do it.

Don let out the smallest snore, and I grinned. He'd fallen asleep before I did. I'd asked him to come and help me sleep once again, and he'd started to and fell asleep almost instantly before his inner fire could lull me to sleep. His hand was on my cheek while his hair hung around his face. He released a breath, stirring the long purple strands. Unable to resist, I slid my fingers through the silky strands, marveling at how soft they were.

I scooted closer and made sure to keep his hand on my cheek. While he wasn't using his gift, his touch alone reassured me. Don's lips parted in his sleep. An urge to press my mouth against his flooded me. Were his lips soft? Warm? How would they feel molded against mine? I had to know. His gentle scent filled my nostrils. I wanted to roll around in it. Cover myself with it.

I was halfway toward kissing him when I finally jerked to a stop. What the hell was I doing? He was asleep. This was not Sleeping Beauty. Besides, touching him in an intimate way like that should freak me the hell out. Shouldn't it? Though I'd touched him before and liked it. Thoughts of me holding his hand in the cafeteria, pressing my forehead against his in my living room, and rubbing my cheek on his uniform in the medbay flooded my mind.

I gaped at Don, clutching his hand to my cheek. My heart thundered in my ears, drowning out any sound, and sweat dripped down my spine.

Fuck my life. I was attracted to Don, but it was more than that. I liked him. His humor. His kindness. His sense of duty. The way his lips quirked in amusement, giving me that perfect crooked smile. He'd been willing to help a complete stranger, an alien, because I needed it. He lost sleep to help me. Who did that? Don did.

This was a mess. When he found out, it was going to be embarrassing. Seth still held my heart, but Don had definitely wheeled inside the walls and set up camp. He'd done it so subtly that I hadn't noticed his claws digging into me, laying claim. It wasn't a huge deal. I'd liked a lot of people, but this was Don. He would know, and my feelings would make it awkward.

Or, my mind unhelpfully supplied, and I told it to shut the fuck up—it wouldn't.

Maybe he wouldn't care. Maybe he would be interested too. Interested in maybe helping me in a different way. I trusted him. I didn't want to, but I did. Don would be the perfect person to work out some issues with. I nodded, coming to a fast decision. I just needed to be fucked and move past the trauma. That would fix everything. I was sure of it.

He wouldn't have to like me back. Actually, it would be easier if he didn't. No commitment. No promises. No nothing. Just how I liked it. Besides, I still wanted to go to Earth—whenever that was, because no one had supplied a timeframe—but if I could work through some of my physical issues beforehand, maybe the transition back home would be easier. I'd be back to normal. Confident and comfortable with whatever the hell I wanted.

Some doubt wiggled and nagged at me, but I pushed it away. This would work. I'd be cured and all it would take was some dick. Easy peasy.

I smiled at Don's sleeping face. He'd be the best person to do this with. He wouldn't hurt me. He would know when something was bothering me, so there would be no hiding. If, for some reason, Don turned on me, I could think of the worst things that had happened to me and perhaps force him away.

But he wouldn't hurt me. I knew that.

Sliding closer, I breathed in his vanilla scent and snuggled against him, burying my face against his neck.

Dontilvynsan

I changed out of my uniform into a pair of soft trousers and a loose shirt. My wings slid out as I stretched. Stars, it had been a long day. We were nearing a space station, and Serlotminden had asked to stop because he wanted to show Bartholomew around. Stopping wasn't necessarily a bad idea, but it did complicate matters.

I'd had to notify my parents and superiors as well as contact the station manager. No one had been against us stopping, as I could pick up a few passengers who wanted to go to Tamkolvanloknol, and ask around about humans being sold. Naldixwuv Station was on the border of Coalition space and was a travel hub.

My inner fire was helpful in this particular situation. I could find somewhere to sit and simply listen. Uncomfortable for me but helpful for my superiors.

I couldn't wait until I returned to my usual work, overseeing some of the most important Drakcon science experiments. It was far more restful for my soul. Except going back would mean not seeing Vince.

Vince.

He was another reason my day had been long. I hadn't seen him since we woke up. Once again, he'd slept near me, his face tucked into the crook of my neck. His lips had been exceedingly close to my scales, and I'd longed to taste them with my own. Only knowing that I didn't have his permission, and that he would dislike it, had stopped me.

I'd laid there as still as possible, watching Vince sleep and listening to the general buzz of his thoughts and the quick flitting of his dreams. When he finally woke up, embarrassment had rolled through him before he had focused oddly hard on breakfast.

Maybe he'd been particularly hungry, which was good because he needed to eat more. Vince had spurned the nutritional supplements, and when he ate with me, he pushed most of his food around without consuming it. His lack of appetite was a worry that was constantly scratching at the back of my thoughts.

Forcing Vince out of my mind, which was quickly becoming a habit, I grabbed my screen and flicked through my most recent notes from Hallonnixmin, Monqilcolnen, and my parents before turning to the reports about my normal work. I'd just started reading a recent report about a slipstream portal opening near the Immortal Planet when the door rang.

"Come," I said, trying to keep the exhaustion from my voice. No matter how long I had worked, I was always on duty. But the familiar rush of thoughts made me groan. *Vince.*

He stepped into the room, fingers playing with his shirt. His pale stomach was showing because of the short black shirt that hung around his small frame, and his tight, stiff black trousers clung to his thin legs.

I swallowed as my tail flicked. He looked good. Vince always did. My arousal faded with the wave of anxiety and nerves coming off him. His thoughts raced so fast, I was having trouble catching more than that he had something he wanted to ask me, and it scared him.

"Vince, are you alright?" I stood, ready to help him if he needed it. He was shaking. What could be bothering him so much? "Vince?"

"I want to ask you something," he said in a rush.

"Alright."

He didn't speak, but an image of him sitting splayed on my lap and snuggled against me flitted through my mind. Embarrassment and longing immediately followed. "Shit," he swore.

What defecation had to do with this was a mystery.

"Shit," Vince repeated, bright red. "Never mind. This was a bad idea." He rushed toward the door before I even had a chance of processing what was going on.

I followed him, soul racing. "Vince, wait. Please."

He didn't stop, but I kept chasing him, listening to the raging embarrassment of me seeing his thoughts. He wasn't mad at me, nor did he blame me—rather, he blamed himself.

When he reached his quarters, he didn't close the door behind him, and I took that as an invitation.

Vince stopped in front of his couch, face bright red. Embarrassment, panic, and fear coiled in his gut like a spring. His muscles were tense. He was ready for me to reject him and his request. I didn't even know what he wanted, besides sitting on my lap. I wasn't, in any way, opposed to that idea.

Hands folded behind my back, I crept closer. "I don't know what you want. I need you to think clearly about it or speak to me, Little Warrior."

Hugging himself, he said in a barely audible voice, "I want to touch you."

My soul throbbed.

"I'm a very physically affectionate person, but after everything…" He lifted and lowered his shoulders. "It doesn't matter. I can't touch people right now, at least not easily, but I thought you could help me work through some of those issues."

Once again, the thought of him straddling my lap reappeared, but it had changed. Instead, he was thinking about me stroking his back as we kissed. My tail flicked. I had to actively keep myself from leaping onto him. My instincts screamed to claim him before someone else could. I fisted my hands and took a deep breath.

The red flush returned, only stronger this time. "I'm not ready for that, but I want to… eventually."

A worry burrowed in my brain, and it wouldn't let go. "Are you doing this so Kalvoxrencol can fuck you?" I would not be alright with that. It would break me if that was what he wanted.

His forehead crinkled as disgust rolled through him like a wave. "God, no. Why would you think that? Kal? That fucker?"

"You thought about it during combat class."

"Oh my god, was that why that person kicked you?" he asked.

I didn't respond, looking away.

Vince laughed, and suddenly, he was right in front of me, looking up at me. "No. It was a random thought. One, I'm definitely not going through with, even if Seth and Kal were interested, which I doubt they are. I want you, Don. I trust you."

His words and the truth of his thoughts washed through me. My breath turned harsh. "I want you as well."

"Good."

"But we need to discuss our permissions first."

"Permissions?"

"Boundaries," I reiterated. "Things you and I are comfortable with and what kind of relationship this will be. It's something that drakcol discuss with every relationship, whether romantic or platonic."

"Makes sense."

"Did you want to do that now?" I asked carefully. I hoped he did, because I wanted to hold him. No, I needed to hold him like I needed my next breath.

I didn't know if I'd ever wanted someone as much as I wanted him. I hadn't had too many partners in my past. My inner fire made people wary of me. The few people I had fucked hadn't been the best experiences for me, which wasn't their fault. Sometimes they thought something off-putting during sex, or afterward, they'd compare me to past experiences or lovers. Then there were the partners who smiled afterward, but were less than pleased with my performance.

Yes, I could hear people's thoughts, but I wasn't omniscient. I didn't know everything they desired, which upset some of my past partners. They'd expected me to be the best experience they'd ever had, but I wasn't. With each one, my confidence flagged until it was a rare experience for me to ask or accept a request to fuck.

Vince was different. His mind was so close to my own, and he didn't care about my inner fire. If I did something he didn't want, he would tell me.

Also, I wanted him. Stars above, I wanted him. I desired him so much, I couldn't help but wonder if this was a bad idea. Vince was leaving. My fucking him wouldn't change that. But it could be the start of me falling in love and considering him my mate. That was a path to disaster. Mating was permanent. Once the bond formed, I was stuck. If that happened and he left, I wouldn't... I wouldn't survive his absence.

His smile brought me back to the present. "Yeah. I want to talk now."

It might be the death of me, but I wanted Vince and I was unwilling to let this opportunity pass me by.

Chapter 16

TALKING BEFORE SNUGGLING.

Vince

We sat on the couch, facing each other. My heart was beating so fast I could barely breathe. I wanted this so badly, but at the same time, I was nervous as hell. I used to be such a physically affectionate person. Holding hands. Hugging. Kissing. Snuggling. Fucking. It didn't matter if they were my friends or some stranger I'd picked up, I wanted to touch them a lot. Now, I hated people touching me. It stirred up memories I would rather not think of.

Don seemed as nervous as I was, because he kept rubbing his wide thighs, his claws catching on the fabric of his pants. I wanted to crawl onto his lap and rub my face against him. He smelled so nice. I wanted to bury my face against his neck and breathe.

His tail flicked, edging toward me before it shot away. "We should talk before we cuddle."

Heat rushed to my face. "Yeah."

"First, I need to know what you want out of this relationship?"

"Nothing permanent," I replied. "I know drakcol only mate once, and I don't want that. I assume you have casual sex relationships."

"We do."

"That's what I want. I mean, I don't want to have sex yet. I want to touch you and be touched. I miss it." I was getting a lot more out of this than Don was, which made me feel like an ass. We might not do more than snuggle, unless you counted him helping me to sleep, for a very long time. Don't get me wrong, I was determined to fuck this trauma right out of me, but it might take a while.

"I'm alright with that. One of my permissions would be about falling in love. I can't care about you like that, Vince, unless you choose to stay. Having a mate bond form, then having you leave me, would destroy me. If you are fine with that, I'm fine and would enjoy a casual relationship with you."

"That's fine." I didn't want him to fall in love with me. I had Seth, and I didn't want to hurt Don when I left.

"I also need more than sex or snuggling. I don't do casual sex without some sort of friendship or talking."

That was easy. I liked talking to and spending time with Don. Besides, we usually saw each other every day. "Sure. We can hang out."

"As you don't want to have sex yet, we can forgo that portion of permissions. When you are interested, let me know and we will change the parameters of our relationship."

I grinned. I liked this. Drakcol had relationships dialed in. Hammering things out in advance was nice, and it soothed some of my anxieties.

"I'm glad," he said, responding to my thoughts. "Did you want to keep this relationship private?"

Seth. He was worried about that. "No. We can tell people." I didn't care. Seth was married, and I wasn't going to hide Don. Nobody liked being pushed away or denied. Since it was perfectly safe to do so, I saw no reason to hide it.

He smiled, and warmth pooled in my gut. God, he was cute.

Don's throat bobbed as his tail wiggled harder. Clearing his throat, he asked, "Are you comfortable with touching in public?"

We had touched a few times in front of people, but I said, "I don't want to do that." It wasn't that I was rejecting Don, but if I freaked out, I wanted to be somewhere away from prying eyes.

"That's fine. What kind of touch are you comfortable with right now? And what don't you want?"

My lips pursed as I thought it over. What was I actually okay with? I wanted a lot. I wanted the whole shebang, sausage and all, but that wasn't happening yet. His eyes shifted to the ceiling as he took several deep breaths, and I smothered a laugh. His being able to hear my thoughts was oddly fun. I like seeing him lose that composed mask he wore. I wondered if we did fuck, if I could get him to come completely undone.

"Vince," he whispered. "Please."

"Sorry." I took a deep breath to focus. "For now, you can touch my face and hands anytime we're alone. I want to stay clothed. Maybe I could put your hands where I want them?" It was a lot to ask, but I wouldn't know what I was comfortable with until we did it.

"I can work with that."

"And kissing? Maybe I can initiate it for right now?" I asked.

"That is acceptable."

"What about you? You have to have things you don't want me to do or places you don't want me to touch." This had to be even, not all about me.

"My tail. I don't mind you holding it, but don't stroke it. It's very sensitive, and I find it arousing."

I nodded, though I was very interested in kissing it. Eventually, maybe.

He cleared his throat as his eyes lifted again. "Yes. Just not unless you want to fuck."

That was reasonable.

"I don't mind if you touch my arm or side in public, but I am the captain, and as such, I do have to remain professional. That also means, when I'm on duty, if you could not intentionally try to distract me, I would appreciate it."

"Like how?" I couldn't control my thoughts all of the time.

"Like when you thought of tweaking my tail as I was talking to my subordinate."

Ah. Yeah, that had been fun, but I understood. "I can still tease you though, right?"

"Of course. I like it."

Good, because I loved messing with him. Playing with Don was quickly becoming one of my favorite things. I swallowed as I looked at his wide lap and my heart thrashed. "Can I..." I trailed off as I pictured climbing onto his lap and pressing against his chest.

"Yes."

Heart in my throat and nerves dancing like electricity through my veins, I stood and went toward him. Don didn't move, except his eyes followed my movements and his tail thrashed. I placed my hands on his shoulders, marveling at the firm muscles beneath my hands, and climbed onto his lap.

It was awkward as I sat on him. Unease rolled through me. I was in a very vulnerable position if he chose to take advantage of it. Don slowly lifted a hand, giving me plenty of time to pull away, and cupped my cheek. General peace blanketed me. I sagged against his chest, boneless.

I shook my head. "I don't want your inner fire."

He yanked away. "My apologies."

I nuzzled his neck. "I'm not mad. I don't want your inner fire. I want you, Don."

"Thank you," he said in a thick voice.

I shrugged.

Warm. I was so warm and comfortable. Heat radiated off of him like a furnace. His lap was easily wide enough for me to sit on, but not so wide that straddling him like this was uncomfortable.

Unable to stop myself, I rubbed my face against his chest and neck. His shirt was soft on my cheek, while his scales had a discernible ridge to them, though they were smooth at the same time. I loved the texture of them on my skin.

Thoughts of being naked and rubbing all over his black scales while kissing the peeking glimpses of red and gold skin ran across my mind, making me groan. Don wasn't far behind. The deep rumble stoked my arousal, though a tinge of discomfort tainted it.

"Vince," he whispered. I felt something rather large harden beneath me, and I tensed. "Don't worry. I won't do anything."

I nodded, but the tension remained. Working through the panic, I grabbed his arms and placed them on my waist. "Hug me."

He surrounded me and lowered his head to my shoulder. The longer he breathed, the more his cock relaxed until it didn't nudge me any longer.

Well, I now knew he was attracted to me.

Don chuckled. "Was that ever in doubt?"

"I'm human and scrawny. It wouldn't be weird if you weren't into me."

Don pulled back to see my face. "I didn't understand that word."

Most of the time the ship's NAID translated what I said well or Don got the context from my mind. I was pretty sure he understood English fairly well because that's what I thought in. But apparently one had squeaked through.

"What word?"

He made some guttural noise that NAID didn't offer any translation for.

I thought through my sentence, then asked, "Scrawny?" When he nodded, I explained. "Small. I'm short and thin. Most drakcol I've seen are huge."

"I understand." Don guided me back to his shoulder, and I settled against him with a groan. How was he this comfortable? He held me loosely in his grasp, but it was safe. "I found you attractive from the beginning."

I smiled against his scales. So I was vain, sue me. I was cute enough to be vain. Feeling brave, I kissed his neck. Don stilled, and I immediately tensed.

"I liked that," he whispered as his arms tightened around my waist.

"Me too," I replied. The scrape of his scales on my sensitive lips was nicer than I had predicted. Needing a distraction, I said, "Talk to me."

"About?"

"Your interests. Work. Anything. I want to know you."

He relaxed beneath me, holding me as close as possible. "I'm rather boring, or so I'm told. I work. A lot. I like music and science. My closest friends are my brothers and my only cousin. I enjoy experiences much like Kalvoxrencol does, but I don't like war simulations. I prefer stories."

"That's not boring," I said, giving him another kiss. Fuck whoever told him he was boring. People could like whatever they liked. He didn't have to be into high-energy activities to be interesting.

Don nuzzled the top of my head. "My work is interesting. I oversee some of our most important and secret science projects."

"Like what?" I asked, then added, "If you can tell me."

"I don't imagine you will tell anyone, but there is only so much I can relate. The most fascinating thing I oversee is the Immortal Planet."

"What?" I slid my arms around him, stroking his back. I felt his wings curl in tighter. I'd wondered if they disappeared into his body like magic, but apparently not. His wings escaped the confines of his shirt, and I brushed my fingers over the supple, leathery membrane.

"Five hundred and twenty-two years ago, we found a trace of something similar to the Crystal. We followed it. Not me personally," he clarified, which was nice because I had no idea how old he was. "I'm forty cycles by your planet's rotation. Drakcol live about the same length as humans."

"I'm thirty-one."

He paused for a second before continuing. "The Immortal Planet has people on the surface who resonate with the same energy as the Crystal."

"Why do you call it the Immortal Planet?"

"We have sent probes close enough to scan the planet. We have to be careful because they are an underdeveloped planet. But the same people are there now as were there five hundred years ago. They haven't aged much. We don't know how long they live or how the Crystal is so similar to them. Some theorize this is where the Crystal originated from."

People that were over five hundred years old. That was unbelievable. "Why don't you take a sample? Seth said we would either be citizens or samples, so why don't you beam someone up here, then wipe their memory? Presto. Mystery solved."

Don gently stroked my back, and I moaned, loving the sensation. He took a shuddering breath before continuing, "We don't like to take people. We can, but we rarely do. Seth was an extraordinary circumstance. Additionally, the Immortal Planet isn't in phase with us."

"What?" This was some *Star Trek* shit.

"They're out of phase with us. It's a different time. We don't know how many years, but enough that the person may be poorly affected if we didn't appropriately plan. We haven't figured out how to do it safely yet. And even if we did, I don't know that we would take a sample without very good reason to."

I was glad that wasn't my problem.

He chuckled and continued to rub my back in long, smooth strokes. Every touch was soothing. I'd missed this. I'd touched Seth and Teddy a bit since I came aboard, but nothing as personal as this. I wanted more, though at the same time, I didn't want to push myself too far. At least not yet.

With a clear thought, I projected the image of me kissing Don. A chaste, quick kiss. His hands stilled before squeezing me. He loosened his hold, though, long before panic could set in.

"Yes," he said.

I leaned back and stared into his deep green eyes, which reminded me of a forest with their flecks of brown and gold. I wanted to lose myself in them. I slid my hands over his shoulders and around his neck. Going up on my knees, I pressed my lips against his in a gentle brush.

My first feeling was arousal. I wanted to deepen the kiss and taste him, to feel his tongue slide along mine, but on the heels of the enticing feeling was fear, as well as unwanted memories of someone smashing their lips to mine as salty tears mixed in with the kiss. I gagged, pulling away.

Don instantly held me close and rested his hand on my cheek. He didn't calm me, though. He waited for me to decide what I wanted. Part of me wanted to fall under the waves of calm. Another was afraid I would get addicted to the sensation like a drug. Instead, I breathed through it, focusing on the warmth of his palm.

It took a minute before I relaxed against his chest. "Sorry."

"Do not apologize for your reaction to what was done to you."

"I'm getting more out of this than you."

His other hand cupped my cheek, so my face rested between his wide palms. "This doesn't have to be an equal exchange. That's not how relationships work, whether friendship or romance. I need you as much as you need me."

I scoffed.

"Do you wish to feel my feelings?"

"What?"

"I can share with you."

I nodded, excited for some reason.

Don stared into my eyes, and something unlocked in my brain. He was happy, content. He liked that I trusted him. He loved the feel of my smaller body on his much larger one. The coolness and smooth texture of my skin entranced him. Memories of the kiss resurfaced, but this time I experienced it from Don's mind. The slight brush had elicited a wave of lust and warmth as his chest pounded.

My pulse elevated at the feeling.

When I'd pulled away, he hadn't cared in regards to himself. All he'd been concerned about was me.

I still felt as if I needed him far more than he needed me.

His thoughts changed to people's reaction to his inner fire, from his brother's occasional annoyance and dislike to people's outright hostility to him.

"You are the only person who hasn't cared," he said, slowly pulling his thoughts away until I was alone once more.

I kissed his neck before wrapping my arms around him, burying my hand in his hair. "Don't let them bother you. There's nothing wrong with you, do you hear me?"

Don cuddled me close while his tail coiled around my ankle.

Chapter 17

SPACE STATION, ANYONE?

Vince

I tried hard not to stare at Don or think about inappropriate things as I watched him in his fighting class, but it was so hard. He was incredibly sexy, even when he was simply standing there instructing people. My eyes kept running over his broad shoulders and muscular chest, and my thoughts whipped back to how it felt to be curled up on his lap, safe.

Swallowing, I readjusted my semi in my tight jeans. I should have worn something else, but I loved dressing in my own clothes and in my own style. It made me feel... well, like me.

I wasn't the only human who'd returned to Earthen fashion, as the drakcol called it. Seth had more hoodies, Caleb wore jeans and henleys, and Teddy would often wear jeans and a plain T-shirt.

Thinking of him, I glanced at Teddy, who was sitting next to me. He hadn't really talked to me much once he learned I was planning on going back to Earth. I got it. We were friends, very close friends, and I'd chosen to leave him. Teddy didn't handle strong emotions well, and he would often turn apathetic when confronted with them.

Caleb wasn't here to distract us today either, adding an extra strain, but Fyn was. He'd mentioned to Seth before they started working out that Caleb had a pain flare because he'd tweaked something, so he was resting. Without Caleb's chatter, the silence between Teddy and I was palpable. I wished Seth was sitting with us, but he was sparring with Mindy while Fyn sparred with someone I didn't recognize. Bimwoxcol was teaching Pierce and Camden how to fight. She'd invited me and Teddy to join her, but we both passed.

Now if it had been Don, I might not have minded. We'd spent almost every night cuddling for the last week or so before he sat with me until I fell asleep. I hadn't kissed him on the lips again, but I'd kissed his neck and chest quite frequently. I liked it. Yesterday, I'd even licked his earlobe, tugging on his long earring, and made him groan. His tapered ears were sensitive, which needed to be explored more. That was something I planned to slowly investigate—one of many things. Then once I'd placed his hands somewhere, Don would rub or pet me, usually my back, arms, or thighs. All of which I enjoyed.

I was steadily growing comfortable with him.

The nightmares were still a thing. He hadn't magically cured me, though I was still hoping some good dicking down would put a major dent into my issues. However, I tried not to have him use his inner fire to send me to sleep unless the nightmares were so bad I'd woken him up. Don had offered to stay the night with me, but I'd refused. I didn't mind when he fell asleep next to the bed before me or after I had a particularly bad dream. But I felt guilty having him on the floor because I couldn't handle him on the bed.

Soon, though. I was sure I would be able to kiss him soon, and maybe after that, I could try to have him sleep next to me, then sex. I swallowed a groan. I wanted to fuck him so badly.

A slam went through the room and made me start.

Teddy grimaced. "That had to hurt."

Kal stood over Don, then crouched. "You aren't paying attention, Captain. Are you alright?"

"I'm fine. You pulled your kick at the last moment." Don grunted as he sat up.

My bad, I silently said, teasing him a little as I thought about licking and sucking on his earlobe. I hadn't meant to distract him, but since I had, I'd use it to my advantage to play with him.

Don glanced in my direction and threw me a small smile before he faced off with Kal again. When Don fought, I couldn't help but watch. But when he and Kal sparred, it was an entirely different matter. They were good. Much better than anyone else. Don was fast and strong, but Kal dodged and threw punches like he could read thoughts, and they both used their tails to their advantage, alerting me to how strong the prehensile appendages were. But it was more than that.

They were graceful, fluid, and seemed to move without tension or thought.

However, no matter what Don did, Kal beat him. It was mind boggling. Kal was shorter and slimmer, not to mention Don could read thoughts.

Begrudgingly, I had to admit Kal was a spectacular fighter.

I liked Don better, so that was something. A small, worthless something, but something.

So I didn't distract Don again, I forced myself to look at Seth. He was a decent fighter, not as good as Mindy, but he was a quick and enthusiastic learner. Mindy would demonstrate something, then Seth would nod and try it.

No one would ever hurt him again.

Maybe I should ask Don to teach me. Or I should keep him as my personal bodyguard. I chuckled at the thought of him in a black suit, earpiece, and sunglasses, calling me odd code names like Falcon or Eagle.

"Still crushing on Seth?" Teddy asked.

I started. No, actually, I'd been thinking of Don again. "He's getting better."

"Serlotminden wants to teach me."

"Are you going to take him up on the offer?"

He shrugged with a grunt—his typical response.

Unable to help it, I looked at Don again. He and Kal were still sparring. His scales gleamed with the exertion and his muscles were pumped. I ripped my gaze away before I thought about inappropriate things like licking him.

"Are you going to go to the space station?" I asked.

"Yeah," Teddy said, eyes going soft. "Serlotminden wants to show me around. Also, Brad, Camden, Roman, and Pierce want to walk around. I figured we could make it a Team Human thing."

"I want to come."

He grinned. "I figured you would. Seth and Caleb are coming too. They're trying to convince Kal and Fyn that we don't need a horde of guards or their presence."

"Alone? We're going to the station alone?" My knees pressed against my chest and I hugged them, balling up. What if someone took us? What if... My mind started to replay what exactly happened when humans were taken.

Teddy grabbed my hand, and I flinched, tensing from the press of his skin to mine. I tried to breathe through the initial panic, but it vibrated under my skin and sent my heart racing. I did better when I initiated physical contact, not that Teddy would know that.

"We'll be fine," he said, his voice ever calm. "It's safe. Mindy wouldn't let me go with everyone if it wasn't."

I nodded, but the wriggling fear didn't abate. I pulled my hand out of his, and he glanced at me, forehead crinkling. I never pulled away first. Teddy wasn't physically affectionate, but he knew I needed it. Or at least I had on Xome. Now... Well, I still needed it, but I didn't want to need it.

"Are you alright?" Teddy asked, his gaze scouring my face.

Thankfully, Don sank down next to me, resting against the wall, and saved me from answering. His long hair was trapped in a messy knot, but a few strands had escaped and stuck to his forehead. I wanted to push them back behind his ears, then trail my fingertips over his piercings before teasing him.

Fuck, what the hell was wrong with me? I clearly needed more physical attention.

Don's lips quirked.

"You did well," I said.

Teddy agreed, "You're so fast."

"Thank you. Kalvoxrencol is better."

"Does that bother you?" It sure as hell bothered me.

"Not at all. He has worked hard for his skill."

Teddy leaned around me, resting his elbows on his knobby knees. He was still far too underweight from our time under Agk's ownership, as well as being stranded on the icy planet. I was too thin as well, but I wasn't actively trying to gain weight like Teddy was.

"Not to be mean, but how does he win?" Teddy asked. "You read minds."

"I take no offense," he replied. "Kalvoxrencol has an annoying habit of letting his mind go blank. He doesn't think when he fights. No plan, just instinct. He perfected this skill to beat me. He's talented enough that he can react to my attacks or attack me with little to no plan. There's also the fact it takes me a second to process what I'm hearing and form a response to it."

Kal was fucking annoying. I wanted to tie an anchor to his ankles and throw him off a cliff into a raging ocean. See if he could fly then. The fucker would drown or crash into the jagged cliff on the way down. I chuckled darkly, then frowned. But with how *perfect* he was, I'm sure the bastard would escape.

Don cast me a look, eyebrows drawing together, and I refused to back down. Yes, he didn't like me plotting his beloved younger brother's demise, which was fair, but I was allowed to think what I wanted. It wasn't like I would *actually* hurt Kal. It would make Seth,

Don, and all of Kal's brothers sad. Besides, I wasn't a murderer. As much as I disliked Kal, it wasn't enough to hurt him.

Now Tryk or Agk? Yeah, I would kill them given the chance. I wouldn't even feel a shred of guilt.

Don's tail coiled around my ankle, and I leaned closer to him, basking in the warmth of his arm and his fragrance. His usual soft scent was stronger with all the sweating he was doing; it was spicier too. I wanted to lick his fucking armpit and taste him.

He coughed, and I grinned, pushing my forehead against his bare arm. I might have said no to physical contact in public, but I liked Don's tail touching me and I liked being able to snuggle with him when I wanted. It was comforting, and I deserved to feel better, right?

Mindy bounced up. "Flower, did you see me?"

"I did," Teddy replied.

"Makes you want me, doesn't it?"

Teddy rolled his eyes. "You're ridiculous."

For whatever reason, that made Mindy grin. He held his hand out, and Teddy took it, slipping away.

"You're going to the station?" Don asked in a low voice.

No one was close enough to hear, so I said, "I don't know. Apparently, it will just be Team Human."

He rested his hand palm up on his thigh in an invitation, probably in response to the sudden trickle of icy fear at his question. I didn't have to take it—Don wouldn't care—but I needed his reassurance. I slid my fingers in between his to interlace them. The burning heat of his palm seared me and soothed the tension from my chest.

"I won't allow anyone to harm you. If I thought the space station was in any way dangerous, we would not be stopping or I wouldn't allow people to disembark. But you don't have to go."

"I want to." I sighed. It was nice that Kal, Fyn, and Mindy wouldn't be hovering. I liked the idea of us humans hanging out and exploring together, and this was the first time I actually *wanted* to do something other than curl into a ball and never move, but what if someone grabbed me? I couldn't go back to that life. I refused to. I would rather die.

Don's breath rushed over my ear. "You are safe, Little Warrior. I promise. No one will ever touch you without your permission again."

I took a shuddering breath. "I believe you."

"If it makes you feel better, I'll be on the station. I have some work. I'll be able to hear you from anywhere on board. If you were in danger, I would know."

"You would come?"

"Yes."

My fear rushed out, leaving me so weightless it was a wonder I didn't start hovering. Don would keep me safe. I trusted it. I believed it.

I sagged against him, my gaze wandering absentmindedly as I ran my fingers over his palm. No one paid any attention to us. I hadn't told anyone about me and Don, not because I was embarrassed or ashamed. I hadn't because no one had asked, and it hadn't come up naturally. I did need to tell Seth and Teddy because they would read into what me and Don were—friends with benefits.

I blinked. Seth was gone. I hadn't noticed him and Kal leaving. I shrugged. I would see him later. It wasn't a big deal. Besides, I liked sitting here with Don.

Resting my chin on his arm, I asked, "Would you teach me to protect myself?"

"If you want."

"I don't know if I want to or not, but it might be nice to know how to fight, if only to kick someone's ass."

"Not Kalvoxrencol's."

I kissed Don's sweaty arm, fighting the urge to lick him. "No, not your precious brother, not that I could beat him."

"You could not, but yes, I'll teach you if you desire."

"Or," I said, grinning at him, "you can protect me."

Don stared at me, tail squeezing my ankle. He eventually said, "I wouldn't mind that either."

I nuzzled his arm. "I'd like that."

He held my hand close to his chest, his heart vibrating beneath me. "As would I."

Dontilvynsan

I was in danger. I held Vince's hand like it was my source of life. When he asked me to protect him, I wanted to offer to do so for the rest of my life. That wasn't possible, because he was leaving and Vince didn't want it.

If I wasn't careful, Vince would steal my soul, and the mate bond would follow.

He nuzzled my arm, enjoying my scent as waves of contentment radiated off him. I should've pulled away to protect myself, but I didn't. I wasn't strong enough. Instead, I rubbed my forehead against his hair, scent marking him.

Chapter 18

SPIDER, PIG, OR RABBIT?

Vince

I walked away from the medbay more irritated than when I'd headed there, which was a fucking feat because I hated going for any reason. Klars was still upset that I wasn't gaining weight. He'd promised, or more like threatened, to appeal to Seth or to take medical action if he didn't see a marked improvement by my next appointment. I'd refused the nutritional slurries, and I wasn't eating much—I had no appetite or interest in food. But I didn't want Seth to find out about anything, nor did I want to put Don in a hard position of keeping his promise to me while fighting Klars.

That meant I was going to have to eat more.

My stomach protested the very thought. I did eat some when I was with Don. He never pressured me, but he would eat and I couldn't seem to stop myself from picking food off of his plate if to do nothing more than make him smile or to tease him. It also helped that he was currently determined to try human cuisine. It was incredibly fun to see him eat different things, half the time attempting to keep his expression bland and not succeeding. Just thinking about it made me smile.

Hands behind my back, I walked down the hallway, which was nearly covered in entirety with vines. The vines were a deep green, a pale blue, and a basic red. They all wove together in an explosion of color, aided by the flowers growing on them. Gardeners were currently pruning them back so they remained on the ceiling and walls and didn't overtake the spongy floor.

It made sense, in a way, for space vessels to be covered in plants. They provided oxygen and cleaned the air. I assumed that none of these plants took much water, but I could be wrong. I paused in my step to round a gardener who was attacking a particularly thick vine, then continued down the hall with nowhere in mind.

I could always return to my room, but there was a chance that I would simply lie in bed and not move. Honestly, that *was* what would happen. I had little urge to do anything, which was so unlike me. I usually flitted around, busy as hell, never stopping. Now, I wanted to be alone and lying on the bed, numb.

Seth was busy. He had to speak with the ruling group of the Drakcol Empire, the Cohort. Caleb was with him. Apparently, Wyn, their friend, and some other drakcol were bringing up concerns of accessibility for the flightless population on the drakcol homeworld. I had no idea what Teddy was doing, besides fucking his husband—that was basically all they did.

People dashed past me, almost running. I didn't really think much of it, because drakcol jogged along the halls all the time. They were all obsessed with fitness to an extreme level—maybe even to an unhealthy level. This time, most people who rushed by were wearing uniforms, not workout clothes.

My pulse picked up as sweat slid down my spine. I felt, all of sudden, like all these running people knew something that I did not. I looked over my shoulder, but the drakcol had disappeared from sight. When I faced forward, I had a split second to see something hurtling toward me.

I shrieked when something smacked into my face and wrapped around my head, sending me to the ground. Pure terror knifed through me, cutting off my breath. I couldn't see. I couldn't react. Something had gotten me. Memories assaulted me and sent my stomach up my throat.

"Pookie," Teddy yelled, yanking the thing off me.

I flipped over and puked. What little I'd ingested this morning splattered the blue moss. Trembling, I vomited again, bile burning my nose. A hand touched my back, and I flinched away, crying, "No!"

"Vince," Teddy whispered. "It's me."

"No," I repeated before puking again. "No." I shook my head. I couldn't do this. I was done. I wanted to be done. I needed to move past this. Why the fuck couldn't I?

"Vince," a deeper voice said, and I looked up.

Don was in front of me, his hair mussed and his scales shiny like he'd been running. I felt my chin tremble, but I fisted my hands and willed my burning eyes to suck the fuck up. He crouched and cupped my cheek, waiting.

Please, I thought. I didn't want to lose it here.

Calm descended, and I took a shuddering breath. My eyes closed, and I instinctively shifted toward Don, needing reassurance from him. His other arm slowly slid around me, then pulled me until I was nestled against his chest with his hand holding my face. His warm scent seeped into my lungs, and finally, I was safe.

"I have you," Don whispered. "I always have you."

I took another intoxicating inhale and shifted back enough to see Teddy, who was holding a literal monster. It was white with floppy ears like a rabbit, eyes that went in two different directions, a pig snout, snaggle teeth, and six spider legs that hugged its body, though each one had tiny paws, complete with toe beans, on the end. It was like a mad scientist had jammed all the spare parts from other experiments together and called it good.

"What the fuck is that?" I asked.

"What the fuck is *that*?" Teddy asked, gesturing to Don and me.

"Oh, yeah. Me and Don are friends with benefits."

Teddy stared at us for a minute, then said, "Okay."

I grinned. "That's it?"

He shrugged. "Am I supposed to say something else?"

I laughed, pushing out of Don's embrace, and stood. I snagged his hand, keeping him close. I wasn't quite ready to say goodbye. "No. Now answer my question."

Teddy held out the monster, whose tongue lolled as it snorted. "This is Pookie. We are currently running from Mindy."

My pulse thrummed. "What? Why? What did he do?"

"It's a sex thing, I believe," Don replied, tightening his hold on my hand.

A deep flush spread over Teddy's cheeks, extending down his neck and up to his ears.

I laughed. "I see. He hunts and gets to keep his prize."

"Something like that," Teddy muttered.

"So, Pookie?" I asked, and when it heard its name, it snorted and its legs thrashed. I flinched and pressed closer to Don.

"She won't hurt you," Teddy said, squeezing her and making her snort. "She loves everybody and wants to play. She didn't mean to scare you. Though that's how she terrified Seth. Caleb finds it funny. He wears her like a hat."

My eyebrows raised. I didn't believe I'd ever heard Teddy talk so much in one go.

"She's not in trouble," Don said, gesturing to the writhing creature in Teddy's grasp. "While many have complained about your pet, Bartholomew, I see no merit in taking her from you."

I snorted. "He means Mindy wouldn't forgive him, and he's a doting older brother who loves his younger brothers."

Don flicked me with his tail, and I grinned at him.

Any tension in Teddy vanished. He set Pookie down, and she bolted toward me. I crouched down, letting go of Don but silently asking him to hold onto me with his tail, which he did, and held out a hand. Her little pig snout twitched and her curly tail wagged. I smiled. She was rather cute when she wasn't acting like a creature from a horror movie who would suck my brains out. I petted her head, and her odd eyes closed as she snorted.

"I like her," I whispered. I hadn't had a pet in so long. I missed it.

"Me too," Teddy replied, moving to crouch on her other side. We both petted and stroked Pookie while she accepted every little morsel of affection. "I couldn't imagine leaving her on that icy planet. Thankfully, we didn't have to."

"There you are," a voice snarled, and I flinched.

Teddy was up in a flash and running away with Pookie at his side. Mindy growled and raced after him.

I swallowed, watching them disappear.

Don grabbed my hand again. "Serlotminden will never harm Bartholomew, and the exercise is good for him. He needs to rebuild his muscles."

While Don didn't remark on my own physique, he did run his eyes over me. I crossed my arms and lifted an eyebrow, daring him to comment.

He smiled. "I was thinking about how well you look today."

Heat slammed my cheeks. I'd picked out this black sundress and fishnet tights hoping he would like them.

With a quirk of his lips, Don stepped closer. His free hand tugged on the hem of my dress. "Do all people wear such clothes?"

"Why?"

"Curiosity. Seth, Caleb, and Bartholomew don't dress as you do."

"I'm more femme than most cis guys."

He blinked.

"Feminine," I reiterated. "I'm not a woman, nor do I want to be one, and I'm not trans femme, but I like soft things and dressing like this." I shrugged, not sure how to exactly explain it.

"I like it."

Once again, heat returned to my face. I pushed him slightly. "If you're not careful, I'll let your compliments go to my head."

Don only moved closer, leaving very little space between us, and not even a tinge of fear plagued me. He was Don; what was there to be afraid of?

He lowered his head, his breath rushing over me as he said, "I think you should let it go straight to your lovely head, Little Warrior."

"Should I?"

"Indeed."

I swallowed. "I'm already dripping in ego. I could get worse."

Lips almost touching my ear, he whispered, "And I'll still be right here beside you, telling you how lovely I find you."

Pulse in my throat and dick hardening, I simply pulled Don into a hug in the middle of the damn hallway and hid my burning face from anyone who happened to wander by.

Chapter 19

DID I SEE A CAT?

Vince

The station was a cylinder with a thick ring around the center that had huge pylons for ships to dock on. We wouldn't see more than this shopping area, and that was perfectly fine with me. I clung to Seth as we walked around the busy station. My eyes were wide as I glanced around. Aliens I'd never seen before and some familiar species filled the space.

There were two levels of shops selling anything that I could possibly imagine. Sometimes, I even had a hard time guessing what was for sale. I spotted clothes, glowing crystals, jewelry, even large-ass beetle-looking aliens selling what smelled like poop. Bars, restaurants, and what might have been a brothel—I tugged Seth away as fast as physically possible. It was a madhouse of activity that was impossible to follow. Every shout, scrape, and whistle made the tension in my muscles ratchet up until I thought I was going to shatter under the strain.

Seth was as tense as I was, but for a very different reason. Seth had social anxiety, and crowds stressed him out; I was worried some asshole was going to abduct and sell me to the highest bidder. I tried to remind myself, repeatedly, that Don was on the station, and everyone had a touchstone. One word and Kal, Fyn, and Mindy would descend for their mates.

It was the one time I was actually happy that Kal was a possessive fucker. I imagined he was hanging around waiting for Seth to call him.

To top it off, Caleb looked fierce as hell in his black tunic and trousers, both topped with black leather armor. He walked with a metal cane that had a white grip, bouncing every few steps in excitement. For once, his wings were properly tucked beneath his shirt; I hoped he hadn't hurt himself to achieve it, but it wasn't my business.

Caleb and Camden had become fast friends in a short time, laughing and joking about everything in loud voices that carried over the bustling crowd and hawkers yelling about their wares.

Brad and Teddy were talking, or more accurately grunting and giving a single sentence every once in a while. They seemed to be getting along, despite their age difference. Roman walked beside them, as silent as ever, but he was watching the crowds, like I was, and his body was tense.

Pierce floated between conversations with ease.

We explored all the market had to see, which was a lot. Seth bought jewelry and clothes for Kal. He offered to get me whatever I wanted, but I was content to look—until I saw a crystal instrument.

It was long, with glowing strings as fine as hair. The shape reminded me of a traditional Korean instrument, a gayageum, but it was made of crystal and shorter, not to mention it glowed when the strings were plucked.

"You want that?" Seth asked. "Why? You were never musical in the past."

"Don. He likes music. I don't even know if he can or would want to play it."

"What's going on with you two?"

Apparently, now was the time to disclose certain things. "We're friends with benefits."

His mouth opened in surprise.

"What? We're consenting adults. We talked about it. Permissions, he called it. I really like those, FYI. He doesn't want anything serious and neither do I, but we get along."

"If it works for you."

"It does."

"Then I'm glad." Seth walked forward and bought the instrument, scanning his touchstone. I had no idea what the cost was, but it had to be substantial. The seller put it into a metal case, and Seth handed it to me. "Here. Give it to Don. Kal would want his brother to have whatever he wants. Don doesn't spoil himself."

"Thanks."

We started forward again. Seth grinned, and I asked, "What?"

"I hated permissions. In the past, I did whatever my partner wanted whether I liked it or not. Kal wouldn't let me do that.

He wouldn't touch me, for the most part, until I told him what I wanted. It helped. I just hated talking about it."

"I liked it. It made me feel safe," I said before thinking about it.

Seth glanced at me, eyes narrowing. Being "safe" had never been a worry of mine in the past. He didn't say anything or ask any questions, and I was glad. I didn't want to talk about it, because *it didn't matter*. Maybe if I told myself that enough, I would believe it.

I froze. "Is that a cat?"

He glanced at a shop with glass doors, which was full of cats with the fanciest cat towers and toys I'd ever seen—like, they were actually trees. The cats even had a damn waterfall and pond with fish moving in it.

"Yeah. Because I brought Lucy, my cat, with me, cats are popular. The Coalition tried to outlaw it, but there was a huge illegal market on cats, so they changed the law. Any cats born in space can be traded, but Earth cats have to be left alone. It's closely regulated, because the Animal Regulation wants to make sure they are properly cared for and not used as breeders."

I wanted one. I could have a pet, an actual Earth pet. A furry friend to snuggle with would be so nice when I needed support or another presence, but I couldn't. I was going home, most likely, probably; I didn't know. This was temporary, though, and animals were a lifelong commitment.

Seth leaned closer, and I tensed as usual, not to mention I pulled back because I didn't want him to touch me, but my pulse remained even, which was odd. Shouldn't I be turned on or feeling something?

"To tell you the truth, I lied to Kal," he whispered. "I told him it was a cultural law not to move when cats sleep on you. Like it's super illegal and no one does it. He believed me. It's spread. Then Caleb made up the fact that we worship the house gods and have shrines with towers, water features, and catnip, not to mention naming towns after cats. When you buy a cat, they literally make you sign a legal document that you won't break the cultural law of Earth. It does deter people from randomly getting one. That, and they are very expensive."

I burst into laughter, and Seth turned bright red. Shock lining my voice, I asked, "You did that?"

"I didn't think it would matter. Caleb also verified it. It was the first thing he told all the humans we rescued about. All of them have agreed to keep it quiet. It's become like a secret that belongs to us."

I liked that. So much had been taken from us. Now this silly lie had become something we all could hold onto.

We moved past the shop, following the group. We all stayed pretty close together, though everyone was shopping on Caleb, Teddy, and Seth's dime. When we agreed to become citizens, we would get a stipend to live on until we could find work or we mated someone who could afford to care for us. From what Caleb and Seth had hinted, it was pretty much expected everyone would touch the Crystal and find their soulmate.

Teddy had point blank refused. He didn't love the soul type testing, because he thought it was stupid, but he utterly refused to touch the Crystal. He didn't want to chance Mindy not being his soulmate. He also didn't want the genetic link and the mind-to-mind talking.

Caleb laughed loudly, his deep voice booming above the crowd. I glanced at him to make sure everything was fine, then paused. Don was sitting at a restaurant. Alone. His eyes were closed, but his tail wiggled and moved incessantly. I bit my lip. He was working, but I would rather hang out with him than wander the station. It felt safer. Besides, it would be fun to see everything through his eyes.

Mindy was supposed to get Teddy at some point anyway, then everyone was going to go back to the ship. But I imagined Caleb would drag Fyn along in exploring the station, and Fyn would invite the rest of the humans because Caleb would want him to. Seth would probably chill in his room, recovering. That was what he used to do, anyway.

"Hey, do you mind if I leave?" I asked.

"Are you going back to the ship? We can all go. We probably shouldn't wander alone."

"No." I gestured to Don.

"Sure. Here." He took the instrument. "I'll see you later."

I gave everyone a quick goodbye before winding through the crowd. I kept Don in my sight at all times. He had to know I was coming, but he didn't help me, because I didn't need it. The closer I got, the more his tail moved. It was like a barometer to what he was feeling. A very cute barometer. I had the utmost urge to kiss and stroke it, but I wouldn't, because Don didn't want me to. Yet. Soon. When we fucked, maybe.

I slid onto the stool next to him. His tail wrapped around my ankle, and I smiled. I didn't say anything to greet him, as he was probably shuffling through the crowd's thoughts. I had no idea what he was looking for, but it had to be important.

A server who was bright orange and fuzzy like moss wandered over. They had four stocky legs that sort of jabbed out of their bullet-shaped body and four pitch-black eyes. They were odd, but perfectly understandable thanks to my touchstone as they asked for my order.

What they served was a mystery, and Don was busy. I didn't really want to eat, but I needed to. I had to gain weight. I asked for whatever they recommended for drakcol, because I could eat pretty much the same things they did. If it would kill me, I assumed Don would stop me from eating it.

His tail squeezed my ankle, and I took that as an affirmative.

The orange alien returned with a plate of noodles smothered in yellow sauce with a large slab of black meat on top. The noodles had the same texture as pasta, and the sauce was surprisingly sweet with a citrus undertone. The meat was gamy, but not bad or underseasoned. I silently ate as I watched the crowd and tried to keep my thoughts as calm as possible to not distract Don.

When I finished, I put my hand on his thick thigh. I didn't want to bother him, but I, for some reason, needed physical reassurance beyond his tail that he was beside me, that I was safe with him, that Don wasn't going to vanish. He didn't react. I had no idea how much time passed with us being quiet and sitting together, but it was pleasant and calming to my tense nerves.

The server didn't bother us more than to bring me red juice with bright green leaves—it was sweet with a minty flavor—and to refill the metal cup when it was empty.

Eventually, I rested my head against Don's arm and breathed in his scent with a low groan. I was happy. It was odd. I hadn't felt this way in so long, and here I was so content sitting with him. We weren't doing anything, and we didn't need to. When I had been on Earth, if I wasn't at work, I was socializing. I went from party to party, event to event. It was a rare night where I sat and did nothing or chilled.

Now I relaxed with Don nightly before he helped me sleep. I loved it. The slow pace. The unhurried need to do anything. I didn't love my lack of willingness to move when I was alone, but that would pass. I was sure of it. I needed time.

If I was going to stay here, I'd have to find an occupation or the nothingness would drive me up the wall, but maybe I didn't need to be as busy as before. I would rather chill with Don. We worked well together like that. He could sing or play something for me, and I would listen and read. I did love to read, even though I'd yet to pick up a book since I'd been here.

We could just be, couldn't we?

How much had I changed in the time I'd been gone? Yeah, a lot had happened, but still... I was me, but I was different too. Who would I have been if I'd never been taken? I couldn't hazard a guess, nor did I even want to try.

Right here, right now, I was safe, happy, and content.

Chapter 20

IS THIS A DATE?

Dontilvynsan

The thoughts around me buzzed like a cloud of insects. I was searching for certain images in the minds of those who wandered by, as I didn't speak all of the languages. Most people thought in a mix of emotion, word, and image, which helped. I paid attention for any chance of humans being sold on this station. If there was, I would find and rescue them.

The Cohort had ordered every Drakcon ship to be on the lookout for humans and to bring them to Tamkolvanloknol if found, at any cost. The Coalition had issued a warning about the trafficking of humans; it was highly illegal. Different species within the Coalition would be keeping an eye out, but illegal sellers would always slip through the nets in place, hence the idea to give bounties for every human returned.

Kalvoxrencol had already repurposed one of the moons around Tamkolvanloknol to be changed into a safe haven for the humans who wanted to stay.

None of the wandering thoughts of the shoppers in the market were as loud as Vince. He was attempting so hard not to distract me, and I loved his hand on my thigh. It was grounding. My mentor had warned me about taking in too much. Other people's thoughts, trauma, and personalities could become my own if I wasn't careful. He'd taught me well about guarding my sanity, but Vince's touch acted as a failsafe, reminding me of who I was.

Vince rested his head against my arm, releasing a long breath, and I struggled to keep my thoughts on the crowd. Waves of happiness and peace rolled off him as he nuzzled me. I caught an errant thought that made me pause and tore my focus to shreds.

If he stayed. Vince wanted a job if he stayed.

The "if" was still there, but the mere contemplation of him thinking about staying made my soul pound. I wanted that. I wanted him to stay here. With me. Where he belonged.

Vince had crawled into my affections with ease, and I feared the marks he'd left on my soul would never fade.

But it was his decision to remain or not, and I wasn't going to try and force his hand or influence his choice. Even if Vince wanted to stay in the end, it didn't mean he would choose or even desire to be with me in a romantic sense.

Knowing my focus was shattered and was something I couldn't recover, I turned toward Vince. "What do you want to do?"

He lifted and lowered his shoulders, face against my arm. I was grateful, for once, that my uniform had sleeves, unlike my casual clothes. The feel of his warm breath and cool skin on my scales would be too much for me to withstand.

"Do you want to explore the station more, or we can go back to the ship to nap?" I asked.

Vince's thoughts were slow and almost blank, though the numbness and void that often plagued him were absent. It felt as if he was going to fall asleep against me at any moment. We could return to his quarters or mine and nap. He'd never stayed in my quarters for more than a passing moment, and I liked the idea of him sleeping in my bed, leaving his scent on my sheets.

Vince perked up slightly at the thought of a nap as the image of us tangled on his bed raced through his thoughts. I suppressed a groan. I wanted that—we hadn't slept next to each other yet—but I would let Vince decide.

A gray cat raced across his thoughts, followed by a shot of longing and the image of us curled up together with one. My head cocked. He wanted a cat. Seth and Kalvoxrencol both enjoyed having Lucy, and Serlotminden and Bartholomew both enjoyed Pookie. Perhaps humans required a pet on some level. They did worship cats—their small house gods.

If Vince desired something, then he should have it. I wouldn't allow him to want for anything.

"I can buy you one," I said. Clothes. He needed clothes. Or jewelry. I didn't wear any, but Vince would look lovely with jewelry. The image of him with long gold earrings and fine necklaces on his delicate throat sent a shiver of lust down my spine. Whatever he wanted or needed was his, and I was more than happy to provide it.

Finances weren't an issue. I received a good pay from my position as a captain in the navy, and I got an allowance from the crown—not to mention my estate on Tamkolvanloknol was profitable. My Vince could have whatever he wished.

"What?" he asked, chin on my arm, eyes heavy.

"A cat."

He chuckled, pushing his forehead into my arm. "You are sweet, but no."

"Why? You want one."

"I do," Vince said, "but they are a lifelong commitment that I can't make right now. It wouldn't be fair."

Reality crashed back onto me with a sharp blade to my soul. Vince was leaving. I was allowing my emotions to get the better of me, but it was hard to contain myself where he was concerned.

"Seth would keep the cat," I reasoned, "or Monqilcolnen, or me if—when you leave."

"Hmm," he replied, eyes closing.

I studied the gentle curve of his cheek and the slope of his nose and the shape of his eyes. He was lovely. But Vince was more than his beautiful face and entrancing form. His strength to survive, his humor, his strong soul, his burning confidence, and his acceptance of my gift were all intoxicating.

His words from some days ago returned to my thoughts: *"I don't want your gift. I want you, Don."*

Pleasure washed through me as I stared at him. How was I going to survive him leaving? I didn't think I was.

I buried the thought with aggressive efficiency. That thought would lead to more dangerous ones with an end result I couldn't handle.

Unable to stop myself, I nuzzled his forehead with my own, scent marking him. I wanted others to smell me on him and the opposite. I pulled back, feeling guilty. Vince had asked me not to touch him in public, but I was having a harder and harder time keeping away from him. Every cell in my body demanded that I press close to Vince and never leave his side.

Vince grinned at me, not upset in the slightest about my attentions. "I want to walk around with you, then nap."

"Anything you desire."

His eyes opened. "What do *you* want? This is not about me. It's about us."

Us. I liked that far more than I should. I leaned closer to him, my hair falling around his face, giving us an illusion of privacy on the busy station. "I want to make you happy, buy you things, lots of things, and then take a nap with you."

He swallowed, cheeks turning red. "Alright."

I smiled, pushing my head against his. "Can I buy you anything I want?"

"Within reason."

I took that as a yes. "Come on."

Vince

Anyone who said they didn't like to be spoiled was lying. Don seemed determined to spoil me. If it was anyone else, I would've thought he wanted something in exchange, but he didn't. Don honestly seemed to enjoy buying me things, and I had no idea why. Yeah, he was nice, but it still seemed odd that he took such enjoyment from finding things to buy for me.

Clothes were first. I had plenty of clothes, but apparently clothes or anything made by a dispenser weren't as durable or as comfortable. Don bought me shirts, pants, skirts, and dresses in several styles and colors. He had yet to see me in any color besides black, and from his choices, it appeared that he wanted to see me in jewel colors. Then he bought me jewelry. I wasn't opposed, but he seemed to like the thin golden necklaces more than I did. Both necklaces hugged my neck and had small diamonds that looked like flashing stars. He'd wanted to buy me earrings, but I didn't have my ears pierced. I also refused to allow him to buy me a ring.

"What else do you need?" he muttered.

I laughed, going up on my toes in front of him. We were weighed down with bags. "I don't need anything else."

He frowned. "What do you want?"

You, I thought, surprised by the intensity of the feeling. I'd never had someone be so nice without expecting anything in return. I was feeling possessive. Shocker. I was a bit unhealthy when it came to people and romance.

"You have me," Don said without stumbling as he stared at the shops, clearly looking for something else to buy me.

"Do I?"

"Yes."

"Good." I took that as tacit permission to be as possessive as I wanted. "I want to go back and nap. With you." My pulse elevated at the thought of us in the same bed, but I needed him stretched out next to me as I fell asleep.

Don smiled and rubbed his forehead against mine. "I want to, but I want to get you a pet first. Something to snuggle with besides me."

"No. It's not fair to them. You will have to do for now."

"Fine."

Feeling brave, I grabbed his hand and intertwined our fingers. "Let's go."

He led us through the crowd, holding tight to my hand and coiling his tail around my ankle. I felt completely safe, even with the numerous aliens around us. Don would protect me. No one would dare to steal me when he was right beside me.

When we got to his ship, we went straight to my room. I dropped everything on the couch and lifted my hands above my head to stretch. I was tired from the amount of walking I'd done. It had been several weeks since I'd been allowed to do more than move from my cell to a customer room. Even since arriving on Don's ship, I hadn't done much either.

Don slowly came up behind me, his steps loud enough for me to hear. I caught sight of his hands reaching toward me. I leaned back. His hands rested on my sides before sliding around me. I groaned, hooking my arms around his neck as best as I could from this position.

"We don't have to, or I could stay on the floor." Don held me securely in his arms while his tail tickled my leg.

"No. I want to." I wanted more than that. I wanted to fuck, but I wasn't ready for that yet. Soon, though. I'd get over it, and Don would help me move forward.

"Alright."

He remained still, holding me. His face burrowed into my neck as he took deep breaths. A growl started low in his chest. I could feel it vibrating against my back. It should freak me out. It didn't. Instead, the sound went straight down to my cock, making it twitch. Don's breath sharpened, and he pulled me closer, allowing me to feel his own cock stiffening.

I wanted to lean into the moment, but the prickle of fear wouldn't be erased. The thought of him leaning over me as we fucked made me panic.

Don instantly let me go and started to step back.

"No," I snapped and grabbed his arms to pull him back. His warmth returned, and I leaned back. "I'm not ready yet, but that doesn't mean I want you to stop touching me."

Don nuzzled my neck. "I was not trying to pressure you."

"I know."

"I want you. That's all," Don said.

I laughed, turning around and hooking my arms around his neck. "I know."

"I care about you."

Heat bloomed in my stomach. "I care about you."

Feeling brave, I arched up and pressed my lips to his. He was so warm and his lips were silky against mine. I groaned. The fear and memories were still there, but I pushed them away. I wanted this. I wanted him. Not some random person. I wanted Don, right here in this moment.

Don kept the pressure soft as he returned my kiss. A moan ripped out of me, and I gripped him, trying to get closer. He growled, and suddenly, the dynamic changed. Don was kissing me like he never wanted to stop. I wrapped my arms around his neck to hold him close, movements frantic. I fisted his hair, and he whimpered. My tongue darted out and claimed his mouth.

His scaled tongue slid over mine, and I moaned, imagining it on my cock. The warm heat of his mouth would be amazing. Don grabbed my ass and lifted me so he didn't have to bend over to accommodate my much shorter height.

Ice shattered the heat of lust and arousal. I pushed away, and Don released me, letting me slide to the ground. I took several steps away from him, panting. His breath wasn't any better than mine and his tail was thrashing.

"My Vince, are you alright?"

I held up a hand to keep him away as I breathed, pushing through the memories of other people's hands on me. My pulse rang in my ears and my muscles were tight. I was trying to remain in one spot, rather than flee or curl into a ball.

I'd been enjoying the kiss until he grabbed me. Hell, I'd more than enjoyed it. My cock had been rock hard and desperate for him.

"Should I leave?" he asked, voice small.

"No." I held out a hand; this time, in silent demand.

Don immediately took it. I pulled him close and pressed my face against his firm chest. I placed his hand on my cheek.

"Me or my gift?"

"You."

I breathed in his light scent and pressed a kiss to his palm. Don nuzzled my head as he took a deep inhale. I stayed like that for a few minutes until I was tired, too tired to keep my eyes open.

Taking his hand in mine, I pulled him toward my bedroom. "Come on."

"Are you sure?"

"Stop asking me. I wouldn't invite you unless I was." In my room, I kicked my shoes off and flopped onto the bed. Don was a lot slower. He was trying not to scare me. I was fine. Honestly. The sudden movement of him grabbing me had startled me, but I'd worked through it.

Don lay on the edge of the bed on his back, tense.

"You don't have to nap with me," I snapped. "If you have somewhere better to be, by all means..." I flicked my hand at the door.

His forehead crinkled. "I want to be here."

I looked at his tense frame. "You could've fooled me."

"I don't want to scare you again."

I scoffed and slid across the bed. Yeah, I was a tad nervous and my body screamed at me to run away, but this was Don. My Don. He wouldn't hurt me. I pushed his arm down flat on the bed before resting against him. His arm came around my waist, hand cupping my hip. He snuggled me close and his tail coiled around my calf.

"Are your wings uncomfortable?" I asked.

"Slightly."

I leaned up. "Let them out."

He sat up enough to let his wings unfold beneath us before lying back down and pulling me against his side. His wings were leathery and warm; I liked the supple texture and the utter heat that enclosed me. Any cold that plagued me was banished in his embrace.

I snuggled as close as possible, closing my eyes. He dragged his forehead over my hair again, and I laughed.

"Why do you keep doing that?" Not that I had any reason to complain. I rubbed my face on him all the time.

"Do you dislike it?" An oddly vulnerable tone had entered his voice.

I leaned my chin on his chest. "No. I like it." I was rewarded with a wide smile, which I loved. Swallowing, I pressed a quick kiss to his lips before lying back down.

"Drakcol have scent glands on our forehead, sides of our necks, and our sides. It's a way of marking you with my scent."

Like a cat? I'd never had a cat, let alone knew much about them, but it seemed like a possessive move.

"Does it bother you now?"

"No." I didn't care if he felt possessive of me. I felt possessive of him. I fisted his shirt. While I was here, Don was mine, and I refused to let him go or share him. Anyone else who wanted him was fuck out of luck. I would literally beat them with a stick if they tried to take him.

"Thank you."

I didn't know what he was thanking me for, because what I was thinking was more than a little unhealthy, but I said, "Thank you for taking me on a date."

"Date?"

"Um," I said, falling asleep. "It's a human courting term."

"Are we courting?"

"I guess. No. Sort of." I shrugged. I didn't know, and I was too tired to figure it out.

Chapter 21

MUSIC.

Dontilvynsan

My arms tightened around a soft frame, and I groaned, nuzzling Vince's silky black hair as I basked in his subtle floral perfume mixed with my own. He didn't react, his body pliant against mine. His thoughts were a low hum, not dreaming. The trust Vince was showing me after everything that had been done to him was utterly amazing. I was humbled by it.

I simply watched him, waiting for him to wake up. I shouldn't have taken a nap with Vince, as I had responsibilities that needed to be seen to, and yet, the greatest pull on my instincts and soul was this man in my arms. There was no higher duty than caring for and protecting Vince.

His eyes fluttered open, and he blinked before grinning and tucking against me. "Donny."

"Did you sleep well, Little Warrior?"

"Yeah," he groaned, arms pulling me until we were flush. "So good."

"I'm glad." I nuzzled his forehead, and Vince silently asked me to kiss it, so I did, pressing my lips against his smooth skin. I traced kisses over his forehead, brushing his back over and over again.

Vince groaned and lifted his face to claim my lips. I sank into him, reveling in the silk of his tongue against mine. He cupped my cheeks, forcing me onto my back and fucking my mouth with his tongue. I surrendered to him and swallowed the desperate noises that attempted to escape at the feel of him. I didn't want him to be put off by whatever groans I made.

He pulled back, panting, and I struggled to not chase him. I needed his lips on mine once more.

Vince stroked my cheek. "I like waking up to you beside me."

"You can have this every day if you wish."

"Can I?" He smirked, fingers pinching my chin. "I don't know, you might be giving me too much."

"Not at all. You can have whatever you want."

He smirked, and my tail wiggled and my gut curled, low and warm. Vince lifted my chin. "That's dangerous to say, Don. I might decide to take everything."

"You can have it all."

Possessive need rolled through him moments before Vince pressed his lips to mine again. "I want it," he whispered, then kissed me again. "I want you beside me every damn day. I want to open my eyes and see your perfect face first thing."

Soul throbbing, I replied, "You can have it."

"Do we need to adjust our permissions?"

I fought a smile. Vince was honoring my needs as much as I was his. "You seem more comfortable about public affection. Can I touch you around others?"

"You can hold my hand." He kissed me. "You can hold me with your tail." Another brush of his lips. "I would prefer to initiate hugs or kisses."

"I'm alright with all that."

"What do you need?"

Him. I needed Vince, and that thought scared me, but it couldn't be banished. Those words couldn't be said, though, so I suppressed them. Instead, I thought about what I truly required at this moment. "I need to spend time with you. I need to care for you, to buy or bring you things. I would also like to spend the night here, even if it's on the floor."

He bobbed his head. "You can have that."

"Sex is still something we need to discuss, if you want to fuck." Vince had thought about fucking many times, but I was unsure if he was *actually* ready to be intimate this soon. It wasn't my place to say, though. Everyone handled trauma differently; everyone healed differently. Only Vince knew if he was ready.

"I want to," Vince said, but a wave of nausea and unease swelled.

"We do not have to, Little Warrior. I'm willing to wait." I would wait for the rest of my life. Vince was worth it.

"I want to," he repeated, firmer, but the discomfort remained.

"What do you like?"

Vince bit his bottom lip. "I..." He swallowed, eyes closing. "I don't know. We need to go slow. Maybe we can start on the couch.

I could—" Vince broke off, breathing hard. "Maybe I can ride you or you can fuck me slowly?"

"I can," I said; however, I was concerned about the dislike and disgust lingering in his thoughts.

"But first," Vince said, kissing me, then pushing off the bed, "I have a gift for you."

I blinked in surprise. It was difficult for people to keep surprises from me due to my inner fire. Vince had to be gaining skills in the ability to think around me. It was impressive for the short amount of time we'd known each other. But much like Kalvoxrencol, he was determined to skirt around my gift and that determination meant he'd perfected the skill rapidly.

A thought of Seth popped into his head before ordering, "Sit down, Donny. I'll be right back." He darted out the front door.

My first instinct was to chase him, but I didn't, even though it irritated me to have him out of my sight. I took a seat on his couch and simply waited, though my inner fire remained trained on Vince's thoughts. With every step, the clarity dimmed, but I was still able to perceive his happiness, which made me smile. There was something perfect about pleasing Vince, and I wished to continue to do so for as long as I was able.

When Vince returned, he was thinking so hard about innocuous things, such as the bland metallic gray of the wall that it nearly made me chuckle. He was attempting to keep this surprise a *surprise*, and for some reason that I couldn't articulate, I loved that.

"Close your eyes," Vince demanded.

"Why?"

"Because I haven't wrapped your gift."

Why would he wrap a gift and what would he even wrap it in?

He had to have caught my confusion, because Vince laughed, and the sound was like the purest magic to my ears. It clung to my soul and made it pound harder.

"Just do it, Donny," Vince said. "It's a human thing."

I indulged him.

His thoughts remained on other things, and I didn't pry, allowing him to keep his secret, but my ears perked at the slight muffled steps, which got closer and closer until I felt him brush against my knees. It took so much more concentration to keep my eyes closed than it should have, but I managed it, barely.

"Look at me," Vince whispered, and my eyes snapped open.

My jaw dropped. In Vince's grasp was a Numxisian harpsichord. I'd never played one before, but I'd heard the music and seen the array of colors that it produced.

Something inside of me shattered, then reformed at the sight of Vince holding the instrument. I'd never received such a thoughtful gift from one who wasn't related to me. It was... I couldn't even say what it was, but I felt light in a way that I never had before.

"This is for me?" I asked, then swallowed to clear the roughness of my voice.

Vince grinned, pressing closer until he was standing in between my legs. "Of course it is. I said as much."

And yet, I struggled to believe it. "I have no words."

A slight divot formed between his eyebrows, and I longed to smooth it away, though I resisted, unsure if my touch would be welcomed.

He bit his full bottom lip and looked down. "Do you dislike it? I can get something better. You don't have to take it. It doesn't matter."

Hurt prodded his mind, telling me how much it did matter to him. I shook my head so quickly it was a miracle my eyes remained in their sockets. "I love it."

His smile bloomed like a flower under the sun and transformed his features. Never in my entire life had I seen someone as beautiful as Vince. His mind had always drawn me in, but now, I could say with some certainty that his aspect was just as magnetic as his thoughts.

This was dangerous. He was dangerous. I needed to flee, or else, I feared, I wouldn't be able to. But I couldn't. No, I refused to. Vince was something special, and I didn't want to fight the gravitational pull that I felt toward him.

"Play something," Vince demanded, pushing the instrument into my lap.

I had no idea how to, but I couldn't deny Vince anything he desired. I glanced from the new instrument to Vince, who sat on the other side of the couch. He tucked one leg under him and brought the other to his chest, resting his chin on his knee. From his thoughts, I knew he wasn't expecting perfection; he merely wanted to hear me, to see me, to be with me.

With a slight smile, I settled the harpsichord on my legs and strummed the fragile strings. A pleasing, light noise trickled out and the base of the instrument flared in a rainbow of colors. Carefully, I pressed on some of the gossamer strings, then strummed with my other hand, listening to the noise.

Vince released a long gust of air and closed his eyes.

Nothing I played was proficient or even good, as I was still figuring out the instrument, but Vince was content and so was I. There was something inexplicably wonderful about spending time together in such a mundane way. It was as if us being together was an everyday occurrence—a thought I very much liked and yet refused to inspect.

When silence reigned for several moments, Vince opened his eyes. His voice wavered and his thoughts twisted and churned like the stormy sea. "Don?"

"Yes, Little Warrior."

He swallowed, shaking as he hugged his leg closer. "I want you to fuck me."

My cock twitched, firming up, but I remained seated and ignored it. Vince's discomfort worried me. "Are you sure?"

"Of course I am," he snapped. "I want you to fuck me. But we don't have to if you don't want me anymore. I'm not a fucking catch. I know that."

I moved closer and slowly laid a hand on his shaking arm. "I will always desire you."

"Then fuck me. I'm ready. I want to get it over with."

That wasn't the most enticing sentiment. I wished for us to be something remarkable, not a chore that must be hastened. Though what did I know? I hadn't pleased most of my past partners. Perhaps

I wasn't good enough to ever be more than a chore. And I'd never been hurt as Vince had. He might need to be fucked to reclaim something he felt he'd lost. I truly didn't know.

"We need to discuss permissions," I said, fighting my own unease at his discomfort.

Trembling and very pale, Vince said, "I don't want to get into too much detail right now. Can I just ride you?"

"Yes." That was a lie. I needed more, but I didn't want to be a bother.

Eyes anywhere but me, he said, "You can use a *condom*. We probably should."

The word "condom" took me a moment to understand, even with NAID assisting, but in the end, I gathered he meant what we called a sleeve. I myself was disease-free, as I'd always worn one in the past and received regular health checks and tests. Not to mention, I hadn't had sex in over a cycle. Vince had nothing to fear from me, but if he felt safer with one, I wouldn't protest.

"I can, but I'm free of disease," I informed him.

"It's not you," he muttered, "who was the whore."

I pressed closer to him and cupped his cheeks, forcing him to look at me. Vince didn't fight my hold, but a tinge of panic sparked in his thoughts. Remaining utterly still, I waited—I would let go if needed—but he relaxed after only a couple of breaths.

I said, voice deep, "There is absolutely nothing wrong or dirty about you. Do you understand?"

"You don't care that I was a whore?"

"I care that you were forced to do things you didn't want to, but I do not find consensual sex work reprehensible. If chosen, I find no reason why someone cannot do that line of work. You did not choose it, Vince. Your hurt is what I care about."

A tear slid down his cheek, but his jaw clenched and his eyes flicked away to the side, refusing to meet my gaze.

I brushed the tip of my nose against his and whispered, "I want all of you."

He swallowed. "Then take me."

Chapter 22

SOMETIMES DESIRE IS NOT ENOUGH.

Dontilvynsan

I could feel the tension in Vince's entire body and mind, but he pressed his shaking lips against mine. I returned the kiss, keeping the pressure soft. I didn't understand why he insisted on us doing this when he was so uncomfortable. I was perfectly content not to have sex until he was ready, even if that was for the rest of our time together. But this wasn't about me or us; this was about his need to overcome what had happened to him.

Which hurt, even if it should not.

However, the desire for this moment to truly be about us together and sharing an intimacy remained.

Vince moaned, pushing me back to climb on my lap. I whimpered, opening my mouth for him. I wanted Vince in every single way possible, but I needed more from this moment. His tongue slicked and swirled around mine as hot arousal flooded his mind, though it didn't outweigh the severe discomfort pulsing inside of him.

Cupping his hips, I pulled him more securely against me, my hard cock pressing against his butt. Vince stilled, and the shaking plaguing his body increased. I ran a hand down his back to comfort him, but he didn't calm, though also didn't move away.

"We don't have to," I whispered against his lips, my breath harsh with desire.

"I'm fine," he bit out, crashing his lips into mine in a feral kiss. "I want you, and you sure as hell want me."

Groaning, I returned his kiss and lost myself into the softness of his plush lips and his smooth tongue. Vince fisted my hair, and I winced at the tight hold but didn't remark on it. I wished we'd had more, or rather *any* conversation about sex permissions. If we had, he would've known I didn't enjoy any pain. But this was about him, not me, not us.

To soften and slow the harsh kiss, I brushed my fingertips along his back and rocked beneath him. Vince broke away from me, gasping. One of his hands gripped my hair even harder while the other dug into my shoulder.

"Is that nice?" I asked, rocking up into him.

His teeth sank into his bottom lip, and he nodded. His hard cock was rubbing against me while I rolled and rutted into him. Vince closed his eyes and held onto me. He was enjoying it. I felt that in his mind as well as saw it from his hard cock that was pushing against his trousers. But the tension and discomfort didn't dissipate no matter how much he liked it.

I wanted to stop. His discomfort was making it difficult for me to continue and it was hurting me. I could put an end to this by simply telling Vince I no longer wished to continue, but he might think I was rejecting him, which I wasn't. Hurting him was destroying me, and that was what I was doing. I was injuring Vince, even though he'd asked for it.

Vince grasped the hem of my shirt and tugged; I leaned forward so he could remove it before claiming his mouth once more. His trembling fingers roved my chest, tracing my scales. He brushed one of my nipples, and I grunted. My nipples weren't that sensitive, but it felt nice to have his fingertips circling the nubs.

He continued his exploration over my chest and down my sides, and I ripped my mouth from his, then swallowed the high-pitched cry that attempted to escape.

"There?" he asked.

"Yes," I panted. "It's where my scent glands are."

His fingers returned, rubbing the spots perfectly until I was wiggling and nearly strangling myself to stay silent.

Shifting back, he yanked his shirt off. I dragged my hands over his fair skin, not able to get over how beautiful he was. His nipples were a lovely pink against his light skin and the nubs were hard peaks. His chest was heaving, showing off his ribs, which practically poked through his skin. Vince truly needed to gain weight, but getting him to eat anything was a feat.

I nuzzled his neck, attempting to calm the rapidly growing panic. Vince cupped the back of my head and tugged me closer. I trailed kisses down his neck to his collarbone, sucking on it. He groaned, gripping me tight. When I moved back, his skin now bore a mark—my mark. Something primal inside of me flared at the sight of Vince's skin carrying my mark while my scent filled the air from his earlier attention to my scent glands.

"Take these off," Vince ordered, pulling on my trousers.

I helped Vince off my lap and stripped bare in front of him. He didn't look at me as he removed his own clothes, and even then, he refused to glance in my direction. I, though, couldn't look away from him. Vince was so delicate and slight. His bones were more prominent around his hips, but he was so soft-looking. His cock was hard and a drop of liquid beaded on his round crown. His shaft was much thinner and shorter than mine, and there was a slight curve. I wanted to drop to my knees and worship him, but I didn't move.

Vince asked, "Do you have lube?"

"Yes." I grabbed some as well as a sleeve. When I handed him the lube, he didn't glance at me. He moved to the couch and got on all fours as he circled his hole with a slick finger. With every touch, his unease was rising.

Vince wasn't ready for this.

"Little Warrior," I whispered, touching his back.

He leaped and skittered away from me, eyes wide and glassy.

"You do not want this."

"I do," he snapped, panting. "Maybe you don't want me anymore, but I do." The tension in his body and his softening cock told a different story.

"We don't have to do this."

"If you don't want me, then fine. I'll just get someone else. It doesn't matter who. I just need a dick."

A knife lodged in my soul, but I pushed my pain away. I came closer, and Vince's breathing increased, as did his terror. When I reached for him, a shriek ripped out of his lips, and he scrambled away until his back crashed into the wall.

"No," he cried, covering his face and drawing his knees to his chest. "No! No. No. No."

The terror was so sharp it sent me to my knees. "Vince, you do not have to do anything you don't want to."

Tears slid down his cheeks. "I want it to be over. I decided I was over it. I did. Not anyone else. Me! This is my body, and I decided it was over."

Slowly, I scooted closer, kneeling in front of him. His face was buried against his knees and his body shook with the strain that was echoing inside of him. Memories from his time on Xome washed through him, and I tried not to focus on them, because I needed to be present.

"Vince, my lovely warrior, you may have decided, but your body has not. There's a wound deep inside of you that needs to be cleaned and healed. It will take time, and more than you deciding you don't wish to feel the pain any longer."

He sobbed, holding himself tighter. "I just want to be done. I want everything to be done. I want you, Don. Why can't I not care about Xome?"

"Because you need to heal. And perhaps you need help."

He peeked up. "Will you help me?"

The absolute trust shining in his eyes and the innocence in his voice had me moving closer. "I will, in any way I can, but you need professional help."

Grunting, he hid against his knees once more. Shame filled him, and I didn't understand.

"There's no need for embarrassment or shame. I've spoken to professionals, as have many people, Vince."

He curled up even more, shaking and crying. Panic was growing with each passing moment. "Help me."

I slid close enough to place my hand on his cheek. The connection flooded me with his fear, his shame, his anger, everything, while I, in turn, gave him my peace, my comfort, my very soul.

His muscles relaxed, and Vince sagged toward me. I scooped him up, setting him on my lap, holding him close, as I continued to feed him my calm.

"Why can't I do this?" he whined.

I nuzzled the top of his head. "Because you are not ready."

"I want to be."

"I know." I pressed a kiss to his hair. "Oh, how I know, Little Warrior. But you are not yet. I shall be here whenever you are, and if that time never comes, I'll still be right here beside you."

More tears slid down Vince's cheek, and I brushed them away, rocking him gently in my embrace. I hummed, pushing the music into him, and Vince relaxed further. I continued to kiss his head and sing him a wordless tune of my affection.

Chapter 23

MIDNIGHT CONFESSIONS.

Vince

We left the station after a couple of days, much to Mindy's annoyance. According to Teddy, Mindy had wanted to explore more with him, while Teddy was perfectly fine with leaving.

Don and I had spent almost every moment together when he wasn't on duty, even after the horribly embarrassing moment where I broke down like a pathetic baby. He'd spent every night in my room, snuggling, playing his new instrument, or simply hanging out with me while I read—finally, picking up a damn book instead of curling up in a ball on the bed. No matter what, though, each and every night, he lay on the bed not far from me and would sing me to sleep. It was a joy to fall asleep and wake up next to him.

Seth had made several remarks on my new colorful clothes and necklaces with a smile, as had Caleb before they shared a look. I'd glared at them both. I liked the delicate chains I wore on my neck. They looked nice, and Don had grinned the first time he saw me wearing them. I never took them off afterward. I wanted to see him smile more, so I kept wearing them regardless of what anyone thought.

Don rarely smiled or laughed, even when he was with his brothers, but he was opening up to me. I wished he would do so with other people, though at the same time, I selfishly liked that I was special. I was fairly certain he stayed aloof because he was constantly guarding against what other people might think. He didn't want to react to other people's thoughts, and he tried to maintain their privacy whenever possible.

Now, I snuggled closer to Don's sleeping form, and his arm pulled me tight against him. There wasn't even a single spark of panic from the movement. I didn't understand how I could sleep with my head on his chest and his arm around my waist—not to mention his tail, which always stayed around my ankle—and feel not even an ounce of fear, but anything more sent me screaming.

I wanted Don. There were no ifs, ands, or buts about it. And yet...

Kissing was getting easier. I liked to sneak kisses in when he least expected it, pressing against his chest and claiming his mouth. I always made sure we were alone or that other people couldn't see, because of his position as captain, and I never tried to distract him. But Don loved when I would kiss him randomly; he'd shared as much.

With every day that passed, the closer we got, and the more I questioned why I freaked out about him being near me. He never brought it up, which I appreciated, but I wondered. That wasn't the only thing I questioned. The more Don wiggled into my heart, the thought of letting him go grew harder and harder.

I liked Don. Actually liked him. He was kind, funny, and calm. God, he was so calm, except when we started to get closer physically. He would try to stay perfectly emotionless, but his stilted breaths and near-silent moans betrayed him.

But I couldn't stay here for him alone, and he hadn't asked me to. He didn't want this to be permanent anyway. Though if I did stay, would he want more with me? Would he desire forever with me? Was I even right to contemplate that? I was a shitfull of issues. Didn't he deserve more?

His face was completely relaxed as his eyes flicked under his lids. I traced my fingertips over his scales. I felt ridiculously possessive of him. The thought of him being with anyone else pissed me off, even though I didn't have the right. We were friends with benefits and nothing more.

Shit, though, I wanted more. How was it he'd snuck into my heart without me knowing? I cared about Seth, but I knew myself enough to know that my feelings had started to dim to a more healthy, friendship level.

Seth was still Seth, though. I was pretty sure I'd always love him on some level, but at the same time, part of that emotion was from what he represented—home, safety, and a time before everything.

Don was different. He was himself, and I liked him. Yeah, I felt safe with him, but I also felt like he got me more than anyone else. I was a bit of an asshole, and he didn't care. I'd been broken more than I even let myself contemplate, and he knew. He knew that I might never be able to... We might never do more, and he didn't care. Don was always here for me.

Of course, enjoying spending time with me wasn't the same as liking me.

I trailed my hand down his chest, loving the scritch, loving the burning heat, loving the physical touch I'd been so starved for. I wanted to fuck him really bad. I'd tried earlier tonight to touch him again without his shirt on while he did the same to me, and I'd freaked out to the point I needed him to help me calm down again.

I didn't know how to move on from this. I wanted to, but my brain kept trying to relive it no matter how many times I buried it. How had Seth moved on? He suffered at the hands of his grandparents and multiple partners, but he was better. He was happy with Kal.

Why couldn't I be happy with Don?

I stared at Don as tears burned the backs of my eyes. I wanted him so bad. I didn't understand why I couldn't do more. He sure as hell deserved better than me. He deserved everything good in this horrid universe.

Don's arms tightened around me as he started to wake up. The one problem with him sleeping beside me was that I woke him up a lot easier. It took only the slightest nightmare. I rubbed his side and nuzzled his neck; he fell back into a deep sleep almost instantly. I'd learned fairly quickly that he liked to have me rub where his scent glands were.

Carefully, I slid out of the bed. Seth. I needed Seth. I needed my best friend. I headed out of my apartment without shoes—I didn't need them with the moss flooring—and only in gray sweats and a loose tank top. I went down the hall toward Seth's room and rang the bell. It was ridiculously late, but he wouldn't care.

The door opened, and I took a step back. Kal was on the other side, his long hair hanging around his naked chest. He had on a loose pair of pants, but they did nothing to hide the muscles Kal was sporting or the large bulge from his dick. Why was this dude so fucking perfect? It made me hate him more.

"Vince?" he asked, brow furrowing. "Are you alright? What's going on? Are you hurt? Where is Dontilvynsan?"

So he was nice. He hated me, but he was still concerned. Kal had a lot to hate about him. Seriously, this fucker was way too perfect.

"Don's fine. I need to talk to Seth. Please," I said, hugging myself.

"Come in." He waved me in and headed toward the open door of their bedroom.

Seth was passed out naked on their bed, sleeping on his stomach, a black cat pressed against him. A tinge of jealousy stabbed me, but it was minimal. I was happy he was happy. Mostly. I was fine with the rest of me that wanted Seth like a petty toddler wanted a lost toy.

Kal closed the bedroom door behind him, which, thank god, hid the sight of Seth's nice ass. He was bulky, my Seth, and he had a fantastic butt. I wandered around the darkened room. It was pretty much the same as mine, but there was a painting off to the side that was incomplete. It was of Seth, lying on his back, smiling. Kal had captured the generous curves of Seth's body and the soft wave of his hair as well as the light in his brown eyes.

Love was so evident in the strokes that I could hardly look away.

"Vince?" Seth walked out of his room alone, which surprised me. He zipped up a hoodie before dragging a hand over his face. "What's up?"

"Kal's work?" I gestured to the painting.

"Yeah. He likes to paint me."

"I don't blame him." I kept staring at the painting as I gripped my biceps. God. I didn't want to talk. I needed to, though; I knew I did. I had to tell someone, anyone. I hadn't even spoken of what happened to me with Don; he'd just caught glimpses in my thoughts. But I needed to admit what happened, because maybe then I could admit it to myself.

I'd pushed away and buried all that I'd experienced on Xome, but it refused to go. The remnants of my trauma clung to me and spread through my veins like a poison. I needed to be rid of it.

Seth said, "Let's go for a walk."

He led me through the basically silent ship until we stopped in the atrium. It wasn't large, but it was enough to host several full-grown trees and ferns, flowers, and vines aplenty. No one was around, and the lights were dimmed, which should've bothered me, but it didn't. The air was heavy with moisture and the freshness of earth. I'd never been a nature person, but it soothed me on some level to be as close to outside as possible.

"Drakcol love plants," Seth said. "They're everywhere. They believe they are the most calming thing in this world."

He wasn't pressuring me, which I appreciated, but I had to say this. But how? I hardly allowed myself to even think of it, let alone admit it.

"When I was first on the *Admiral Ven*, the ship that brought me here," Seth started, "I was terrified of Kal, of being here, of what life would be like afterward. Everything. But I got through it."

"It's not the same," I said. He'd been taken by his soulmate, who loved him; I'd been taken by someone who saw me as profit.

"You're right." Seth grabbed a deep red leaf, chewing on his bottom lip. "I hid a lot. In my room. In the garden. I was afraid Kal would hurt me. He never did."

"I was raped," I said suddenly, the words bursting out of me.

Seth gaped at me for a second, staring.

I looked away, ashamed. Maybe he didn't understand like I'd hoped.

Before I knew what was happening, Seth had his arms wrapped around me, holding me close. I closed my eyes, leaning into the comfort of his hold. He was here with me, and that was everything I needed.

The story of what had happened spilled out of me faster than I thought possible as tears slid down my cheeks and grief tore me apart. Every pain, every shadow, every punishment, every customer, everything came out, and Seth didn't flinch.

We ended up on the ground, leaning against a tree as Seth rocked me. I had my face buried against him, and he held me close. Seth didn't say anything, but what could he say? Empty platitudes would've pissed me off, and he didn't do that. He was just there, letting me process what happened however I wanted.

I wiped my dripping nose on his shoulder, and Seth laughed, tousling my hair. He kissed my temple. "Shit, Vince, still doing that?"

I'd done that often when we were kids. I'd believed in the philosophy that if I licked it first, no one else would want it as a child. Seth had fallen into that category. Now, it was a disgusting habit.

"I guess."

"Thank you for telling me."

"You suspected, didn't you?"

He nodded. "I knew something had happened. You've always been super affectionate with me more than anyone else, and you tense when I touch you or sometimes pull away. At first, I thought it might just be me, but you also did it with Teddy, so I knew something had happened."

I sighed, head going back against the rough bark as I leaned into Seth's side. "How did you get over it?"

"What?"

"Everything that was done to you."

Seth shook his head. "I didn't for a long time, but I've had years, Vince. You've had weeks. And I was still struggling when I met Kal. I can't hear you-know-who's name without getting upset. But I had help."

"Kal?"

"Yeah. He helped, but no. I've started seeing someone."

I looked at him.

"Fyn has a therapist for his depression. Caleb got one to help with getting used to his new body. I have one that's helped me process.

There's no quick fix to the shit that life throws at you. You have to work at getting through it."

"Great. Just what I want to hear. More work ahead. Perfect."

He chuckled. "Sorry, Vinnie."

Tears came to my eyes at the old nickname. One more confession was needed, because I *had* to fucking move on. I looked straight at him and said the three words that I had never, not once, gotten out. "I love you."

"I love you too," he said with a smile.

I shook my head. "I am in love with you. I have been for years."

His expression fell. "Vince."

"I know you love Kal, and that's fine." I hugged my knees, laughing. "God, I've wanted to tell you for years."

"I never knew." His eyes were wet.

Fuck. I hadn't wanted to upset him. "Don't cry. Please don't cry. I can't take that. No tears."

He wiped his round cheeks. "Sorry."

I bumped his shoulder. "It's fine. I'm ready to get over you. I need to. I just want to be friends, but I needed to say the words out loud once. I'm a selfish dick like that."

"You're not."

"I am. I wanted to take you from Kal, but he's so damn perfect."

Seth burst into laughter. "He's pretty great."

I shoved him gently, and Seth laughed again. I said, smiling, "Thanks."

"For what?"

"Being my friend."

"That's not going to change. Not ever." He shifted to his knees so he could face me. "I'm sorry for cutting you off. I shouldn't have. I can blame everything that happened on... Travis, but honestly, what I did to you was horrible and I'm sorry."

"I'm sorry I didn't want to be friends afterward."

"I got why you didn't."

He settled beside me again, and I curled into his side. I felt lighter. Everything still sucked, but I felt a lot lighter. Someone knew; someone I trusted.

"I'm going home," I whispered.

"Yeah, it's late and you should get some sleep. Don's probably worried about you. I know he's been sleeping in your room. The brothers like to gossip."

I shook my head. "I'm going back to Earth."

His eyes turned glassy. "What?"

"I can't stay. I'm going home."

"Is it because of me?"

"No," I said. "I want to forget, and going to Earth will let me do that."

"But you won't remember seeing me again."

"I won't, but you will. You and Teddy are happy and safe. That's enough for me. I want to go back so I can forget. That's how I can move on. How I'll finally be at peace and back to my old self."

"That's not enough for me," he whispered. "I need you, Vinnie."

Tears burned the backs of my eyes. I had an impossible time not giving Seth whatever he wanted.

"Please don't leave."

I pushed my face against his shoulder, sobbing. "I need to."

Seth pulled me close. "I won't stop you, even though I want to, but I will sure as hell miss you."

"I will miss you too, even if I won't remember seeing you again, seeing you safe, seeing you happy. I will always miss you, Seth."

Dontilvynsan

"Captain Dontilvynsan," NAID said, making me jolt.

I immediately reached for Vince to soothe him back to sleep, and froze, soul racing. He was gone. I blinked, sitting up. Where was he?

"Captain Dontilvynsan," NAID said again.

"Yes?"

"Prince Kalvoxrencol is attempting to reach you."

He must have tried to ping me on my touchstone, but I hadn't heard. "Put him through."

My youngest brother appeared on the screen across from Vince's bed. "Sorry to wake you."

"It's fine. What's wrong, Pest?"

"Vince came to speak to Seth. He looked upset. I didn't want you to wake up and not know where he was."

My brothers knew I'd been sleeping in Vince's room. I hadn't bothered to hide it, and Serlotminden had caught me leaving one morning. He'd teased me fiercely, but I wasn't embarrassed about our relationship. Vince cared about me. He'd called me "his" once. I wanted to be his permanently, but that wouldn't happen, so I was keeping tight control of my emotions.

"I would've worried," I conceded. "Do you know what he wanted?"

"To steal my mate maybe," he grumbled. If Kalvoxrencol truly believed that, he wouldn't have let Seth out of his sight. I remained silent, waiting. He continued, "I don't know."

Was Vince upset at our latest failed attempt? We'd been kissing when he asked to take off my shirt. I'd agreed, cautiously, hoping he wasn't going to initiate sex that he wasn't ready for, and then he'd taken off his own. My eyes had feasted on the sight of his bare skin and the trail of hair down his stomach. We'd gone back to kissing, but when our bare chests touched, he'd panicked.

Vince had climbed off my lap so fast, he'd fallen. He'd been unable to calm down until he begged for my help. He'd kept apologizing over and over again. I hadn't cared besides the fact he was terrified. After we dressed, I'd pulled him onto my lap and held him close, sharing my thoughts with him. Vince loved when I opened up to him. He'd fallen asleep like that.

I'd never been as open with someone as I was with Vince. He was the only one I'd ever shared my thoughts and general feelings with, because I trusted him. He wasn't going to get annoyed or hate me.

I lay back on the soft bed, waiting for Vince to return. A sudden flare of agony and grief pierced my brain like a knife. I clutched my head, groaning. Vince. He was in pain—horrible pain. I was out the door without a single thought besides finding and protecting him.

I found Vince in the atrium with Seth. He was sobbing as Seth held him, rocking him gently and placing kisses on the top of Vince's head. I wanted to rip Seth away and soothe Vince myself, but I grabbed ahold of the violent instinct. Warrior souls were naturally protective, and Vince called to my instincts more than anyone. But Seth wasn't a threat to what was mine.

Seth was helping him, I realized as Vince told him what had happened on Xome. Something inside me uncoiled. He'd needed to actually talk about it, and Seth was the best choice, above Bartholomew, even above me. They were best friends, and Seth understood what it was like to be hurt. They trusted each other.

Slowly, I backed out of the atrium. I would wait for Vince in his room.

When he did come back, Vince raced into the bedroom and threw himself at me. I held him close. "I have you."

He snuggled. "Don't let me go."

I nuzzled his head. "Never."

"I mean it, Don."

"As do I, Little Warrior."

Vince looked up, eyes wet. "It wasn't my fault, was it?"

He was thinking of what had happened on Xome. I'd caught the occasional stray thought that he was culpable in his assault because he hadn't fought hard enough or long enough, and now, I was being able to see the entire scope of his thoughts. How this entire situation was something Vince blamed himself for, which was utterly false.

I cupped the back of his head. "None, and I mean absolutely none, of this is your fault, Vince. You were taken. You were hurt. You survived. You are not to blame for what others did to you."

His breath sped up and his hand fisted on my chest. "It wasn't my fault."

"No, it wasn't."

He was practically panting as he said again, "It wasn't my fault."

I didn't think Vince was talking to me anymore.

The first tear slid down his cheek. "None of this was my damn fault. None of it."

Tugging him closer, I kissed his forehead. Vince shivered. A sob broke out of him, and I kissed him again. More tears landed on my chest as Vince wept, curling against me.

Chapter 24

HALFWAY THERE.

Vince

I was sitting with Seth while he talked to the gathering of humans. Brad, Camden, Roman, and Pierce were firmly on Team Human, and I thought there were a couple of other people coming toward their side. I wasn't, as much as Caleb protested, but I supported Seth. Also, I was attempting to leave my room and do something. I mean, I was reading now and staying out of my bed, but I was trying to engage as much as I could.

After telling Seth I loved him and everything that had happened, our relationship had gotten a ton easier.

In an effort to move past Xome or at minimum accept what had happened to me, I'd started talking to Camden and Pierce. They'd both been in brothels like me, and our experiences were similar. I wasn't cured, but it helped. They'd already made a support group of sorts and invited me to join.

I'd been almost hurt they hadn't asked me before, but they hadn't wanted to impose. I'd held myself apart from the other humans from

Xome and clung to Seth and Teddy or stayed in my room. I told myself I wouldn't have come earlier even if they'd asked, and it was true. I hadn't been ready to talk. Hell, I still wasn't ready, but this was something that I needed to do.

Don spent every night in my room now, but we hadn't done anything, even kissing had been minimal. I felt insanely guilty that I clung to him, but I didn't want to lose him. He was mine. For now.

My eyes flicked to Teddy, who was across the table. He hadn't spoken to me much since I'd told him I was going home. I hadn't even told him about what happened on Xome. I should've; I needed to, but it was hard. I didn't want to dump my trauma on him when he was lugging around his own. But he was my friend, and I didn't want him to think I was abandoning him.

Teddy spoke up for the first time, "We won't have to touch the Crystal, right? I don't fucking want to."

"I have spoken to the Cohort, and no one will be forced," Seth informed us. "You will be soul tested, but you don't have to touch the actual Crystal."

He frowned at the soul testing bit, but his shoulders relaxed.

I was right there with Teddy. I didn't want to know who my soulmate was, or if I even had one. Honestly, anyone besides Don would piss me off. Besides, I was going home. It would hurt whoever my soulmate was.

And knowing my luck, it would be someone like Mindy, and I would hurt Teddy. That was literally the last thing I needed. Also, Mindy. I shuddered at the sunshine man who bounced around with

Caleb, the two of them laughing like idiots while Teddy and I shook our heads. I couldn't handle that, nor would I want to.

"Anyone who wants to touch the Crystal and seek their soulmate can," Seth said. "I can explain the process." No one said anything, so Seth added, "We can also talk in private if anyone is feeling shy."

Seth gripped my hand, and I pulled it onto my lap, smoothing my fingers over his palm. He struggled with this whole leader thing, but god, he was good at it.

"It's time for your combat class," I said, saving him.

"Right," he said. "Does anyone want to join me?"

Teddy, Brad, Pierce, Roman, and Camden immediately jumped up. *Team Human, go*, I thought. A couple of others joined more slowly.

Seth looked at me, and I shook my head. I wanted some downtime. I'd been spending basically all of my time with Seth or Don, barring a few times with the other humans or Don's family. While I needed to interact with people, part of me longed to be in my well-lit room alone.

When they left, Teddy hung back. His hands were buried in his pockets, and his eyes were looking anywhere beside me. He asked, "Are you okay?"

"No," I said, finally being somewhat honest.

He came to my side and bumped my arm with his. "Want to talk about it?"

I closed my eyes, then glanced around the cafeteria. There were a few people, but no one close by, but their presence was enough to have me nodding toward the door. We stepped outside, and I turned toward the elevator. After the door closed, I didn't ask NAID to send the elevator to a floor. I leaned back against the vines covering the walls. There was literally no escape from the plants, but I didn't mind it. Not really.

Teddy didn't talk either. He rested against the wall and simply breathed with me. It was... soothing.

"It was a lot, huh?" I finally broke the silence.

"What?"

"Xome."

He nodded and confessed, "I have nightmares."

"Me too."

"I see them," Teddy whispered.

"Who?" I looked at him, but he was staring at the floor, shoulders shaking.

"Everyone I killed. All of the people I locked in that damn incinerator. Their ghosts haunt me."

Fighting through any unease I had about touching, I snagged Teddy and hauled him into my arms. "It was not your fault," I growled. "Do you hear me, Bartholomew? What happened on Xome wasn't your fault."

"I locked the door."

"And I didn't fight."

Teddy backed up. "What? I didn't give you a choice."

"That's not what I'm talking about." I sank to the floor, and Teddy was right behind me. I drew my knees to my chest and said, "I was sold to a brothel after you were abducted."

"Fuck."

"Yep."

"That's why you want to go home," Teddy said baldly, and I chuckled. He always shot straight to the heart of the matter.

"Yep," I repeated.

"Fuck," he repeated as well and pushed his fingers through the short amount of black hair he had. "I'm sorry I was an ass about you going home."

"You didn't know."

"And you didn't tell me."

I looked at him. "I couldn't get the words out."

"That, I understand."

"It wasn't your fault," I said, resting my head on his shoulder.

"It wasn't yours either."

Tears welled in my eyes, and I fought them, but they slipped out. Teddy didn't say anything, letting me weep, and I wasn't alone. He cried silently, his tears dripping onto me.

The door opened, and I expected to see Don, but I was surprised when Mindy was in front of us.

He crouched. "Flower? Vince? Are you well?"

"Yeah," Teddy said. "Just human stuff."

Inappropriate laughter bubbled in my gut, but all I could think about was a woman saying "lady stuff." I wiped my face and said, "You heard him. Human stuff. Don't worry about it." I slipped out of the elevator, but I turned in time to see Mindy holding Teddy close. He was so gentle with my friend. I wanted to believe that Mindy wasn't an asshole to Teddy, but I didn't trust him yet, not like I did Don.

When the elevator came back, I went to my room and flopped onto the couch. I grabbed the tablet Don had given me and looked at the map that showed where we were in relation to the drakcol home planet with its fucking long name.

Halfway. We were halfway there.

Time was running out with Don. Sure, it would be a while before a ship headed back to Earth, but me and Don were coming to an end. Once he was home, he would be back to his normal routine, and I'd be left behind until I went home. I didn't blame him. Much. He had a life there, and people he was close with.

My chest tightened and my hands curled into fists. I hated the thought of anyone else touching him, which wasn't fair. I'd always been more possessive than was strictly healthy, but with Don it was another level. I didn't want to share him.

He's a person, not a pizza. He's not yours to hog, I told myself. But just like pizza, that's exactly what I wanted to do. Don was mine.

Not that I could touch him.

I groaned, rolling over. We barely even snuggled anymore, except when I was going to sleep. I wanted to touch him. I wanted to blow him. I wanted to fuck him. But I didn't want him to touch me.

I sat up, mouth opening. What if I touched him and he didn't touch me? I wanted to. God, I really did. And if he didn't touch me, maybe I wouldn't freak out.

It could work. It really could. I'd have to ask Don if he was comfortable with me loving on him. I couldn't imagine he would say no. Who said no to a no-need-to-reciprocate blow job? But what if he did? I needed him so badly.

All I had to do was ask. The worst Don could say was no, right?

Dontilvynsan

I stepped out of the shower and dried my hair with a cloth to get out as much moisture as possible before pulling on some soft trousers and a loose shirt. Vince hadn't been at the combat class, not that I was teaching him—he hadn't decided if he wanted me to. But I was used to him coming to watch me, and I liked it, as much as it was a distraction. Seth had said Vince was taking some time for himself, which raised an immediate worry. More often than not, one of us had to drag Vince out of his room or initiate spending time with him. Too often he was trapped in his head and his thoughts weren't always pleasant. I hadn't sensed anything horrible coming from Vince's distant thoughts, but I was still concerned.

He'd been distant since we failed to move closer. He felt guilty, even though he had no reason to. I wasn't in a rush, and if we never fucked, I was content with this. Every moment with Vince was a precious gift that I would treasure.

Something flitted across my thoughts. Vince. I blinked. He was close. I stepped out of the bedroom, and he was sitting on my couch, playing on my screen. My soul leaped at the sight. He rarely came to my quarters, but I'd added him to my security and my full system so he could get to me whenever he needed or buy whatever he wanted with my money.

"Vince," I said, self-conscious for some reason. I cast my gaze around my room. Nothing was out of place or untidy, yet the nervous energy remained.

He looked up with a smile. "Hey, Sweetheart."

I paused at the endearment. That was new. I knew what the word sweet meant. Heart was the human equivalent of the drakcol's soul, while their soul was some intangible force. Humans were very confusing. What I didn't know was what they meant together. NAID was giving a rather straightforward translation, but from Vince's thoughts, it was well meant.

"What are you doing here? Not that it bothers me," I said quickly, tail wiggling and wings readjusting on my back. "I like you here. In my quarters. With me. Now. It's all wonderful."

Vince chuckled. "Calm down. I'm not mad."

I relaxed in a rush and moved toward him. I bent slowly, giving him plenty of time to move away if he wanted, and pressed a kiss on his forehead. My damp hair fell around his face and tickled him, making Vince squirm, though he grabbed my cheeks and pulled me down to his mouth.

We met in a gentle kiss. I relished every feel of his soft lips on mine. It had been several days since we'd kissed, and I'd missed it terribly. I never wanted to move away. This. This right here was perfect, and I feared when he was gone, I would miss Vince to the point of pain.

He shifted away first, and it took every fiber of self control not to chase his mouth. A growl formed in my chest, but I swallowed it as best I could. Vince didn't seem bothered by the noise, as he stroked my cheeks and traced my features. His thoughts were scattered, but not upset. He was determined. About what, I wasn't sure.

"What's bothering you?" I asked, hoping his thoughts would show me. My very soul curled at the thought of him hurting.

"Nothing really." Vince took a deep breath and released me, but I didn't move away, needing to be close to him. "I want to touch you."

"You know you can."

He shook his head as his thoughts formed a very clear picture of him sucking me. My own cock began to lift as desperate need flowed through my veins.

A slight flush darkened his cheeks as he said, "I see you're interested."

"I think you need to expand on your thought." I *did not* want a repeat of him forcing himself to fuck. Vince had hated it, and that had broken me in a way that I didn't wish to experience again.

Vince motioned to the couch, and I took a seat. He said, "I know we need to talk about permissions and all that, which we didn't do last time. That was a mistake. I'm sorry, Donny."

I shook my head, tail coiling around his ankle. "You have nothing to apologize for."

"I do, and I'm truly sorry. I should've talked with you. You needed it, and I ignored that. I'm really sorry."

"I accept your apology."

"Thank you, Sweetheart." Vince took another deep breath and placed a hand on his chest. "I want to try something that I think will work."

I tilted my head, listening to the flow of his thoughts.

Vince continued, "I want to touch you, Don, but I don't want you to touch me. Not that you want to."

"I want to," I said immediately to comfort him. Stars above, I wanted to. It was an ache in my soul to feel his skin against my scales. I realized a moment too late I'd said the wrong thing when Vince hugged himself and disappointment shot through him.

"No, my Vince, that's not what I meant. I mean, I did." I ran my hand through my hair. How did such a small creature upset my usual calm so easily? "I mean, I do want to touch you, but I understand why you don't want me to and I'm alright with it."

"You might be able to touch me, but we'll have to go slow," Vince said. "I need more time. I realize that now."

"And that's fine." Anything was better than hearing him scream in terror.

His thoughts turned to the scenario he was thinking about. Me naked on the couch as he explored my frame with his tongue and fingers. He was completely clothed, which seemed to relax him, and my hands were against the couch.

"I understand."

"Are you alright with it?"

"Yes," I answered, because I was. "Permission-wise, I will keep my hands to my sides and you can touch me wherever."

"Your tail?"

I chuckled—he was very interested in touching my tail. "Yes."

"Anything you don't want?"

"I don't enjoy pain or being insulted. Shame is not something I enjoy." I'd had more than enough partners shame me that I didn't enjoy it, even when it was meant to tease or titillate.

"Do you want me to be gentle?" he asked, head tilting.

"I do," I replied in a hoarse voice. Most expected that because of my large size, I preferred rough fucking or even being the one in control. I didn't. I liked when things were gentle and I enjoyed being on the bottom, though I was versatile. Not that any of that mattered. Vince wasn't interested in penetrative sex at the moment.

Vince smiled. "I can do that. I want to be sweet to you."

My cock lifted the rest of the way.

His eyes connected with the tenting on the front of my trousers, and he licked his lips as a rush of lust swept through him. His own cock started growing, and his voice was husky when he asked, "Do you want to do this?"

"Yes."

"Take off your clothes," he ordered, and I followed without hesitation.

Chapter 25

OUR FIRST TIME.

Vince

Don lay on the couch, one hundred percent naked, and fuck, he was fine. His long damp hair draped over his heaving chest. He was solid. I'd known he was muscular and had caught sight of him without his clothes on, though I hadn't taken any time to study him, but I liked now that I could appreciate every aspect of his body. His bulging muscles under his scales. The hard planes of his abs. The thick, corded muscles of his arms. His trim waist. His wide thighs and strong calves.

He was hung. Don's cock was huge and pressing against his stomach. He was much thicker and longer than a human, which wasn't too shocking. Drakcol were larger than humans, and he was proportionally bigger. The head was tapered to a point with a slit that was already leaking copious amounts of pre-cum. The scales on his cock were closer together and more delicate looking, not showing any glimpses of mottled skin, and his balls were heavy and round.

I licked my lips, wanting to taste him, but I ignored it and my own throbbing dick and continued looking, down to his thick thighs, muscular calves, strong ankles, and large feet. His toes were tipped with small, pointed claws. Finally, I returned to his face, and Don was panting, eyes blown wide.

"You're gorgeous," I told him.

Don swallowed; his tail thrashed beneath him and his cock twitched, then another stream of pre-cum dripped onto his stomach. I grinned. He liked compliments. That was easy enough. Don was amazing.

I bent over him and pressed my lips to his, keeping the kiss soft. I wanted to be sweet to him. I wanted to give Don whatever he needed, because he deserved it. He groaned and his tail curled around my wrist before whipping away. I chuckled. He couldn't help it.

"I can't. My apologies," he whispered before chasing my lips.

The kiss remained slow as I invaded his mouth, swiping my tongue over his. Don ceded complete control to me, and I moaned at the trust. My fingers slid down his neck, and his breath sharpened when I stroked his chest, circling one of his nipples. Every touch and pinch was gentle. I didn't want to hurt him in the slightest.

Don wanted me to be soft with him, and I would. He was my delicate sweetheart.

I broke off and moved to kiss along his sharp jaw and down his neck. Don turned his head to give me more room. I licked and kissed my way down, feeling the smoothness of his scales while tracing the perceivable ridge around them with my tongue.

When I reached his nipples, I laved my tongue over one, and Don gave a low cry. Every noise he made, while quiet, was music to my ears. I liked that *I* was the one pleasing him. Not someone else. Just me. I nipped at the bud, and he jerked, but I didn't think I'd hurt him.

I looked at him, and his eyes were blown wide while he panted harshly. Arousal looked good on him. Kissing the bud, I said, "Tell me if I hurt you or do something you don't like. I can't read your mind, Sweetheart, and I want you to enjoy this."

"I will and I am," he said in a rough voice.

Reassured, I continued with my slow exploration. I latched onto his other nipple, giving it the same loving treatment as the first and trailed my fingers over the scent glands on his sides.

"Yes, my Vince," he said. "More, please."

I rubbed my face on his side. I couldn't smell anything besides his normal vanilla scent, but Don growled, his hips arching and tail thrashing. My cock twitched at the noise as pre-cum stuck the tip to my briefs. I liked the noise. A lot. I nuzzled his stomach and continued my way down, tongue running over his hard abs. I licked his navel, which made him breathe harder.

Reaching his cock, I rubbed my fingers through the pre-cum sliding out of his slit, way more than a human would ever produce, but it was hella hot.

"Please," he begged.

"Soon." I spread the viscous liquid over my hand to ease the glide of my palm and pumped him from his thick base to his tapered tip.

A deep cry escaped from his lips, and his hips lifted to follow my hand.

"You are huge," I told him. "I would struggle to get this in my ass without a lot of prep."

"I would take care of you," Don said. "If that's what you wanted."

I kissed the tip of his cock, lapping up the liquid. The sweet taste made me moan wantonly. "That's because you're sweet, Don. You are as sweet as you taste, and you are just as good."

A shudder went through him, and his tail coiled around me again. How starved was he for compliments? Don was one of the best people I'd ever met; he should be swimming in admirers.

Well, he would never lack for admiration with me. I would give him what he needed, and more than that, what he deserved.

Don whimpered, "Vince."

His tail tightened around my arm, coiling upward. He started to pull it away, but I caught it, sliding my hand down the length. He jerked and his chest heaved. I ran my nails over the soft scales, and he moaned, finally gaining the volume I desired.

"Don't try to control your tail," I told him. "I don't mind you touching me with it."

I pressed a kiss to the royal purple tuft. My eyes remained on his, making sure he was alright with my actions. Don's tongue escaped from the confines of his mouth and licked his lips. The sight of his black tongue covered in scales made me swallow. God, my cock would feel nice in his mouth. But not yet.

I kissed and licked his tail as far up as I could before releasing the appendage. It immediately wrapped around my wrist. I straightened to push his legs further apart—Don instantly complied.

"Good job," I whispered, kissing his thigh. Don shuddered and more pre-cum leaked out of his cock. I grinned. My Don loved to be told how good he was, and I was happy to tell him. "Are you my good boy?"

He whined.

"You are, and I'm going to take care of you." I settled in between his legs, and Don rocked his hips, making his cock bob.

I pushed his hips down. "Soon, Sweetheart. I won't leave you desperate. I promise."

I slid my hands over his thighs, running my fingertips over the inner part. Just like humans, it was more sensitive, if his vocal reaction was anything to go by. The tight pucker of his ass twitched. Part of me wanted to have him roll over so I could eat him out, but I decided it was time to stop teasing him.

Sucking on the tip of his cock, I circled his rim with my finger, encouraged by the grunts and cries coming out of his lips. "You were so patient, so good," I told him.

"I don't mind. I like you touching me."

I kissed his hip. "Now, I'm going to suck you until you beg to come."

Dontilvynsan

I was losing my mind. Vince was relentlessly working my cock. He couldn't get the entire thing into his mouth, but he sucked as much as he could, cheeks hollowing with the pressure he was exerting, and pumped the rest of my shaft with one of his hands. His other hand cradled and played with my balls before moving down to my hole. He didn't push inside of me like I wanted, but he circled it in mind-numbing slowness that sparked a fire in my veins.

Every touch of his mouth, stroke of his tongue, and circling of his fingertip built the pressure in my spine and had my balls high and tight as my orgasm swelled, shoving me toward the edge. I couldn't stop the moans from ripping out of my throat, and each one sent a wave of lust through Vince.

He tongued my slit, and I jerked. "My Vince."

Vince slid off me, and I protested. Stars, I was close. I needed him back on me.

He rubbed my glistening tip on his impossibly smooth cheek. "I like you calling me that."

"W-what?" I asked, panting, unable to think with the amount of pleasure wracking my body. My cock was so hard it hurt. I needed release, and I needed it now.

"Yours. I like it," he said in a low voice.

My soul stilled. I hadn't realized what I'd called him. Fear flitted through my thoughts. How far had Vince crawled into my soul?

His mouth returned to my cock, and he moaned around me, sending vibrations up the shaft. All thought left my mind at the pleasure of the wet heat of his mouth and the silk of his tongue. It took all of my control to keep from thrusting into his mouth to chase my pleasure or burying my hands in his black hair to force him to take all of me.

"Please, Vince," I begged, not caring about the neediness in my voice.

He sucked me harder, tongue working on the underside of my cock, as he pumped me faster, moving in tandem with his mouth. His finger pressed against my hole, and I groaned.

"I'm coming," I warned him, trying to pull out of his mouth.

A wave of possessive need rushed over my thoughts as Vince silently snarled, *Mine.*

His claim sent me over the edge, and I immediately thought, *Yours.* I found my release with a bellow as I jerked under him, spurts of seed coming out of me. My eyes scrunched closed, depriving me of the sight of him swallowing my release, and buzzing filled my ears.

Vince worked me through my orgasm, milking every drop from me, until all tension leached out of me and I was boneless beneath him. He licked me clean, making me shiver, then started pressing kisses over everywhere he could reach.

"So good, Sweetheart. You were so good. You were such a good boy."

The compliments plus his happy thoughts soothed me. Vince had enjoyed sucking me as much as I loved the attention.

I slowly lifted my hand, giving him a chance to move away, and cupped his cheek. *Mine.* Vince was mine, and I was his. I'd tried to deny my growing feelings for him, but I couldn't. I wanted to take care of him, protect him, and belong to him. Sadness and fear raged under my scales.

He was leaving, but I knew without a doubt, he was my mate. Once that bond had been made, it was permanent.

I dragged my thumb over his cheek, and Vince leaned into my touch, beaming. I said, voice rough, "Your turn."

He shook his head, though his hard cock pressed against my thigh. "I'm not ready for you to blow me."

Blowing. Humans. They were so odd with their many inaccurate words.

"I know." I carefully made the connection between us, forcing my happiness and contentment at his touch to the forefront and my doubts and fears to the back. I thought of him stroking himself while I watched.

Vince worked at the button of his trousers and shoved them down. His cock popped out. The tip was red and leaking, and I spotted thick veins around his shaft, making me want to trace them with my tongue. The patch of hair that was above his cock made me moan. I wanted to bury my face in it and worship him.

I said, "Give me your hand."

Vince held one out. I lifted it to my mouth, licking his palm and sucking on his fingers, able to taste myself on him. He moaned as I got his hand nice and wet.

"There," I told him. "Now let me see you come."

With hard jerks, Vince pumped himself as he leaned over me. I watched while he worked quickly, chasing his release. His frantic cries grew louder and louder as pleasure swelled in his mind. His thoughts were locked onto my face while he pumped himself harder and faster.

"Don," he groaned between clenched teeth when his cock spurted ropes of thick, white seed onto my stomach.

He fell on top of me, and I pulled him close. I nuzzled his sweaty hair. Vince stroked my chest and neck as he panted. "I liked that."

"As did I," I replied. I did, immensely, but worry churned in my gut. Vince was mine, and I was going to have to let him go. This was precisely what I hadn't wanted, but it was foolish to be upset at Vince—I was lost the moment I saw him.

"I want to stay here tonight," he said, cuddling closer.

I kissed his head. "You're always welcome."

"You are way too kind to me."

"Not at all." We drakcol took care of our mates, and I would take care of Vince as long as I had him.

Chapter 26

A DELIGHTFUL INTERLUDE.

Dontilvynsan

Vince was pressed against the arm of the couch, eyes flicking over his screen. He was sitting with his legs crossed at the ankle, and he was wearing a short red dress that I'd bought him, which I loved, but my focus was on his mind, which was alive with images and emotions. I'd recently discovered a love of Vince reading. His thoughts almost pictured the scenes like it was happening and I could feel his growing excitement, worry, fear, or in some cases, arousal.

I didn't always know what every creature Vince read about was, in this case, men who turned into large, hairy predators. But he was enjoying the mystery, the romance, and the sex if his emotions were anything to go by.

Originally, I'd been playing my new harpsichord and watching an instructional video as I tried to gain some proficiency with the instrument, but I became almost immediately distracted by Vince. When he'd picked up his screen to start reading—something that

I adored he did now—I hadn't noticed much. But the book had moved into a sex scene that Vince had very much enjoyed, and it had distracted me.

Now, I was just lying on his lap, eyes closed, and reading along with him. The images and emotions raced across his thoughts as the story picked up. My own soul started to thud against my ribs, vibrating in a rapid beat, as the story grew nearer and nearer to the climax, and to another sex scene, I assumed, from the way the two men were speaking to each other. I licked my lips, tail whipping, more than a little excited.

All of sudden, it all stopped so fast I groaned from the rough transition. What had happened?

Vince stared down at me, his eyebrows pulled together. He stroked my cheek, and I released the slightest moan. The feel of his skin on my scales would never become old.

"You stopped playing," Vince remarked, continuing to stroke my face with the barest of touches.

"Yes," I replied, voice rough from his ministrations. "Quite some time ago."

"Why?"

"You were distracting me."

He laughed, and I swore my soul leaped in my chest. That noise was as perfect as he was. Vince said, "It's a good book."

"I was enjoying it as well."

A smirk firmly in place, he asked, "Which part?"

I looked away, my tail flicking.

"You're not getting away that easily," Vince teased, pulling my chin so I looked back in his direction.

I simply smiled at him. Things had gotten so much easier of late. Since Vince had admitted what had happened, since he'd talked to Seth and Teddy, since he'd started talking to Camden and Pierce, since we'd had sex—everything. There was a lightness to him that hadn't been there. I'd caught glimpses of it previously, but now, I was truly seeing it. Vince was starting to heal. It was going to be a very long journey, but he'd taken a step, and that made me beyond happy.

"I enjoyed the whole story," I eventually said.

"Hmm, I'm sure." Vince bent over me, and my pulse skittered at his close proximity. He whispered, "Tell me the truth like the good boy you are."

My cock took notice and started to grow. I couldn't say why I liked my Vince calling me a good boy, but I did—a lot. I swallowed, his nearly black eyes boring into me. I forced out, "The sex scenes."

Why my enjoyment of them should embarrass me was also a mystery. Sex wasn't shamed in Drakcon culture, nor was I young anymore. But some part of me felt fragile admitting that I liked it in front of Vince. Perhaps it was the content of the sex scenes themselves—one partner dominating the other.

I had no trouble imagining Vince telling me what to do, as he'd already done that, and taking me from behind, folded over a large red chair called a Chesterfield, though far more gently than the fucking in his book.

Vince rewarded me with a kiss and warm brush of happiness in his thoughts. He said, "Let's finish this, then I want you to play for me."

"I would like that." This simple domesticity was starting to become a routine, and I feared when it was gone, I would not survive.

Vince

I was lying on my stomach on Don's bed, watching him get dressed. Over the last couple of days, I'd sucked him off before jerking myself a handful of times, but last night had been the first time on the bed. I was getting better with him. I'd even managed to get my shirt off last night. Next, I wanted him to touch my chest.

I was accepting, though, that I needed to go slower and give myself some grace. I couldn't immediately jump into everything. Talking with Camden and Pierce almost everyday was helping with that too. They understood in a way that no one else did, even Seth and Teddy. They'd helped me realize this trauma was going to take more time and hell of a lot more work than I wanted to overcome.

But I'd like to think that I helped them too. Both Camden and Pierce were struggling, though differently than me. Sometimes when we got together it was laughter, and other times hard discussions of what *actually* happened, and occasionally we just sat together, all struggling with our own experiences.

Another thing that was helping was Don letting me have control while we planned what we were going to do beforehand, with him reading my thoughts and sharing his own. It had eased most of my tension. We never deviated from the plan unless one of us proposed a new change and the other agreed.

Not the most spontaneous, but spontaneity wasn't something I was currently comfortable with.

We hadn't had a thorough permission conversation, because at any given moment I never knew what I would be okay with, but this sharing and planning was protecting us both and allowing us to enjoy a wonderful intimacy that was feeding my touched-starved self.

"I'll never make it to Command on time if you keep thinking about fucking me," Don commented.

I laughed. "I wouldn't mind that."

Don kneeled on the bed, shirtless, and kissed me. I gripped his cheeks, deepening the kiss, and his long earrings tickled my cheeks and his hair formed a curtain around us. I tried to pull him all the way onto the bed, but he wouldn't be moved.

"No, I need to go to my duty shift, and you promised to meet Camden and Pierce in the canteen."

He was right. Of course. I licked my lips, and Don swallowed. I chuckled. God. He made me happy. It was indescribable how happy and safe I felt with him. "I will try not to distract you today."

"Thank you."

I gave him a quick kiss. "Bye, Sweetheart."

When he left, I took a leisurely shower before yanking on some clothes. Camden, Pierce, and I were supposed to meet for breakfast. I'd originally planned to spend time with Seth and Teddy this morning, but Seth had successfully wrangled one of the doctors from the nesting facility back on the drakcol homeworld into agreeing to speak with him, yet again, about his growing child.

Apparently, everything in the doctor's house had gone haywire, which I hadn't thought much about, but Seth had clued me in that Edith had probably done it because he'd complained about not being able to speak to the doctors. It had to be nice to have a scary supercomputer sidekick to bully people.

Teddy had then decided he and Mindy needed to go running, a.k.a foreplay chasing before they fucked, though he'd extracted a promise from me that I wouldn't stay holed up in my room.

So I reached out to Camden and Pierce, who were both game for breakfast. Afterward, Brad, Roman, Seth, Teddy, and some of the other humans would join us. The experience suites were booked, but we figured we'd hang out in my room and drink. Nothing like being abducted as a reason to start day drinking, though I'd been avoiding drinking away my issues. With friends, though, it seemed less toxic and more like a fun time.

I stepped into the cafeteria and immediately spotted Camden with his towering height and blonde hair, and Pierce with her deep red curls.

"Hey," I called, sliding onto the stool next to them.

"Hey," Camden said while Pierce grinned at me.

"You seem happy," she commented.

"I am. Why wouldn't I be?"

"Well, besides the fact we were all abducted," Camden said, "you walked around with a stick up your ass the first couple weeks. Now you're all smiley. It's disconcerting."

I rolled my eyes. I was allowed to be happy. If part of that was due to Don, then so be it. "How are you guys?"

"I'm fine," Camden said. "No nightmares last night." Like me, he'd been having nightmares nearly every night. "Brad never complains when I wake him up, but I feel bad." He ran a hand through his golden hair, and I swore it practically glowed in the artificial light. No one should look that good, but he did. "I've been talking to an Amorian therapist."

"You have?" I asked.

He nodded. "Klars offered it, and why wouldn't I take him up on his offer? I need help processing everything."

"Yeah, but..." I trailed off. Therapy had never been *my* thing.

Camden frowned, crossing his arms. "There's nothing wrong with therapy."

"I didn't say there was," I snapped.

"I heard a tone. I need help and I refuse to be ashamed of it."

"And I'm not shaming you. I didn't say anything."

"Seriously," Pierce said, "both of you need to calm the fuck down. Vince, you were shaming. Own it. Think about why you are, then work on it. Camden, drop the attitude. We're all in this together."

I glanced at Pierce, but she was staring at the table.

Camden scooted closer. "Are you alright?"

"Perfectly," she replied. "I'm not allowed to call you two out on your bullshit?"

She was, and did so frequently; I just hadn't expected it to be so harsh, anymore than Camden had.

He moved even closer. "You look upset."

Pierce sighed, running a fair hand through her red curls. "Me and Bimwoxcol have been sleeping together."

"Okay," I said. She was getting some, good for her.

"She's also sleeping with other people," Pierce said.

Camden asked, "What? How could she do that to you?"

"Didn't she tell you that in the permission discussion?" I asked. Drakcol talked about everything. There was no way Bimwoxcol would start fucking Pierce without telling her about the other people.

Pierce nodded. "Of course she did."

Camden raised his eyebrows. He *wasn't* sleeping with a drakcol apparently.

"I just didn't expect it to bother me," Pierce continued, waving a hand. "I've never had a casual relationship before, but after everything, I thought it would be nice. I wanted my needs met without even a hint of pressure, and she's nice and caring, and most of all, safe."

"Did you talk to her? Drakcol are pretty open about discussing everything." I mean, Don was. I assumed it was fairly normal, especially from what Seth had said.

"Yeah, she doesn't want a serious relationship either." Pierce looked away, eyes growing moist. "I thought I was the same, but I've really started to care about her. I want more. I want to be the only person she's with." A tear slipped down her freckled cheek.

Panic, sheer male panic, grew under my skin and curled in my stomach. I hated when anyone cried, but when a woman did, it bothered me on a different level. You would think being gay would take that away, but nope. I glanced at Camden and he had the same deer in headlights look as me.

She started laughing wetly and wiped her cheeks. "God, you guys are useless."

"Tears and comforting people aren't my thing. Can I interest you in a sarcastic remark?" I offered.

"No thanks." Pierce took a deep breath. "It's fine. I should've known this was what was going to happen. Bimwoxcol warned me she was sleeping with other people and intended on continuing those relationships. Deep down, I thought I would be different, which isn't fair to her. She's allowed to sleep with whoever she wants."

Camden patted her shoulder awkwardly. "Cry it out, I guess."

My heart raced, and my mind whipped to my own situation. Don currently wasn't sleeping with anyone else besides me, but he hadn't said he wouldn't either. We were friends with benefits. It was wrong to try and make this exclusive, but damnit, that was what I wanted.

I hated the thought of anyone else touching Don, or seeing that half-smile that formed when I complimented him, or hearing the quiet moans he gave as I pleased him, or sharing his gentle thoughts. Don was mine, but I sure as hell couldn't keep him, because I was going home.

"Do you guys ever consider going back?" I asked when there was a lull in the conversation.

"To Earth?" Pierce asked.

"Yeah."

"Of course, I did," Camden said. "Part of me wants to go home because I have a younger brother that I miss terribly, but I have a shit ton of student loans, a dead end job, no healthcare, and deadbeat parents. Here, I actually have a chance to get ahead. I think in the end, I'll be happier here. But I still miss my brother."

I looked at Pierce, and she sighed. "I almost decided to go back. I still could, but... This is a chance to do something I would've never dreamed of. Will I miss my family? Hell yeah. Do I feel selfish staying? Yep. But after everything that happened I don't feel like I can go back. I'm a different person now, and I don't want to erase that. Are you going back?"

"Probably."

"Why?" she asked.

"I'm going back to erase the person I've become," I whispered. Pierce wanted to stay to remain the person she'd become; I wanted to go back to be the person I used to be.

Camden and Pierce shared a look. Out of everyone, they understood, but it looked like they didn't agree.

"You can, of course, do what you want," Camden started, "and I don't blame you for going back, but are you sure that's what you want? You can't take it back. You can stay here, or, well, on their planet, for a bit before you decide. I'm guessing you don't like therapy, but it would help, Vince."

"You have Seth and Teddy." Pierce tried to take my hand, but I pulled away. "You have us."

I couldn't stay for them, any more than for Don. I had to stay for myself, and I didn't know what I wanted. Part of me cringed at the thought of never seeing Earth or my family again. Another part of me hated the thought of leaving Don, Seth, and Teddy. I had no idea what to do.

Thankfully, the door opened and a herd of humans came in led by Caleb.

"Come on," Caleb called.

I leaped up and moved to Teddy's side, hooking an arm around his waist. He gave me a grunt before draping an arm over my shoulder. I hugged him, then slid away before I got uncomfortable.

"Let's go," I said, leading the way to my room with Seth's hand in mine.

Kal swore at me as he lifted a drunk Seth into his arms.

I laughed, feeling hot and fuzzy. "He had fun."

"I did," Seth shouted, making Pierce, who lay on the floor, groan.

The afternoon had turned to drinking games, which got out of hand, and then turned into a night of drinking, leading to the natural conclusion of most people passed out on my living room floor. The only sober one was Caleb, and he was loud enough without alcohol.

Seth mashed his lips to Kal's, and I rolled my eyes. Seth was a happy drunk. Kal pulled away. "You are too drunk for that."

"Spoilsport," he said, giggling, which made me laugh.

"I like that. Spoilsport. Ruining our fun," I said.

"So true." Seth squished Kal's face between his hands. "But he's so cute."

I gagged. "Not really."

"Yes, he is," Seth yelled.

I laughed, falling back against the wall. "I'm not into blue."

Seth burst into laughter.

Kal shook his head and looked at everyone who was passed out, then at Caleb. "What am I supposed to do with you and Bartholomew?"

"Fyn's coming to get me, and I'm sure Mindy will get Teddy. Nice of you to care about the others."

"They're not my brothers. You and Bartholomew are," Kal said.

"Teddy can stay with me," I said, waving a hand. "We've slept together before."

Kal whipped toward me, and Caleb said in a light tone, "I wouldn't advertise that in front of Don or Mindy."

I shrugged. Who fucking cared? They both knew we'd shared a cell at Agk's fighting ring. When it had gotten cold, we'd snuggled. When I had a bad day, Teddy had held me. We'd slept together a lot.

"We've slept together," Seth said, waving a hand between us.

"What?" Kal barked.

I nodded. Seth had lived with me and my parents when his asshole grandparents had kicked him out as a teenager. He'd stayed in my room, and we'd shared a bed most nights.

I shifted to my knees to prod Teddy. "Wake up. The bed's over there. Come on."

Teddy groaned and grabbed me, making me teeter. I hugged him close, relishing the feel of him. We somehow managed to get to our feet, stumbling toward my empty bedroom and crashing onto bed.

Teddy yanked off his shirt. "It's hot."

I grunted. Teddy curled around me, and the first spark of panic broke through my drunken haze, but it faded and I snuggled against him while basking in his comfort.

"I'm pinging Serlotminden," Kal said from the living room.

"You should call Don too," Caleb added, who was probably still on the couch. "He'll want to know."

I heard Seth complaining the whole way out of the room that he wasn't tired before the door whooshed closed.

Teddy groaned and rolled out of my arms. "It's too hot." He kicked off his pants, sprawling on the bed.

I pushed on his chest. "You're naked."

"Am not." He snapped his briefs. "See."

"Barely." I flopped onto my back, and Teddy dragged me closer. I wanted to move away, but I was so tired. My eyes could barely stay open.

"Where is my husband?" Mindy asked in his peppy voice. I moaned in protest, burying my face against Teddy; he held me closer.

A growl sounded, and suddenly, Teddy was out of my arms and Mindy was hovering over me. Icy fear pumped through my veins. I screamed, scuttling toward the edge of the bed. I had to get away. He was going to hurt me.

Strong arms snagged me and yanked me into a solid body, moments before a hand cupped my cheek and waves of peace crashed over me. "Don," I cried, wiggling to wrap my arms around his neck as I tried to get as close as physically possible.

"I have you, my Vince. You are safe."

"I didn't mean to scare him," Mindy whispered.

Don growled.

"Enough, Dontilvynsan," a calm voice said. I looked up, and Fyn stood in the doorway. "He didn't mean to, and Vince is safe." He brushed a hand through Don's hair.

I slapped him away. "Mine."

Don stilled beneath me, and Fyn blinked.

Hand buried in Don's hair, I said again to make sure everyone understood, "Mine. All mine."

"It's fine, Vince."

"No," I snapped, hugging Don closer. Everything felt stronger and my mind was full of fluff, though oddly focused. Don was fucking mine, and I wasn't going to share him with anyone. I smashed my lips into his, then gentled my touch as I remembered he didn't like it hard.

Soft. Soft. Soft. I repeated it over and over. I would be gentle with my Don.

He pulled back. "Not right now."

I snorted and tears started to form in my eyes. Why didn't he understand? I wanted to make him happy. He was mine. I would take care of him. I would. I sniffed, and Don made a distressed noise in the back of his throat.

"Is he crying?" Mindy asked while Teddy complained about being hot. "No, keep your undershorts on."

"He's crying," Caleb yelled. "What did you do to him?"

Sobs tore out of my mouth, and I held Don. I didn't want to share him. I wanted to take care of him. Why was he rejecting me? Was I not good enough? Was I too damaged? Was I too dirty?

"Nothing," Fyn said. "I promise, Little Soul. I touched Dontilvynsan's hair, and Vince slapped my hand away."

Caleb hissed. "Are you alright?"

"It didn't hurt. Vince was making a point. He doesn't want me to touch Dontilvynsan."

"Oh," Caleb said. "Why is Teddy naked?"

"I'm not sure," Fyn replied. "Something about being uncomfortable. Who knows with humans?"

Caleb smacked Fyn's arm, but Fyn smirked at his mate, taking his tail.

There was shuffling, and Teddy groaned, "I don't want them. It's hot."

"I can't take you back to our room with your butt showing."

"It's a nice ass," Caleb teased, and Mindy growled. "What? It is. I'm gay. I know my asses. I'm an ass man, and Teddy has a nice ass. Not as nice as Seth's, but it's nice. I could rank everyone's asses. That might be fun."

Fyn chuckled. "I don't believe that anyone but me would enjoy that."

"Your ass is number one," Caleb said.

I wiped a line of snot on Don's shoulder, ignoring Caleb's rambling about butts. No one's ass was as nice as Don's, and it was mine. All mine. I kept crying, and Don held the back of my head and rocked me in soothing motions.

"I'm taking Vince back to my room."

"What about the other humans?" Fyn asked.

"They'll be fine," Caleb said with a wave of his hand. "Trust me. This is probably not the first time they've woken up on the floor with a hangover. Heaven knows, I have many times."

Don lifted me, and I hooked my legs around his waist. When he turned toward the door, I gripped his hair and declared, "See. Mine."

Fyn lifted his eyebrows, and Caleb laughed. Mindy was still fighting with Teddy about putting on his clothes, so he didn't acknowledge me.

As Don walked toward his room, I pressed my face against his neck and breathed him in; my eyes grew heavy. I brushed his hair back and whispered, "I don't want to share you."

"You will have to with my brothers."

I shook my head. "You don't understand."

"What? I can't read your thoughts. They're too muddled."

"I don't want you to fuck anyone else. I promise I'll get there. Don't leave me."

"Vince." We stepped into his room, and he went to the bedroom and tried to put me down, but I clung to him like a koala.

"No," I cried as tears began to run down my cheeks. I couldn't take his rejection. I wasn't good enough, but I wanted Don.

Don sat down, and I remained on his lap. He ran his fingers through my short hair. "Little Warrior, I'm not going to leave you. I'm not in a rush. Whether you get there or not is fine."

"You don't understand," I sobbed. "You don't understand."

"You are a horrible drunk," he muttered.

I sat back and gripped his cheeks. "I want you to be mine. No one else's. Bimwoxcol is fucking other people beside Pierce. I don't want that. Just me."

"Alright," he said. "Just you."

"No. It's not fair. I'm being unreasonable," I said, chest heaving.

"I have no idea what you want right now," he said with a breathy laugh.

I hugged him again, fisting his hair. "We're friends with benefits. I know that, but the thought of you with anyone else makes me mad. While I'm here, while I have my memory, I want to be the only one touching you like this. Just me, Donny."

Don kissed my neck, arms tight around me. "I don't want anyone else. Just you, Vince. Only you."

Chapter 27

HUNGOVER

Dontilvynsan

I held Vince against me as he drooled on my shoulder. Any time I tried to move to take care of him, like wipe his face, he gripped my shirt and started to cry. All while I snuggled him, his words circled my thoughts. My soul pounded with warmth. Vince had claimed me. Completely. I wished it was forever, but he was giving me everything he could in this moment.

My fingers trailed over his back, feeling the smoothness of his shirt. I wished it was his skin, but I was content he was beside me. My Vince. I rubbed my cheek against his hair. His gentle scent bore the barest tinge of my own, but I wanted it to be stronger. Until any drakcol could scent me on him, I wouldn't be satisfied.

He whimpered in his sleep when a dream started, rolling onto his back.

"Hush, my Mate. I am here. You are safe." I forced him onto his side against me. I didn't want him to choke on his own vomit—something Kalvoxrencol had pinged to warn me about. I dragged my claws through his hair, scratching his scalp, careful not to hurt him.

Vince calmed without use of my inner fire and pressed closer to me, his fingers gripping my shirt.

Often I felt as if I was nothing more than my inner fire. My family cared about me beside my gift, and in some cases, in spite of it. Some of my past partners had only sought me out because of my inner fire. My early work in the navy was because of it. Vince was different. He cared about me for me.

The easy compliments he gave. All were sincere. From how he liked my smile to how smart he thought I was. Vince never held back. The gentle touches. Slowly, he was becoming more and more comfortable with me. As he did, Vince was happy to stake his claim with a soft touch on my arm or a brush of his lips.

His fierce claiming of me was something I desperately needed; something I'd never known I needed until I'd met him.

Suddenly, Vince sat up, eyes wide. "I don't feel good."

Before I was able to react, he vomited. The foul-smelling liquid splattered me and the bed. His eyes grew wide, and tears began to gather.

"Don't cry. It's alright. I'm not mad. I won't hurt you." In his current inebriated state, I couldn't read his mind. It was all blurry.

"I'm so sorry," he sobbed, chest heaving. Vince gagged moments before he vomited again, spewing on me and the sheets. I got up and snagged an empty planter, shoving it into his arms. Vince puked again. I had no idea how this much liquid was in his stomach.

"I'm sorry," he said again, tears running down his cheeks and snot leaking from his nose.

"It's fine." I brushed a hand through his hair, breathing through my mouth. Love wasn't all smiles, apparently. It was vomit too. When he continued to sob, I said, "You need to stop or you're going to make yourself sick."

"I want to look pretty for you."

"What?" I asked with a slight chuckle.

"You're too perfect. I want to be pretty."

"You are pretty."

"No, no, I'm not. I smell." His head fell back as he sobbed.

Unable to stop it, I broke into laughter. I cupped his cheeks, ignoring the vomit on both of us. "Where is my confident Little Warrior?"

"I don't know." He kept crying and crying.

"You shouldn't drink like this again if it's going to upset you."

Vince continued, "I want you to like me."

"I do."

"I want you to think I'm pretty."

"I do, Vince."

He cried, "Why am I not good enough?"

I truly didn't understand. Vince had never seemed like he cared what anyone thought. I pulled him closer. "You are. You're the only person for me."

He sniffed, wiping his tears before dragging his dripping nose over the shoulder of my shirt. My nose crinkled in disgust, but I wasn't going to say anything to him in this state.

"You never cared about this before that I know of," I said, brushing his hair back "Why are you upset?"

"I like you best."

My soul pounded. "What about Seth?"

"I *like* you best," he repeated. "Seth is Seth." Vince waved his hand like that explained everything. "He's always going to be Seth. But you are Don. My Don. And I like you best. I want you to like me best."

"I do." I kissed his cheek. "I do."

Vince finally calmed down, head on my chest.

We were both covered in vomit, as was the bed, and all of it smelled horribly, making my stomach churn. Carefully, I maneuvered him to the bathroom and had him sit with the planter on his lap. The easiest thing would be to put him in the shower with me. In his current state, I could probably convince him to get naked, but he hadn't given me his permission to do so. I didn't want to take advantage of him, or when he woke up, for him to never trust me again.

So I took a shower, alone, while I made him sit in the bathroom because he kept vomiting occasionally. Once I was clean, I tied my hair back and pulled on fresh clothes. I got a cloth wet and wiped him off, though his shirt was filthy. I pulled it off, and Vince didn't react. I yanked one of my own over his head, and he drowned in the excess fabric. I growled at the sight of him in my clothes.

When we returned to my room, I stripped the bed and put new bedding on.

"I'm sorry," he whispered.

I kissed his cheek. "Don't be. I will always take care of you."

He lay down, and I rolled him toward me on his side. Vince rubbed my shirt and frowned. He tugged on the hem, and I caught his hands. "No. You are too drunk."

"I don't want to fuck," he snapped, though it was wet as if he was about to start crying again. "I want to touch you."

"Vince, I don't want you to wake up tomorrow and be upset with me."

"No," he wailed, yanking on my shirt. "Just you. I want to feel you against my face. I need it."

Relenting, I leaned up and pulled my shirt off. Vince sighed, pressing against me. His eyes closed, and he held me as close as possible. "Mine."

"Yes," I said with a chuckle. "Yours. All yours."

Vince

Groaning, I held my head. My mouth was literal trash and also bone dry. Everything hurt. I wanted to curl into a ball and die. God. Dying had to be less painful than this. It had to be.

Arms surrounded me, and I started, yanking away, which ripped a whine from my throat as my stomach threatened to escape.

"It's me," Don whispered.

I blurrily looked at him, confused. An odd sensation went through me. Don looked as he usually did, though his royal purple hair was tied back, not hanging free. He was shirtless, but that wasn't weird either. I'd asked him to sleep next to me without his shirt on before. I liked the feel of his scales against my hand or face.

No, it was none of that. But for the life of me, I couldn't remember how I'd gotten into his room or when. The last thing I remembered was drinking in my room with everyone.

"You were drunk," Don said, voice low and soft as he settled me against him.

I closed my eyes, head pounding.

"Kalvoxrencol pinged me, and I brought you here."

Nothing besides a vague sense of unease, like I'd done something really *really* stupid, was coming to mind.

"You need to drink water. Kalvoxrencol says that's how to cure human hangovers." Don gently set me away from him, then moved toward the dispenser on the wall. "I confess, I haven't researched much about human care, but I will."

"I should be able to take care of my own damn self, but research away. It's not like I can stop you," I muttered. What the hell had I forgotten? Had I done something embarrassing with Seth and Teddy? This was Don's ship, so I imagined if we had done something truly asinine he would've told me already.

As I shifted on the bed, my shirt caught under me, making me tug on the fabric. "What the hell?" I asked, looking down at the mass of cloth around me. I recognized it. "Why am I wearing your shirt?"

Don's tail flicked as he handed me the glass of water. "You vomited on your clothes last night. Your shirt got the brunt of it, so I put you in one of mine."

Like a floodgate being released, everything I'd done last night came pouring back. Smacking Fyn. Calling Don mine. Asking him not to fuck anyone else. Puking on him.

Fucking hell and all the good things in the universe, I'd puked on him. Multiple times. He'd seen me vomit. There was no way to recover from that. Abandon ship, call the reaper, put a fucking fork in me. This whole whatever-we-were was done.

I groaned, shoving the water onto the nightstand, and buried my face in the pillow to hide my burning cheeks.

The bed shifted when Don moved behind me. He nuzzled my back while his tail coiled around my leg. "Don't be embarrassed."

Unlikely. Of course I was embarrassed. I wished a black hole would suck me in so I didn't have to face him.

"I wouldn't like that," he said. "I would miss you dreadfully."

Resentment pooled in my stomach. I couldn't even be embarrassed in private.

It was instantaneous. The moment he heard my thoughts, Don drew away.

"No," I growled, rolling over. I snagged his hand, but he didn't look at me, expression completely blank. "No, Sweetheart. I didn't mean it. I'm just fucking embarrassed. I love you hearing me. You know that."

Don nodded, but the damage was done. It had been bound to happen sometime. I couldn't police my thoughts constantly. That was impossible. Nevertheless, I didn't want to hurt him.

"Please?" I asked as I conjured the image of him lying on the bed next to me. "Please, Sweetheart. I'm sorry. I didn't mean it."

He settled beside me, and I pressed against him, breathing in his light scent. Nothing else calmed me down like he did. I kissed his chest. "I'm sorry."

"It's fine, Vince."

"No, it fucking isn't. You're allowed to be mad at me for hurting your feelings, Don. Yes, I cannot control all of my thoughts, and I'm going to think shit things at times, but I never want to hurt you."

He kissed the top of my head. "I forgive you."

"I'm embarrassed because I puked on you after making unreasonable demands and smacking your brother. Caleb's going to be pissed I hit Fyn."

"I liked you claiming me, though if you could refrain from hurting my brothers, I would appreciate it. Even Kalvoxrencol," he said, making me frown; I still kind of wanted to kill him, not that I would, but I sure as hell would keep planning it mentally.

Don continued, "I don't want anyone else, Vince, so your request isn't unreasonable. I would also prefer if I was the only person you were having sex with."

"I don't want anyone else," I said with a shrug. Why would I want anyone besides Don? I was a possessive asshole. I could only focus my attention on one person at a time for the most part, except for Seth. Though even with Seth, I didn't want to sleep with him anymore.

A smile tugged at the corner of Don's lips and his grip tightened a bit. "As for the vomiting, I don't care. You are mine to take care of."

I swallowed as an unnamed emotion clawed at my throat. "I'm yours?"

"If you want to be."

Hell yes, I wanted to be.

Head aching, I rolled onto Don, and he kept his hands at his sides, although his tail tightened around my ankle. "You are mine."

Don's expression turned utterly serious as he said, "I am yours, Vince. No one else's. Completely and utterly yours."

Grinning, I settled on his chest and closed my eyes. Hangover be damned. I was happy as could be. Don was mine for as long as I wanted to keep him.

Chapter 28

THE BEST CURE TO A HANGOVER.

Vince

Everything fucking hurt. I didn't even want to breathe, and Don was the only good thing in the hangover crapstorm that made me want to vomit and question whether I was a good person or not.

He didn't say anything about my roiling emotions and gently stroked my back or occasionally planted kisses on my head.

"You have duty on Command," I told him, clutching him. I sure as hell didn't want Don to leave, but at the same time, he was the captain of this ship and couldn't neglect his duty because his *special* friend wasn't feeling well.

"I asked Bimwoxcol to take over Command today."

"Donny, you can't do that."

"I can and did. You are ill."

I wasn't ill. I was currently suffering from the consequences of poor decisions and a lack of respect for alcohol. But sure, that was the same thing.

"You need to drink some water and perhaps eat something." Don moved out of my embrace and brought me another glass of water and a piece of flatbread.

Neither sounded appetizing to my rolling stomach. I sat up with a groan, though the sight of Don's generous shirt gathered around my much slighter form made me smile. I inhaled the fabric, then looked up, blushing.

Don was watching me with a possessive grin.

"Thanks," I squeaked as I took the water and food. I nibbled on the soft bread, ignoring Don, which was basically impossible.

"I like you in my clothes," he whispered close to my ear, setting my face even more aflame. I was fucking blushing. What the hell was he doing to me? "Even more, I like that *you* like wearing my clothes."

Now my face was an inferno. Perfect.

Keeping my eyes in front of me, I tried to drink the water and eat the bread. From past experience, a bit of food, water, and maybe some painkillers and I'd be right as rain. When I finished, Don whisked the cup away before settling beside me again. I curled next to his side, pressing my face into him to drown out the light.

His claws scraped at my scalp. "I can turn off all of the lights if you need, my Vince."

"I'm fine." I was as long as I kept my eyes closed and buried against him. Besides, I hated the thought of the world being dark around me. I couldn't even stand the possibility of it.

As time passed, the water and food combo dulled my headache, but I felt no urge to move. None at all. Snuggling against Don was one of the best feelings in the world.

Don suddenly moved, and I groaned in protest. He kissed the top of my head and said, "I know. Someone is pinging me. Hold on."

I didn't care who was fucking pinging him. If it wasn't an emergency, I wanted to hog all of Don's free time.

He dropped the touchstone, and his lips found mine. I returned the kiss with a groan, rolling on top of him; I did better when I was in control. Don didn't fight the move. His wings sprawled under him and his tail curled around my leg.

The kiss turned hot as I pushed my tongue into his mouth and swiped along his scaled one. I groaned at the feel. Someday, I would feel it on my cock.

"Anytime you want," he said, breathlessly.

I hardened in a flash. I rubbed on him, seeking friction for relief. Need rushed through me—need to be close to him, to feel Don against me. I grabbed his hand and pressed it against my cheek. I turned from his mouth to brush a kiss to his palm.

A soft moan broke out of Don. I loved his noise. Each and every one was a gift.

"Let me hear you," I whispered. "I love your voice."

He panted. Something started to prod my backside, and I grinned, grinding down. "Good job," I told him. "Absolutely perfect. You are such a good boy for me."

Don's green eyes practically glowed as he stared at me. "Please."

"What, Sweetheart?"

"Let me share my thoughts."

I kissed his jaw, trailing up his face. "Of course."

A lock released in the back of my mind, and Don flooded in. I couldn't understand his words because he thought in Drakconese, but his emotions. Fuck, they were potent. His lust was foremost, as I imagined mine was, but the softer feeling of care and amazement of me wanting him were beneath it.

Clearly he needed more compliments.

"My perfect Don," I whispered. "You're the prize, not me. Thank you for being mine." I couldn't keep him for forever, which hurt more than I thought, but for the time I had him, I'd treasure the hell out of Don.

I kissed his throat, making sure to keep his hand on me, so I'd feel if I did something he didn't like. I kept every touch of my hands and lips soft. The more gentle I was, the more Don came apart beneath me.

His hard cock pressed against me, straining against his pants. Mine throbbed in need while the slick tip stuck to my briefs. I needed release, and so did he, but it was more than that. I needed Don.

As clear as I could, I formed a picture of what I wanted in my mind as I sucked on one of his nipples. Don's throat bobbed, and heat blasted me from his thoughts. I nipped him. "You like my idea?"

"Will you be alright?"

"I think so."

Sitting up, I tugged my shirt off before bending back over to kiss his chest. I put one of Don's hands on my back while the other stayed on my face. My nipples scraped against his warm scales, and I moaned at the sensation. Don arched under me as it moved through him.

With every touch, I felt his pleasure while he experienced mine until we blended into a single unit. It was hard to differentiate what I was feeling from Don, but I didn't want to anyway. I wanted to fuse myself to Don, so there was no escape for either of us.

I sat up, breaking the connection, which made Don whimper. "I know, Sweetheart, but I need you and we have too many clothes on." I undid the buttons on my pants before scrambling off him and kicking them off. I yanked on Don's pants next. He lifted his hips, allowing me to get them off.

Securing the lube, I scooped up a generous amount and pumped him. Don cried out, hips following me. "Does that feel good?"

"Yes. Please, Vince."

"Good boy."

Don was so good at begging. I nipped his hip and kept working his dick as I watched him come undone. When his eyes were wide and his movements jerky, I knew he was close. I didn't want him to come this soon.

I gently tugged on his balls. "Wait for me."

"I will, my Vince."

I slicked up my own dick and straddled Don again. His cock slid into my crack, and I bobbed up, making it slide. He moaned. I put his hands on my hips, and I did it again. My head went back at the sensation of his scales scraping against me.

"I want to feel with you," Don said, cupping my cheek.

The connection snapped into place, and I cried out. Every feeling was tenfold as I rocked. I pumped my own cock in time with my movements.

Don's tail coiled around my shaft. "Let me. Please."

I let go, and his tail squeezed me in time. Pleasure swelled with each movement. My balls drew up tight as my muscles tightened. Between the sensation of Don's tail working me and his cock sliding over my crack and brushing my clenching hole, not to mention his feelings flitting through my mind, my orgasm built incredibly fast until I crashed over with a scream. Don came with me, cum splattering my back while mine painted his stomach.

Boneless, I collapsed on him. Don trembled beneath me as his thoughts settled into mindless joy and sated comfort. I groaned, nuzzling his broad chest. I kissed him. "So good. You are such a fucking good boy."

Us touching like this, skin to scales, I thought wouldn't be possible, but Don made it so much easier.

His hand gently slid up and down my back, feeling my bare skin. Don cupped my ass, and I sighed, relaxing. With slow movements, he explored me, and I didn't freak out. It might have been a combination of his lazy thoughts joining with mine and the after-sex glow. Or it was that I simply trusted Don.

"Perfect way to get rid of a hangover," I said.

He chuckled. "I will remember that, my Vince."

Chapter 29

WHAT'S BETTER THAN AN AWKWARD CONVERSATION?

Dontilvynsan

After we cleaned up, we returned to bed. Vince remained right against me, running his fingers over me. He hadn't redressed, and when I touched him, he leaned into me while his thoughts remained calm and pleased.

His fingers moved over my side, and I fought a growl. I loved when he touched my scent glands. Instinct demanded I cover my mate in my scent so everyone knew he was mine, but Vince didn't know he was my mate. He still thought this was temporary. I had no plans to disillusion him from that assumption.

As much as Vince claimed to be unkind, I knew the truth. He was genuinely nice and he cared. A lot. He cared about Camden and Pierce. He cared about Teddy. He loved Seth. And he truly cared deeply about me. If he knew his leaving would permanently injure me, which it would, he would stay.

I feared if he stayed here for me, he would regret it. Though hope at him remaining wouldn't completely go away. I couldn't help but wonder if Vince overcame some of his issues or came to terms with what had happened to him, then maybe he would stay by my side where he belonged.

Someone rang the chime, and Vince groaned. I kissed his head, my tail tightening around his calf. "Don't worry. No one will bother us unless it's an emergency, and if it was, NAID would've pinged me."

A wave of possessive need washed through Vince and made me smile in contentment. He wanted me with an almost feral intensity. I loved it. I ran my hand over his back, marveling at the smooth chill of his skin. I'd never experienced anything like this ever before. Vince kissed my shoulder and snuggled closer.

The person kept ringing the door, and we ignored it. It was probably one of my brothers, and I didn't bother to check with either NAID or my inner fire—I didn't want to deal with any of them. Not right now. All that mattered was Vince. We were running out of time, and I wanted to spend every moment I had with him.

NAID appeared on the screen in front of my bed, and Vince squeaked, even though NAID literally couldn't care whether he wore clothes or not. I pulled the sheet up to cover him while keeping him close.

"What, NAID?"

"The princes Serlotminden, Zoltilvoxfyn, and Kalvoxrencol are outside your room. They wish to speak with you."

"I bet they do. Nosy assholes," Vince grumbled, making me chuckle.

I nuzzled the top of his head, scent marking him, which soothed my soul. My Vince. "NAID, tell them I'm unavailable."

Warmth rushed through Vince and into me. Content. He was happy. We could always be like this to some extent if he chose to remain, but I wouldn't pressure him. This was his decision, and I couldn't take it from him no matter how much I wished to.

"Dontilvynsan, stop fucking Vince and open the door," Kalvoxrencol shouted, living up to his endearment of "Pest."

Visions of stabbing Kalvoxrencol flitted through Vince's mind.

"As irritating as he is, I would rather you not kill my younger brother."

"Then tell him to fuck off," Vince growled. "We're spending the day together, and I'm not sharing. Besides, Seth and Teddy are probably hungover. Kal and Mindy should be with them."

As I slid out of bed, Vince kissed my arm and snagged my tail, gently holding it. "Come back soon."

I kissed his head. "I will."

Tugging on trousers and a shirt, I stepped into the shared space and opened the door. The trio of my younger brothers all stood there—Kalvoxrencol at the forefront.

"What?" I asked, examining their thoughts. All were worried about something. Me. Vince wasn't far from their thoughts either.

"We need to talk," Kalvoxrencol said. Even though he was the youngest, Pest often led the way, especially with Zoltilvoxfyn. Serlotminden followed them unless he disagreed.

"I'm spending the day with Vince," I said, leaning against the door jamb.

"Please, Captain," Zoltilvoxfyn said. Setlotminden stared at me, expectantly. They all knew I had a hard time saying no to any of them.

I fought a groan. "We cannot be gone for long. Vince needs me."

"We won't," Serlotminden said.

"Give me a moment." I left my brothers where they were and returned to Vince. He was on his stomach, dozing on my pillow. I crouched next to the bed and kissed his forehead. Vince smiled. He'd become so dear to me in such a short amount of time. I could hardly believe it, but trying to imagine my life without him was painful. "My Vince, my brothers need to speak to me. Now."

"Fine. I'll share you with them." Vince laughed, teasing me. He cupped my cheeks and kissed me. "Will I see you later?"

"You will. Very soon. Wait for me here."

He grunted, eyes closing, and snuggled closer to my pillow.

After I slipped on my shoes, I left my quarters and followed my brothers down the hall to Zoltilvoxfyn's quarters. Caleb was nowhere to be seen, but he'd been the only one not to drink last night, which meant he was more likely to be upright at this hour. Also, knowing him, he'd probably stolen Pookie and was playing with Bartholomew's pet.

Serlotminden turned to the screen on the wall, and I frowned. Hallonnixmin, my older brother, and Monqilcolnen, my sole cousin, stared back at me on the split screen. Hallonnixmin was back at the palace while Monqilcolnen was on the *Admiral Ven*.

This was an ambush.

I kept my expression utterly blank as I stared at my older brother and cousin. They knew me far better than anyone else. Hallonnixmin resembled Kalvoxrencol the most, though he had a shade darker scales and his hair was the same shade of purple as mine. His green eyes matched mine, and he shared our father's long nose, wide forehead, and strong chin. He didn't take his eyes off me, running a hand through his perpetually messy hair. His hair wasn't the only messy thing about him, which had led me to giving him the endearment of "Slob" when we were children.

Monqilcolnen could've passed for our brother, though his father was our father's older brother. His dark green scales, silver hair, and yellow eyes set him apart from us, but his features were similar and had the same strength, though harsher. He simply remained quiet, watching me.

My gaze moved to my little brothers. I knew what they wanted. I knew their concerns. It didn't matter. Nothing would take Vince from me nor return my soul to me. Vince owned it, and I wouldn't change it even if I could.

"We've told them everything," Kalvoxrencol said.

"Which is what, Pest?" I asked. Even annoyed, I would never injure Kalvoxrencol intentionally. He'd hurt himself enough in the past. My gaze wandered to my two other little brothers. They'd also struggled in different ways, as everyone did, but it would take something far greater than annoyance for me to try and injure them.

"How you are around Vince, and how he acts around you," Kalvoxrencol continued.

Hallonnixmin took control of the conversation. "What's going on, and be honest with us, Dontilvynsan?"

I would not deny my mate nor my affection for him, but I wasn't ready to tell them, because they would worry. I feared, as well, that they'd try to convince Vince to stay against his will.

Kalvoxrencol stared at me for several moments before he snagged Zoltilvoxfyn and Serlotminden's arms, tugging them out of the room. Serlotminden protested loudly while Zoltilvoxfyn calmly stated these were, in fact, his quarters.

When the door closed behind my little brothers, I sagged onto the couch.

"Come on, Captain," Monqilcolnen said in a soft voice. "Tell us what's going on."

"I'm in love with Vince, and he's returning to Earth," I said simply, as if it was nothing. As if it wasn't tearing my very soul to irreparable shreds.

Monqilcolnen closed his eyes. "I wondered, when they were talking to us."

"Are you sure he's going back?" Hallonnixmin asked.

"Yes." I had no doubts. I hoped he would stay, but I knew he would not. Vince still hoped to return to the person he'd once been, and I was unsure of how to convince him that he *was* still that person. I'd witnessed so many memories of him from the past, through his own mind and Seth's. Vince was the same, just older and wiser and wounded.

"And he is your mate?" Hallonnixmin asked, shoving his hand through his hair once again and making his long gold earrings sway.

"Yes."

"Four humans," Monqilcolnen said with a slight smile.

Unable to help it, I chuckled. Both Hallonnixmin and Monqilcolnen joined in. All three of my younger brothers had successfully mated with humans, and my mate was a human as well. What were the chances?

"There's something about them. I cannot exactly define what, but it's enticing," I confessed.

"I believe it is the Crystal," Monqilcolnen said.

"What do you mean?" I asked.

Monqilcolnen had the strongest spiritual soul ever tested. He understood the Crystal like no one else who'd ever been born. "Our inner fire was gifted to us by the Crystal, but we cannot speak to it. Humans can. There's something that allows them to interact with the Crystal in a way that we cannot. I believe we are drawn to them because of it."

A fascinating theory to be sure, but Vince was my perfect mate. I did not need the Crystal to tell me otherwise. "Perhaps," I told Monqilcolnen, "you will take a liking to one of the humans I'm bringing home."

His expression remained unchanged, but he said, "I do not believe so."

I lifted my eyebrows in question, wondering what he was thinking, but he didn't explain. Monqilcolnen's inner fire was perfect intuition. He didn't have visions of what would happen, like his father did, but sometimes he simply knew something for no reason that any of us understood.

"So. Vince," Hallonnixmin said, bringing the conversation to the matter at hand. "Does he know you are mated to him and that it's permanent?"

"He's aware that drakcol mate for life, but no, he doesn't know he's my mate. When we discussed permissions before fucking, I told him that it couldn't be more unless he wished to stay."

"Zoltilvoxfyn said he claimed you," Monqilcolnen remarked.

"He was drunk." As much as it hurt to say, I told them the truth. "Vince doesn't want to stay with me forever. He cares about me. He is possessive of me. But he doesn't want forever and he thinks I'm the same."

"Have you told him differently?" Hallonnixmin asked, frowning.

"No. I don't want to influence his decision to stay."

Monqilcolnen shook his head, sending his long hair over his broad shoulders. After me, he was the next largest. "I can understand that, but you will not survive this, Captain. I know you. You've never allowed yourself to care about anyone besides your family. Now that you've fallen in love, you will be fierce in it. Drakcol struggle to live without their mates, and you will not survive the separation."

"I am aware."

Hallonnixmin growled, his tail thrashing while his wings spread protectively. "I will not lose you because you don't want to inconvenience anyone." I started to protest, but he cut me off with a sharp slash of his arm. "No. You have always acted as if your every need was a bother, but it's not. Tell Vince what you need, then let him decide."

"You also need to tell Serlotminden, Zoltilvoxfyn, and Kalvoxrencol," Monqilcolnen added. "No secrets."

That was hypocritical of him. Monqilcolnen kept secrets from all of us. He hadn't even shared his inner fire with my three younger brothers until recently.

He must have read my expression because he tilted his head in concession. "I know, but they need to know."

"I'm afraid they will try and force Vince to stay."

"They won't," Hallonnixmin said. "Have faith in them."

"Alright."

"And talk to Vince. Don't give him the illusion of a choice. If he truly cares about you, as you say, then he would want to know what his leaving would do to you."

My eyes closed. I didn't know if I could do as Monqilcolnen wanted, but I would think on it.

A scream sounded over the screen, and Hallonnixmin glanced over his shoulder. "My children are attempting to kill each other." He shook his head and quickly said, "Tell him, Captain." He ended his connection before Monqilcolnen or I could say anything.

I crossed my arms and waited for Monqilcolnen to say something further, but he surprised me.

"Vince is Seth's age, yes?" he asked.

I blinked. "He's nine cycles younger than me."

"That is quite a bit of time."

I lifted my palms. Time was time. Yes, I was older than him and our age difference was larger than the typical couple, but we suited each other. "Vince and I are both adults, and we know what we want. I don't feel guilty or... odd for being attracted to him."

Monqilcolnen pursed his lips, but other than that, his expression remained calm.

"Why do you want to know?" I asked.

"No reason."

I doubted that, but without being physically next to him, my inner fire was useless to find the reason.

Chapter 30

AWKWARD CONVERSATION, TAKE TWO.

Vince

I lounged for a bit after Don left, before getting up and taking another shower. I didn't know how long he'd be gone, but I wanted to hang out when he returned. Doing something. Doing nothing. It didn't matter. All that mattered was the time we spent together.

Sitting on the couch, I ran my fingers over the strings on the harpsichord and watched as the instrument lit up in a multitude of colors, which made me grin. Don was insisting he learn how to play because I'd bought him the instrument. Though technically Seth bought it, or Kal, if I wanted to look at it that way, which I didn't. I might be giving up Seth, but I still didn't like Kal.

As I strummed the fragile strings, my mind wandered back to this morning with Don. Sex was getting easier. I trusted him not to deviate from what we planned. While I enjoyed everything that we did, I wanted more.

The thought of Don on top of me, pressing into me, made bile climb my throat and sweat slide down my back. I quickly pushed the image and unease away by taking a deep inhale of Don's fragrance. I didn't want him to sense my fear and come running. I wasn't sure how far he could sense me from, but he always seemed to appear when I freaked out.

Don being on top or inside of me wasn't going to happen, no matter how much I wanted it. At least not yet. My body was insistent on remembering everything, even though I was beyond done and wanted it to go away. Perhaps Camden was right about needing to talk to someone, but I didn't want to. I didn't have anything against therapy per se; it just wasn't something kindly talked about when I was growing up, and I'd never seen a point to it. Then again, I hadn't had the trauma I did now.

Man, I felt like such a dick, especially for how I'd spoken to Camden.

Could therapy even help me have sex with Don? And how in the fucking hell did I ask a therapist about that? I would die of embarrassment.

Though we were already halfway back to the drakcol home planet. How much longer did we have if I wanted to have Don fuck me? And did I really want to leave him? Could I leave him?

I sank to the couch, hands falling into my lap. I didn't want to part from Don. The very thought made my chest tighten and tears burn my eyes. I pushed the sensations away. We would be planetside for months, maybe even years, before the drakcol sent a ship to Earth. We had plenty of time.

Penetrative sex would happen between us.

What if I was on top?

The thought of Don beneath me, his long hair spread out on the pillow as he made his soft noises, sent my heart racing. My cock twitched, then began to harden in a hurry. Though all of the touching made me a tad uncomfortable, scales to skin sometimes triggered me. It wasn't limited to scales, but too much touch set me off at the most random of times.

The image of Don on his hands and knees, tail wrapped around my arm, as I fucked him filtered in, and I groaned. Fuck. I wanted to do that. I wanted to feel his hole squeezing me while I sank into the warm heat of him. I palmed my erection through my jeans, shaking. I almost stood to go back to the bedroom to jerk off, but I held off.

Would Don want to? He might, but then again, what if he didn't bottom? I didn't top often—because of my small size people often assumed I would always be the bottom—and some guys weren't versatile like I was.

A chime interrupted my thoughts. My cock was hard and pressing against my stiff black jeans. I took several calming breaths and tried to relax, which didn't help. In the end, I readjusted, hiding my straining cock, and called, "Enter."

The door slid open, and Seth stumbled in, pale and sporting stubble. I held out my arms, and he crashed onto the couch, snuggling close. I had a single moment of fear before it rushed away. I brushed his impossibly soft brown hair back as he settled against my shoulder.

"Are you still hungover?"

He grunted.

I wanted to chuckle, but I swallowed it so I didn't hurt his head. Seth had never handled alcohol well. That hadn't changed. "Didn't Kal take care of you?"

"Yeah."

"Still hungover, though?"

"I drank more than you," he groaned.

With soft touches, I continued to finger-comb his hair while my thoughts circled around Don. Before he got back, I'd have to put some distance between me and Seth or at least, think hard about how I wasn't as strongly attracted to him. I didn't want to hurt Don. Besides, he was truly the only person I wanted right now.

"Can I ask you something?" I said in a quiet voice.

"If you have to."

I laughed, and Seth groaned. I swallowed it, then whispered, "Do you top with Kal?"

He jerked back, face red. "W-what?"

"Do you fuck Kal or do you always bottom?" I guessed Seth was versatile, though he never talked about sex. Not from prudishness, but rather from pure discomfort.

"Why would you want to know that?" He fluffed the front of his hoodie, and the action made me smile. Travis had never let him wear hoodies. Seth had reclaimed a part of himself since that abusive relationship, and the very sight of it soothed something inside of me. While Kal could fall off a cliff and die, I was pleased to know that Seth was safe.

"It's important."

Seth fisted the front of his hoodie, cheeks on fire. "I top more often than I bottom. Kal prefers to bottom most of the time, and I take far more prep than he does."

I nodded; Don might be willing to bottom. Or was this just something Kal was fine with? "Do you think Don would bottom with me?"

"W-what?" Seth asked again.

Poor guy. I was pushing him far out of his comfort zone. Caleb or Teddy might be a better source of sex information, but I didn't know Caleb well and Teddy hadn't been with Mindy long. Besides, Seth was the one who knew everything. He was the leader of Team Human after all.

"I want to have sex, but I can't stomach the thought of Don inside me. Not yet."

He closed his eyes and took a deep breath, squeezing the life out of his hoodie. "You need to ask him."

I frowned.

"I'm serious, Vince. Drakcol are super open about sex. If he doesn't want to, he'll tell you directly. I'm sure you've discussed permissions and all that."

"Yeah. We haven't gotten super in depth, because I don't know what will or won't upset me until we do it."

"Make sense." Seth glanced at me, face as red as a tomato. "Ask Don. He won't be mad. At most, he'll say no, then you know."

"Thanks," I said, bumping his shoulder. "I know sex is one of the things you hate talking about."

"Caleb would be far better. He has no shame. He'll tell you whatever you want to know and what you don't want to know. Also, he's in a drakcol body."

True. My lips pursed. He would know what feels good, and he probably wouldn't care if I asked.

"I didn't come because I wasn't feeling well."

My forehead crinkled. "What's going on?"

He chewed on his lower lip, and I raised my eyebrows. He squeaked, "Kal and his brothers are worried."

"About?" I could feel my hackles rising. Don was mine, and I sure as hell wasn't letting him go because his younger brothers didn't like us together.

"I've told you drakcol only mate once."

"I know, but Don doesn't feel that way about me."

Seth touched the thin gold necklaces I was wearing. "He's buying you things."

"So?"

"That's what Kal did when he was pursuing me." Before I could say anything, he continued, "He's scent marking you. Kal noticed. You claimed him when you were drunk."

I stood. "You don't know what you're talking about," I snapped, then immediately felt guilty when Seth flinched. "Look, Don said he didn't want more. We're just..." What were we? We sure as hell felt more than friends with benefits. "I don't know what we are, but I'm not Don's mate. I'm going home."

"I know," he whispered, "but what if he considers you his mate? Drakcol don't do well with separation. Some don't survive."

Panic raced like electricity down my veins. Would something happen to Don if I left? I could never live with myself if it did. Of course, I wouldn't know if it did because I wouldn't have my memories.

Seth said, moving behind me, "I wanted to warn you about the possibility, but Don would've told you if you were his mate."

Trying to lighten the mood, I teased, "You just want me to stay."

"I do. I really do, but I wouldn't lie about this."

I faced him, taking his hand and swinging it between us. "I know."

"Do you like him?"

"Of course I do." I liked Don more than I'd ever liked anyone, except Seth.

"Maybe this could be a permanent thing between you two?"

Maybe. But did I want that? And more importantly did Don?

Dontilvynsan

When I stepped into the room, Vince's thoughts and emotions were all over the place. The sole clear thing I got from his mind was that Seth had been here, in my quarters, and he'd said something to confuse Vince.

Had Seth started to care for Vince in the same way?

Jealousy ripped through me.

I moved toward Vince, instinct demanding I claim him. Vince, in turn, raced toward me and threw his arms around my shoulders to yank me down, lips finding mine. I paused at the searing kiss, lust rushing through me and settling in my cock.

Without thinking, I lifted Vince. He didn't hesitate to wrap his legs around my waist. His cock was hard against my stomach while his thoughts whirled around going to the bedroom and sucking each other off—something I was more than fine with.

As I carried him to my bedroom, I kept a tight hold on him. I didn't care what Seth had said. Vince was mine. Until he decided to leave, I would keep him, and no one would take him from me.

Chapter 31

ANOTHER PLANET, OR BY ANOTHER NAME—A DELAY IN DISGUISE.

Dontilvynsan

I kissed my way down Vince's back as I stood. He'd been sleeping in my room for the past week since my brothers confronted me and since that mysterious conversation between Seth and Vince had taken place—the one Vince hadn't thought about or told me about.

The only time he'd returned to his quarters was to get his stuff, putting his shiny pillows on my couch and his pink blankets on my bed and a large pillow he'd told me was meant for the floor near the wall. His clothes now filled my closet, and his hygiene products were in my bathroom. He'd effectively moved into my quarters, and I couldn't have been more pleased about it. Falling asleep and waking up next to him was a dream.

Rather unwillingly, I put on my uniform before leaving the room and Vince behind until lunch when he would meet me in the canteen. Even having just left, my thoughts turned toward him and my senses stretched through the walls to him, needing to be connected to him. As he was asleep, I didn't feel much besides his general presence.

Disappointed, I moved to the lift while I recalled how his thoughts kept skittering around something. I respected his privacy, not digging for what I wanted to know, as much as it pained me.

With every day that we spent together, Vince was getting better at avoiding my inner fire, reminding me heavily of Kalvoxrencol. Out of all my brothers, he was the best at evading me; Vince was becoming his equal in shocking time.

The two of them, while they would both hate the comparison, were similar in the oddest ways.

When the door opened to the command floor, I pushed Vince from my thoughts as much as I could—he wouldn't leave completely, not ever.

"Captain on deck," Bimwoxcol said when I entered.

"Return," I ordered right away. "Status."

Bimwoxcol rambled off the same information as yesterday, not a surprise. If there had been something new, I would've been informed already. We were in Coalition space, not far from the Drakcol Empire. I didn't expect any trouble, though I always remained vigilant.

I took my seat, grabbing my screen to look through the notes and reports that had come across my system. Both Hallonnixmin and Monqilcolnen had sent me notes that were almost identical. They wanted to know if I'd told my brothers yet and spoken with Vince. I ignored them, because I'd done neither.

All of my younger brothers had attacked me at various times to find out what was going on, and I'd rebuffed them. Zoltilvoxfyn and Serlotminden were more annoyed at my evasion; Kalvoxrencol was hurt, which tugged at my soul. I would have to tell them soon.

Though, interestingly enough, I worried about what Kalvoxrencol would do more than any of my other brothers. He was viciously protective of us. If he thought Vince's departure would injure me, he wouldn't hesitate to act. Not to mention, he wanted Vince to no longer present a threat in regard to Seth.

The door to Command opened, and I paid it no mind. If someone was late for their duty shift, Bimwoxcol would handle it. All crew schedules and problems fell to her unless it was severe enough for me to interfere.

"Captain," Serlotminden said, which made me swallow a groan. Now they were ambushing me while I was on duty? That was too far. Though as I stood, I blinked. He wasn't here about Vince and I.

"Serlotminden, what do you need?"

The image of a planet flitted through his thoughts as he asked, "Can I speak to you alone?"

I gestured to the door. My office was right down the hall. We stepped into the room, and I guessed, "You have a request."

He grinned. "You always know what people want."

Not always. Vince was hiding something, and I desperately wanted to know what. "You want something about a planet."

"Yes. Inogga is near here, and it has beautiful hot springs. I want to take Bartholomew." The image of Bartholomew naked in the pure blue water as they fucked raced through my little brother's thoughts, making me wince. "Sorry," he said when he caught my expression. Serlotminden tried to think about other things, but it always came back to Bartholomew and him smiling as they loved.

The absolute worst part of my gift, but it was hardly new.

"This is not a pleasure trip," I said. Inogga was four days—one way—out of our way. While it was still in Coalition space, it was hardly on our route.

"I know, but the warm water might be nice for Caleb, and Bartholomew would love it." When I stared at him, he grinned. "Vince would like it. He might even want to rent a private hot spring for the two of you."

I frowned at his obvious ploy, but that didn't stop his words from working. Thoughts of Vince resting against the rough rocks, blue water lapping around his narrow hips as he went on and on about the warmth and comfort. He would like it, whether we fucked or not.

It would be nice to simply hold him and talk about whatever he wished or to simply take him because it would bring him pleasure.

"I cannot go off route simply because you or maybe I wish to. This is a navy vessel, and I have to justify how and why I go where I do." I might be the captain, but I didn't own this ship—the Drakcol Empire did.

"You can't find a reason?" he asked, eyes big as his tail flicked.

I fought a growl. My brothers knew I had a hard time saying no to them.

"Eight days travel and maybe a week there. It's a *small* delay," Speedy said.

My thoughts latched onto the word delay. We were over halfway home, which meant me and Vince were closer than ever to separating. If I could concoct a reason to take this trip, then it would stall our return, granting me more days with Vince, which I needed. More time to find my voice to tell him what I wanted and hope that he returned it.

⸺

I dried my hair, then lay down next to Vince on the bed. We hadn't done much tonight. He'd spent time with Camden and Pierce—their support group, I believed Vince called it—before returning late. I'd practiced the harpsichord. I was struggling to gain any proficiency with the instrument and I kept breaking the delicate strings, but it would take time. More than that, I was determined.

Now we were going to bed. I had another early duty tomorrow. I'd spent a good portion of the day—once I'd reviewed the most urgent reports—searching for a reason to go to Inogga. The only one I found was that some sidlis researchers were requesting samples of the water and some of the plants. It was an academy level mission, which we would normally send some cadets to do, but I could justify traveling there, especially if Doctor Muznim wrote something about Caleb benefiting from the healing water.

Everyone catered to the humans because they spoke to the Crystal. If Seth merely said he wanted to travel there, the Ranks and the Cohort would order me to go. Though I doubted he wanted to. He wanted to go home to his unborn kit.

Vince kissed my chest, and I turned my thoughts to him. I gave him a smile, cupping the back of his head. He didn't have any interest that I could hear in fucking, and I was tired, but I relished the feel of him next to me.

"What's going on, Sweetheart?"

"What do you mean?"

"You've been distant all day." A spike of worry shot through him. *Is he mad at me*? he wondered, and I kissed his forehead, instinct surging to the forefront. Drakcol cared for our mates, and I'd left mine worried.

"Serlotminden made a request, and I've been thinking about whether I can do it or not."

Vince looked up at me, a cute wrinkle marring his forehead. I kissed him, unable to stop myself. He returned it with gentle pressure, and his fingers skated over my side, making my tail thrash. If he didn't stop, I would become aroused, and I didn't want to pressure him for anything.

Lying back, I continued, "He wants to visit a planet four days out of our way that has lovely hot springs."

"He wants to fuck Teddy with pretty surroundings," Vince surmised.

"Yes, and I have to justify going with my superiors."

"Will you get in trouble?"

"Possibly, unless I can find a reason or ask Seth to lie and say he wants to go."

Sleep began to tug on Vince. "Then don't do it. You're more important."

I smiled at his assertion. The problem was I wanted to go. "Would you like to see Inogga?"

He shrugged. "It might be fun."

"Then I will find a way."

Vince sat up, frowning, and I had no idea why. Annoyance flared in his thoughts, and I tried to pull back, but he wouldn't let me. "What do *you* want?"

"What?"

"Donny, you always do what I want. You're doing what your brothers want. What do you want?"

You, I thought, but didn't, couldn't, say.

"Be selfish," he said when I didn't respond. "Be completely selfish. I have been, many times with you, so don't filter what you want. Just tell me." Vince lifted my hand to his face, and I knew what he wanted. He wanted to feel my honesty, and I was terrified. I didn't want to scare him away.

"Trust me," Vince whispered, kissing my palm. "Just trust me, Sweetheart."

I made the connection, shaking. "I want to go. I want to bathe in the hot springs with you." The image of me kissing his pale back as the water lapped around his firm butt rose from the depths.

"What else?"

I swallowed, fear building.

Vince kissed me. "Trust me. Please."

"You," I forced out. "I want you."

He blinked. "You have me."

"I don't want you to go back to Earth. I want you to stay with me. Forever." I forced down the words about him already being my mate because I didn't want to scare him.

His thoughts were frozen for several moments before he thought over my words. Vince released a long breath before sliding onto my chest and kissing me. "Thank you for trusting me. Thank you for being selfish with me. I need to hear what you want, Don, and I think you need to say it even more."

"And?"

"I can't decide this now," Vince replied. "I've been wavering because I care about you, more than I ever thought possible. I want to stay with you and Seth and Teddy and everyone else, but this is a choice I have to make for me."

My eyes dropped, and I pulled my hand away, though not quick enough. Vince kissed my neck, rubbing his cheek on the side near my scent glands, but it didn't soothe me as usual.

"I shouldn't have said anything. My apologies," I said.

He grabbed my cheeks, his grip a tad harder than he usually used on me. Vince growled, and my cock twitched. He said, "Don't. I want to know, and you're allowed to feel and want what you do. I'm just not going to lie to you. I can't say yes right now, but that doesn't mean I'm mad or want you to keep it to yourself.

"I care about you, and I want you to talk to me. Please don't stop or pull away. I need to know this isn't all about me or what I want." Vince turned my face so he could kiss my cheek. "You are very important to me, and you are the main reason I want to stay. But I'm still scared and I hate remembering what happened. I need to think about it."

I could feel his sincerity like sunlight warming my scales. Vince wasn't upset. If anything, he was happy, flattered even, that I wanted him. Though shock underlay everything. It was like he couldn't believe how much I craved him, which was ridiculous. He was perfect for me.

Trailing my fingers over his back, I said, "Thank you."

"No, thank you."

Unable to help myself, I said, "I'm yours, Vince."

He paused. "What do you mean by that?"

Was he questioning whether I claimed him as my mate or not? Perhaps one of my brothers had already spoken to him, even though I hadn't told them anything. "You asked me to be yours as long as you're here, and I am," I replied. It wasn't the whole truth, but I didn't want to overwhelm him.

"And I'm yours."

My soul pounded. Stars above, I wished with every fragment of my being that was true.

Chapter 32

I'M GLAD MINDY GOT HIS WAY.

Vince

I stepped off the shuttle, holding Don's hand, my mouth hanging open. Mindy, or rather Don, had gotten his way, and we'd traveled to Inogga on a pointless mission that barely justified the trip. Seth had complained—if his quiet, almost non-existent frustration could be called complaining—about the departure from our route, but Mindy had begged him not to say anything, then I'd mentioned how much Don wanted this. Seth, being a truly nice person, relented. That and I was pretty sure Kal had convinced him the hot springs would be fun.

But fuck Kal. It was me and Mindy in the end, or so I was choosing to believe.

Snow was everywhere, and it was bitterly cold outside of the shuttle, but a clear path stretched from the landing pad to what looked like the mouth of a cave. We'd landed near where there was supposedly a resort on the side of a towering mountain with a jagged peak. The opening to the cave was decorated with twisted ropes that stretched across it; each rope had a small square of red cloth that fluttered in the light breeze. Massive braziers sat on either side of the entrance, welcoming us. Coniferous-looking trees, though a deep orange, were scattered around the snowy peak.

Some of the crew had been sent to gather the samples before taking their shore leave, and the rest would be spread out all over the small planet. Several hot springs adorned the planet's surface, some near boiling and others at more bearable temperatures.

Don had chosen this resort for the temperature of the springs as well as the seclusion. Selfishly, I wanted him to have picked the isolation so he wouldn't be distracted from me, but it wasn't that simple. Here, security was easier to arrange for us, the humans who'd decided to come to the surface, as well as easy access to a shuttle port.

A light breeze flared, and the crisp air sent a shudder down my spine while turning my breath into a cloud. A slight sulfur tinge wrinkled my nose; I supposed it was from the hot springs that were somewhere.

"Do you like it?" Don asked, tail twitching and voice apprehensive.

Shouldn't he know? I'd gotten better at evading his inner fire when I wanted to hide something, but I hadn't tried to keep this from him. I wiggled in front of him, slinging my arms around him, uncaring about the people beside us. "I love it."

The corner of his lips tugged up, giving me the crooked smile I adored. If we were alone, it would've been a full-blown thing; however, it made my pulse leap. His tail coiled around my calf and drew me even closer. "I pleased you."

"Yeah. You pleased me." Something nameless and soft curled in my chest as I stared into his burning green eyes.

Mindy had his arms around Teddy, bouncing a bit. "Do you love it? Isn't it perfect?" he asked in garbled English. "Didn't I promise to bring you to a hot spring?"

In true Teddy fashion, he grunted.

Mindy frowned, and I had to fight a smile. Teddy didn't talk a lot, but I imagined, much like Don, he was more expressive when they were alone.

Caleb and Fyn wasted no time, rushing off toward the trees while Caleb went on and on about how amazing everything was. Seth stepped out shivering while Kal tried to ply him with more layers, even though Seth already resembled an overstuffed ravioli, growling at the cold temperature.

Don cupped my cheek, thumb running over it and creating tingles that shot downward. His voice was deep with need as he asked, "Do you wish to see our quarters?"

I grinned. "Yep."

He took my hand and headed inside.

Dontilvynsan

My mate was stretched out on the soft white furs beside me. The room was a rough-rock cave that would've been gloomy if not for the fake torches lining the walls. I'd requested more light, knowing Vince couldn't handle the dark, and the staff had complied. The cave was a single open space with a generous fireplace, a massive stone tub along with necessities, and a pile of furs.

I kissed Vince's back, and he groaned. My hair tickled his skin as I moved down his spine, nibbling and licking as I went. I was careful not to put any weight on him. Vince did well enough with me touching and kissing him as long as he didn't feel trapped or covered. Nonetheless, I kept careful watch on his thoughts and emotions. At the slightest discomfort, I would stop.

We'd fucked, barely getting into the room before Vince had launched at me. He'd been on top as he rubbed my cock against his. It had been quick and frantic, filled with desperation, but satisfying.

Moving to his side, I trailed my lips over his skin, relishing the smooth texture.

He rolled, disrupting my worship, and wrapped his arms around me. I snuggled close, gripping his back. Time was running short. I couldn't imagine him not being by my side, which seemed ridiculous—I hadn't known of his existence only a few months ago. Yet it was true. Vince had become completely integral to my happiness and my life.

"Sweetheart," Vince said, running his fingers through my hair.

I rubbed my forehead on his chest. My own scent had started to mingle heavily with Vince's, but I needed more. I needed to reassure my instincts that Vince was mine, even though logically I knew it wasn't true.

"What's wrong?" he asked, fingers massaging my scalp.

I groaned, pressing closer. Vince continued his ministrations, not saying anything, but his question hung in the air. Kissing his chest before I rested my chin on him to meet his gaze. Vince's fingers skittered over my face, making my eyes close.

"What?" Vince asked again.

Unable to help myself, I kissed him. "We're going to be home soon."

"I know," he said, fingers never stopping as they traced my features. "But it will be a while before the first ship heads to Earth. Months, at least, I imagine."

"Yes, but I won't be able to stay planetside with you."

He stilled. "What?"

"I'll have to leave after a week, maybe two if I'm lucky."

"Why?" Vince gripped my hair more tightly than usual—or than was comfortable—but I didn't mind, because I sensed his panic. I nuzzled him, and he relaxed his hold with an unspoken apology. I kissed his chest, so he knew I wasn't upset.

"I have already been away from my duties for longer than usual. I have to return to them."

Fear. Panic. Anger. Possessive need. They all flashed through Vince, followed by his utter unwillingness to let me go. I smiled, pressing my forehead against his sternum. Vince didn't want me as I did him, but he did care about me.

"No. I don't want you to."

I kissed his chest again, not able to get enough of him. "I don't have a choice, my Vince. If I could pick, I would choose to remain by your side, but I cannot. Nor do I wish to give up my commission."

"I would never ask you to."

"I know."

"I just—" He broke off with a loud breath.

I didn't press, just observed his emotions swirl and change as his thoughts raced, making it difficult for me to comprehend what was going on within his mind.

Vince closed his eyes. "I want more time."

Part of me selfishly wanted to insist he stay, but I understood why Vince didn't want to. Though, at the same time, I wanted him to remain with me. I needed him to choose me.

Not saying anything, I rested my cheek on his chest, listening to his heart pound. The thump was so different from the thrum of a drakcol's soul, but I loved it. Vince ran his fingers through my hair as we lay next to the crackling fire, simply existing with each other.

Chapter 33

HOT SPRINGS.

Vince

I leaned against the pure white side of the hot spring, swallowing my moans. The hot springs were as glorious as I'd been led to believe. There were private ones, public ones, inside ones, outside ones, and all were fucking lovely. I was in an outside public spring. The snow covered the ground, though the resort had cleared a path leading to the pools, flat gray stepping stones leading the way to the edge. The water was robin's egg blue and perfectly warm, though it did have a sulfur odor that you couldn't get away from.

From the flush on Teddy's cheeks last night, it was safe to say Mindy had gotten the fuck he'd wanted. I'd decided to rent a private hot spring for me and Don.

But it was only humans this morning. Seth had been hard to convince to come and bathe with us, but he'd finally agreed. Caleb leaned back against the edge, arms spread. Camden, Pierce, Shannon, and Roman were chatting. Brad and Teddy grunted in their usual conversational tone. The other humans moved around the pool in groups, chatting and laughing.

All the hot springs were mixed gender and everyone was sans clothes. At first, I'd thought it might be odd, but Pierce had just raced in, boobs bouncing in a way that had to be uncomfortable. After that, everyone else hadn't cared. Even shy Seth had walked in without covering himself, though he'd been bright red.

I moved around the pool until I was next to Seth, who was in the water up to his neck, trying to hide most likely. I asked, "Glad you came?"

"Yes, though Kal threatened to challenge you or anyone who stared at me too long."

I burst into laughter, and Seth followed suit. Seth could protect himself, something I was supremely glad for, but Kal was overprotective to the extreme.

My head went back, resting on the lip of the spring. "Don's leaving."

"What?" Seth asked, water splashing as he sat up straight. "You two are breaking up? I don't believe it."

I gripped the thin chains around my neck. I never took off the two necklaces he'd given me. Not ever. "We're not breaking up. We're not together."

"That's a fucking lie. You're basically living together."

I hadn't slept in my apartment or even been back since I'd gotten drunk, except to get all my clothes and stuff. It felt natural to sleep in Don's room, whether we were going to fuck or not. I said, "That's not what I was talking about, anyway."

"Then what did you mean?"

"He's going to leave shortly after we get back to the Drakcon home world. He has responsibilities."

Seth nodded, chewing on his bottom lip. "That makes sense."

A growl started in the back of my throat. "It might make sense, but I don't like it. I thought he would stay until I left."

"Until you leave? So is this about Don, or about you being upset that he's not catering to you?"

I frowned, but Seth didn't relent, staring directly at me. I was a selfish bastard. I knew it. Seth knew it. Hell, everyone but Don knew it. More like he refused to accept it.

"Both, I guess," I confessed. "I want him to stay because I like him and I don't want him to leave. I want more time."

"How much time?"

Forever, I thought, and my heart thudded. I wanted forever, but I was terrified of staying, because the trauma was still there. Nightmares continued to plague me almost every night. The thought of people touching me made me feel sick, let alone the panic that ensued when someone grabbed me. I couldn't even think about Don fucking me without a cold sweat. Everything that had happened remained, and I didn't want it to.

"You can't ask him to stay or give up his duty when you can't even answer that question, Vinnie," Seth said gently. "Don cares about you."

"I know."

He wanted me to stay. He wanted me for the rest of his life, which shocked me. Who would want me? Don knew me, my baggage, my fears, and he desired me, and more than that, cared about me. I had a hard time believing that.

"I want to ask you a question," Seth said, voice careful. "If you don't want to answer or this is totally inappropriate, tell me."

I frowned. Seth usually never asked hard questions. Though looking at his red face, he wasn't exactly comfortable. I nodded. "Ask away."

Seth played with the water, eyes averted.

I nudged him. "It's really fine."

With a deep breath, he asked in such a quiet voice that I had to lean toward him to hear, "Is your wanting to leave about forgetting everything, or about not wanting to commit to Don?"

Angry words battled to escape, but I swallowed them, not wanting to hurt Seth. I said, tone rough, "Of course this is about forgetting. I don't expect you to understand."

His shoulders hunched. "I don't, exactly. I've never been hurt like that. But I do know you. You never committed to anyone in the past. When relationships got too serious, you'd run. I just want to make sure that's not what's happening." Seth glanced at me. "I'm pretty sure Don wants to remain with you."

There was some truth to what Seth had said. In the past, I'd never been in a long-term relationship, but that was because I'd been in love with Seth. Now, that wasn't the issue.

If I did stay, it didn't mean I had to remain in a relationship with Don. I scoffed. I would. I couldn't imagine not being with him or allowing anyone else to touch him. Don was mine. I recognized how unhealthy and possessive I was, but it didn't change my feelings. If

I stayed, Don and I would be a couple; we would become mates—I had no doubt about that.

Fear coiled in my gut at the mere thought of being Don's mate. The permanence. I would never be able to escape, not even if he got tired of dealing with my past or all the baggage that came with me. And what if some soulmate showed up one day, but we were already mated? Everyone would be hurt.

A hand gently grabbed mine, and I sighed.

"You don't have to answer," Seth said. "If you would think about it?"

"I will," I whispered.

———

After a long day of wandering the snowy woods, it was nice to relax in a private hot spring with Don. I was straddling his lap, head on his shoulder. He traced his fingers up and down my spine as we simply cuddled. We'd barely even spoken when we'd climbed in. I'd merely settled on his lap and snuggled close.

My thoughts were blissfully empty. The water was bone-melting hot, hella relaxing, but I wouldn't be able to stay for *that* long. However, it was nice, and Don was comfortable. I was safe, utterly safe. Don would never let anyone hurt me.

He kissed the top of my head, probably in response to my thoughts, but he didn't speak.

I nuzzled his shoulder, kissing the joint, before going back to resting.

"Did you have a pleasant day?" Don asked after a moment.

Memories of the day whirled before my eyes. Seth knocking Kal into a snow drift. Fyn and Caleb disappearing when they found a cave with glowing moss. Mindy retelling stories from the planet he and Teddy had crash landed on. Don holding my hand. He'd stayed by my side for the whole of the day. No matter what we'd done, he was there.

"I did," I said with a smile, kissing him again. I laved my tongue over his smooth scales, unable to help myself. He tasted of salt and sulfur, but not unpleasantly so.

"Don't," Don said, and I flinched at the rejection. He caught my chin and ran his nose along mine. "I liked it, my Vince, but too much, and you will get sick from the water. It's not meant to be consumed."

Worrywart, I thought.

Don grunted, but his fingers returned to my back, brushing over my skin.

Either he'd understood what I said, or, more likely, he'd gotten the context from my thoughts.

He skated over the knobs on my spine. "You're finally gaining weight."

It had gotten easier to eat. I refused to drink those slurries Klars recommended, but I was eating all three of my daily meals with Don. And I often had snacks as well when I was hanging out with Teddy and his demon pet or Seth and his cat, who I hadn't caught more than a glimpse of.

"Yep, though, just so you know, humans don't like to discuss weight."

"I apologize."

I nipped him, careful to keep the pressure soft. "It's fine, Sweetheart. I don't mind, but some do. It's better not to talk about it."

"I shall refrain in the future."

"You can with me, if you want." I looked at him. "I know you like that you can't see all my bones anymore. Though I wasn't nearly as bad as Teddy. He used to give me his food, which is why he was so much thinner than I was."

His thumb rubbed over my bottom lip. "I don't care how you look, Vince. I care about you being healthy."

My Don worried about everything. I snuggled against him, warm. Part of me wanted to initiate something. Frotting would be hot, in the best way, but another part of me worried someone might see us. I wasn't embarrassed about my attraction to Don or the fact we fucked. I didn't want to chance anyone seeing us, even though this was supposedly a private space. Every one of Don's intimate expressions and noises belonged to me; I didn't want to share them.

Don growled, kissing the top of my head.

I chuckled. My possessiveness might be toxic by human standards, but Don seemed to like it.

"I do," he said in a gravelly voice. "I need it."

"Me too," I whispered. My eyes ran over his strong features as my fingers followed the same path. Don bit my forefinger when it brushed his lips. Helpless but to confess it, I said, "You are so beautiful."

He squeaked. An honest-to-god squeak. I laughed, loving that sound.

"You are, Dontilvynsan," I said, using his full name. I rarely said it, but I did love how it rolled off my tongue. Seth might struggle with the long names, but I didn't, and Don's was lovely. "So beautiful. I've never seen anyone as pretty as you."

His breathing turned harsh, and he looked away.

He was embarrassed. Don hadn't been complimented enough in his lifetime, and I aimed to change that. Everything I said was the truth, and he deserved to hear it.

"But you're more than beautiful," I said, kissing his neck. "You're kind, smart, funny, caring, and so giving. You are lovely inside and out, Sweetheart. I've never met someone like you."

Swallowing, Don lifted his hand, and I placed it against my cheek. A wave of embarrassment crashed over me. My compliments were overwhelming him, but beneath the discomfort and unfamiliarity was happiness.

I kissed his palm. "Do not doubt your worth. You are more than your gift and what you do for people. You're unbelievably you, and that alone makes you special."

"Thank you," he whispered.

"No thanks needed. It's nothing but the truth."

Don trembled, and I knew it was enough right now. He couldn't handle anymore. I went up on my knees and claimed his lips. He groaned, and I pillaged his mouth, claiming him softly but no less thoroughly or possessively. Grabbing his free hand, I placed it on my ass. I had a single moment of fear before it faded.

His fingers wandered over the round globe of my ass cheek but didn't really go anywhere.

"Room," I whispered. "I want to go to our room."

With one last kiss on my lips, Don stood and helped me out of the hot spring.

Chapter 34

ONE AT LAST.

Dontilvynsan

Our mouths crashed together the instant we entered our room. I directed Vince toward the furs, and he moaned against my mouth. He frantically shoved my robe off before yanking his own off. His hands wrapped around me, rubbing on my sides.

I growled, and my cock leaped, swelling with my burgeoning desire. Vince ripped his lips from mine, and I moaned, trying to extend the kiss. He evaded me and shoved me toward the furs. I complied, settling on my back. My wings sprawled out beneath me and my tail thrashed.

He stared at my erect cock, leaking pre-seed. I needed my mate. "Vince."

He bit his lip, and thoughts flashed through his mind. I frowned, only catching the thought of me on my hands and knees and the overwhelming feeling of nervousness. Vince wanted to ask me something, but he was unsure of how I would respond.

"Vince, what is it?"

"I want to fuck you."

My breath left my lungs, and my soul raced. "I very much want that."

Kneeling between my legs, he reached for my hand. I gave it to him as well as curling my tail around his ankle.

"I want you to be on your hands and knees while I fuck you from behind," he said. I could feel the desire for my body and his worry I would say no or be offended by him simply asking. Vince continued before I could even say anything, "I want to be in you, but I can't do it face to face. I'm worried it will trigger me."

I frowned. He didn't want to see me?

Feeling me through the connection I'd established, Vince shook his head, then explained, "I want to see you, Don. I won't be thinking about anyone else. I'm more nervous about the amount of skin to scales ratio." He swallowed. "Do you even bottom?"

"I'm versatile." In many ways, I preferred to bottom. I rarely got the opportunity.

"Do you want me to fuck you?"

"More than anything."

Vince grinned, kissing my palm. We wouldn't be able to stay connected like this, sharing every emotion and sensation, but it didn't matter.

He sent me the scenario he wanted to try, and I agreed.

"On your hands and knees," Vince ordered, voice rough.

I pulled my hand, reluctantly, from his cheek and rolled over. Vince groaned; he was pleased at the sight of my firm ass on display for him. My tail flicked in excitement. I forced my wings to retract, though. I wouldn't risk injuring Vince with my sharp talons.

Vince grabbed my tail, his touch exceedingly soft. I whimpered. My tail had always been incredibly sensitive, and I loved it being played with. Thankfully, Vince liked to touch it as much as I loved him to.

He ran his fingers over the appendage, his grasp whisper soft. My breath turned harsh, and Vince kept stroking my tail, pumping it like he would if it was my cock. Pre-seed leaked out of my slit at the sensations running up my spine, splattering the furs beneath me.

Patiently, Vince kissed the tip of my tail and gently brushed his lips up the length, taking his time. His wet tongue swiped at the base, and I moaned, trying to keep the volume down.

"I want to hear you," Vince muttered, tongue licking the sensitive scales where my tail connected to my spine. "Your every noise is mine."

I cried out, and feral joy ripped through Vince.

"More," he demanded. "Don't silence yourself, Sweetheart." Vince kissed one of my butt cheeks. "I don't know if someone's told you they didn't like your noise, but fuck them. I love all of it, Don."

More than one person had told me my noises were off-putting, so I tried to remain as quiet as possible when I had sex. Vince, though, was different. He was mine, and I was his.

Not restraining myself, I let the animalistic cries tear out of my throat. With each one, I felt Vince's enjoyment and hot arousal.

His hands slid up and down my thighs, teasing the sensitive scales. His fingers moved up, and his thumbs spread my cheeks apart, and Vince moaned. "God, even your hole is beautiful."

I jerked at the compliment, my cock releasing a spurt of pre-seed.

Vince chuckled, his breath washing over my entrance, making it twitch. "You like me telling you how pretty you are, don't you?"

"Yes." I loved it.

Puncturing each word with a kiss on my hole, he whispered, "You are so fucking gorgeous, Dontilvynsan."

Moans ripped out of my throat. I bowed my head and arched my back, presenting my butt to him.

"Good boy. You are such a good boy for me," Vince said against me right before he swiped his silky tongue over my waiting hole.

"*Nngh*," I whined.

"Such a good boy."

I whimpered.

Vince held me tight, keeping me in place, but not hard enough to cause even a twinge of pain. He was always so careful with me. With every gentle swipe, he stole my thoughts and made me writhe. He didn't relent, kissing, nibbling, and sucking on my entrance.

The tip of his tongue slid into my loosened hole, and I cried out, "My Vince."

He fucked me with his tongue as his thumbs kept me wide open for him.

I'd never had anyone do this for me, and the pleasure was mind-numbing as his tongue relentlessly worked on me. I could not stop the moans or pleas for more escaping out of my throat. My pleasure was growing with every passing second, making my control slip.

Vince suddenly growled low in his chest. "I feel you," he whispered. "I feel you."

Unable to respond, because he attacked me with new vigor, I simply moaned. I didn't bother to try and control my pleasure as Vince kept tongue-fucking my hole while whispering how good I was for him. My balls were hugging the base of my shaft, and pre-seed continuously leaked from the tip.

Eventually, he pulled back, and I whimpered, wiggling my butt. I wanted him to return. Vince kissed my back. "Soon, Sweetheart," he said, clearly feeling my desires. He grabbed the lube from where we'd tossed it earlier and put some on his fingers before he speared my entrance.

I groaned at the invasion, loving the stretch.

Vince slid his lubed finger in and out of my hole before adding a second, then third finger. I was groaning so loud I worried that someone would hear, but at the same time, I couldn't care less. He was my mate, and he was inside of me, claiming me with his talented fingers.

"Your ass is swallowing my fingers so good."

I cried out.

"Good boy. Louder for me."

I was near sobbing from the warm pleasure.

He laughed, nipping my butt.

My tail thrashed, and Vince froze as fear shot through him. A hazy memory of an alien with a spiked tail above him played through his thoughts. I stilled, panting. I tried to control my pleasure with deep breaths to help calm Vince if he needed it.

"We can stop," I said. My breath was equally harsh, but mine was from pleasure, while his was from fear.

"No. I want this. I want you."

"I know, Vince, and you have me. We have time."

His fingers slid out from my hole, and he lay over my back, nuzzling my spine. He was so small against me, but I felt so safe with him like this. Vince took deep breaths, and I didn't move. He would tell me what he needed if he needed anything more than being present from me.

"I want to continue," Vince whispered.

"Then fuck me."

Vince chuckled. He kissed my back. "I want your lovely tail to wrap around your cock."

I swallowed and my cock bucked at the thought. "Slick it up for me, please."

"Such a polite boy, aren't you?" Vince asked, kissing down my back, and I whimpered. He rubbed lube over my tail, then kissed the base near my spine. "Jerk yourself."

My tail coiled around my own cock, and I cried at the warmth. I milked it, my butt wiggling.

Vince pressed more kisses to my back. "I love seeing you like this, needy, desperate. You deserve to feel good, Sweetheart."

"You make me feel good," I replied.

"I will."

His words sent a jolt down my spine.

I felt the head of Vince's cock press against me, and I bore down; he slid in with little trouble. I moaned at the stretch, at him inside of me. I was full. Perfectly, and wonderfully filled by my mate.

"Vince," I cried.

He gripped my hips, panting. "Fuck, Don. You are so warm and tight. Your ass took me so well. It's like you were made to be fucked with my cock." Vince pulled out, then snapped his hips back into me.

"I was. Yours," I cried out.

"Mine," he growled, pounding into me. "You're my good boy, and no one else's."

I couldn't respond, because Vince set up a quick pace as he rutted into me. With every smack of his hips, he tagged that cluster of nerves, making pleasure swell. Between that and my own tail jerking me, I was edging closer to my release faster than ever.

"I want to hear you come," Vince said. "I need it, Sweetheart." He continued to fuck me, nice and fast. I whimpered. He bent over me as far as he could, kissing my spine.

"Vince. My Vince."

"Come, Don."

With a loud shout, my release rushed over me. My hole clenched around him as seed erupted from the tip of my cock, spilling over my tail and onto the furs. Buzzing filled my ears with the pleasure flooding me.

Vince pounded my ass a couple more times before he cried out, "Don."

His cock jerked inside of me, filling me with his warm seed and coating my insides. I whined at the sensation, and Vince grunted face against my back, his breath swirling over my scales.

Slowly, he pulled out of me, and I wanted to ask him to stay inside of me, but I didn't want to bother him or force him to do something that he didn't want. Besides, he would never be able to stay inside me for as long as I wanted. I rolled to my side and reached for Vince, shaking. I needed him against me after such a strong release. He didn't deny me, cuddling close.

Cupping my cheeks, Vince said, "God, your release was so beautiful."

Heat filled me.

His thumbs brushed my cheekbones, and Vince placed a gentle kiss on my lips. "Never keep your noises from me, Don. I love hearing them, and you shouldn't have to worry about what you sound like when we're fucking."

"Thank you."

Vince curled close, head tucked under my chin. His fingers ran over my chest as his breath began to slow. In a sleep laced voice, he said, "We should get cleaned up."

His seed was leaking out of my hole, and I quite liked the sensation. "Later."

"It'll be a *bitch* to clean your scales if my cum dries."

I frowned at the word "bitch." There were several meanings supplied by NAID from a mean woman to a female dog, which I had no idea what that was, but from his thoughts, I guessed he meant hard.

"Later. Sleep, Vince."

He grunted, holding me tight as waves of sleep dragged him away.

Only a few minutes later, my touchstone pinged. Serlotminden's voice called my name. "Yes?" I answered in a low voice to not wake Vince.

"I assume your two had a great fuck," my younger brother said.

"What?" I asked. How had he known?

Serlotminden laughed. "Did you forget you share your strong feelings with us sometimes?"

Embarrassment washed through me. "No, I didn't forget. My apologies."

"Don't worry about it," he said. "I got really turned on, and me and Bartholomew had a lovely time. Since Zoltilvoxfyn and Kalvoxrencol are not answering my pings, I'm going to guess they're still fucking."

I held Vince close, running my hand over his arm to soothe my raging embarrassment. I'd never felt this strongly about someone before, so I'd never worried about my brothers catching my strong arousal. But between my love for Vince and my brothers close proximity, it had only been a matter of time.

"Captain, you still there?" Serlotminden asked.

"Yes, Speedy."

"I wanted to make sure you're alright," he said.

I wasn't. If Vince chose to go home, I wouldn't survive. Yes, he would still be alive, but the separation would be torture, and it would kill me in the end. Forcing calm into my voice, I said, "Vince fucked me. It was our first time having penetrative sex."

"Good for you," he said. "I'm assuming you two had fun."

"We did." I kissed Vince's head.

"I'm happy for you two."

"Me too, Speedy. I've never been this happy before." Why I was telling this all to Serlotminden was a mystery, but not seeing him or sensing his thoughts was making it easier.

"I hope he stays."

I kissed Vince again, breathing in his scent, which was laced with the bitter and sweet notes of our spend and sweat. "I do as well."

Chapter 35

PARADISE.

Dontilvynsan

My hands were braced on the edge of the tub as Vince scrubbed me clean. I swallowed, trying to control my cock, which wanted to harden. Sex wasn't on his mind, not even close. Vince seemed to take almost an indescribable amount of joy from simply cleaning me, caring for me, loving on me. His lathered hands scrubbed at my scales between my butt cheeks and my inner thighs. True to his word, cleaning his seed from last night off my scales was proving difficult, but he didn't care.

Vince washed me thoroughly and relaxed thoughts floated through his head. The act of caring for me pleased him greatly, and it made tears burn my eyes. He didn't expect sex, he didn't expect repayment, and all he wanted was to take care of me. I didn't understand it.

"I have you," Vince whispered, placing a kiss on my back.

"How did you know?" I hadn't made a noise to alert him to my sweeping emotions.

Vince kissed me again. "Letting other people take care of you can be hard, Don, but I want to. Rely on me. I've spent every moment of this journey leaning on you, but I want to be there for you too."

I didn't know why letting someone take care of me was so difficult, but it was. I'd spent my life taking care of others—my younger brothers, my fellow soldiers, and now my mate. It seemed almost wrong to allow Vince to care for me when I could be caring for him.

"Let me wash you," I said, changing the subject.

He kissed my back. "No."

"Vince," I said, swallowing as tension filled my muscles.

With a long breath, he rubbed his face against my lower back, hands finally stilling. "Sweetheart, I want to take care of you. Please let me. I need this."

I could feel his desperation to care for me. It was hard, though. But I couldn't deny my mate something he required, and deep down, I was certain I needed this more than he did.

"Alright."

With another gentle kiss, he continued his ministrations. Vince's every touch was soft as he scrubbed me clean, no speck left unwashed. He even made me sit so he could wash my hair. His fingers rubbed the products through the long strands, then massaged my scalp while he hummed a light tune. It didn't have a true melody, but I joined him, humming along, and soon we found a rhythm all our own—one I would never forget.

Unable to stop it, my cock lifted, poking out of the water. Beads of pre-seed slid out of the slit as Vince massaged my scalp. I swallowed a needy groan. I wanted him to fuck me again. Because of my large size, I wasn't often on the bottom or snuggled or treated gently, all of which I craved. Vince easily and happily met those needs.

My tail coiling around Vince's wrist, I scoured his thoughts—sex wasn't on his mind. Loving on me was.

"Close your eyes, Sweetheart," Vince said right before I heard metal scraping on stone. He had to be grabbing the detachable nozzle on the side of the tub. I complied, and warm water rushed over my hair as Vince washed the cleanser off. I only opened my eyes when I heard the metal of the nozzle hit the side of the tub once again.

The water sloshed over the sides as Vince climbed around me. I averted my gaze when he moved directly in front of me—my needy cock was obvious.

Soft fingers grabbed my chin, and Vince made me look at him. He kissed me, then muttered against my lips, "Did you need me to take care of that?"

"If you want."

Vince frowned, and I blinked at the frustration that rushed through his mind. "Don," he said, "what do you want? I want to take care of you. If you want sex, tell me. I might not always say yes, just like you don't have to when I ask, but you sure as hell can ask. I want you to."

"I want to have sex," I said, not sure why the words were hard. Vince was mine. I loved him. He cared about me. He wouldn't be upset if I asked, but I couldn't stop the tension forming.

"So do I," Vince replied, kissing me. He pulled back after the barest moment, eyebrows pulled together. He reached for my hand, bringing it to my cheek. "Sweetheart, why are you so tense?"

I didn't want to share my feelings with him. I wasn't in control. Vince frowned but didn't press when I refused to make the connection between us.

"What's going on?" His eyes widened. "Did a past partner get mad at you for asking or expressing what you needed?"

Rage, pure and unfettered, flowed through Vince. The potency as well as his desire to murder whoever hurt me made me blink.

"No, my Vince," I replied, drawing him onto my lap. We both ignored my aching cock as he snuggled against me, holding me securely in his embrace. I ran my fingers through his short hair, tugging on the black strands, and tried to organize my thoughts.

"I've never been in a long-term relationship, or in one even like this," I said carefully. Vince and I had never defined exactly what *this* was. "No one hurt me as people hurt you, so I feel almost bad even discussing this."

Vince frowned. "This isn't the pity *olympics*. Just because I had something horrible happen to me doesn't invalidate what happened to you." He pressed a hard kiss to my collar bone. "I want to know."

"Olympics" was a foreign word and NAID supplied: competition and events. I couldn't help but wonder if humans competed for who had the worst trauma. That seemed quite horrific in my mind, but they did have entertainment programs about murder. As a whole, humans were odd.

I continued to stroke Vince, more for my own comfort than his. The feel of his silky skin beneath my scales calmed me. "Many of my past partners were unkind at times."

"Why?"

"My gift. They expected more."

He stared at me, confusion clear in his thoughts.

I brushed his bottom lip. "They expected me to be the best lover, which I was not."

He kissed the pad of my thumb. "You're the best lover I've ever had, by far."

I preened at the compliment while, at the same time, doubt surged. Vince was being completely honest, but I couldn't help but think he hadn't been with many people. Though I hardly wanted to contemplate who he'd fucked in the past. That would only anger me.

"Almost none of them were outright mean, but I sensed their frustration or disappointment. Some had told me I sounded odd or was too needy, so I tried to be quiet and not ask. I let them lead. No matter how many permissions we discussed, I kept being a lackluster lover. It got to the point I rarely accepted when people expressed an interesting in me fucking them, especially when most of the time I would rather someone fuck me."

Vince's wet arms came around my neck, and he went up on his knees to kiss my lips. His tongue invaded my mouth and his thoughts stabbed me. *They were wrong. You are perfect.* I moaned, hands moving tentatively to his butt. Vince didn't even slow and

fucked me with his tongue, claiming me with a resounding, *Mine.*
All mine.

Vince

I held Don's hand when we went down for breakfast, finally. We'd
stroked each other off in the tub after he'd told me a little about his
past sex partners. Even thinking about what they'd said to Don or
how they made him feel had hot lava pouring through my veins. I
wanted to find them and murder them.

Don kissed the top of my head, no doubt sensing my murderous
intentions. He was by far the better half of this couple, but I didn't
fucking care. I was fine with being the asshole if it meant keeping
Don's emotions safe from selfish pricks.

We weren't the only ones late. Fyn and Caleb were just sitting
down as we entered the private dining room. Kal was fussing over
a bright red Seth, and Mindy was kissing Teddy, who didn't seem to
care about the audience. Everyone looked oddly happy.

"Did something happen?" I asked Don in a low voice.

His tail twitched, and his eyes purposefully moved away from me.
He cleared his throat. "We all had a good night."

What the fuck did that mean? I mean, it was probably the
obvious—we were all on a vacation of sorts and had fucked our
partners. But a single glance at Don, who seemed oddly tense, had
me questioning exactly what he meant.

He refused to look at me, and I felt tension in the hand I held, so I let it go. It didn't matter. Everyone was in a good mood, which meant we were all having fun.

I took a seat around the low wooden table. The floor was stone and freezing under my ass—the thin cushion did nothing to keep the chill away. Fake torches, like in our room, lined the walls. On the wall to the right of the entrance was a waterfall that let off steam into the pool that surrounded the eating area. The water put enough moisture in the room that all of the drakcol had beads of moisture gathering on their scales.

Don made a plate for me—grain, berries, and some type of bright red meat. I shot him a smile, and he dipped his head in what I knew was embarrassment. His tail coiled around my wrist, and I rubbed the tip instinctively, making his breath increase. I stopped because he didn't like me to touch his tail when other people were present and sex wasn't an option.

He kissed my temple, no doubt from my thoughts, and I beamed.

"I'm fine, Kal," Seth said, drawing my attention away from Don. Kal was frowning at Seth, who readjusted once again, and began to fuss over him, straightening his clothes and adding more food to his plate. Seth caught Kal's hands, giving him a soft smile.

Dontilvynsan's tail tightened around my wrist, but I thought, *I'm fine, Sweetheart*. I wasn't jealous of Kal and Seth anymore, at least not how Don thought. I was jealous of their relationship. I wanted the same thing with Don, though at the same time, it freaked me out.

His tail flicked the back of my hand, soothing the stress out of my muscles. I leaned against Don's shoulder and nibbled on the strange meat. It wasn't cooked. The flesh was firm and tasted salty and fresh like fish. I put it down. I wasn't a fan of raw fish, especially for breakfast, but the berries and grain were tasty.

Fyn was feeding bits of food to Caleb across the table from us, and Serlotminden and Teddy hadn't stopped making out yet. Kal continued to fuss over Seth, who would shift every few seconds—like his ass was sore.

I chuckled, catching Seth's gaze, and he flushed clear to the roots of his hair. Yeah, they'd had a good night. They'd all had a good night. My forehead creased as I recalled feeling Don's heightened emotions when we'd fucked.

His head dipped and his hands curled into fists.

"Sweetheart," I said in a lowered voice. "It's fine. I don't care."

Don had lost control last night. He'd told me once that his emotions sometimes spilled over to those closest to him, and no one was closer to him than his brothers, except possibly me, if I allowed myself that arrogant thought. I almost laughed. Of course I allowed it. Hell, I reveled in it because I wanted that thought to be true. I wanted to be closer to Don than anyone else in this entire universe, even his brothers.

He was mine.

Don nuzzled my temple. "Just yours."

"So," I said, "what are we doing today?"

"I think me and Kal are going to hang around the cave, lodge, resort, thing, here," Seth muttered, flushed.

"Seth is very tired," Kal added, which made the red in Seth's cheeks deepen.

I chuckled, lifting my eyebrows. "Oh, I bet. So very *very* tired."

Seth squeaked, and I laughed, wrapping an arm around Don to squeeze him to make sure he was joining into the fun.

"Everyone seems... tired," Don added, earning a laugh from each of his brothers.

Caleb piped up, "Me and Sunshine are going to explore the other cave system that we found yesterday. There's so much glowing moss. Several varieties. Fyn thinks it can be spliced into the moss that covers most ship floors, which means it would glow if there were power outages."

"Impressive," Teddy said.

Caleb beamed, hugging his mate, who grunted and wiggled in the no doubt too-strong hold. "My Sunshine is the smartest person."

Serlotminden ran a hand through Teddy's extremely short curls. "That he is. Bartholomew and I are hiking to a secluded spring."

More fucking, it seemed.

I rested my chin on Don's bicep. "What do you want to do?"

"Spend the day with you."

I pressed my face into his arm to hide my smile, but nothing could hide the fierce joy burning through me at his words. Snuggling next to Don, watching my closest friends with their partners, and basking in the comfortable atmosphere was as close to paradise as I would ever get, and I wanted more.

Chapter 36

WHAT DID YOU JUST SAY?

vince

It had been a week since we left Inogga, but I was still basking in the warmth of the vacation. It had been six days and five nights of me and Don with very few distractions. We'd fucked, talked, and explored to our hearts' content.

Now, with my chin in my palm, I watched Don get dressed. He'd woken me up when he slid out from beneath me. I slept better when I was draped across him like a blanket, and he didn't mind. He pulled on his uniform, tugging his long hair out from beneath the collar. My eyes wandered over his broad form, lingering on his taut ass and swishing tail.

"Vince," Don groaned. "Please."

I smirked. My thoughts had started to wander to the pleasant memories of me fucking Don. We hadn't had sex face to face yet. I'd tried, but it unnerved me, which frustrated me. I wanted to watch his face as I pounded his ass, to see how he looked when he came. I needed it. I needed every aspect of Don, all of him.

Don gripped my chin, gently guiding me back so I lay on the bed. He carefully hovered over me, not covering or putting any weight on me. He pressed his lips to mine, and I moaned. My hands slid up his sides to his neck, feeling his earrings drag over the backs of them, to bury in his hair, not caring that I was mussing it. His scaled tongue slipped between my lips, and I opened for him, welcoming him. He kept the pace slow and the pressure soft, but every nibble and swipe made me harden and ache for him.

Panting, he pulled away to rest his forehead on mine. "I have to go, Vince."

"I know."

He rubbed his forehead on me, and I smiled, loving the thought of him claiming me. Don kissed my forehead, still holding my chin, then looked into my eyes and said, "We'll get there."

I knew he was referring to us fucking face to face. "I want to."

"And we will. Don't trouble yourself about it, my Vince."

I smiled. "Go to Command before I yank you into this bed and fuck you senseless."

"I want that."

I tugged on him, but he resisted.

"I *want* that, but I need to go."

"Fine. Lunch, though?"

"Yes." Don planted one more kiss on my lips before heading toward the door. "Please, don't distract me today."

"I'll try to be good."

When the door closed, I rolled over, hugging Don's pillow. I lazed in bed because I could, and why the hell not? I had nothing to do. Don's scent invaded my nose and made me groan, my cock hardening.

Unabashed, I kicked off my sweats and slid a hand down my body to my aching cock. I rubbed my thumb over the seeping slit, circling the crown to spread the liquid around. My thoughts went back to Don, his small smile, the loud moans he made beneath my hands, and the way he made me feel—safe, cared for.

I jerked my cock, groaning. "Don."

I pictured him below me, smiling, his long purple hair spreading over the pillow. My fingers slipped down to my balls, tugging on them a bit and making me moan, then went down lower to circle my rim. A sick feeling welled in my stomach. *This is my body*, I thought. I forced myself to continue touching and rubbing my entrance, but I couldn't. I didn't like it. I couldn't make myself do it. I just couldn't.

Moving away from my ass, I grabbed my balls and tugged on them. I groaned at the feel, playing with them as I pictured Don.

"Donny, Sweetheart," I moaned.

Gripping my cock, I pumped it from base to tip and screamed for Don. I sped up, stroking my shaft with desperation, until I erupted, splattering my hand and stomach.

Panting, I shivered. I wished Don was beside me and dragging me into his secure embrace, but he was working. My eyes flicked to his pillow, and I laid my hand on it. I wanted to fuck Don face to face, yes, but I also worried that wouldn't be enough, that he'd want to fuck me. I'd been getting better about him leaning over me, but the thought of him pressing into me made my pulse skitter.

I wasn't ready, but we were running out of time.

Soon we would be back on the drakcol homeworld, and Don would leave to wherever his orders took him. I wouldn't see him again before I left for Earth.

The thought made my heart clench and fear dance along my veins. I didn't want to leave Don, but I didn't want to stay—or at least I didn't think I did. It was all so confusing, and my opinion changed almost daily.

Frustrated, I got out of bed and headed to the shower for my first of the day. Flicking on the water, I stepped under the stream. Thank god the drakcol loved water. Many other species used subsonic showers that disinfected you and cleaned the dirt, but it wasn't the same. I scrubbed my hand through my short hair, tilting my face into the warm stream.

Everything was so mixed up inside. I had no idea what I did or didn't want. If I stayed, I'd have Don. He would be mine, and not just for now but forever. I swallowed as a tremor went down my spine. That thought delighted and terrified me.

Groaning, I rested my head against the rough rock. Was it the memories I was running from, or Don?

"Fuck," I growled. I was afraid I knew the answer, and it wasn't the one I actually wanted to admit.

Dontilvynsan

Vince was trying to send me to insanity. I'd just made it Command when he started, I assumed, to masturbate. I trusted him enough to know he wasn't fucking someone else. Besides, I'd left him needy because I was due on shift.

I sat on my stool at the front of Command, hand fisted on my thigh, and pretended to read my notes. The words were meaningless because I sensed Vince's pleasure as well as heard him call my name. Me. He was pleasuring himself and thinking of me.

My cock threatened to swell with the waves of pleasure rushing through me. Only a couple of weeks ago, I hadn't been able to feel Vince like I did now. We'd been growing closer, and the closer we got the more attuned I grew to him. He was my mate, my love, my soul, and my reason for breath. I wanted to be near him at all times, in any way possible.

A groan built in my throat as Vince's pleasure swelled, reaching his climax. I took a deep breath to calm myself. Hopefully, now sated, he wouldn't try and chase another release. Vince had a lengthier refractory period than I did, so I'd have a reprieve.

"Captain, are you well?" Bimwoxcol asked.

I faced my commander. "Yes."

Her eyes flicked to my fisted hand and my thrashing tail. "As you say."

I was not alright. I wanted to run to my quarters and curl around my mate. Even if he didn't want to fuck, I had the urge to smooth my hands over him until he was boneless beside me, sated and happy.

Refocusing, I flicked through my notes. The usual inquiries from Monqilcolnen and Hallonnixmin wondering if I'd informed our brothers about Vince and my attachment to him—I had not. My parents checking in. My superiors. I froze on a letter from the high commandant of the Drakcon Navy. Garqixren didn't often send me a note. I had only spoken to her once in my entire career—there had been no need to speak to her more than that.

When I quickly scanned the letter, the contents sent my soul pounding. I stood.

"Captain departing," Bimwoxcol called.

I waved my hand, not even paying attention to them. I was out the door, down the corridor, and in my quarters before I could even breathe. I didn't see Vince in the shared space and I tore into the bedroom, hearing the flowing water from the shower. Vince was in the middle of washing his hair.

My arms went around him, the water soaking my uniform.

Vince jolted. "Fuck, Sweetheart. You scared the shit out of me."

His spike of fear and pulse didn't even register in my senses in the wake of my own terror. I forced Vince around, trying to get as close to him as possible, and pressed into him until he hit the rough wall. I wasn't close enough. Vince. I needed more. So much more. I wanted to crawl inside of him and never separate.

"Don!" His voice finally broke through my fear when he yanked on my hair—the sharp pain enough to shock me. Vince was panting, shaking, and fear was flooding his mind.

I shook my head, backing away. I'd scared him. I. Me. I'd scared Vince.

He held onto me, not letting me move away. "Breathe."

I took a small breath, the water coursing down my cheeks like tears.

Vince slowly released my hair to cup my cheeks. "There we go." Low levels of fear tainted his thoughts, but he was calming as I was. He brushed his thumbs over my cheeks. "There you are, Sweetheart. Just breathe. I'm here. You're here. We keep each other safe."

I dropped my head to his shoulder, shaking. Vince ran his hand through my hair. He conjured the song we'd made back on Inogga together. The wordless tune slipped into me, and my thoughts followed along. The longer he hummed, the more I relaxed.

My Vince was soothing me with my own inner fire.

After a few minutes, he led me out of the shower and into the bedroom. Without a word, he undid my uniform, tossing it in the laundry chute, then he rubbed a towel over my hair. I could detect a slight tremor in his hands.

Grabbing one, I kissed his palm. "I'm sorry, my Vince. I didn't mean to."

"I know," he replied. "Was this because I jerked off?"

"No," I said, "though I did feel it." I kissed his palm again. "You seemed to enjoy yourself."

I earned a smile. "I did." Vince brushed his thumb over my lips. "I thought about you."

Even though I'd known that, his words made warmth flood my soul. I nuzzled his forehead, spreading my scent. Even that small claim helped settle me.

"What scared you?" Vince asked, stealing all the heat and comfort.

Slowly, keeping my eyes on his, I stepped closer to Vince until I was pressed against him. He wound his arms around my waist, holding me. The feel of his wet skin flush against my scales soothed something deep within me. My mate. I needed him. It scared me how much I did. I could hardly believe how important he had become in such a short amount of time, but he had and there was no arguing against it.

"I received a note from the commandant of the Drakcon Navy," I said.

"Oh?"

I burrowed my face in his neck. Time was running out for us, and one day soon the cool feel of him in my arms would be a distant memory unless Vince chose me.

"Sweetheart, talk to me." Vince held the back of my head, fisting my hair.

"She's ordering me back to the Immortal Planet. She wants me to drop you all off at the next Drakcon space station and leave. You will all stay there until the *Admiral Ven* can come get you."

"What?" Vince asked, thoughts spiraling so fast I couldn't catch a single one.

"Yes."

"How long?"

"Two days."

Vince wrapped his other arm around me, practically scaling me as he plastered himself against my chest. "No."

"I can't refuse, Vince," I replied in a broken voice.

I understood why Garqixren wanted me to return to the Immortal Planet. A portal had opened near it, and sensors indicated something had crashed onto the surface. The planet had moved further out of phase, not allowing us to get a true reading, but the navy wanted the planet guarded and studied. It was important—but so was Vince.

"No," Vince merely said again. Disbelief, anger, fear, possessive need, and a far stronger and fiery emotion filled him. If I was bold enough, I would call it love, but Vince had never thought, let alone said he loved me, nor had I to him.

Stroking his back, I continued, "I won't return before the *Admiral Ven* leaves for Earth. There's no way. The Immortal Planet is on the edge of our territory, and no one will relieve me so soon."

His grip tightened, almost painfully so. "No," Vince snapped. "No."

I didn't know if he could find another word in his shock, but I had nothing else to say. When Vince calmed, I'd ask him to choose me, but I had little hope that he would. Why would he choose me over his home and his desire to forget? The answer was: he wouldn't.

With Vince in my arms, I lay down, keeping my mate close. My duty could wait, my responsibilities could wait, everything could wait until I was sure my Vince didn't need me any longer.

Chapter 37

DECISIONS.

Vince

Dontilvynsan lay on the bed across from me. He'd fallen asleep well before I had. We'd spent the day together, regardless of his duties, which he really shouldn't have ignored. But he hadn't left, merely passed the responsibilities off. Of course I hadn't encouraged him to leave, even though I probably should have. I hadn't been able to let him go, though. I'd had to physically hold onto him, utterly terrified. The panic was so strong, even now, that I couldn't bear him out of my sight.

I ran a feather-light touch over his face, tracing the planes and edges. I loved the sharpness of his cheekbones, the length of his nose, the fullness of his lips, and the strength of his jaw. Don was perfect, like, completely perfect, and yet I was frightened of staying with him.

If I was honest with myself, I loved Don. It wasn't shocking or at all surprising. I apparently had a habit of falling in love with the worst person possible, though that wasn't fair. Don was sweet, kind, and perfect for me. He wasn't the problem—I was.

My fingers stopped on the corner of his lips where they would often quirk in amusement. No, Dontilvynsan wasn't the problem. He hadn't said he loved me, but he cared about me, deeply, and he wanted me for the rest of our lives. Me? I was a mess.

All I had was fear. Fear of the future. Fear that the memories would never abate. Fear that Don would get tired of me. Fear that some soulmate would show up for Don and make all of us miserable. Fear that I wasn't good enough for him. Fear that I was too broken to be whole again. Fear of everything.

I was so damn afraid, and I fucking hated it.

I wanted to choose hope. I wanted to choose love. I wanted to choose Dontilvynsan. But the thought made my pulse pound and sent tremors through me.

I was a fucking coward.

Closing my eyes against the tears, I tried to take control of my breathing so I didn't wake Don. He woke up at the slightest nightmare or shift in my emotions, but I'd been running high all day and he'd fallen asleep to me being terrified, so maybe he wouldn't.

Don stirred, reaching for me. "My Vince, are you having a nightmare?"

Sleep laced his voice and his movements were jerky. He wasn't quite cognizant yet. I shifted against him to press needy kisses to the underside of his jaw. My tongue traced the scales over his pulse point.

"Vince?"

I didn't respond, just continued to kiss his neck, laving my tongue over his scales. I slid up and nibbled his earlobe, teeth catching on the long earring. I tugged on it. Don took a sharp breath, but it wasn't from pain—drakcol ears were sensitive. I licked and bit my way up his ear until I reached the tip. I took it into my mouth and sucked—hard.

"Vince," Don cried, cupping my ass.

I needed him. Now. I needed to be inside him, to feel his hot channel squeezing me as desperate cries slipped out of his lips.

"Yes," he said, breathless. "Yes, Vince."

Securing the lube, I kissed my way down his chest, yanked his sleep pants off, and palmed his thick thighs apart. His cock bucked, hard and leaking. I fondled his heavy balls, playing with the delicate scales, and Don panted. I wished I had more patience to slowly work him into a frenzy, but I didn't.

"Fuck me, Vince," Don said. "Take what you need from me. I'm yours."

I kissed his thigh, pressing my nose against the hard muscle. My Don. I nipped him, careful not to hurt him. I would never hurt him—well, physically.

"Stop thinking or worrying and fuck me, Vince." Don pushed his fingers through my hair. "The future will keep. Right here and right now, it's just you and me. No one and nothing else. Just us."

He was right. I needed Dontilvynsan and he needed me. I kissed the weeping tip of his cock. "Just us."

"Just us," he repeated, cupping my chin.

I opened the lube and put a generous amount on my fingers before circling the tight ring of his ass. He moaned, and I savored the sound. Each and every noise was mine, and I wanted them. I kissed his thigh, licking the scales, and worked my finger in and out of his hole. Don never stopped making noise. His cock bucked with his rocking hips, leaking pre-cum out of his slit.

I licked the tip, groaning at the sweet taste on my tongue.

"Vince, my Vince," Don panted.

Pushing a second finger inside of him, I kept opening Don up for me steadily. He really didn't require the prep, but I was nervous I'd hurt him somehow if I didn't stretch him more.

"Please," he begged.

I kissed his needy cock. "Soon, Sweetheart."

When my three fingers easily slid in and out of his channel, I lined up my dick. Don's green eyes locked onto mine. I swallowed as nerves slid down my spine with a tremor. I gripped his hips. This moment belonged to us. There was no room for the future, for my worries or Don's, for the past, or for anyone who'd hurt me. The only thing in the moment was me and Don, nothing else.

Gently, I thrusted into him, eyes on his. I shivered at the all-encompassing heat and the tight grip of his hole. Don hooked his thick thighs around my hips, and his tail slid over the back of my thigh to my ass before going down again. He stretched out a hand, and I grabbed it, placing it on my cheek.

His emotions flooded my mind. I groaned. Pulling out, I pushed back in with a grunt. Don moaned when I was buried to the root, hitting that spot deep inside of him. Being connected like this was so personal and intense with our joined pleasure. I kept my eyes on his, silently begging him not to look away from me. I needed to see that it was him I was with, and no one else.

"I have you," he whispered. "I'm right here, my Vince."

I felt the backs of my eyes burn, but I didn't stop, hips smacking into his. Don planted his feet wider, thrusting up to meet my downward push. Soon we were moving in a perfect symphony. The wet sound of my cock sliding into his hole and the slapping of our bodies filled my ears, along with my grunts and Don's loud cries.

Bending over him, I kissed his chest. "Don."

His hands ran over my back. "I'm here."

Our eyes never separated as we fucked, each movement slow and long. Don's thick cock rubbed on my stomach. With our connected emotions, I felt his pleasure from me invading his body and his dick dragging through the trail of hair on my lower stomach.

Grunting, I picked up speed, pounding into Don, chasing my release. His hole tightened around me, and I grunted. My balls hugged my shaft as my orgasm barreled down my spine.

"Yes, Vince," Don cried, wrapping his arm tight around my neck. "Yes."

Unable to hold back any longer, I tipped over the edge, plunging deep into him. My pleasure ripped Don's from him without me even stroking him. He shrieked beneath me, his cock kicking and warm cum painting our stomachs.

I shook as I slid out of Don, and he whimpered. I kissed my way down his chest, licking his release off his scales and cleaning his cock. He writhed under me, too sensitive, but I wanted to lap up every drop of the sweet liquid. His hand still held my cheek, connecting us, so I felt it, but I couldn't resist.

Once he was clean, I lay on top of him and tucked my head under his chin. I needed to be close to him after everything. Tears burned the backs of my eyes, and yet I felt so safe cuddled against him.

Smoothing a hand over his chest, I breathed in his scent and planted a kiss on his collar bone. Don deserved my truth, even if he didn't want it.

He tensed beneath me; I rubbed his chest to calm him, but it didn't help.

"Tell me," he whispered.

"I love you, Dontilvynsan."

Pleasure so intense I felt it in my toes crashed through me. Don kissed the top of my head.

I stifled a cry and smoothed my hand over his scales again. "I love you, Don. More than Seth. More than anyone. You are the brightest star in my sky."

"My Vince."

"B-but," I said, voice breaking. "I can't stay with you."

Pain so strong it stole my breath shredded me for the barest instant before Don yanked his hand away, severing the connection between us. "What?"

I sat up, facing him. "I love you, Sweetheart, but I can't stay."

"Why not?" Don also sat, his tail utterly limp and his wings hugging his broad shoulders. His face was completely blank, which let me know how much I was hurting him, even if I hadn't caught a glimpse of his emotions.

I grabbed his hand, and Don didn't pull away, but he remained limp in my grasp. Lifting his hand, I brushed my thumb over his prominent knuckles, then peppered kisses on the back. I shouldn't, but I had to touch him.

"Sweetheart, I'm not forever."

"I don't understand."

"If I stayed, we'd become mates, wouldn't we?"

"Yes," Don said without hesitation.

"Drakcol mate for life."

"Yes," he replied, even though it hadn't been a question.

"Humans don't."

"I'm aware."

Sighing, I closed my eyes. "I can't promise forever, Don. I can't be with you." Looking right at him, I continued, "This has nothing to do with you, and everything to do with me. You're amazing, but I'm a mess. I would only hurt you."

"I don't believe that."

"What you believe doesn't matter," I said, squeezing his fingers. "I know me, and me? I'm not good enough for you. We're not meant to be. You deserve much better."

"I want *you*," Don said, reaching for me. I didn't fight him when he pulled me onto his lap. "I want you, Vince."

I buried my hands in his hair, kissing his neck. God, I loved him, but it wasn't enough. "This is my choice. I need to go home. I need to forget. What was done will never leave me, and I don't know if I can live with it. I shouldn't have to. I can't be the burden you have to lug around for your entire life." I laughed like it was a joke, but neither of us had a lick of humor.

"It would never be like that." His arms trembled, and he burrowed his face in the crook of my neck. "I will always choose you."

My heart was breaking, but I'd made my decision. Not saying anything, I kissed his temple. *I will always love you more than anyone else in this universe, Dontilvynsan. I promise.*

"You can't promise that," he whispered.

I smiled, recalling when he'd promised no one would ever touch me again without my permission. I repeated his words, "I can, and I am."

I stared at the bedroom door. Don had left over an hour ago. He'd held me for a while, then without a word slipped out of bed, got dressed, and left. I didn't blame him. I'd broken his heart. But what he didn't know or refused to accept was I was protecting him from me. While I hated—no, that was too weak a word for what I felt—the thought of someone else touching him, Don deserved more than I could give him.

Sliding out of bed, I went to the living room to wait for him, though I wasn't sure he was going to come back. There was also the possibility that one of his brothers or Seth would ask me to leave Don's rooms. None of them would be dicks about it—Don wouldn't let them—but it would be more than fair of him to want me to vacate his space.

My eyes ran over the living room that I'd made my own. Most of this stuff was from the dispenser, but some I'd picked up at the station. The bright beaded pillows, the blankets, Don's harpsichord, my tarot cards—this space felt more like home than anywhere in my entire life. I didn't want to leave, and I was far too selfish a person to abandon this apartment or Don unless I was forced.

Once again, my gaze settled on my tarot cards. My feet moving of their own accord, I stopped in front of the low table. The deck was harmlessly sitting on the edge in a neat pile. I'd brought them with me when I moved from my room to Don's, but I hadn't done another reading for him or one for myself. I wasn't able to. I was afraid.

I scoffed. What else was new?

My lips curled into a deep scowl. Grabbing the useless cards, I chucked them across the room with a scream. What was the point? Nothing mattered. I was a fucking coward who couldn't get over my damn issues. I grabbed one of the pillows and threw it. Heat pulsed in my stomach. It wasn't enough.

Screaming, I threw every stupid thing I'd gotten out of the dispenser or from the station on the floor. I ripped and threw and destroyed the room that had become my home, just like I'd destroyed everything else.

I should've fought. I should've screamed. I should've fucking died on Xome and then none of this would be happening.

When I reached the harpsichord, I seized it and lifted it above my head. The fragile crystal would shatter into a million pieces without the slightest provocation. My grasp trembled as I simply held it aloft. One motion. One flick. One tiny inconsequential movement and I would break one of the few remaining things that tied me to Don and this place.

"Fuck," I yelled, sliding to the floor and clasping the instrument to my chest. "Fuck it all to hell." I bent over it, tears streaming down my cheeks. I sobbed, shoulders shaking, as grief rolled through me like an endless fog, drawing me back into the void of darkness that I thought had vanished.

No matter how much I cried, the door didn't open, Don didn't come back, and I remained alone.

Chapter 38

IS THIS TRULY GOODBYE?

Vince

I folded one of my shirts and dropped it into the bin with the same fervor as one preparing for a funeral. I'd collected an impressive amount of shit that I had to now pack up. I mean, it was utterly pointless because I couldn't take any of it with me when I returned to Earth, but I refused to leave Don with this mess, like the one I had the other night. I'd passed out before he returned, and he had put me to bed and cleaned everything up without a word, much like how he'd left.

A sudden dark cloud surrounded me. It really hadn't left since... well since I'd fucking destroyed Don's living room. I clutched the rocks I'd taken from Inogga. When we'd left, I'd wanted to take a piece of paradise. I dropped them into the bin. I should have just left them there.

Paradise wasn't a real place.

I shoved more clothes into the bin, ones that Don had bought me. After I'd made my decision, I should've gone back to my room, but like an asshole, I'd offered to leave, and Don, being the fucking saint he was, had refused to let me go. I hadn't even fought him or tried to insist, because the thought of not seeing him made me sick. It had been quiet, though. He hadn't been mean or passive aggressive about my choice, more sad than anything.

Unlike Zoltilvoxfyn, Serlotminden, and Caleb—they wouldn't talk to me. Teddy had continued to act the same, as had Seth. But the aforementioned people scowled and growled. Don had told them to stop; he was still protecting me.

The one who shocked me was Kalvoxrencol. He'd merely watched me with a cocked head like he was trying to figure something out, but he'd been polite. It made me hate him more than ever. I deserved every harsh word, and the rat bastard wouldn't give it to me. I swore he wasn't being a dick just to mess with me. I wanted to punch him in the face with a knife.

I sighed, folding another shirt before dropping it into the bin. It hardly mattered. I wouldn't be staying in the palace with them. The emperor had secured a building for the humans to live in while the moon settlement was being built. Those who were returning to Earth would travel on the *Admiral Ven*, and the rest would eventually move to the moon if they wished or stay on Tamkolvanloknol.

The door opened, and Don walked in. I gave him a sad smile, gripping the thin gold chains around my neck. I should probably give them back, but I didn't want to. He brushed a hand through my hair, and like the shameless whore I was, I leaned into the touch.

"They were a gift and you should keep them," Don said, working his fingers over my scalp.

"I like them."

"And I want you to have them," he said, cupping my cheek.

Unable to stop myself, I kissed his palm. Don smiled, but it was tinged with sadness, and I understood. I should stop touching him, but I couldn't. I needed to feel his scales on my skin.

Don crouched and pressed a gentle kiss to my lips, which I returned. "I want you to keep touching me, Vince."

I leaned forward to kiss him again.

"I also want you to stay in the palace, in my room."

"Don," I started.

He silenced me with a kiss. "No, my Vince. I need it. I need to know you're somewhere safe. Besides, you'll be closer to Seth and Teddy, which you need."

I wrapped my arms around his neck. "Why are you so nice?"

Don didn't reply, but he hooked his arms around me and stood, carrying me to the bedroom. I didn't fight, nor did I have an interest in doing so. We hadn't fucked since I told him I wanted to return to Earth, but I wanted to have sex, and yet I didn't want to force Don into anything.

We lay side by side, with Don simply holding me. He didn't initiate anything and he must've heard me, which meant he didn't want more at the moment. I was fine with that, but... our moments were almost up.

"We're docking soon, aren't we?" I asked, trailing my hand over his back.

His arms tightened, drawing me even closer to his broad chest.

I took that as a yes. I had to finish packing, as did the others. It would be a few days before we moved completely to the station, but as soon as we did, Don would leave. I, and the others, would be on the station for several days to a couple of weeks as we waited for the *Admiral Ven* to arrive and take us back to the drakcol homeworld.

Fear slid down my spine. What if someone tried to grab me?

Don kissed the top of my head. "You'll be safe. I promise. My brothers will protect you, and Kalvoxrencol has already said you'll stay with him and Seth."

Fun. I got to look forward to listening to them fuck. I was *sure* that would make me want to murder Kal less. Not.

He rubbed my head with his forehead, scent marking me. I shifted my hand to his side, sliding under his uniform to touch his bare scales. Don groaned, then gave a mewl when I traced where his glands were to help release his scent. I wanted to smell like Don. I wanted everyone to know that he was mine and I was his for as long as I was here.

I swallowed. He wouldn't be, though. As soon as we separated, he would be free to seek others. I should be happy for him, or at least not a possessive dick that wanted to keep Don all to myself, but I couldn't. He was mine, and I didn't share.

"I will seek no one else, Vince."

"No," I said, meeting his gaze. "That's not fair of me to ask."

"Fair or not. I won't. I want you alone."

I kissed his chin. "Will you talk to me every day?"

"Yes. I need that as well. Every day, face to face. We can also send notes throughout the day."

That was better than nothing.

I nuzzled his chest, planting a kiss on the scales near his collar. I groaned at the feeling, my hips automatically canting toward him.

Don cupped the back of my head. "Vince, I can't."

"It's fine." It was. Did I want Don? Yes. Did I want to fuck him so I could feel connected to him? Also yes. But I understood why he didn't want to, and I wasn't going to pressure him. I placed another kiss on his neck, then snuggled against his chest, simply running my hand over his chest, side, and back, touching him everywhere I could reach.

Don took a deep inhale, his nose pressed against my hair. His tail coiled up my leg and his wings slipped out, one covering me. I burrowed into him. If I could freeze time, right here, right now, I would in a heartbeat. This moment with Don in my arms was everything, and I never wanted it to end.

"It doesn't have to," he whispered.

I sighed. It didn't. It was ending because of my choice, and yet at the same time, I couldn't stay. I'd only hurt Don. He deserved better than me.

His fingers dug into my back. "I want you. Only you and no one else."

"I know." We'd had this conversation, and nothing had changed from the last time.

He kissed the top of my head and didn't say any more, for what more was there to say?

Dontilvynsan

This was death. I truly felt as if I was dying. Yesterday, we'd docked at the Varjuntet Station. In a handful of days, Vince would disembark from my ship, and I would never see him again. I could not even imagine it. The mere thought was enough to send me to my knees.

My brothers wanted me to tell Vince he was my mate, but Vince had made it clear he didn't want to stay and that he would be happiest returning home. How could I guilt him into remaining when what he wanted was to leave?

Hallonnixmin had been furious, though, so in an effort to force me to speak, he'd told our younger brothers. All of them had sided with Hallonnixmin and Monqilcolnen—they wanted me to force Vince to stay. They all feared that I'd wither when Vince left.

Some drakcol survived the loss of their mate, but most did not. They faded. It was hard to keep breathing when your reason for life was no longer by your side. Vince would still be alive, but he'd be out of reach and separated from me forever. Those mates who weren't bound by the Crystal could travel and live apart due to work or life circumstances, and some did, but it was different—they were still together.

Vince would be gone, unattainable, lost to me.

I didn't think I would survive long. The grief would shred me, but perhaps I'd surprise myself and find the will to continue on. I doubted it. The moment Vince returned to Earth, I was fairly certain my days would be numbered.

Of course, my brothers didn't want that, nor would my parents when they found out. I wouldn't be swayed, though. Vince and his needs were far more important. He didn't want to remain with me, and I'd let him go.

I tried to force my thoughts from Vince as I looked at the many notes regarding the offloading of passengers and the few repairs we needed done before we left. The communication dish and long-range sensors had continued to act up, but the nodes we needed were in short supply currently.

I stared at the request form to up our importance on the restock list, but my brain did not wish to cooperate. My thoughts and senses flew to Vince. He was in our room, packing. I felt his general melancholy, the gaping void had returned, nearly consuming him, but not his individual thoughts.

Vince loved me, and he wanted to stay and he didn't at the same time. Part of me wanted to take advantage of his indecision, but I wouldn't. I wanted him to choose me for me. I didn't want guilt to drive him to my side. I wanted to be loved and chosen for who I was.

A chime sounded at my office door. I resituated on the stool, dropping the screen onto my metal desk with a loud clack, and called, "Enter."

The door opened, and Kalvoxrencol stepped inside. I swallowed an annoyed growl. Every single one of my brothers and Monqilcolnen had pestered me about speaking to Vince. So far they'd honored my wishes to remain quiet, but I didn't trust them to continue that silence.

Kalvoxrencol's thoughts were oddly quiet. All I caught was low-level concerns about Seth, their child, and about how he was hungry. I wanted to snarl. No one was better at evading me than Kalvoxrencol. I contained it, though. I would never injure him, no matter how annoying he was.

"Pest," I greeted, keeping my expression bland.

He took a seat on one of the stools in front of my desk, his jewelry jingling. A gold necklace with a rough purple stone the same shade as his eyes stood out from the rest of the silver jewelry. Seth had gifted it to him not long after they were mated, and Kalvoxrencol never took it off.

Kalvoxrencol snorted, tail flicking. "You can hide your emotions behind this calm facade all you want, Captain, but I see through it. It's destroying you. The thought of Vince leaving is killing you."

I tilted my head in concession, offering my throat. I wouldn't lie about it, at least not to them.

"I remember when I was wooing Seth. The thought of us separating was enough to send a shard of agony to my soul, and he never actively planned to leave as your Vince is."

I swallowed, struggling to keep my calm. I'd painfully thickened my usual static shield over the last couple of days to the point I barely perceived the others around me, because I didn't want Vince or my brothers to become victims to the agony encasing me.

"Talk to me," Kalvoxrencol said, and I wanted to laugh. How many times had I begged him to talk to us throughout his life, and how many times had he spurned us? Nevertheless, he'd changed, and I refused to bring up his past.

I pushed a hand through my hair, letting my wings slide out, keeping them in a relaxed position. "He wants to leave, Pest. He told me this."

"But he doesn't know that he's your mate."

"He does not," I replied. "But does it truly matter? Vince wants to go home. He says he's not forever."

Kalvoxrencol crossed his arms, eyes narrowing. That was his thinking face. I'd seen it many times in my life. His thoughts bounced, and I didn't try to track them. I was too tired. Sleep had been torture. Vince had been draped over me as usual, and I had simply lain beneath him, tracing the line of his spine and savoring the feel of his cool skin against my scales because it would soon be a thing of memory.

"I cannot say what you should or shouldn't do, Dontilvynsan, but don't give up. Vince cares for you, that is obvious. Tell him exactly what you need. He won't know unless you tell him. You need him to stay, and maybe he needs you to need him."

I looked away.

"Some people need to be needed," he said. "I did; I do." Kalvoxrencol stood. "Maybe he needs permission to stay, to want you. Not all of us feel worthy of the gifts we are given." His tail coiled around mine before he left me to my thoughts.

Chapter 39

NOT YOU. ANYONE BUT YOU.

Vince

I numbly walked around the station that was to be our home for a few weeks. It was on the edge of Drakcon territory and another alien species' space, which was not part of the Coalition—I hadn't bothered to catch the name, as what was the fucking point? There weren't as many plants, which surprised me, and the aliens walking around seemed more leery, eyes flicking back and forth. Conversations were muted and not as loud or joyous. Something about this place was darker or rougher than the other station, but maybe it was more my utter dread of being here without Don.

Wary, I stayed close to Don. He had meetings on the station and had offered to bring me with him. The offer was more than a simple offer—he needed me to stay with him. I was much the same way.

It was difficult to let Don out of my sight. When I couldn't see him, that worthless void filled me again, blotting out any light. I believed he was struggling more than I was, even though he didn't say anything.

Don was talking with the station manager about room placements. He wanted all of us humans—well, not me—placed in a single room in between his brothers. We humans needed to be protected. All of us had been taken against our wills in the past, and we were nervous about it happening again.

His tail flicked against my ankle, tightening in response to my thoughts, while his hand gripped mine. Don didn't waver in his conversation, but I smiled at him, resting my head against his shoulder. When we stood or walked side by side like this, it made me aware of how much larger Don was than me, but he was so gentle. I didn't fear him in the slightest. I had no reason to.

That trust, which at first had been terrifying, wasn't anymore. He'd proved time and time again that he would never harm me.

No. I was the one who hurt people.

He squeezed my hand again.

I forced myself to think about something else, so I didn't distract him. My eyes flicked over the station, taking in the aliens and numerous shops. Much like the other station, this one was a cylinder with a docking ring surrounding it. We were in the center, which was filled with shops and restaurants. People of all shapes and sizes meandered around, speaking in so many different languages that NAID didn't or couldn't translate.

None of them truly bothered me, even with their sketchy air. In my time being away from Earth, I'd gotten used to seeing the variety of aliens who lived out among the stars. Besides, I was safe.

I rubbed my temple on Don's shoulder, listening to the timbre of his voice even though I didn't pay attention to his words. I couldn't care less about what he was talking about, sadly, but I did like listening to him. He was so good at his job, even the boring bits. Fuck, I'd be bad at it. I'd tell everyone to handle their own shit and to leave me alone.

Not Don, though. He took everything about his job seriously, though he'd played hooky with me a couple of times. He was so good at it. Who knew competence was sexy, but it was.

A deep rumble came from Don, and I grinned. I was distracting him yet again. I sent him a silent apology and tried to focus on something else besides Don.

Blindly, I stared at the crowd. A spindly figure walked across my vision and sent a tremor up my spine. My breath turned harsh, and I had to fight not to scale Don like a fucking tree.

An alien who haunted my dreams like a monster under the bed was right in front of me. Xoi. The same aliens who'd stolen me from Earth. Their oblong heads like watermelons, their pencil necks, their thin bodies that didn't seem possible, and the horrible spandex jumpsuits they wore—all terrified me.

The scorching flames on my arms as Agk ordered me to burn a dead body, followed by him hitting me and Teddy. More corpses. More flames. A not-dead alien writhing on the flames. Then Tryk buying me, throwing me to other aliens. The darkness. The never-ending darkness as hunger curled in my gut. Pain. Screaming. Begging to die. More darkness. There was no freedom from it.

I shook, my eyes unable to leave the two aliens who walked across the station marketplace without a care in the world. Rage boiled in my stomach, mixing with potent terror. I wanted to flee and, at the same time, grab a weapon and shoot them in their fucking heads. I wanted to see those watermelons explode and spatter the gray metal wall.

Arms encased me, dragging me against a solid chest. "You are safe."

Xoi were here.

"They're not a part of the Coalition," Don said, "but they are allowed in our and Coalition space to trade, as long as they follow the laws."

I didn't care. I wanted to kill them all.

Don shushed me, rocking me in his embrace.

His touch and scent normally soothed me, but it didn't this time. Memories crashed over me, making my stomach roil. I pushed away from him. "I'm going to puke."

He dragged me to the closest trash can barely in time before I bent over the metal receptacle and vomited. Tears burned my eyes and the acidic bile made my nose sting. Memories swelled, pushing over the dam I'd constructed to hold them back.

I was back in the hold of the cargo ship. The juddering floor. The moans of my fellow captives. The stink of body odor, sewage, and death. Over a hundred of us were jammed into the tight hold with no place to lie down. Teddy. I'd latched onto him and hadn't let go, even when they dragged us out and sprayed us with a cleansing foam that burned or when they shoved us into an auction.

Vomit continued to come up. Tears ran down my cheeks. Everything that followed shredded me. The fights. The dead bodies. Being sold again. Being starved. Being hurt. Being used.

Something warm cupped my cheek and waves of calm like the tide of the ocean washed over me, soothing the memories, stealing them away.

"I have you," Don whispered. He picked me up, and I whimpered when the connection broke between us. "I have you, my Vince. Let me take you home."

A shot of longing for our room pierced me so strongly that I clutched the front of his shirt and begged, "Please."

He pressed a kiss to my forehead. "Hold on."

I didn't care about the looks we received or how it appeared to have the captain of the ship carry me through the halls. All I knew was I needed Don; he was all I needed or wanted.

Suddenly, like time had skipped, I was in our bedroom. Don settled me on the bed, and I reached for him. I needed to know he was here, that I was safe. He lay down beside me and pulled me into his embrace. I snuggled close, trying to burrow inside of him.

Don cupped my cheek and more calm washed over me. I groaned. It had been some time since I'd needed his gift, but I did need it, and I felt bad about it.

He kissed my temple. "Don't. I'm happy to offer assistance whenever you need it."

I climbed on top of him, draping across his broad chest, and went boneless with my eyes closed. I was safe. All of the memories receded beneath the gentle warmth of Don.

Dontilvynsan

I pinged Serlotminden and asked him to finish meeting with the various station management I was supposed to. He readily agreed; he was a diplomat, though he did tell me he was going to leave Bartholomew with either Zoltilvoxfyn or Kalvoxrencol. He didn't want his mate anywhere near the xoi anymore than I did.

Afterward, I simply ran a hand over Vince's back while I kept my other hand and emotions latched to him. He was calm, utterly so, now. If I broke the connection, I was unsure he would remain that way. I wasn't doing much at the moment besides stabilizing him, but that might be enough to keep him calm.

Sliding under his shirt, I tucked my hand against his skin. Vince relaxed even further. He was draped across me, and his familiar weight was comforting. Vince needed me, and I loved that he did. Guilt made me swallow. I felt horrible that I liked him needing me, but at the same time, I thought back to what Kalvoxrencol had told me. Sometimes people needed to be needed, and I did.

Did Vince? Did he need me to give him permission to have me? Did he need the reassurance that I needed him as much as he did me? I'd told him that I wanted him. Wasn't that enough?

Vince nuzzled my neck and planted a kiss on my jaw. I swallowed as arousal and desperation raced through him. His cock hardened against my stomach as he licked and kissed down my neck.

"Don," he whispered in a husky voice.

He wanted to fuck so we could connect. We hadn't had sex since he told me he wanted to go home. It wasn't that I didn't want to—I did; I loved Vince—but I couldn't help but wonder if it would be the last time, and my instincts rebelled against such a notion. Though if we didn't fuck again before I left, then the time he told me he loved me would be our last.

I cupped his butt and turned my head to meet his lips. "Yes, Vince."

I gave him the image of me on my hands and knees and him taking me from behind. Vince groaned. I licked the seam of his mouth before tangling our tongues. After a moment, I pulled away from him and yanked my clothes off. Naked, I turned around for my mate. He peppered kisses along my butt.

"Don," he moaned. "My good boy."

"Take me, Vince."

And he did while part of me died, terrified this would be the last time I ever felt my mate deep inside me.

Chapter 40

NOT AGAIN, PLEASE.

Vince

I watched Don as he got dressed. We'd fucked once from behind, then after a bit, we'd fucked again, face to face. I'd needed to see Don, to see his face as I felt him squeezing me. I had to know it was him and not anyone else. Afterward, he'd spent most of the morning and early afternoon with me, but now he had to go back to the station. Mindy had covered as much as possible for Don, but he couldn't do everything. I didn't plan to move from being curled against his pillow, breathing in his scent.

Don tugged his long hair out of the back of his uniform. He faced me, putting one knee on the bed, and kissed me.

I groaned, cupping his cheeks. The kiss wasn't the chaste one I'd been expecting. Don leaned into me, lips demanding. When his tongue prodded me, I opened for him without hesitation. His scaled tongue scraped against mine, making me moan. His kiss was claiming and insistent, but not the slightest bit harsh.

My gentle Don. He loved me being soft with him, but he gave it right back to me.

"Stay," I asked, even though it wasn't fair and he couldn't.

"Vince," he moaned against my lips before he captured me again. His kiss was just as fierce and demanding. I wrapped my arms around his neck to draw him closer. I didn't want him to leave, to be anywhere the xoi were.

Fear raced through my veins. What would happen when Don wasn't here? I couldn't live with something happening to him.

"Hush," Don whispered, pressing his lips against mine. "You're safe. No one will touch you again without your permission."

"You promise?"

"I promise." Don cupped my cheeks and pressed yet another kiss to my lips. "I have to go."

He did, but I selfishly wanted to hog all of his time. He nuzzled my forehead, probably in response to my thoughts. I clung to him, gripping his sides. I hated how needy I was. When I was on Earth, I hadn't needed anyone. I knew how to keep myself safe, how to take care of myself, and I didn't have to rely on anyone for anything. Now, I was dependent on Don, and part of me hated it; I was a burden.

"No," he said, lifting my chin so our eyes met. "You are not a burden, Vince. You're mine and I'm yours. We take care of each other. I need you as much as you need me."

I didn't believe that.

"It's the truth," he said.

I went up on my knees to hug Don, then pressed a loud smack to his neck. "You need to go."

"Are you going to stay here?"

"Yes." I had no intention of leaving this room. Maybe ever.

He carded his fingers through my hair. "I will be back."

My eyes stayed on Don until he disappeared from view. I flopped back onto the bed and curled around his pillow, taking in his scent. The soft sheets and the cozy blanket lured me into a relaxed state. Sleep started to drag me away, and I didn't fight it. If I slept, I'd feel better, and Don would be back by the time I woke up.

A chime sounded, and I groaned, pulling the pillow over my head. Maybe they would go away? The chime sounded again, then NAID said, "Vince Lyford."

I flopped onto my back. "Yes?"

"Prince Consort Seth Harris would like to speak with you."

I'd never heard Seth's title before. It was... odd. Shaking it off, I said, "Let him in."

I forced myself out of bed and went to the living room. Seth was on the couch. He was red-faced. "Sorry," he said. "I didn't realize you were sleeping."

"I wasn't." I mean, I'd been about four seconds from falling asleep, but whatever.

Seth smiled, but it was tight like he thought I was lying. I shifted to his side and snuggled against his shoulder. He slipped an arm around my waist. I had one moment of tension before it passed, and I could relax, pushing away my first instinct of fear.

"I wanted to check on you," Seth said after a moment. "Kal saw Don carrying you, and I was worried. I wanted to come right away, but Kal said Don would want to take care of you."

"He took good care of me." Very *very* good care of me.

"Are you okay?" Seth asked.

"Yeah." I was mainly. I'd be better if Don was here right now, holding me, but I was fine.

His hand went up and down my arm. "Do you need to not stay at this station? I could ask the Cohort. They're pretty accommodating to us humans."

More like they were very invested in Seth. For whatever reason, Seth would say something, and the drakcol would jump to do it for him. It was weird, but if it worked to our advantage, then I wouldn't complain.

Part of me wanted to accept Seth's offer. He could probably convince the Cohort to allow Don to take us back to the Drakcon homeworld, and that meant more time with him, not to mention away from the xoi.

But I couldn't. I couldn't force Don, and if I did, it could affect his career, which I never wanted to do.

"No, but thanks. We'll be fine," I said. "The xoi won't take any of us again."

"They won't," Seth agreed.

I smiled, but I wanted to snap at Seth. He'd never been taken by the xoi. Kal had abducted him because he wanted to claim Seth as his soulmate. It was different. But I contained it. Seth wasn't agreeing because he lumped his abduction in with ours; he was agreeing to comfort me. Still, it rankled. He'd been met with love, and I'd been met with blood, death, and rape.

We stayed silent for quite some time, each lost in our own thoughts. After a bit, Seth gently moved me from his side.

"Seth?"

"Camden and Pierce talked to me."

I groaned, covering my eyes. I'd been avoiding them like the plague since I had finally made my decision. Out of everyone, they got what I'd been through, and I didn't want to have to justify my reasoning.

"They're concerned."

"I'm fine," I snapped, hugging myself. I wasn't. Fuck. I was numb most of the time. I hated myself. I hated everything but Don.

He stared at me, then said, "Okay."

When he stood, I asked, "Where are you going?"

"I promised to meet Kal. We're going to the space station. Kal wants to help Don and Mindy with some of the preparations for us transferring to the station," he answered.

I grabbed his hand. "You should stay on the ship."

"Kal would never let anything happen to me."

"Still."

Seth tugged on me. "I'll be fine. You can come if you want, but you don't have to."

On one hand, I'd feel better if I went with Seth because I could guarantee he came back. On the other, I wanted to stay right here in mine and Don's room—where I was safe.

"We'll stay together?" I asked.

"Of course."

"Fine."

———

The station was as busy as last time, but everything was different now. Every alien was more sinister and every shadow held a hidden threat. My eyes whipped back and forth, searching. Every noise or brushing pass of someone near me made me jump and sent my pulse skyrocketing. We'd only been on the station for maybe fifteen minutes, and I was desperate to return to my room.

It was a miracle Dontilvynsan hadn't sensed me and come running.

Kal glanced at me for the umpteenth time. Maybe he was the reason Don wasn't coming to get me. If he could sense me, he'd sense his little brother. When I showed up at their room, Kal had been upset about Seth inviting me to go along with them. He'd worried Don would be mad at him, which, to be fair, was possible, but it was my choice. And fuck Kal. If Don was angry, it was Kal's problem, not mine.

I clutched Seth's hand tighter, ignoring the sweat that gathered on his palm. Kal held Seth's other hand and one of his ankles with his tail. Between the two of us, Seth almost looked like a child. However, I didn't want to let go of him. He was my lifeline, and I had to make sure he came back.

People pressed around us, making Seth draw closer to Kal, who murmured to him. The crowd itself didn't bother me; it was the general threat they represented that upset me.

We wound through the busy space until we came to a small hallway. Kal opened the third door to the right, and I saw Serlotminden as well as a handful of other people sitting around the table. I looked for Don, but he wasn't there. I was one part sad and two parts relieved. I was ninety-eight percent sure that me being here would piss him off. Not because he didn't want to see me, but rather, because he was afraid of me getting upset.

Mindy's eyes widened when he saw me and Seth. "Why did you bring him?"

Nope. Not Seth. Just me. Don's brothers were pissed at me for leaving, and it seemed they didn't want me around. Whatever. Fuck them all. I was protecting Don. They didn't have to see that.

"Dontilvynsan will kill you if anything happens to him," Mindy hissed. "Take him back, Pest. Now."

So... he was afraid for Don.

"Vince made his decision to come. If Captain has a problem with it, he can come and take Vince back himself," Kal replied calmly. "Besides, I would never let anything happen to Vince. Seth would never forgive me."

Seth swatted his husband. "You would be upset too."

Kal grunted.

I was with Kal. He didn't care about me anymore than I cared about him—which was none at all. We only cared because Seth did.

The other aliens in the room didn't react to the hushed conversation. I didn't know the name of their species, but I'd seen them before. They looked like living trees with bark-like skin, gossamer clothes, and green hair. One was a hulking alien with four arms, purple skin, and two tall horns like an antelope. But most people around the table were drakcol.

The meeting commenced with little fanfare. Seth stayed plastered to Kal, and I sat fairly close to Seth's other side. Mindy, who didn't seem happy about it, sat to the right of me. The two brothers boxed us humans in, protecting us from any possible threat.

Mindy, who'd always seemed like a ray of sunshine with extra sunshine shooting out of his ass, sat there, arms crossed and expression hard. He was angry I was hurting his brother, and I got it—more than that, I didn't hold it against him. I was angry I was hurting Don too, but I was so fucking tired of being terrified, and I was worried that if I stayed, I would hurt Don far *far* worse.

My eyes drifted to the open door, hoping to catch a glimpse of Don, but I didn't. The meeting dragged on, and I paid absolutely no attention to it. I wanted to return to my room or to Don's side. Once upon a time, I'd loved rushing about and being busy, but now, I missed the slow days of us traveling and relaxing.

When Kal, Seth, and Mindy stood, I followed suit. Mindy gave another warning, which I ignored, and Kal led me and Seth out without remarking. I kept hold of Seth as we wandered through the busy area. Kal had another meeting, and me and Seth were tagging along.

A flash of purple and black caught my eyes. I whipped around. Don. He was there. I could see the back of his head moving through the crowd. Why hadn't he come and said hello or grabbed me? Was he angry?

Don, I yelled at his retreating back.

He didn't react.

I pulled out of Seth's grip.

"Vince?" Seth asked.

"Vince!" Kal yelled.

"I see Don," I called back, slipping through the crowd.

"Come back," Kal snarled, but I ignored him.

Don was right there.

I tracked his much taller head through the mass of people, ignoring the crush of bodies, the odd odors, and the snarls as I shoved people out of the way. I caught up and froze. The alien with purple hair was Don's height, but they weren't Don. They had deep black skin, four golden eyes without pupils, slits for a nose, and no lips.

"What?" they snapped.

My hand hovered in the air and my pulse thundered in my ears. I had left Seth and Kal. I was alone on a space station with xoi, and the person I'd chased was not Don.

"Weird fucker," the alien grumbled, walking away.

I stayed frozen in one spot as I struggled to breathe, fighting off the black dots floating through my vision and the white noise clogging my ears. No. This wasn't happening. I was fine. Everything was fine. I just had to remain calm.

Turning around, I looked around for Kal or Seth, but I didn't see either of them in the sea of people who crashed around me. I wasn't even sure what direction to look or head toward; I'd paid no attention to where I'd run, following that alien... The alien who *was not* Don.

I took a deep breath to try and still the shaking in my hands. I just had to find the ship, and I would. It would be fine. I was hardly helpless. At that thought, my hand dove into my pocket; I had my touchstone.

"Seth Harris," I said, moving toward the wall.

"Vince," Seth shouted, his voice reverberating in my skull from the touchstone in my grasp. "Where the fuck are you? Why did you run?"

"I thought I saw Don. It wasn't him."

Seth sighed. "Vince."

"Can you come get me? I'm next to a shop selling beetles. Why the hell do people buy beetles the size of puppies? They're terrifying. Who wants a beetle that big?"

"I don't know. Aliens are weird. We are coming. Don't move. I mean it, Vince. Stay put. If Don was here, he would come. Don't run off no matter who you see."

"I won't."

"You better not," Seth said before disconnecting.

I leaned against the wall, putting my bitch-face on, and crossed my arms. I felt like an idiot for rushing off when I thought I saw Don. It had been like an hour, and I hated being apart. How the fuck was I going to survive an unknown amount of time on the drakcol planet, then six months to Earth—all without Don.

My eyes closed. I didn't know if I could do this. I couldn't leave him. I couldn't. But if I stayed, I'd be a fucking selfish bastard. Don deserved someone better than me. I wasn't sure I would ever be able to function independently. I wasn't sure I could return to who I

remembered myself being. But maybe I didn't need to. I was still...
me. Both versions.

Someone grabbed my arm so fast that I had no chance to act. They
wrenched it behind my back. I thrashed, heart pounding. "Let me
go, you bastard."

"Fucking xoi. I knew they cheated me of all my property," the
gravelly voice said, grip tightening.

Panic like lightning sparked through my veins. No. Not again.
Never again. I tried to yank away, making my shoulder pop
sickeningly, and ripped a scream from my throat. The alien kept hold
of me, dragging me by my damaged arm.

"No. Help!" I shouted.

The massive alien slapped me across my face and stars danced
before my eyes and blood filled my mouth.

The alien grabbed my biceps and picked me up off the ground
with ease. He was huge, at least seven feet tall. He had four arms, red
cracked skin, and twelve black beady eyes. His face was utterly flat,
except for a set of sharp mandibles coming out of his mouth.

"Shut up. Unless you would like me to kill you now," he ordered,
mandibles clicking.

Don! I screamed. Not again. Never again. I would rather die.

Chapter 41

BROKEN PROMISE.

Dontilvynsan

Vince was anxious. I could feel him from here on the station, which was odd, but I'd left him upset. I hadn't wanted to leave him, but I had responsibilities. I did my best to focus on my meetings, arranging rooms, security, and food for the humans and my brothers until the *Admiral Ven* came for them. Talvax and her ship, as well as Monqilcolnen, should be here in a handful of weeks, and they would take my brothers and the humans to Tamkolvanloknol.

For now, the humans would remain in their quarters as much as possible, even with the extra security I was hiring and the station security. This station was under the Drakcol Empire and run by drakcol, but other aliens were very populous here and this station bordered unfriendly space. I didn't trust anyone to keep the humans, let alone my mate, safe.

Don! Vince shrieked.

I staggered. Commander Hyn of the station reached out to stabilize me, but I waved them off. Vince. Something was wrong with Vince. I ran out of the room, ignoring the calls that followed me. I didn't care about my meeting or anything else. My mate needed me.

I wove through the crowd, snarling when people blocked my way. Vince kept screaming for me. He was here on the station, and I had no idea why. He was supposed to stay in our quarters. What could've drawn him here not long after I'd left him?

His cries filled my mind, and he was getting further away. I didn't know where he was, but I could feel him and I would find him. I would track him to the end of known space and further to find him. Nothing in this universe would keep me from my mate.

I ripped down a corridor. He had to be here. Somewhere. This was the docking ring. Whoever had him was trying to take him away. I growled. That would never happen.

Don, Vince called out.

Now that I was racing around the docking ring, his voice was getting closer. My feet pounded on the metal floors and flowers and vines on the walls flew past me as I tried to hone in on Vince. I skidded to a stop when I came to a fork in the docking ring. One path continued along the ring, and the spoke went off to docking for several different ships.

Vince screamed, and I turned down the spoke, hearing him in my mind and with my ears. I was close.

"Shut up," a deep voice snarled, followed by a harsh slap and a subsequent yelp.

Anger unlike anything I'd ever known surged through me. There was Vince in the hands of an alien. Blood dribbled out of Vince's mouth and the entire left side of his face was bruised. I roared and was across the corridor without thought. I ripped the alien away and threw him toward the wall. He collided with a thud, and a haze of flowers erupted off the damaged vines.

I put myself between Vince and the alien. Panting, I growled, wings out and tail thrashing. I would kill this person for hurting Vince.

Vince

"Don," I whispered.

He didn't react.

The alien got to his feet and yanked out a blaster. I screamed, terrified that Don would be injured, but Don didn't flinch. He slapped the blaster away and punched my would-be kidnapper straight in the face. Don's tail latched around the alien, throwing them. Crouching, Don snarled. The alien growled, and they collided in a mass of limbs.

My heart pounded. I couldn't help. Fighting wasn't my thing, and the alien was huge, though Don wasn't much smaller. With my good hand, I grabbed my touchstone.

"Kalvoxrencol," I called. As much as I would rather talk to Seth, I needed help, and no one was a better fighter than Kal.

"Vince, where are you?" he snarled, sounding as angry as Don.

I screamed when Don crashed into the wall, green blood dotting his side. My kidnapper had a knife. "Kal," I cried. "Someone stole me. Don's here. We need help. *Please*."

"I'm coming. So are Serlotminden and Zoltilvoxfyn. Hold on, Vince. We are coming, brother."

"Don," I yelled; he was on the ground, bleeding quite profusely. The alien had stabbed him. I dropped my touchstone and raced in front of Don, throwing myself at the alien. "Leave him alone!"

The red alien tossed me aside with ease. Don staggered to his feet. He bared his teeth and launched at the alien, his hands cupping their jaw. He shoved the alien back against the wall. Don didn't seem to be doing anything, but the alien started to scream. Don held on, growling. The alien thrashed, but eventually, their eyes closed and they slumped.

Don didn't let go or stop growling.

"Don," I whispered, trying to get to my feet. My ribs ached, my face throbbed, my left eye was swollen closed, and I was pretty sure my shoulder was dislocated, not to mention the plethora of bruises and scrapes.

He didn't release my would-be kidnapper.

"Sweetheart," I said, trying to get up again but failing. I whimpered. "Sweetheart, I need you."

Instantly, he dropped the alien and prowled toward me. A deep prey instinct told me to run, but my lizard brain could go fuck itself. Don was mine, and he sure as hell wouldn't hurt me. I reached for him, and Don swept me into his embrace.

Even with the tension in his muscles, he was exceedingly gentle. I pressed against him, breathing hard. My fingers slid down, finding the wound on his side. I pressed my palm against it; blood leaked between my fingers.

"Sweetheart, you're hurt."

Don didn't answer; he was cupping my chin and staring at my bruised face.

"I'm fine, Don. You're not."

He ignored me.

I didn't know how much he was actually understanding at this exact second. I pressed his hand against my uninjured cheek. He needed me. A connection formed between us. I could sense his anger, terror, need, pain, and so much more. I rested my forehead against him and thought about soothing things: the ocean, Don singing to me, Don playing the harpsichord, us snuggling, and many other things, all while our song played in the background.

"Dontilvynsan," voices yelled.

Don snarled, but I kept hold of him.

"We're safe," I whispered. "We keep each other safe."

Kal stood in the front and held out his hands. "You know us, Captain. Everything's fine. You and Vince need treatment."

Don's arm tightened its hold on me.

Seth peeked around Kal. "Don, calm down. Vince is hurt, and you're bleeding everywhere." His voice shook a tad, but he stepped forward, pushing Kal's hands away. "Don, trust us. I know you do. So stop. Just stop. Vince needs help."

Looking down at me, Don frowned. I went up on my toes, ignoring the pain, and kissed his lips. "Mine. All mine."

"Yours."

"Good. Now we need treatment," I said. "And that fucker has more humans somewhere."

Kal growled. "Zoltilvoxfyn, have them lock the station down. No one is leaving or coming until we find them all."

"Of course." Fyn darted off.

Commander Bimwoxcol and a few other drakcol I didn't know stepped forward, taking my would-be kidnapper into custody. Mindy was barking orders while Kal came toward us slowly.

I kept Don's hand on my cheek to keep him calm. "Come on, Sweetheart."

Dontilvynsan

I lay in the medbay, eyes on Vince. Doctor Muznim and Physician Klars had tried to move him out of my sight, and I'd snarled, ushering them away. Vince had calmed me down again, choosing a bed right next to mine. I had to keep him within sight.

My soul was throbbing in pain. I'd broken my promise. Someone had hurt Vince, and I hadn't protected him. I'd failed. I paid no attention to the assistant working on my stab wound. Muznim had wanted to heal me first, but I refused. Vince was more important.

With his arm bound to his chest, Vince moved toward me. His face was still bruised and his movements were jerky. It would take time for him to heal. Amorians weren't as advanced in medicine as we were, but their techniques and medicine were usable and helpful to humans. Not all Drakcon technology could safely be used on humans.

MARS QUINN

He climbed onto the bed beside me, and I hauled him closer, careful to be gentle. Vince rested a hand over my throbbing soul. "Are you alright?"

"Yes."

"He was stabbed. Several scales were broken, and he has some internal damage from the knife as well as broken ribs and bruised organs," Muznim answered, looking at her screen.

Vince gripped my shirt. "But he'll be fine, right?"

"Yes," she said. "Captain Dontilvynsan will make a full recovery. He simply needs rest."

My mate glared at me. "You heard her. Rest."

I ran a hand through his hair. "As you wish, my Vince."

Chapter 42

RECOVERY AND DECISIONS.

Vince

Don was on strict bedrest; he wasn't taking it well. But I didn't care. I would sit on him if I had to. The doctor didn't want him moving around too much, and Don would follow what she'd prescribed to the letter.

Currently, Kal was leading the search for the other humans, and I had no doubt he'd find them all. I might hate the bastard—though I was softening from how fast he came to protect Don—but Kal was dedicated to finding the humans and protecting them.

Right now, my main concern was Don. He needed to heal, and I would be damned if I let anything happen to him.

My arm was bound to my chest to keep my shoulder from moving. Klars had put on several nanite plasters to speed up my healing. I only had to wear them for a few days—he wasn't actually certain about the timeline. Until then, he wanted me to move my arm as little as possible, to allow the medicine and tech in the plasters to heal me.

I gathered up the bandage supplies, cleanser, and oil for Don's side. Where the alien bastard had stabbed Don were several broken scales. Depending on the extent of the injury, the scales didn't always come back—Caleb had several spots without scales—but the skin underneath was sensitive to the extreme. Cold, heat, dry weather were a few things that could harm the exposed skin.

The oil Dr. Muznim had provided should help his scales regrow, but she couldn't say for certain. I would, of course, do everything to help him heal.

I set everything on the ground beside the couch, and Don looked my way, tail flicking. I caught the wiggling appendage and pressed a kiss to the tip. "Don't glare, Sweetheart. I need to take care of you. Doctor's orders, which you promised to follow."

"What's one more broken promise?" he muttered.

"What?" I asked, leaning over him. He'd never broken a promise to me.

His eyes shifted to the side.

"Sweetheart?" I asked, but he didn't look at me or move to lift his hand and make a connection between us. He hadn't formed a connection since the incident, and I missed it. Was he mad at me? I'd gone to the station when I'd promised to stay in our room. I was the reason he was attacked.

"I let you be hurt," he whispered.

"What?"

His luminous green eyes met mine, stark and full of pain. "That person hurt you, and I did nothing."

"You saved me."

"I swore no one would ever touch you again without permission, and someone did."

Fuck, Don was adorable. I pressed my mouth to his. He grunted in surprise. I took advantage of it, forcing my tongue inside. God, he was warm. I laid siege, plundering him until Don was shaking beneath me.

I pulled back, and he followed. Smiling, I brushed my fingers along his cheekbones. "You didn't fail me, Don. I left the ship. I left Kal and Seth's side. I was the idiot who risked myself. You saved me." I gave him a harsh kiss, though I tempered it to not hurt him. "You saved me, Don. I'm not mad. I don't blame you. You didn't break your promise. Do you understand me?"

He didn't meet my gaze.

I grabbed his chin and forced him to meet my eye. "Do you understand, Dontilvynsan?"

"I understand, my Vince."

"Good boy." My fingers slid through his long hair, and I trailed kisses along his jaw. "It's all fine."

Don gave me his throat, and I lowered to kiss down the column of his neck. When I reached his chest, I grabbed the base of his shirt and tugged. He leaned up so I could slip it off.

"Good job," I told him, and he wiggled. I didn't have to look to know his cock was starting to harden. "My perfect, good Dontilvynsan. You're so sexy, you know that?"

"Vince," he groaned.

"You're such a good boy." I placed kisses down his chest, licking and biting as I went, until I reached the bandage. Carefully, I peeled it away. A slash marred his side. The scales had been plucked so all that remained was his red and gold mottled skin. Getting the towel wet, I cleaned the injury, skin, and surrounding scales with the cleanser the doctor had provided.

"If I was a drakcol, I'd lick this, wouldn't I?" I asked, dropping the towel.

"You would," he replied, breath harsh.

When we returned to our room after the doctor released us, Don had insisted on licking my every bruise and scrape. He'd wanted to bathe my shoulder, but the plasters had been in the way.

"Do you want me to?" I asked.

His eyes widened and his breath came out in rough gasps. I peeked at his groin, and the tenting told me all I needed to know. I bent down and kissed the exposed skin. Don released a strangled cry. I smirked before giving him a tentative lick, and he arched, but his moaning turned pain.

I pressed him back down. "Don't hurt yourself, Don. Let me take care of you."

He panted. "My Vince."

I returned, growing bolder. I traced the sealed injury with my tongue. It was rough from being closed with a laser, but it was healing—that was all that mattered. His mottled skin was impossibly soft and silky. I could hardly believe it. I kept the pressure gentle, but I cleaned every spec of exposed skin.

Don only grew louder, making me smirk. I loved that I was the only one who made him like this.

With one last kiss, I pulled away and cleaned the area again. Instinct or not, mouths were disgusting cesspools of germs. Patting it dry with a soft towel, I inspected the sealed stab wound—I had to make sure it wasn't peeling open. Dr. Muznim had shown me exactly how to take care of Don, and I intended to follow her instructions. Nothing would happen to him on my watch. I put some oil on a cloth and rubbed the skin and surrounding scales. When I was finished, I put a clean plaster on.

"There. Perfect, just like you," I said.

He whimpered. His cock was straining against the fabric of his pants.

I grinned. My sweetheart needed release, and I was more than happy to help. I moved to his chest, kissing my way down.

"My Vince, you're hurt."

"I'm fine," I murmured between kisses. As long as I didn't use my injured arm, I could suck him off, which I wanted, more like needed. I undid his pants and started to pull them down. Don helped me, shimmying them off, though the second he grunted in pain, I shoved his hands away. I could do it.

His cock slapped his hard stomach, and I sighed. He was a thing of beauty. A bead of liquid came out of his slit. I licked my lips. "You look good enough to eat."

Don moaned, and another bead of pre-cum slipped out and down his length.

I bent down and licked the tip, tasting the sweetness. I didn't give Don any time to enjoy the prelude, just swallowed him as far as I could. He was too long and wide for me to take him to the root, but I took him as deep as possible and worked the rest with my free hand. I was used to being able to pump him with two hands, but that wasn't going to work right now. Still, I could make sure he enjoyed it—I was a skilled cocksucker.

Up and down, I bobbed, cheeks hollow. My tongue slicked over the underside of his cock, and just like humans, it was sensitive. Don cried out. I groaned at the sound, making him whimper. He buried a hand in my hair, not forcing me, but keeping me in place and connecting us even closer.

I licked the crown of his cock, prodding the slit.

"Vince," Don said, almost yelling.

"Come, Sweetheart. I want to drink your release. Come for me."

My mouth had just enclosed around him again when he cried and warmth rushed over my tongue. I moaned from the sweet taste and swallowed as fast as possible to not waste a single drop.

Don sagged back, panting. I cleaned him off, making him squirm, which I ignored, then crawled up beside him. He wrapped an arm around me and his tail coiled around my ankle.

"Now you," he said, breath harsh.

I nuzzled his neck. "I'm okay."

"Vince."

I kissed him, silencing him. "Sweetheart, I'm fine. I want to take care of you. Sleep."

Don fought me for a couple more minutes, but I kept petting his chest and nuzzling his neck, and predictably, he fell asleep. When I was certain he was deep asleep, I sat up to stare at him. My gaze slid to the metal crate with my stuff. Was I actually going to leave Don?

Anytime we were apart, I missed him so impossibly much. How was I supposed to survive months or even a year or two in the drakcol homeworld, then six months to Earth without him?

I couldn't. I loved Don and I was unwilling to let him go. I was that selfish. Don sure as hell deserved better, but fuck anyone who thought they could take him from me. And yeah, I'd spend my life needing him and being a burden to him, dragging around my baggage, but I loved him and couldn't live without him.

But what if Don's soulmate came for him? Panic pounded in my chest. If it happened after Don and I were mates, they'd be fuck out of luck, but it would be horrible for all of us. If it happened before... My knees shook. Don would leave me. And why wouldn't he? I was a mess. Why would he stay when his soulmate showed up? Someone who wasn't dragging around a gazillion pounds of crap.

"Vince," Don muttered, reaching for me. "Are you having a nightmare?"

I'd had nightmares, bad ones, every night since I was kidnapped, but that wasn't the problem. I walked over to him and cuddled close. "No, Sweetheart. I'm fine."

He placed a sloppy kiss on my forehead, not truly awake. "Sleep, my Vince."

Pressing close, I closed my eyes and breathed in his vanilla scent. "I love you."

Don moaned, but he didn't return the sentiment. Yet. He would, and we had time. Plenty of time. Because I wasn't leaving. I would kill that stupid soulmate if I had to. Don was mine. I did not deserve him, but I was sure as hell keeping him.

Chapter 43

MORE FUCKING DECISIONS.

Dontilvynsan

I moaned, and Vince growled around my cock, sending vibrations up my shaft. I'd moved, which he didn't like, because it hurt me. Every time he cleaned my injury and oiled my skin, he sucked me off, though he never let me reciprocate.

His silky tongue moved over my length, and I cried out, balls high and tight. I was close. Vince worked his tongue over the head of my cock, and I whimpered, then loudly yelled when he licked the slit.

"Vince, please!"

Soon, he thought. Vince was enjoying sucking me, but he liked pushing me toward my breaking point. All I could think about was his tongue on my bare skin. It had felt amazing. I'd never experienced anything like it.

Vince kept sucking and stroking my cock until I struggled to keep still, constantly begging him. He moved to the tapered crown and ordered, *Come for me, my Don.*

I came with a shout, head arching back as my hand fisted in his hair and my tail strangled his wrist. Pleasure zinged along my nerves, burning me. The waves of my orgasm dragged me under. It took me some time to come back to awareness. Vince, like always, was licking all of my seed off. I squirmed, sensitive, but he continued until he was done, then lay against my side.

"Please, my Vince," I asked. He hadn't had any release since his injury.

"No. Klars said my shoulder plasters can come off today, and I want to fuck you. So nope. I'm saving it."

I ran my hand over his back. "I would like that."

He kissed my chest. "Of course you would."

I kept him close against me as Vince nuzzled my neck and smoothed his hand over my side. I groaned.

Vince smiled against my neck. "Sleep."

My eyes started to close, but a random thought passed through Vince's head. He planned to go to the medbay after I fell asleep, then check in with Seth on how the hunt for the humans was going. Seth was probably on board, but he might be with Kalvoxrencol. The thought of Vince being on the station without me made my eyes snap open and my breath harshen.

"Sweetheart?"

"I will go with you."

"What?" he asked.

"I will go with you to the medbay, then to see Seth."

"You're not jealous, right?"

"No," I answered. "I know you love me, Vince."

He smiled, kissing the corner of my mouth, and my soul picked up. It took very little to stir me. I ran a hand over his back, and he arched into my touch. I couldn't help but think of how terrified he used to be of me when we first met, and now, he loved me and my touch.

"I want to go with you," I said, palming the back of his head. "Please, Vince."

"Why? I'm just going to the medbay. It's not a big deal."

"I need to make sure you're healing."

Vince kissed me. "You like to worry, my Don."

My soul stuttered.

"But fine. As long as we walk slowly. I don't want you to strain your injury."

"I can do that."

Vince

Klars walked around me. He looked so human, even though he wasn't. Amorians were apparently closely related to humans in the grand evolutionary scheme of the universe or some shit. They were faster, stronger, and had better sight I believed, not mentioning the dots that went down in a V to their nose and then another V on the sides of their mouth. The dots could rip open and reveal fangs and tentacles, according to Seth, but I was pretty sure he was shitting me.

Don said from behind me, "He's not."

My eyes widened in surprise.

"It's the truth," he said.

Klars glanced at us, probably confused by the one-sided conversation. I ignored him, since I didn't really like him anyway, and reached for Don with my good hand. He was pacing far too much as he waited for the results. Klars had merely scanned me. Nothing more. I was fine, even if the plasters had to stay on for a few more days.

He stood in between my legs, and I wrapped my arm around him, chin on his chest. I told him, "I love you."

Don bent to place his head on mine.

Apparently, I only had to say it once, and the words wouldn't stop coming out. I'd never told anyone I was with that I loved them, besides Seth, and that didn't count. Of course, I never loved someone like I loved Don.

His hand ran over my back, and he rubbed his forehead against mine. "Vince." He didn't say anything more than my name, but it was enough.

Klars returned, tablet in his pale hands. "From my scans, our techniques are not working as well on you, which I should've anticipated since the plasters on your hands hadn't worked quite as planned."

"What does that mean?" Don demanded, tail thrashing. "Vince will be fine, right?"

"Yes," he replied, not even looking at us, eyes on the tablet. "The plasters will take more time than I estimated, but he should make a full recovery. The bruises are fading, the scratches look excellent, and his scan is promising. Vince simply needs time." Klars tucked the tablet under his arm and smiled kindly at me. "Another week at the most, and you will be back to normal."

Well, I wouldn't be fucking Don tonight.

He pulled me closer. "Don't worry. We still can."

I frowned. It was fine if we didn't fuck; we had time.

Don looked at Klars and asked again, "But my Vince will be fine?"

"Yes. The damage, while colorful, wasn't as bad as it could've been. Arachlyns are exceedingly strong, and humans, from my study, are quite fragile."

Don straightened like a bolt of electricity had shocked him. I shot Klars a glare, and dragged Don closer. Fucking Klars. This was why I didn't like that fake, smiley asshole. He didn't need to scare Don. I was fine, and humans weren't weaklings.

I arched up and dragged Don down, planting a kiss on his lips. "I am fine," I whispered against him. To Klars, I said, "Shut the fuck up."

He simply lifted his eyebrows. "Captain Dontilvynsan, I believe Dr. Muznim said you should be resting."

I could feel a growl vibrating in his chest, and I tugged Don closer before he did something stupid. Growling at the humans' personal healer, the one chosen to keep oh-so-precious Seth alive wasn't a good idea, nor good for his job.

The growl died, probably because of my thoughts. "Come, my Vince," Don said.

Standing, I grabbed his hand, and we headed out of the medbay. I needed to tuck Don back in bed, then go see Seth; I should probably also call Teddy. He'd been holed up in his room. The captive humans somewhere were probably triggering him too.

"I'll go with you."

"Sweetheart, I'm fine." When Don didn't say anything, I glanced at him. His eyebrows were furrowed and his tail was near strangling my ankle. He was scared. I stopped and grabbed his face. "I promise not to leave the ship, Donny. I'm going to stay right here with you."

He frowned.

"You need to nap, and I'm sure go over reports or whatnot." I kissed him. "I'll come back."

Don nuzzled me. "Fine, my Vince. I will do as you say."

———

I sat on Seth's couch. Predictably, he had a live feed of his baby on the TV. The entire station was on lockdown as they searched for the humans. Scans had revealed nothing, but there were humans somewhere. Kal had ordered a full search. Seth was hopeful they would find the other humans soon.

I gripped my necklaces and announced, "I'm going to stay."

Seth jerked toward me. "What?"

"I'm going to stay here with Don, with you, with Teddy."

A smile spread over his face. "You are?"

"Yeah."

He dragged me into his arms. I stiffened before forcing myself to relax. "I mean, Don deserves more than me, but I can't leave him. I love him, Seth."

"What do you mean he deserves more? There's nothing wrong with you."

There were lots of things wrong with me, and Don was literally the best person I'd ever met.

"Vince?"

"What?"

"Don's lucky to have you."

I wasn't going to fight with him. Seth was way too nice, and he'd never come to my way of thinking. "Anyway, I haven't told him yet, but I thought about getting him a ring and asking him if he wants to be husbands, I guess."

"I'm pretty sure, he'll say yes."

"Me too." While Don hadn't told me that he loved me, he'd said we would be mates if I stayed. That was basically the human equivalent of marriage.

Seth squeezed me. "I'm so happy for you, and me. My baby needs their uncle, and I want my best friend."

I rolled my eyes. Seth and his kid, who would've thought? "How do I get a ring?"

He pointed to the dispenser. "NAID will have Don's measurements, so making a ring won't be hard. If you want something special engraved in it, just fool around with a design and NAID will implement it."

"Oh. Right."

"I did learn that from you," Seth replied, looking at his kid again.

The blob looked the exact same. I wasn't sure what I was even looking at.

I grabbed Seth's tablet, and sketched something. I wasn't great, but I only wanted stars on the inside of his band, so it didn't take much skill. Then I simply went to the dispenser and ordered a gold ring the size of his left ring finger.

With a quick goodbye, I went back to our apartment, the ring burning a hole in my pocket. Don might deserve better, but he wanted me. We were going to be together, no matter how guilty I felt about it.

Chapter 44

WHAT ARE YOU SAYING?

Dontilvynsan

I was sitting on my and Vince's bed, trying to read the reports Kalvoxrencol had sent, but I couldn't pay attention. Vince had shredded my focus. He was still injured. Klars had incorrectly estimated the amount of time it would take for Vince to recuperate, and it gutted me he remained in pain. I'd promised him that no one would ever touch him without his express permission and someone had. As much as Vince might say it wasn't my fault, it was.

My eyes locked onto the metal container that was full of Vince's stuff. He hadn't added anything to it, as far as I knew, since we'd been injured. I wanted to dump it on the floor and demand he stay, and yet, part of me wondered if it was best he was going home. By his own admission, Vince thought he would be happier on Earth than here with me.

The main door opened, and I looked toward the bedroom door, waiting. Vince appeared a moment later, and something inside of me relaxed. I almost wanted to laugh. I was contemplating sending him home, not that it was my choice, but I couldn't stand the thought of him being away from me.

Vince pressed a kiss to my forehead, and I breathed him in. "You're back."

"I told you I would be," Vince said.

He headed toward his crate, and my stomach clenched. Vince's thoughts were peaceful, if not a tad excited. Did he want to leave that badly? He reached into the crate and grabbed a folded shirt and set it on the floor. I frowned. Vince kept pulling clothes out, then when the stack began to teeter, he stood and disappeared into the closet.

My soul pounded. Vince was unpacking. "My Vince?"

"Hmm."

"What are you doing?"

Vince looked at me like I was ridiculous; his thoughts echoed his confusion. "Unpacking. I have been. For days."

"What?" My voice broke.

"Unpacking. It's not revolutionary. I'm putting my things back where they used to be."

Soul thrashing, I couldn't get a single word out.

He moved toward me, cupping my cheek. I leaned into his touch, rubbing on his palm. Vince asked, "You didn't notice?"

"No."

Carefully, he climbed onto my lap, and I hooked my arms around his waist, pleased when there wasn't even a tinge of fear within his mind. He pushed his hand into my hair, and I groaned. Every touch was amazing, and I would never tire of it or take the show of trust for granted.

"I'm staying," Vince said, swallowing. "I'm staying with you."

My soul stopped in my chest before it sped up so fast I could feel my pulse throbbing in my neck. "You are?"

"Yes," he said. While his voice was happy, his thoughts were nervous. Did he actually want to stay or had one of my brothers said something to him?

"My Vince, why are you scared?"

He frowned, then chuckled. "I should know better than to hide from you. I'm worried you'll say no. I'd understand if you did. I'm... complicated, and being with me will be burdensome. But..." He lifted and lowered his shoulders. "I love you, and I'm selfish."

Joy so fierce it stole my thoughts and breath consumed me. I pressed my lips against his, claiming him. Vince moaned, fingers buried in my hair. My tongue slipped into the wet warmth of his mouth and fucked him. My Vince. He was mine—now and forever.

Eventually thoughts began to break through the strength of my emotions. Vince thought he was a burden. Vince had doubts about staying rattling through him. Did he actually want this?

I pulled back, pressing my forehead against his, panting. "Vince." I didn't want to say anything to make him change his mind, but I had to. He was more important than me, as was his happiness. "Vince, do you think you'll be happier with me?"

He leaned back. "What do you mean?"

"Will you be happier here than on Earth?"

Frowning, he answered, "In ways, yes. I'll miss Earth, but you're here."

"What will you miss?"

A sad smile tugged at his lips. "Being able to keep myself safe."

I stared at him.

He laughed, kissing me. "It sounds ridiculous. But on Earth, I know how to read the room to keep myself safe, usually from homophobic pricks, but I didn't worry like here. I wasn't afraid all the time. Here, it's different. I'm not really ever safe unless I stay right here, beside you." Vince kissed me. "Not that I mind. I like being right here next to you."

"If you went to Earth, would you be happier? Safer?"

"No," he said slowly. "You're here, Donny."

While Vince was saying one thing, his thoughts were all over the place. He only felt safe with me. He loved me. He would miss me too much if he left. He felt unworthy. He felt upset about not banishing the memories of what happened. He was pissed they would keep coming back. He wished we could go to Earth together. He wanted more time. He wanted less time.

Vince didn't actually know what he wanted. And if he stayed with me, I feared he'd come to regret it one day. I would never survive that resentment from my mate, and by then, we would be publicly acknowledged as mates and he wouldn't be able to leave me or go back to Earth.

Also, would my inner fire start to grate on him? I'd seen that annoyance when he couldn't be embarrassed in private. How many more situations like that would happen? Would I spend our days counting down when he started to hate me?

But most importantly, did Vince truly love me or did he simply love the peace that I provided? I wasn't certain if Vince even knew the answer to that question. He was so confused, so unsure, so unhappy, so scared. Vince was so many emotions that I could hardly breathe.

My soul shattered in my chest. I was going to have to let Vince go.

"Maybe you shouldn't stay," I said carefully.

White-hot pain flashed through Vince. "What?"

"If you would be happier on Earth, then you should go."

Vince shoved my hands away and slid off my lap, breath harsh. "You want me to leave?"

"No!" I growled. I took a deep breath to calm myself. "I want you to be happy and safe. Wherever that might be, even if it's not by my side."

He gripped his necklaces, panting. His thoughts were a roiling mess of hurt.

"Vince, I want you to stay," I told him again. "I do. But I want you to be safe. I don't wish you to regret your decision. I couldn't handle that or the subsequent resentment. It would kill me."

"I can't know the future, Don. I don't know if I'll regret it or not. I can't know, and neither can you," he snapped. "All I know is right now. And right now, I want to be with you and you don't want me to."

"Vince—"

"I offered myself, and you rejected me."

"Vince," I started again, but he wouldn't let me.

He shoved a hand through his short black hair. "Don, why can't you be fine with right now?"

"Because I have to think of the future, for both of us."

"Mindy and Kal can accept when Teddy and Seth say they'll love them forever, even though they can't promise that. Why can't you?"

"I'm not my brothers, and you are not Seth or Bartholomew. You, by your own words, would feel safer on Earth. What am I to say to that? I need you to be safe. I need you to be happy. And, Vince, you do not know what you want."

He shook his head, coming closer. "I know what I want. I want you. You're the one who doesn't know what you want or... maybe you do. Maybe you've decided I'm too much work or that now, presented with forever, you're not ready to commit."

I got to my feet stiffly. "That's not it. I want you, Vince."

"Then why are you rejecting me?"

Cupping his cheek, I wiped the tears that had started to spill away with my thumb, careful not to cut him with my claw. "I'm not. I would be with you forever, but I'm afraid you're picking me because of what happened, not because you truly want me. I don't want you to choose me out of fear. I want you to be happy."

Vince pressed against me, and I wound my arms around him. I loved him so dearly, but his needs would always take precedence over mine. There was also a small worm of fear that refused to be banished that Vince didn't truly want me.

"This has happened relatively fast," he said, voice muffled. "I came and then we were together."

I ran my fingers through his hair. It hadn't felt fast to me, but I felt his pain dimming.

"Maybe we need time."

"What do you mean, my Vince?"

He took a deep breath and leaned back to give me a shaky smile. "Maybe we should stick to the original plan? I'll go back to your homeworld, and you'll go about your duty." He nodded. "It's for the best, I think."

A claw shredded my gut more painful than the knife that stabbed me days ago, more painful than anything I'd ever experienced. "Is that what you wish?"

"Yes." Vince smiled.

"So you and I will be no more."

"No." He went up on his toes to kiss me. "No, you're fucking mine. We are not breaking up." A thought of an angry man with wet-looking hair, screaming, 'We were on a break' popped into his mind, and I had no idea what to make of it. "We're just pausing or taking a breath. We're together. I'll stay in your room, and we'll talk every single day, but we'll take a moment to both think about what we want."

Before I could say anything, NAID said, "Captain, Prince Kalvoxrencol needs to speak with you. He found the humans."

"Go," Vince said, patting my chest. "Sweetheart, it'll be alright."

Swallowing a growl, I kissed him, then slowly walked out the room while the feeling I was losing something infinitely precious swept through me.

Chapter 45

THE END OF WHAT IS.

Vince

Don was a fucking bastard. I fought to keep my thoughts calm, so he wouldn't feel me and become distracted. The poor rescued humans needed all of his focus, not me and my pissed off self. I chucked my clothes back into the crate without bothering to fold them. Who fucking cared about wrinkles? Not me.

I sank to the floor, and simply breathed instead of sobbing like I wanted to. My hand snaked into my pocket to draw out the ring. I'd wanted Don to be my husband. I wanted to spend the rest of my life with him, but he had doubts. Part of me wanted to yell at him, but another part understood.

For drakcol, they mated once and that was it. Once Don fell in love with me, we'd be together forever. Separating mates had the potential to kill them.

We humans could fall out of love. Of course he was nervous. Not to mention I was a walking disaster. He wasn't only signing up for the potential of me hating him because I was stuck with him, he was also agreeing to being with me and all my baggage for the rest of his life.

It was no wonder he needed a second to think about it.

A little separation, perspective might be good for the both of us. Our relationship had started very quickly after we met. I'd never been one to mind jumping into bed with someone... Well, now it was different. With what had happened to me and with Don coming into my life, he was the only person who would ever be in my bed for the rest of my life, as far as I was concerned.

But maybe some time apart would allow us to connect on a different level, and for Don to grow assured of how much I loved him. Besides, a bit of quiet would be nice. Of course we would be traveling back to Tamkolvanloknol with a group of traumatized humans, so peace and quiet might not be on the menu.

I covered my eyes and rocked. No. All of this was shit. I wanted Don, and the rat bastard didn't want me. Panting, I promised myself that I wouldn't cry. That I wouldn't succumb to the urge to lie down and never move again. I was fine. I was perfectly fine. I'd leave Don, and we would either be fine in the end, or the fucker had earned a stalker for the rest of his life.

The bell rang.

"NAID," I snapped. "Who is it?"

"Prince Consort Seth Harris," the computer responded.

"Let him in."

The main door whooshed open, and Seth called out, "Vince?"

"In the bedroom. Don't worry, I'm decent."

Seth chuckled and appeared as I was chucking more of my crap into the bin. His eyebrows drew together. "Weren't you unpacking?"

I snorted and threw shirt after shirt into the metal crate, each giving a satisfying slap. "Nope."

"Vince, what happened?" Seth rested a hand on me to stop my frantic movements.

With a deep breath, I shoved the hurt down. Don wasn't rejecting me. He simply needed time, and I could—would give him that. He was worth every effort, every risk, every sacrifice—Don was worth everything. Whatever he needed, I would give to him and more. Or so I told myself.

"Don wants me to go home."

Seth's mouth fell open. "What the fuck did you just say?"

I laughed, a true one. "That was my response. He thinks I'll be happier and safer. And I might be. But he's here, and I don't want to leave him."

"But *he* wants you to?"

"No, yes, maybe." I ran a hand through my hair, then took another breath. I had to keep my emotions relatively calm. Don would expect some anger and frustration, but too much and it would distract him from the humans who needed his full focus. "He needs time, I think. This is all happening super fast."

"That... I guess that makes sense," Seth said. "But you don't want time."

"I want Don."

Seth frowned. "That fucking bastard."

I almost laughed, but it turned into a sob of pain. Don wasn't rejecting me, but it felt like he was, and, fuck, it hurt.

Arms surrounded me and drew me in tight. "He broke your heart."

I slapped away the tears. "No. He didn't. We just need time."

"So what are you going to do?"

"Give him what he needs. I'll go back to Tamkolvanloknol, and Don will go wherever he's been ordered to go. When he comes back, we'll try again."

"And if the ship leaves for Earth before then?"

I glared at him. "I'm not leaving Don. If he needs time, he has it. But make no mistake, Seth, Don is fucking mine and no one will take him from me."

Seth shook his head. "It's no wonder Don likes you. Drakcol have a thing for possessive people."

Well, that suited me just fine.

Suddenly, Seth reached into his pocket and pulled out a touchstone. "Kal? What's wrong?" He paused for several seconds. "I did tell you I figured that would happen." Another pause. "Yes, yes, you didn't want to risk me. Mindy and Fyn can bring me onto the station." He slid the light blue stone back into his pocket.

"What?" I asked.

"It's the humans. Kal found them."

"I know that."

"There's a little over three hundred," he continued, "and they've been shoved into a rather small space."

I swallowed as memories surfaced. I knew exactly what that felt like.

"Kal didn't want me to go, because—" He cut off to wave at my still visible bruises and my bound arm.

"Naturally."

"But none of them will talk to him or Don, so they need a human, like I told Kal." Seth shook his head, but he was smiling and blushing like a teenager. "He wants to keep me safe."

Red flag, thy name is Kal. Though that was a bit hypocritical coming from me. We were both overly protective. I hated the thought of Don on the space station as well. He'd been hurt and was recovering.

Seth stood. "I have to go. Did you want to come?"

I immediately shook my head. It wasn't that I didn't care, because I did, but the thought of seeing a bunch of dirty, terrified humans shoved into a small space was too much. It reminded me too much of what happened to me, and I couldn't do it, as much as I wanted to.

"If you need me, call," Seth said, hesitating at the door.

I waved him off, and Seth left. I continued to throw my things into the crate, trying very hard not to be mad or hurt.

Less than five minutes passed before the chime sounded again. I fought a snarl. I wanted to be left alone, but clearly, that wasn't going to happen. I shouted, "Come in."

"Vince?" Teddy called.

"Bedroom," I yelled, throwing more shit into the crate.

His eyes followed the steady stream of shirts that landed in the crate. "Seth called. They found the humans."

"Yep."

"They're safe, I guess."

"Yep." I didn't want to talk about them.

"Seth told me about Don."

I threw a sweater into the bin harder than needed, the metal from the zipper smacking into the side. "He wants me to go home. What else is there to say?"

Teddy nodded and sat on the bed. "You were planning on staying?"

Guilt smacked me. I hadn't told Teddy. I should have, but I was a bastard like that. Also, I hadn't wanted to bother him, especially with the xoi here, the captive humans, and all that. I said, "It hasn't been that long."

"Hmm."

Sighing, I faced him. "I'm sorry, alright. Everything has happened so quickly. I did plan to tell you that I'm staying."

"Even with Don and you breaking up?"

"We're not breaking up," I snapped, then took a deep breath and shoved a hand through my hair. "No matter what, I'm staying."

He stared at me for several long moments, then asked, "Do you want Mindy to beat him up?"

I burst into laughter and sat on the ground across from Teddy. "Do you think he could?"

"No, and I doubt he would either."

"Yeah, probably not." These siblings were very close. My eyes closed and I hugged my knees to my chest. "I'll be okay. Me and Don will be fine too."

"Thanks for staying," Teddy whispered. "I need you."

Tears burned my eyes from that admission. He didn't do emotion, so saying that had cost him. I gave Teddy a wide smile. "I need you too. You're one of my best friends."

Teddy smiled. "We'll be okay. I know the start wasn't great, but…" He waved around. "Things are working out."

I fought a sob. It would all work out as long as Don chose me. I nodded. "We'll make it."

———

I lay in bed alone. It was late, and Don hadn't come back. I wasn't sure if he was going to or not. I'd heard nothing about the humans, besides the fact Seth had gotten them calmed down and Klars was checking them out.

The door opened, and the bed dipped before fingers skated through my hair. "You're back," I said.

"Yes," Don whispered. "I had to get the station security set up for the humans as well as everyone else's arrangements."

"Why?"

"The Cohort ordered two additional ships to come to protect the humans while the *Admiral Ven* travels here. The ships will be here tomorrow. After that, there will be no reason for me to stay."

"I see."

Don paused, then moved away. I heard him going through the motions to go to bed. He settled behind me, not reaching for me. He was giving me space, but I didn't want space. I rolled over and draped across his chest, like usual. His arms came around me, and he nuzzled the top of my head.

Taking a deep inhale of his soft vanilla scent, I said, "We'll be alright, Sweetheart. I promise."

We would survive, even if it wasn't fun.

He cupped the back of my head. "Sleep, my Vince."

Cuddling into his warm embrace, I closed my eyes. Me and Don would be fine. Everything would be just fine, eventually.

Chapter 46

TIME FLIES WHETHER YOU WANT IT TO OR NOT.

Dontilvynsan

"He's so cute, Don. He's got blue scales, a little bit lighter than Kal's, but his brown hair and eyes are all Seth. God, I just want to smoosh his face," Vince gushed, lying on our bed back at the palace. I was still aboard my ship, far away from him, and it had been months since I'd seen Vince with my own eyes.

No matter how much time passed, I couldn't stop thinking about the day I'd left Vince. His sadness about being separated, his terror of staying on the station, his utter unwillingness to let me go. I'd kissed him, not caring who was watching, needing to be close with my mate, and Vince had held onto me while he silently asked that I demand he stay. I hadn't, and I regretted it everyday since, but, at the same time, it had been the right thing to do. Vince needed to make his own decision, and I needed to be chosen for who I was.

"He's the cutest baby," Vince said, hugging himself.

"Kalvoxrencol sent me several images of their kit," I replied, smiling as Vince grinned. "Have they picked a name?"

"No. Seth's determined to name him Bob. Seriously? Who names their kid Bob?"

No drakcol of Kalvoxrencol's station would.

"Kal's refusing. It's become a silent battle between them. Well, one of them. Kal literally cannot stay silent."

"Seth still can't let anyone besides Kalvoxrencol hold their child?" I asked.

It had been a week since the kit's birth, and I'd received multiple notes about Seth refusing to allow anyone to hold the baby besides him and his mate. Kalvoxrencol had merely said Seth needed time. His mate was utterly terrified something would happen to their child. This was the first human and drakcol hybrid, though I doubted the last. None of the seeker souls knew if the baby would be alright or if something would happen. Seth had a hard time accepting that. Naturally, he loved his child.

"Not yet," Vince said. "Well, he's letting me and Wyn hold the baby. Other than that, no. I think Fyn's really hurt. He and Seth are close."

I imagined my younger brother was, and yet, out of everyone, Zoltilvoxfyn understood Seth and the way he battled his mind.

"But Seth's talking to his therapist. I think he'll get there. It'll take time. He hasn't left Bob alone for even a minute yet."

"So you're calling him Bob?" I asked, rolling to my side and staring at Vince's lovely face. I missed him. It was a constant ache in my soul, and the separation was starting to affect me. Every breath wasn't enough, and my guts were constantly churning, making it difficult to eat. Every night when I tried to sleep, my arms would reach for him, and when he wasn't there, it would hurt like it was the first time. It wasn't getting better, but rather, becoming worse.

"You know Seth will win this fight. They might make his name ridiculously long, but Seth will be calling his son Bob."

"You're probably correct."

"Do you want kids?"

I ran my eyes over my beautiful mate and replied, "Perhaps."

"What does that mean?"

Resting my cheek in my hand, I said, "When I was younger, I wanted to be a father because of how much I adored my younger brothers. Then when all of them so despised my inner fire over the years, I rethought it."

"Those bastards."

I smiled at how protective he was of me. "It wouldn't be pleasant for a child to have your father be aware of your every thought and emotion. There would be no privacy. I would love that child, and having them hate me for something I couldn't control would destroy me."

My mate frowned. "You don't know they would."

I lifted an eyebrow.

"Fine," Vince said, voice rough, "the kids will hate it at some point, but that doesn't mean you shouldn't have them. You'll be an amazing father, Dontilvynsan. You are so sweet and understanding and kind." He shook his head. "I can imagine how soft and lovely you'll be."

When my mate left, it would hardly matter. I would never have a child without Vince. I simply said, "Thank you."

Vince's smile turned gentle. His hand stretched toward the screen. "I miss you."

A groan formed in the back of my throat. "I miss you, my Vince." Miss was far too small of a word. It was an all-consuming black hole of need.

His eyes closed, and his breathing began to deepen. The hour was late, and he'd been busy and would be busy... without me. Stars, that thought burned. It wasn't that I disliked Vince having things to do, but it was difficult how well he was doing without me, while I was struggling to cope without him by my side. This space in our relationship without clear guidelines of what we were was hard for me.

Vince had said we were the same as before. He wasn't courting anyone else, as far as I was aware, and neither was I. I scoffed. I didn't want anyone else. Vince was my soul.

He jerked, eyes opening, and he blinked rapidly. "Sorry, Sweetheart, I'm just tired."

"It's fine. Sleep."

"No," he groaned, flopping, which made me smile. Almost anything he did made me smile. "I miss you. I wanted to jerk off together."

That was something we did often. Vince loved to watch me and I him as we chased our pleasure.

"Tomorrow," I said. I fought a growl. It had been six months of tomorrows already.

"When are you coming home?"

"I do not know." I wished to say I was heading toward him right now, but that wasn't true. There had been strange activity on the Immortal Planet, and the Cohort and the Council of Seekers were hesitant to have me end my vigil. They were sending out a ship to form a base on the most distant moon of the planet, so the planet could be protected and observed constantly, something we hadn't done before, because we didn't want to chance interference.

"Seth's going with the ship to Earth," Vince muttered.

The air left my lungs like I'd been hit in the gut. "What? When are you leaving?"

"A month, I think," he replied, yawning. "Seth and Kal are going. Fyn and Caleb aren't. It's not safe for Caleb to travel so long. Mindy and Teddy are on the fence."

I frowned. I didn't understand what fencing had to do with this situation.

"Wyn's going. He said he would never let Seth and his child out of his sight for a year or more. Teddy and Caleb do have a huge list of 'samples' they want Seth to 'collect.' For Teddy, I think it's going to come down to whether the Cohort will allow him to get his family. He wants to talk to them and see if they want to come back to Tamkolvanloknol. Oh, Camden is also petitioning for his brother to come back with him. Poor Shannon has been asking every day for the ship to leave sooner. She misses her wife and kids, and I don't really blame her."

I tried to find something to say, but panic rang in my ears so loud that I couldn't seem to find any thoughts. Vince was leaving for

Earth in a month. It would take longer than that for me to return home, even if I was allowed to.

"Pierce isn't going. She's been spending time with Caleb and his sister-not-sister Tinlorray." Vince wiggled his eyebrows. "I suspect we'll hear wedding bells soon enough." When I didn't respond, he said, "They'll be mates, Sweetheart."

I grunted.

"Anyway, the *Admiral Ven* has to rush, I guess," Vince said, yawning. "With the xoi taking so many humans, the Cohort needs to claim Earth." He laughed.

I swallowed at the sound. How many more times would I hear it? "What?"

His eyes cracked open. "Did you know they are declaring Seth the leader of Earth?"

"The Cohort is?"

"Yeah. I guess to claim Earth as under drakcol protection they have to say Seth is the leader, and since he's mated to Kal, the planet belongs to the Drakcol Empire. They're doing some fast wording that I'm sure Caleb gave them. It's a ploy to establish a base nearby, but undetectable by human tech. It should keep any xoi ships away. The vveki apparently support it. They want to stop illegal trafficking of Earth spiders. One of the priests went so far to say he had a vision of the goddess telling him Seth was the earthen ruler."

Vince broke into a fit of laughter. "God, Seth's so uncomfortable. He wanted so badly for Teddy to be the one they used, but all the humans we've rescued and who want to stay have huddled under Seth's protection. I think it's because he's so normal. Everyone's comfortable with him. And Seth's so terrified of power he's never going to misuse it."

It didn't surprise me that the vveki had supported the claiming of Earth. If it worked, the Coalition would turn it into a reserve of sorts, to keep the remaining humans safe until they were ready to travel among the stars. The vveki had great camouflaging technology—it was how they survived. They were a small unassuming race, but they were insanely intelligent.

"Did you know the vveki inject themselves with spider venom to speak to their goddess?" Vince asked. "It kills some of them. But they call it dying in her embrace. It's so sought after that they have to limit it to a select few who build up an immunity."

"I did."

He grinned. "You're so smart, Sweetheart."

Warmth flooded me at the compliment, even though my first instinct was to deny it.

Vince snuggled closer to the screen. "I'm falling asleep."

"Then go to sleep."

He shook his head. "I miss you. I want to talk to you."

"And I shall be here tomorrow."

"I know, but all I can do is send messages until tomorrow night. That's not enough."

It wasn't, but it was all we had. During the day we would exchange countless notes. Vince would send some as innocuous as what he was eating, which I liked because it alerted me to the fact he was taking care of himself, or what his plans were. I would send him snippets of my day, omitting how increasingly hard it was to be apart from him. Then every night we would see each other. Sometimes we stared at each other, others we talked, and most nights we pleasured ourselves. With each release, it made me more lonely for him.

"Sleep, my Vince. I shall stay here until you fall asleep."

He grunted, squishing a pillow to his chest. "I love you."

I wanted to return the words, but then he would know he was my mate. "I am yours," I told him, and he smiled.

It didn't take long for him to fall asleep, but I didn't end the session. Instead I got as close as possible to the screen and listened to my mate breathe. The sound was the most wondrous thing I'd ever heard in my life, and I never wanted to stop hearing it for as long as I lived.

Vince

I bounced Bob—or Bobbinvoxlyn— in my arms as Seth slowly moved around his and Kal's apartment, straightening shit up. I had no idea how much of a mess babies made before Seth had one. It made me a tad hesitant about having one with Don, but I wanted to see his face on my own child, so I would get over it. Besides, the image of the massive Don so gently holding our baby wouldn't leave my thoughts. One day, we'd have one, maybe two.

Kal had stepped out for a moment to speak to his father about the coming journey and smooth over the fact that in the three weeks since Bob's birth only I, Wyn, and Fyn had held him, beside Kal and Seth himself obviously.

Seth was trying, but he was paranoid as hell about his kid. He knew he had to loosen up for the good of his baby, but knowing something and getting your brain to calm down about it were two very different things.

He wasn't the only one who was paranoid. Wyn checked in often to make sure Bob was healthy, Urgg called at least once a day—I loved the barbarus who was Seth's mentor as well as his friend, and I couldn't wait to meet them in person—and Edith had constant sensors on him. Bob was going to grow up surrounded by overprotective adults.

I figured once Kal and Seth had another, which they both wanted, and other humans started popping out hybrids, everyone would calm the fuck down. Until then, Bob was going to be a spoiled little monster. As he should be.

Grinning, I ran my finger down the center of his forehead to the tip of his nose. He was adorable. A perfect mix of Kal and Seth, leaning more to Seth's features, which I highly approved of.

"I can't believe I'm not going to see you or this little tyke for a year, at least. Maybe two. He's going to be huge by the time you get back," I said. I would miss Seth fiercely, but I couldn't go. I didn't want to be separated from Don for that long. Six, almost seven, months was more than enough. I was getting desperate for him. Talking to him over video chat wasn't enough. I needed to hear him in person, to feel the rumble of amusement in his chest, and experience the scrape of his scales against my skin.

Selfishly, I also wanted him back because I'd slept horribly since we'd separated. Nightmares plagued me almost nightly. I'd wake up terrified, and Don wouldn't be there. But it was more than that; I missed spending time with him.

"I can't believe I have to go," Seth said, sitting next to me. His brown eyes were ringed with dark circles and his shoulders were slumped in obvious exhaustion. "I don't want to."

"I know." I bumped his shoulder with mine. "But think of all the hoodies you can steal."

He chuckled. "You just want me to bring back chocolate."

I'd made an extensive list of plants and things I wanted, as had Caleb, Teddy, and Seth. Of course, the Council of Seekers wanted their own samples, and Fyn had requested certain plant samples he wanted—flowers mainly.

"I do want chocolate and coffee."

Seth leaned back against the other arm of the couch, as I was on the part that had a back. It was Kal's invention. Part of the couch had a back where us humans could lounge and the rest was backless for drakcol. I'd ordered one for mine and Don's room already.

"I'm glad it's the *Admiral Ven* we're traveling on. I'm used to it. And I'm also glad you're staying, though," he said.

"Why?"

"You can head the human sanctuary project on the moon and get everything ready."

Buildings were slowly going up, and plans for where the fields would go were being drawn. Part of the sample taking was for us humans. All plants taken from Earth would be exclusively for human usage. It was so we could then make businesses off the products and make money. The drakcol were trying to set us up as much as possible because they saw this whole fiasco as their fault. If Kal hadn't taken Seth, none of this would've happened.

I never thought I'd be grateful for Seth being abducted, but I couldn't imagine not being with Don.

The door opened, and Kal strode in. He went straight to Seth, gently stroking his cheek while his tail curled about Seth's ankle. "Husband."

Seth blushed like a kid.

God, they were sickeningly adorable. I fucking hated it.

Well, that wasn't accurate. I was jealous. Ridiculously jealous. I wanted to curl up on Don's lap making people sick with how sickening we were being. Was that too much to ask?

"Mate," Kal whispered against Seth's ear, "you need to go nap. You didn't sleep last night."

Seth looked at Bob, who was passed out in my arms, and worried at the hem of his hoodie.

"I have him," I said. "You know I'd never let anything happen to my nephew. Besides, Edith is always around." At her name, a blue head popped in and out of the TV-sized screen. "Wyn will probably stop by, and as useless as Kal is, he's here."

Kal lifted his lip at me in a soundless snarl, but it was nothing compared to the scowl Seth shot my way.

"Kal is not useless."

"Oh," I said, like I was shocked he was defending his husband. "If he isn't, then why are you afraid to nap? Bob is Kal's kid too. If he's not useless, then go take a nap."

Seth frowned. "I hate you sometimes."

I grinned. "I know."

He stood and gave Kal a half-hug and cast one more nervous glance at Bob before he went to lie down.

When the door clicked closed, Kal said, "That was well done."

I lifted my eyebrow. "It's like I know him or something."

He frowned and planted himself not far from me as we both stared blankly ahead. We didn't necessarily hate each other anymore, but we would never be best friends, which was fair.

"So you're staying," he finally said, breaking the silence.

"Yep."

"Does Dontilvynsan know?"

"No," I said sarcastically. "He has no idea. I'm merely living in his apartment and spending his money."

"You should tell him."

So Kal didn't get sarcasm. More reasons to dislike him. "He knows, Kal," I said. "I told him that before we separated, and just a few nights ago, I talked about how everyone was leaving." I didn't specifically say that I was waiting for him in the conversation, I thought—I'd been half asleep—but I knew I'd mentioned who was going and whatnot. Don knew I was his. I'd told him.

"Are you sure?"

"Say whatever it is that you want to," I snapped.

Bob scrunched his little face up, and I bounced him, my arm burning. Kal reached over and pulled his infant into his arms, soothing the child back to sleep. If Seth heard Bob cry, he wouldn't be able to nap.

"Dontilvynsan hasn't spoken to us much, and when he has, he's been... odd."

A needle punctured my heart. "What?"

"There's something wrong, but I can't say what it is. He won't talk to us, and you haven't said exactly what happened between the two of you."

I'd told Seth, Teddy, Camden, and Pierce the generals of it, but I hadn't told the particulars to any of the brothers, because they'd been pricks to me—so fuck them. But it seemed Don had kept quiet too, which was what probably made them all be horrible to me in the first place.

While Kal would literally be the last person in the entire fucking universe I would choose to talk to, I had to say something. He knew Don, as much as I hated to admit it.

"I'm sure you're aware I have some issues." God, it was like glass coming out.

"Seth nor Dontilvynsan have told me, but I have a guess about what might have happened to you."

Fuck it. "I was raped, okay? A lot. It messed me up."

Kal's face turned so kind that I wanted to sock him. If he hadn't been holding Bob, I might have.

"Anyway, it left me lots of *gifts* that keep on giving," I spat out, crossing my arms. "Don helps."

"His inner fire."

"At first," I admitted, "but then it was just him. Only him." I smiled at the thought of curling up on his lap. There was no place I felt safer or happier. "I wanted to go to Earth to erase my memories

of what happened after I'd been abducted, but I fell in love with
Don. When I told him I wanted to stay, he told me to go home."

"What?" Kal barked, making Bob open his eyes and release a small
cry. Kal was up on his feet in a flash, rocking his child while his eyes
flicked to the bedroom door. The second Bob quieted, Kal repeated,
"What?"

"I offered myself to Don, and he said no."

"He said no?"

"Are you going to repeat everything I say?" I asked but didn't give
him time for a response. "I told him I would, in some ways, feel safer
on Earth. Don wants me, which he made a point to say." I glared
at Kal for good measure in case he thought I'd forced his brother to
be with me. "But he wanted me to go back to where I would be the
happiest. Honestly, he couldn't accept the fact that I *might* not like
being here in the future or resent him for staying.

"I can't predict what I will or won't feel," I said. "And unlike you
and Mindy, he couldn't get past it. So we decided that we needed
some space. Our relationship happened super quickly, and we both
needed to think about what we want. We're still together, but we're
taking a breath."

Kal stared at me like I was a moron.

I stood. "You know what? I'm out."

"Vince," he called. "Stop. Please."

It was the "please" that made me freeze at the door.

"I forget that humans don't understand us, much like we don't
always understand you."

I turned around, and Kal walked toward me. I refused to flinch or cower, not that I actually thought he would harm me. Annoying as he was, I was far more likely to punch Kal than he was me. Stupid for such a small guy as I was, but, hey, that was me.

"Dontilvynsan would give up everything for you. His happiness, his peace, his soul, and even his life would be nothing compared to yours in his mind. If you would feel safer on Earth, then of course he is going to insist you go. You are the most important thing to him."

My pulse thudded in my ears. And I asked, even though I was fairly certain I knew the answer, "What are you saying?"

"You're Dontilvynsan's mate."

I had no words, but Kal apparently did.

"We've known for a while, and by we, I mean myself, the rest of my brothers and Monqilcolnen."

Those fucking fuckers of fucktown.

"Dontilvynsan told us not to tell you. He didn't want to pressure you into staying."

"So," I started, holding up a hand, "he was going to let me get on a ship to Earth, knowing it might kill him?"

"Yes."

"I'm going to kill him," I growled. "That bastard. What? Did he think you lot wouldn't break down and tell me before I wiped my goddamn memory? Of course you would, and then I would've been pissed the whole way back to him. That selfless asshole. Why doesn't he value himself? I'm going to kill him. I swear I'm going to strangle him within an inch of his life, then make him promise to never lie to me again."

I glanced at Kal, and his expression was murderous. I took a step back, swallowing.

"You will not harm my brother," he all but snarled, tail thrashing.

So drakcol also didn't understand hyperbole. Fantastic. "I'm not serious, Kal. I would never hurt Don. Not ever. I love him."

"Humans sometimes hurt those they claim to love."

My eyes flicked to the bedroom door. Seth had lived through such situations. I shook my head. "I'm not like them. When humans are angry, we sometimes spout things we don't actually mean. Ask Don yourself. I have never hurt him, and I never will. I'm just mad—furious really. I'd give up everything for him."

Kal forced a smile, but I could tell he was pissed because the barest amount of light gathered under his scales, and his tail flicked incessantly. He took a deep breath before he said, in an almost normal voice, "Dontilvynsan has always acted as if his only worth is what he can do for others. You, being his mate, would be the hardest for him to burden."

Don being a burden? Kal had to be kidding. Don could never be a burden. He was sweet, funny, smart, kind, and loyal to a fault. I loved him. Something clicked in my brain, and my pulse raced. If *I* didn't think Don was a burden, then maybe, just maybe, he didn't think me and my problems were one either. Maybe, like me, he simply wanted me and the rest didn't truly matter... It was too much to hope for, but maybe.

"He would hate thinking you were only staying because he needed you to," Kal continued.

That I got. Everyone wanted to be chosen, not to be the last pick in dodgeball that someone was forced to be with. While it had been a shock, falling in love with Don had been a sequence of choices, none of which I regretted.

I nodded. "I get it."

"So what are you going to do?"

"Hmm, make him suffer."

Kal growled, and I smirked. God, he was easy now that I knew what button to push.

"I'm going to think about how I can make sure Don knows I'm choosing him," I said with a shrug.

He smiled, the first real one he'd ever shot in my direction, and it made me want to punch him. "Good," he said. "You can always seek the Crystal. It's very romantic."

I rolled my eyes. Nothing like a floating rock to spell romance. "Yes, and when it spits out some random dude or Mindy as my mate, I'm sure everyone will be *thrilled*."

"You don't believe Dontilvynsan is your soulmate?"

"I don't think it matters. I pick Don, soulmate or not. But if you think some mystical bond will make him assured of me, then I'll think about it." In some ways it would be nice if I was Don's soulmate. I'd no longer worry about some random person showing up and trying to steal him.

Kal pursed his lips, as if he was truly thinking about it. "I believe it might comfort Dontilvynsan. He would know you are his, never to be taken away. Possession is a strong need for us drakcol."

That I knew. Well, it might not be a bad idea, unless the Crystal screwed me over, then it would suck ass.

"I'll think about it," I said before slipping out the door.

Chapter 47

THIS MIGHT NOT BE A GREAT IDEA.

Dontilvynsan

Vince had been distant the last few days. We'd talked every night, but it had been stilted and his thoughts had obviously been elsewhere. I'd never missed my inner fire more. I needed to know what was bothering him. Perhaps nothing was. He could merely be excited to start the journey back to Earth.

I closed my eyes against the fresh wave of pain.

"Captain?" Commander Bimwoxcol asked in a low voice that would be heard by my ears alone. "Are you well? Perhaps you should visit Doctor Muznim. You've been looking rather strained lately."

That was one way to put it. I'd lost weight between my churning gut and my inability to sleep. It was starting to affect my work. Concentrating was becoming difficult, and out here on the edge of Drakcon space, that was dangerous. I couldn't in good conscience endanger my crew.

I had two options: pass temporary command to Commander Bimwoxcol, or confess to my parents and superiors who Vince was to me. The latter presented its own issues. My parents would never allow Vince to leave, at least not without explaining exactly what it meant that he was my mate. They would present him the information, much like if I'd sought the Crystal and it revealed Vince as mine, then allow him to make a decision. But Vince would never choose his happiness or safety over my life.

Nevertheless, I had to do something.

"Commander, when are the support ships arriving?" I asked.

Construction on the moon base had begun, but additional ships to patrol the area had been requested. The Immortal Planet was out of phase for the moment, but the satellite showed anomalous readings consistent with xoi technology as well as some readings consistent with the Crystal. We couldn't allow anything else to infect the planet. When the planet returned to our sensors, we would find a way to extract anything that didn't belong.

"Ten days."

My tail flicked in acknowledgment. When they arrived, I was going home. Vince wouldn't be there when I returned, but I was still going. I could do this no longer. I opened my mouth to say as much, when a light flashed on the main screen.

A sudden flux appeared in the sensors, originating from the planet. It wasn't supposed to come into phase yet, and it didn't appear to be doing so. But these readings...

"Take the ship back," I ordered. We moved further away from the planet, but the wave kept coming. "Full speed."

It didn't help. Whatever this wave was, it was moving faster than we were.

"Brace for impact," I ordered.

A charge went through the ship and raced along our systems. Sparks shot into the air and a fire erupted from one of the consoles. I gripped the arms on my stool and rode it out until the whole ship went dark.

"Report," I barked.

Bimwoxcol said, "Most of our internal and external sensors are offline, and NAID is not responding."

"Life support?"

"Operational."

I allowed myself a moment to collect my thoughts, then began issuing orders. "Form a search team to look for injured crew members, then our first priority needs to be reinitializing NAID."

"Understood."

"And someone tell me what that was!" I snarled as I started working on my console.

Vince

"Please," I asked again.

Seth groaned and chucked another onesie-like baby outfit into a metal container. "No, Vince. Do you know how busy I am? Do you know how much shit babies require, and how much I have to pack up to go on the ship to Earth?"

True. Babies seemed to have a lot of accessories. Bob was currently with Kal and Fyn, who were walking through the garden; Fyn and Kal needed some time to actually hang out together. Often they got busy with their mates and lives, but the brothers needed each other. I thought it was sweet. Besides, Seth allowing Bob outside without him was a huge step.

"I did a tarot reading, and it even helped me decide this," I said. Finally, I'd been able to do a reading for myself... and it had felt liberating. I was reclaiming parts of myself that I'd thought were lost, and I was no longer afraid of the future.

"I forgot you did that," Seth commented, glancing at me.

"Want me to do one for you?"

"So it manipulates me into doing what you want?" he asked with a chuckle.

I shrugged.

He sank to the couch beside me, scrubbing a hand through his hair.

"What?" I asked.

"The Council of Seekers doesn't want me and Kal to take Bob with us. They want us to leave him here."

"Why?" I couldn't picture Kal or Seth leaving their kid, who was only a few weeks old alone, for over a year.

"He's the first hybrid. They don't know how he's going to age or if any genetic problems will appear. Dr. Qinlin will be on the *Admiral Ven* and so will Klars, but that might not be enough. I'm terrified something will happen to Bob, but I can't leave him. But Earth needs me too."

I draped an arm over his shoulders. "Bob is fine."

While I couldn't promise the future, that kid was happy and active—way more so than a human baby after only a few weeks. The kid was aging like a drakcol so far, which was probably a good thing. Human newborns didn't do much other than sleep, shit, and cry.

"I'm not going to tell you not to worry. Of course you're scared, but I think you and Kal are right. He should go with you, and you do need to go, Seth. We have to protect Earth and keep anyone else from getting abducted."

"Thanks." He pushed a hand through his hair. "I think I needed to hear that." He started to pack again. The ship was leaving sooner rather than later. Earth needed to be protected and the Vvekian Authority was sending ships to travel with the *Admiral Ven*—they would meet part way.

"So," I started, "can you take me to the Grand Sanctuary?"

He sighed. "Why do *I* have to take you?"

"I can visit without you, but the Ranks won't let us humans appeal to the Crystal whenever we want anymore."

At first, any human could appeal at any time, but a huge population of drakcol complained. They couldn't appeal willy nilly—no one could, besides royalty. The general populace had to wait for one of four days per year when they could be presented to the Crystal. The Cohort ruled humans would have to do the same as any other citizen. But if Seth went, as a prince consort and beloved of the Ranks and Cohort alike, they would grant me permission. It was weird how much people catered to Seth. He would never take advantage of it, being far too kind, but I was more than happy to.

"So you want to skirt the rules?"

"This shocks you?" I asked, smirking.

"Not really." He chuckled. "Why do you have to do it now? Why not wait?"

"Kal said he thinks it will help Don calm down if we're bound."

"So wait until he comes back," Seth commented, chucking even more baby crap, including several adorable teddy bears, into a metal crate. Really, how much shit did one kid need? This seemed excessive, but I supposed my nephew deserved anything and everything. He was Seth's kid after all.

"What if he's not my mate?"

Holding a blanket to his chest, he asked, "Do you think that's possible?"

"I don't know." I really didn't, but I had shit-tastic luck. "If he's not, I want to break the human or drakcol's heart *before* he comes home."

"And if they're not on this planet?"

"Then I'll tell Don, and I still break the fucker's heart. As far as I'm concerned, no one but Don will ever touch or see my ass again. He's it."

"Not how I would put it," Seth remarked, blushing.

"It's how I say it." It was the truth. Don was it. He was the only person I would ever want. I didn't care if the Crystal chose someone else, I would not accept them. For the rest of my life, I would have one person, so if I had another *soulmate* they were fuck out of luck. Don was mine, and I was Don's.

Seth glanced at me, lips pursed. He had an inordinate need to please people. I didn't want to take advantage of it. Seth was far too important for me to use like a common household appliance. Yet...

I needed him to take me. I wouldn't have access any other way. Don could seek the Crystal when he returned, but he wouldn't, because he wouldn't want to trap me. My Dontilvynsan was exceedingly self-sacrificing.

No. I had to do this. I had to be the one who chose him.

He shoved a hand through his hair, making the brown strands stick up. "Fine. I will go, even though they'll want to talk to me." His face scrunched like he couldn't think of anything worse. In his defense, I didn't want to talk to anyone from the Ranks either.

"Thanks."

With a small smile, he said, "I would do anything for you, Vince."

I impulsively wrapped my arms around him, not flinching too hard when he returned the hug. I planted a kiss on his cheek with a loud smack before I said, "Thank you. I would do anything for you too."

We headed out of the palace to the Grand Sanctuary, which was on the grounds. I'd never been inside the towering glass structure, which almost looked like a church with its steep roof, nor had I seen the Crystal. When I'd been soul tested after our arrival, along with all of the other new humans except Teddy, who'd plain refused, a priest had merely held a square piece of glowing glass for us to touch. There had been no need to see the Crystal. Some of the other humans had gone for curiosity's sake—it was a giant floating rock—but I hadn't cared.

Now, I wanted it to link Don and me together forever.

The glass doors, seamless with the walls, opened, and the first thing I noticed was the amount of plants everywhere. Vines, flowers, ferns, bushes—hell, even trees filled the structure. The glass walls and cathedral ceiling gave it an airy, light feel. On one side of the building was a room filled with consoles. There was also a darkened doorway that appeared to lead downward. Where? No idea, and I didn't really care.

In the center of the sanctuary floated a massive crystal. It was bright white and let off a low throbbing hum.

I swallowed, unable to take my eyes off of it. "That's it?"

"Yep," Seth replied.

Before he could say more, a lanky drakcol with light gray scales and lavender hair rushed toward us. He sloppily offered Seth his throat. "Prince Consort Seth. It is an honor. A great honor. I wasn't—we weren't expecting you. What can we—I do for you?"

The man was practically vibrating with excitement, his cat-eye pupils blown wide, and his tail thrashed. It was so awkward, like watching someone meet their favorite celebrity.

Seth was bright red and his fingers were worrying the hem of his hoodie. I had two seconds before he bolted or called Kal. If Kal knew I'd brought Seth here, I would never hear the end of it. The Ranks had been trying to get their claws into Seth since the beginning because of his dark red soul—he was a pure warrior, which meant a lot to them.

I'd also tested as a warrior, but I was medium red—a respectable warrior, but nothing to write home about.

"Seth was kind enough to bring me. I'm Vince Lyford."

The drakcol offered his throat again. "I'm Dax. I don't believe you've been one of the humans to visit."

"I haven't. First time here. So exciting and all that. Me and Seth were best friends back on Earth," I said, dropping my connection in the hopes Seth's presence alone would be enough to entice this priest to give me what I wanted.

Dax offered me his throat again, bouncing on his feet as his tail writhed. "You knew Prince Consort Seth on Earth?"

"Yep," I said. Seth was growing more uncomfortable by the second. "We grew up together. Anyway, I was hoping to seek the Crystal for my mate, and whatnot."

Dax looked between me and the Crystal. "We're not supposed to allow humans to have access to it whenever anymore."

"I know that, but Seth is leaving for Earth, and I'm staying. He wanted to see me find my mate before he left," I lied. Seth glanced sharply at me, but he didn't refute my words. "I would hate to disappoint him. Wouldn't you?"

Poor Dax looked so upset at the prospect of Seth disliking him that I almost told him I was lying, but I held my peace. I was fine with being an asshole. Mostly.

Looking between me and the peacefully humming Crystal, Dax said, "I suppose it couldn't hurt anything. Great Mother and the Cohort would probably make an exception for Prince Consort Seth's wishes."

They would. They all loved him.

"So what do I do?" I asked. We needed to get this show on the road before someone older and not as naive as this priest appeared and stopped it.

Standing to his full height, which was somewhere around six-five, he said, "Approach the Crystal with a pure soul seeking your other half. Only with them will you truly be whole."

Yeah, that was garbage about being whole—people didn't need someone else to be whole—but I sincerely wanted to find my soulmate. I walked up to the Crystal, leaving Seth behind with the enthusiastic Dax.

The closer I got, the faster the thrumming pulse of the Crystal grew.

Nerves twisting my gut, making my stomach threaten to escape from my mouth. I swallowed it. Don was the best, and he needed me to do this, to not be worried about forever or if I was a burden to him, which I truly was beginning to believe that he didn't see me that way. But if this rock gave me someone else, it would hurt him and me. I planted a hand on the Crystal.

You had better give me Dontilvynsan, I thought as my eyes began to flutter closed and my other hand came to rest on the perfectly smooth surface.

Vince, a voice made of hundreds, if not thousands, of people said. *Vince Lyford, warrior, conqueror, survivor. You are seen, you are wanted, you are not broken. Seek what has been given and return to forge your paths together.*

I jerked back, panting. "Fuck, that was intense."

Dax piped up, "Your search has begun with the light of Crystal to guide you."

"Do you know who my soulmate is?" I demanded, walking toward Dax and Seth.

When I came to Seth's side, he snagged my hand in silent support. I looked back at the Crystal, which was harmlessly floating there. Part of me wanted something dramatic to happen, like it changing color or shaking or causing an earthquake. It did none of that. In fact, there was literally no change to reflect what had happened.

Boring.

Then again—I glanced up at the glass ceiling—it was probably good it hadn't done any of those things, because I would have died from glass shards raining down on me.

"If they are drakcol or one of the humans here, we will know in a moment, as they have been soul tested. If not, then we will know a general direction you must follow." He glanced at the console, then proclaimed. "Your soulmate is Prince Dontilvynsan."

I released a huge sigh of relief. Thank fucking god. I'd been almost positive, but how could I actually know when a magical crystal was involved?

The door whooshed open, and I groaned. In came Kal and he was looking pissed. How in the hell did he even know where we—or more accurately, Seth—was? Did he have a tracker implanted in Seth? I wouldn't put it past him. Kal was a possessive fucker. On his heels was Fyn, holding Bob.

"Prince Zoltilvoxfyn and Kalvoxrencol," Dax squeaked, offering his throat. "It is so lovely for you to visit."

Yeah, he didn't sound any more happy than I felt. Of course, Dax had just done something wrong at my behest. I supposed I could let him get in trouble for me, but I wasn't that much of an asshole—I would take the blame.

"Kal," Seth breathed and rushed over to him.

Kal instantly pulled Seth closer and growled at me.

I crossed my arms. "I was just following your advice, asshole."

He paused. "You sought the Crystal?"

Fyn sidled up right next to Kal, handing Bob to Seth, and asked, "Who is your soulmate?"

They both looked at Dax, who cowered under their stares. I frowned at them. "Leave the poor guy alone. All of this is my fault, not his. If you're going to blame someone, blame me. Alright?"

"And your soulmate?" Fyn asked again.

"It's Don. I guess you're stuck with me. Suck on that, bitches."

Relaxed smiles spread over both their faces. Fyn whispered, "Thank the Crystal."

"Stars," Kal groaned, shoving a hand in his hair. "Captain is going to be so relieved."

Interesting. None of Don's brothers were particularly fond of me, but I guessed their love for their brother outweighed any dislike of me.

Seth smiled, holding Bob close. "I'm happy for you, Vinnie."

"Me too. Now Don just needs to come home."

Chapter 48

LIMPING HOME.

Dontilvynsan

Our ship's NAID and touchstones were functioning on the ship, but NAID had said it could not connect to the hub. Our long-distance communication and sensors were dead. The communication node that had been malfunctioning was destroyed, and there was a Coalition-wide shortage for the part. The long-range sensors ran along the same hub in the ship and also had been fried in the blast from the planet.

Unfortunately, we were flying blind.

My first instinct had been to order us to head toward home. I wanted to see Vince and I couldn't even speak to him now—his time here was so short—but I reined in the impulse. The Immortal Planet was my responsibility, and even if I left right this instant, I wouldn't see my mate before he departed to Earth. So I remained, even though it felt as if it was going to kill me.

I had to wait for the relief ships to arrive and hope that, by some miracle, they had the parts we needed, or else we were going to have to stop at the closest Drakcon station for repair or head directly home without long-range sensors. I could pass reports to my parents and superiors when the relief ships arrived, but I wouldn't be able to do the same with personal notes, as they wouldn't remain in my private system and might be reviewed by others in the transfer. We royals had strict rules on the lines of communication we could use. Besides, sending notes wasn't the same thing as seeing Vince and helping him fall asleep. I needed that.

Time passed slowly, and I buried myself in repairing what I could on my ship. It was better than focusing on never seeing my mate again.

When the relief ships arrived, they had what we needed to repair the long-range sensors, but not our communication. Such an innocuous thing as a part shortage, and it was separating me from Vince. I wanted to scream, but I contained it. Instead, I passed on notes of what was going on, turned over what we knew about the current flux of the Immortal Planet, and headed home.

When we passed a Drakcon ship, I used it to retrieve my notes and send more reports. One that I received stopped my soul from beating and sent shards of ice through me. Father had sent me a note. They had finalized plans, and the *Admiral Ven* was on its way to Earth. Kalvoxrencol, Seth, Serlotminden, and Bartholomew were going. He'd said nothing of Vince, and I hadn't expected him to.

My Vince was gone, and he wasn't coming back. Everything in me wanted to curl into a ball and never move again. I couldn't. My family needed me, but the emptiness of separation ate at me, and soon I would give into it. The despair was so thick, I had a hard time breathing. I now understood why drakcol didn't continue on if their mate rejected them or they died.

When we finally came to the Tanlyn Station orbiting Tamkolvanloknol, I turned over the ship to Commander Bimwoxcol. Father had allowed me to come down to the planet, but he wanted my ship to remain ready while it was repaired and the systems were studied to try and figure out what exactly had happened on the Immortal Planet.

Bimwoxcol rode down with me in the lift toward the docking area. Before the door opened, she handed me a screen. "The files you requested."

"Thank you." I tucked it under my arm and kept staring at the doors in front of me. It was a fight to stay focused on the matter at hand. My mind wanted to dwell on Vince's departure and the fact that I would never see him smile with my own eyes again. Yes, I would be able to speak to him now, for as long as he wished to, but it wouldn't be the same. His thoughts would never brush mine; I would never touch the smooth softness of his skin; I would never hold my mate again.

I didn't know how I would survive.

When the door opened, Commander Bimwoxcol placed a hand on my arm to stall me. "I hope you find what you need, Captain."

I wouldn't. He was gone. I merely replied, "Thank you."

Without a backward glance, I headed to the space station. I barely paid attention to the bright yellow ensign who greeted me and led me toward the shuttle. He kept up a steady chatter, reminding me of my mate-brother Caleb, who never ceased talking.

In the shuttle, I leaned back against the bulkhead, exhausted. My eyes closed, the ship vibrating beneath me. Every moment seemed to stretch. The short ride felt like days instead of the true time.

The ensign, whose name I hadn't gotten, began the non-stop chatter as he led me out of the shuttle. I bid him a quick goodbye. I didn't require an escort to the home I'd lived in my entire life. I looked at the palace with its towering spires, balconies, terrace jungles, and lights glimmering from the many, many windows.

The hour was late, or early depending on how you wanted to look at it, but the moons hadn't set yet. Two people I recognized were standing on the edge of the shuttle port—Zoltilvoxfyn and Caleb. Even exhausted, I was beyond pleased to see them. Both of their familiar thoughts rushed over me. Caleb thought in a mix of English and Drakconese, and his mind bounced from topics so quickly it was dizzying for me. Zoltilvoxfyn was more sedate in his thoughts, but worry at my appearance was the foremost. I was unsurprised.

"You look like shit," Caleb blurted out, and I shook my head, swallowing a chuckle. Zoltilvoxfyn shot him a look, but Caleb just said, "He does."

I reached for them, curling my tail around Zoltilvoxfyn's and resting a gentle hand on Caleb's shoulder. He flinched, pain radiating through the joint. I pulled away instantly. Caleb's body had been in a severe accident before he'd come to inhabit it, and pain flares were normal for him. Annoyance flashed through him at my inner fire, but it didn't bother me—I was too used to it.

"Vince is safe," Zoltilvoxfyn said.

"Thank you," I replied, closing my eyes. He would've known that Vince would be my primary concern.

My little brother gave me a small smile, and something relaxed in my gut. It hadn't just been Vince who I'd missed or who I was worried about. I put a hand behind his neck to draw him closer. I rubbed my forehead on his, scent marking him. In my current state, I needed the comfort.

Zoltilvoxfyn's nose flared as his tail writhed, clearly unhappy, but he did not pull away or deny me. It had been a long time since my younger brothers had tolerated me scent marking them. Kalvoxrencol had balked at it far younger than any of my other brothers, while Serlotminden allowed it far longer than normal. But I needed to reassure myself that he was here, well, and safe.

When I pulled away, I peeked at Caleb—most mates wouldn't tolerate another, even family, scent marking their mate. Caleb, being Caleb, bounced as much as he was capable of and said, "You two are so adorable. I'm almost tempted to have kids so I would have sons as cute as you two. I just want to squeeze you both!"

I stepped back.

Wrapping his arms around his mate, Zoltilvoxfyn said, "You should get some sleep. You look…"

"Like shit," Caleb supplied.

"Thank you," I replied, lifting an eyebrow.

Caleb grinned. Nothing but love and affection came off him, though his words, while light, were filled with worry. Both him and Zoltilvoxfyn were concerned about me, and I didn't blame them.

My scales had lost some of their sheen with malnutrition, and I had lost weight.

I cupped Zoltilvoxfyn's cheek, patting him. I wouldn't lie and say I was fine, but I didn't want him to worry unduly. "I will rest."

"I doubt it," Caleb said in a singing voice.

I frowned. Why wouldn't I sleep? Caleb's thoughts didn't illuminate me, as Zoltilvoxfyn had brushed his lower stomach to quiet his mate, and now his thoughts were solely on my brother's cock in his mouth. I shook my head. Ignoring them, I started toward the palace and my quarters.

There were few people in the corridors because of the hour, but that suited me fine. It meant less mental static for me to navigate or to tax my precarious calm. With Zoltilvoxfyn in close proximity and his own struggles with all-consuming moroseness, I didn't want to harm him.

My door loomed before me, and I closed my eyes. Vince wouldn't be inside. He had been, but he wasn't there now, nor would he ever be again. I opened the door and growled, my cock hardening in a flash. Vince. His perfect floral scent clung to every fiber of my quarters, which had been redecorated in my absence. I didn't scent anyone else, not that I expected to—Vince had said we still belonged to each other alone, but it comforted me nonetheless.

Tears came to my eyes. Caleb was right. I wouldn't sleep. I wanted to drink in Vince's smell, and, with a glance down at my throbbing cock, I realized I'd have to calm myself before sleep was possible.

I moved to our bedroom, and as I opened the door, I froze. Every muscle in my body tensed as my soul throbbed in my chest so hard

I feared it would rip free. A figure was lying on the bed, hugging a pillow that was oddly enough dressed in one of my tunics. He grunted in his sleep, and I lurched forward, desperate to cover his body with mine.

Vince. Vince. Vince. His name was a mantra that wouldn't stop.

Every instinct demanded I claim him. Now. A growl started in my throat as I stalked toward his slight form. It had been so agonizingly long since I'd seen my mate. I curled my hands into fists, forcing myself to stop. If I grabbed Vince, I would scare him.

Breathing in through my nose, I panted, shaking. I didn't know how much longer I could hold off. I needed my mate, and I needed him now. Trying to temper myself, I crept forward and fell to the floor beside the bed. I leaned toward him, face as close to him as I could from my position. I brushed his cheek and groaned. His skin was softer than I remembered.

Unable to hold back any longer, I climbed part-way onto the bed and pressed my lips against his cheek. A moan ripped out of me. He was so smooth and soft. Mine. Vince was mine. He shifted under me. I pressed into him, dragging my claws through his hair. The black strands were far longer than when I'd left, and even since I'd last seen him.

Vince started, panic building. I latched onto the emotion, trying to force myself away. But when his deep brown eyes landed on me, joy rushed through him and every drop of fear leached out of him.

"Sweetheart," he cried, then suddenly his mouth was on mine.

His thoughts radiated happiness and relief, but mostly need. My mate needed me as much as I did him. He moaned, and I flicked his

bottom lip with my tongue. He grunted as he yanked me closer to
him. I covered his body with mine, tensing. He didn't normally like
me on top, but Vince didn't react. His tongue thrust into my mouth
as he cradled the back of my head, fingers sliding through my hair.

"Don," he moaned. "I missed you."

Tears rushed to my eyes at his words. I trailed my lips over his
cheek and down his neck, tongue flicking out to taste him. Vince
arched when I found a sensitive spot. I bit him, not enough to mark
him. He cried out, pulling me closer. Vince began to writhe beneath
me, his hard cock pressing against me.

"Clothes," he ordered, hands dragging down my back. "Now."

I leaned back, staring at my mate. His round pupils were blown
wide with arousal and his breath was harsh. He didn't have a single
stitch of clothing on, allowing me to see all of his glorious pale skin.
His cock jutted up toward his stomach, the head red and swollen,
and it leaked pre-seed all over him.

Slowly, I pulled off my clothes, and Vince's eyes narrowed while
he took me in. I expected some thoughts on my weight loss, but all
I sensed was more arousal and possessive need.

He thought, *Mine*.

"Yours," I replied without hesitation. I stretched my wings out
and reveled in the sharp gasp he gave. Vince loved my wings. Smiling,
I slid off him and pulled off my trousers. His eyes were locked on my
butt from his thoughts. My tail flicked. I wanted my mate inside of
me, claiming me.

"Don," he moaned, voice and thoughts growing desperate.

"Yes," I said, in response to his thoughts about what he wanted.

He reached for the lube, which was already on the bed, and slicked himself up, cock glistening. "Don," Vince said, reaching for me.

He wanted to make sure I was ready for him, but I couldn't hold on any longer. I straddled him and reached back for his cock. I angled it toward me and started to lower onto him.

Vince moaned, hands clamping my hips. "Sweetheart."

There was a flash of stretch from the sudden intrusion that passed quickly; I didn't require as much prep as human males did. I lowered and lifted, keeping my eyes on him, until he filled me completely. Vince panted beneath me, gripping me. His touch was a tad harder than usual, but not enough to cause pain.

I watched my mate as I rode him, hips rocking and rolling. We'd never done this before, as Vince didn't like anyone else in control, but he wasn't struggling this time. He was grunting and groaning, thrusting up into me.

When the head of his cock brushed my cluster of nerves, I cried out.

"So beautiful," Vince said. "You are so fucking beautiful."

Heat filled me at the compliment.

"Ride me, Don," he ordered, "like you want me to fill your hole with so much cum that you will never be free of it."

I whimpered, and began to slide up and down his thick cock faster.

"Do you like it?" he asked. "Did you miss this?"

"Yes," I cried. "You fill me perfectly. I'm so full. I needed this. I needed you."

"Good boy." Vince grinned, thrusting up into me. "My Don."

My eyes closed as I moaned.

He bucked under me, pushing harder into me. "Look at me, Sweetheart. I need to see that it's you."

I looked at my mate. Peace filled him at the sight of my eyes. We worked in a perfect rhythm, rocking into each other at a slow, unhurried pace. I'd expected our fucking to be frantic, but Vince was calm, as if this was expected or the normal outcome of me waking him, not as if I had been gone for so long.

Moans and cries slipped out of my lips with every thrust because his crown hit me perfectly each time. My cock was hard beyond belief, but Vince didn't touch me. If he did, I'd explode in an instant. Pre-seed leaked out of my tip, covering us.

Vince gripped behind my neck, yanking me into a kiss. I cried into his mouth at the change in angle. His tongue fucked me while his cock claimed my hole. My cock dragged over the line of hair down his stomach and it was enough. My balls hugged my shaft, and I was moments from spilling my seed.

"Vince," I bit out against his lips.

He captured my mouth again, not willing to surrender me. I came against his stomach as Vince continued to fuck me, and his mouth swallowed my cries of pleasure. My release was so intense that I couldn't hear or see, only feel what my Vince was ripping from my body. He pumped two more times before his seed filled my hole.

When Vince slid out, I whimpered, bearing down to keep him inside of me. I needed to be connected.

"Hush," he whispered, kissing my chest. Gently, Vince helped me roll over and he sprawled on top of me. "I'm here. You're here. We're here."

I wrapped my arms around him, shaking. "Vince."

"It's all fine, Sweetheart."

I held him close. He was here, with me. Everything was so much better than I'd ever thought it would be.

Vince fell asleep long before I did. I fought sleep to listen to him breathe and feel his familiar weight on top of me. I'd thought I would never experience it again, and now, here he was.

I would never let him go again. I would tell Vince what I needed so he never left, and I would never, not even if ordered, go anywhere he couldn't be beside me again.

Chapter 49

IT WASN'T A DREAM.

Vince

I was warm. Utterly and completely warm. I hadn't been this warm since Don had left. Hell. Merely thinking about him was enough to send tears to the backs of my eyes. I needed him back. I needed him here. But his ship was experiencing some kind of technological difficulty, so we couldn't even talk. I couldn't even send a message.

Oh, I'd kicked up a fuss about that, multiple times, but privacy concerns, royalty, customs, blah blah blah. Caleb and Seth had tried to explain it, even bringing in Jalqyn, who handled press relations for the royal family, to explain it to me in detail, but I hadn't cared. I wanted Don. It might have helped if the emperor and empress had known who I was; they didn't and wouldn't until Don could tell them. However, I fucking hated not being able to talk to Don, but whatever, he would come back when he could.

Still, it didn't stop the desperate need I had for him.

Something ran down my back, firm and familiar. The movement sent visceral terror through me. I was lying on someone. I scrambled up, breath harsh, but before I could get away, a hand cupped my cheek, forcing me to look at the person beneath me.

"Me or my gift?" the most perfect voice in the entire fucking universe asked.

Tears raced to my eyes. "You. Just you."

He was here. How was he here? I'd had a dream of him coming home and fucking him, but Don, my Don, was actually here.

His thumb traced over my cheek as he wore a soft smile. "It wasn't a dream, my Vince. I was here. With you."

A flush rushed to my cheeks. Don had ridden me. I hadn't thought we'd get there with him on top, but it hadn't freaked me out. In fact, it had been hot as fuck. Don smirked in response to my thoughts. His thumb kept tracing my face as his other hand slid up and down my back.

I kissed him. "I missed you."

"I missed you more than air."

My blush deepened. Fuck, he was adorable. How was Don this adorable? Don grinned, arching up to lick my cheek with his scaled tongue. A groan ripped out of my mouth, and my dick twitched in need.

"Yes," he muttered against my skin as his lips trailed over me. "Whatever you want, yes."

I laughed. "Anything?"

"Anything." His lips latched onto my Adam's apple and sucked, hard. I grunted, grinding against him. Don's hand flattened on the small of my back as he worked the skin on my throat. When he finally pulled away, I was panting, and my cock was rock hard and leaking all over him.

I formed a very clear picture of what I wanted, and his head tilted as his eyes narrowed.

"Are you sure?"

"Yes," I answered. I wanted this—no. I needed this.

"I don't want to upset you."

"You won't," I said, but when he frowned, I modified it, "or rather, I'll tell you if you do or I need to stop." I took a deep breath. "This is something I've been working through, with the help of my therapist."

His eyes widened. "You're talking to someone."

"Camden and Pierce wouldn't stop bothering me, and even Teddy, Seth, and Caleb kept bringing it up."

He cocked an eyebrow.

"Fine," I snapped. "I want to get better. For me. For you. For us. I want a future where I know how to handle my past. It might always bother me on some level, but now, I'm building tools to keep my past where it belongs and a healthy perspective. I'm not ready for everything and I don't know if I ever will be, but I am ready for this."

Don brushed a kiss on my cheek. "I'm proud of you."

Something about that simple assertion sent heat flooding through my body. "I want you, Dontilvynsan."

Don groaned, and I smiled, easily propped up on him—he was significantly larger than me. Though even as I thought about it, my fingers trailed over his sides where his scent glands were and I frowned. Dontilvynsan was a lot thinner than I remembered.

"Sweetheart?"

"I'm fine," he whispered, kissing my neck.

He wasn't. The more I studied him, the more I found changes. His scales were far rougher and duller than usual. He'd lost weight. His eyes looked so tired. I could see the strain in his muscles. Don wasn't alright, by any stretch of the word.

Don pressed a gentle kiss to my lips. "I'm with you, so I am well."

I buried my hands in his hair and molded my lips to his, keeping the touch soft and slow. I scraped my nails over his scalp, and Don moaned against me. I grinned, swallowing the noise. It was mine. All of it was mine. I pushed my tongue into his mouth and tangled it with his. Every movement stirred my desire, ramping it up until I was desperate.

He gently cupped my ass, and I pushed up into him, wanting his touch. Pulling my mouth from his, I asked, "Do you want to?"

"More than anything."

I grinned at his needy tone. "That's because you're my good boy."

Don moaned, low and loud.

Getting up, I resituated until I was on my knees over his face, hands gripping the headboard. Don was already reaching for my hips, trying to pull me down. I smiled down at him. "You want me so bad, huh?"

"Yes," he panted. "I want to taste you. Please."

In all our time together, Don had never eaten my ass. Hell, I could hardly even have him touch it. I wasn't ready for him to fuck me, and honestly, I might not ever be and I was okay with that. What me and Don had was enough. It was healthy, intimate, and our sex was good for us, which was all that mattered.

"Please, Little Warrior," Don begged.

"Oh, Donny, you are so sweet."

Another whimpering moan came out of him.

I lowered, slightly nervous, but the position made me feel better because, even now, I was in control.

His tongue dragged over my taint and hole, and my hands gripped the headboard as I cried out. Fuck. That felt amazing. It had been forever since someone had done this to me, and Don's tongue with its scales provided the perfect amount of scritch and pressure.

He growled under me, and I laughed. Gripping his hair, I said, "You're the best. You know it. Now, lick me."

Don followed my command.

I writhed and wriggled on his face, trying not to hurt him, but it felt so damn good—impossibly good. "Good boy," I said breathlessly. "Don't stop."

He didn't.

My cock was hard and dripping, and my hole was getting sloppy from his saliva. Gently, he sucked on my rim, and I whined. It was just too good. Nibbling, sucking, licking, Don continued to pleasure me with no intent to stop. When his tongue prodded my hole, I froze and so did he.

I shook my head, pulse racing and not in a good way. "I can't, Sweetheart."

Don tentatively licked me again, and I moaned.

"Yes, Donny, yes."

He continued feasting on me without penetrating me. I wasn't ready, and he didn't seem to care.

Eventually, I went up on my knees, taking my hole out of his reach, and he growled, trying to pull me against him again.

I smirked down at him. "Did my good boy like licking me?"

"Yes," he said, voice rough.

I cupped his cheek, my smile softening. "Good. Now I want you to ride me again because that was the most beautiful thing I've ever seen."

He swallowed.

My Don still didn't handle compliments well.

I lay on my back, and Don didn't hesitate to straddle me, his weight pressing me into the bed.

"Give me a moment," I whispered, breathing through the initial panic. I was safe. I was making a choice. This was my body. I wanted this. Hell, I'd thought last night was a dream come true. I'd jerked off multiple times thinking about this. I paused. Shit. I turned my head to the side to the pillow I was half on—the one dressed in Don's shirt. "I can explain," I squeaked, blushing.

Don's rumbly laugh vibrated through me, and he bent over me to kiss the sensitive skin behind my ear, nipping at the lobe. "I'm sure you can."

"I missed you." It was the best explanation I had. I'd put his shirt on a pillow, then would bang one out, pretending he was holding me, loving me, keeping me safe.

"I missed you. Desperately." He buried his face against my neck. "I cannot be away from you again, Vince. Not ever."

I beamed, tightening my hold—not enough to hurt him but enough to keep him close. "Not ever."

Taking one of his hands, I slid it down my body, panting. Don groaned, and it made my cock twitch. I loved his noise—every groan, every moan, every gasp, they were all mine and I cherished them. I was the only one who would ever make Don cry with pleasure. I was the only one who would ever hear them.

"Yes," he murmured against my lips, breath as harsh as mine.

I guided his hand to my aching cock, and he gripped the base, pumping me.

"*Ugh*, Sweetheart."

He kept slowly jerking me. "Vince, I want to taste you."

"Yeah."

Don kissed down my body, his tongue flicking out and scraping against my skin. Every brush of his tongue drew a cry from my lips. I kept a hand on his head, gripping the silky strands to ground myself. It was easier when I could see Don's eyes and know it was him, but holding him helped.

"It's me," he whispered against my nipple, making the nub tighten. "It's me."

"I know, Sweetheart."

He latched onto my nipple, and I arched. "Fuck." I was sensitive. "Don," I cried as his tongue flicked. He sucked and nipped until I was writhing under him, cock leaking pre-cum everywhere. Don pulled back with a pop, and the cold air made the abused nipple sting pleasantly. He shifted to the other one to do the same thing.

With every touch, he was driving me to the edge. I was calling his name, rocking against him in an attempt to seek friction of any kind, even though I didn't want to come yet. I wanted to be buried in his hole while he rode me, seeking only the pleasure I could give him.

"Vince," he groaned, and I smirked.

"You like that thought, don't you?" I asked. "You like how much I want you."

"Yes." He placed his chin on my stomach, looking at me.

I brushed my fingers through his purple hair. "You love that I'm hard and aching for you."

"Yes," he replied with a moan.

"That's because you're my good boy."

Don didn't reply but let out a lewd noise that had my dick throbbing.

At the sight of those perfect green eyes latched onto my face and the feel of his rough breath on my skin, I cupped his cheek. "I love you."

"I love you too."

My heart thrashed against my ribs. I wanted to yank him up and press my lips against his, but Don wiggled away. He kissed down my stomach, dragging his tongue over the trail of hair that led to my cock.

"I adore this," he commented, nuzzling my hair.

"Good, because I'm not shaving."

Don frowned. "I don't want you to get rid of it." He kissed the bush at the root of my cock, making me groan. God, he was so close to where I wanted. "I love it."

Words were impossible because Don licked my weeping tip.

"*Ungh*," I grunted.

The friction of his scales on my sensitive glans was almost too much. Don sucked my cock into his mouth, working his tongue over my shaft as he slid down. The wet heat of his mouth made me cry out as I fisted his hair. It took every ounce of control I had to not thrust up into his mouth and chase the touch.

He bobbed up and down, cheeks hollow as he took more of my cock until the head hit the back of his throat, making him gag and pull off. Don tried again and gagged once more. Tension began building in his shoulders and his tail started flicking. He was worried I was going to get mad, like his other partners had gotten.

I cupped his chin, but he wouldn't meet my eyes and said in a rush, "I'll get it, my Vince."

"Fuck that."

His eyes jerked to mine.

I ran my thumb over his bottom lip. "I'm so turned on, Sweetheart. You're so fucking good. I don't need you to deep throat me, and if you did, I would come in an instant, spilling my cum down that pretty throat of yours."

Don's eyes turned wet, and it broke my heart. I swore if those fuckers who'd hurt him appeared, I would rip them a new one. Don was utterly perfect, and how dare they make him feel less than?

He pressed the sweetest kiss to my leaking cock. "I love you."

I grinned, unable to stop it. "I love *you*."

Don sucked my cock again, making me cry out his name as I fisted his hair. His hands worked whatever couldn't fit into his mouth until I was screaming. "Sweetheart, stop," I begged. "I'll come if you don't stop."

He pulled off with a groan. "Next time, I want to drink your seed."

"Yes." If he sucked me like that, he could have whatever the hell he wanted.

"You are so beautiful," Don whispered, as if he was afraid of my response.

I smiled. "Just for you."

Don ducked his head.

God, he was adorable.

I pulled him up, and Don didn't resist. He straddled my waist, those perfect green eyes on me. Pulling the lube out from under my Don-fuck-pillow, I put some on my fingers. "Go up on your knees."

When he did, I reached between them, seeking his entrance. The second I brushed it, Don gasped, making me smile. His tail whipped back and forth and his wings spread as I circled his rim in irritating slowness before pushing inside of his impossible heat. He released a low cry, and I pumped in and out of him. Don truly didn't need prep to take me, but I enjoyed fingering him. It was incredibly hot to watch him buck and whine on my fingers.

"You are perfect," I whispered, pulling out. "My perfect good boy. Ride me."

Don mewled and gripped my cock, angling it to his hole, and sank down. I clung to his hips as the tight heat encased me. Fuck. I would never tire of just how welcoming Don's body was. He bent over me, claiming my lips. Tongues tangling, I slowly rutted up into him, keeping my arms wrapped around him. I wanted to be as close as possible. I wanted to be one person. I wanted to be one goddamn soul.

He whimpered.

"Just like that," I told him as we slowly fucked—or rather, made love. Because that was what we were doing. We were making love. "Good boy, my Donny, my Sweetheart, my Dontilvynsan."

"Vince," he cried, pushing down harder on me.

"Fuck. Fuck," I whispered as he continued to roll his hips riding me. My orgasm was barreling down my spine, and it was hard to hold it back. I didn't want this to end. I wanted more of him and me together.

"Vince," he cried.

Words were impossible for me as I called for him. His pace picked up as he pounded down onto me. Neither of us were going to last long at this speed. We were too desperate for each other. I fisted a hand in his hair, bucking up into him, needing him, craving him.

"My Vince," he cried and his hole gripped me impossibly tight.

"Don," I screamed as my orgasm crested, sending me over the edge, filling him full of my cum.

He grunted, riding me through my mind-numbingly good release until he sagged on top of me. I groaned, going boneless. Don breathed heavily as he practically crushed me beneath his weight.

Slowly, he pulled off of me, making me hiss from sensitivity, but I wrapped my legs around his hips. I wanted him to stay on me for now. I needed his weight to ground me, so I didn't float away on the waves of pleasure he'd brought me.

Don kissed every inch he could reach and nuzzled me, scent marking. We'd been apart for enough time that I doubted I smelled like him anymore, which wouldn't do. I rubbed his sides to help spread his smell.

He chuckled. "I love that you love me scent marking you."

"I'm yours. I want to smell like you."

A growl came out of his lips, and I grinned, kissing his neck.

"All yours, Dontilvynsan. All yours."

Sniffling, he buried his face against me, and I held him securely, brushing my fingers through his hair. "All yours, Sweetheart. All yours."

Chapter 50

TRUST IS A TWO-WAY STREET.

Dontilvynsan

Vince was asleep on top of me. The sun was high and wind fluttered the sheer curtains that framed the two tall windows on the back wall of our bedroom, bringing in a fresh scent every few minutes. I shook my head. Our bedroom. And it truly was. He'd changed it some since I'd last been here.

The large four-poster bed covered in vines and flowers was the same, but the covers were now a dark yellow with a subtle geometric pattern, and the sheets were crisp white. The terrace outside the windows was filled with colorful flowers like usual, but there was a chair, with a back, on it for Vince. Even the walls, which had been bare, now had art hanging on them. My mate had made himself comfortable.

My mate. I smiled as I ran my hand down his thin back, and he grunted, nuzzling closer to me. I cradled the back of his head, tail coiling around his leg.

He'd wanted to clean up after we'd fucked, but I'd needed to hold him. I couldn't bear the thought of him out of my arms even for a moment. Besides, there was some primal instinct that was satisfied by feeling his seed leak out of me. I needed it, as much as I needed to have my seed on his skin, even though it would be difficult to clean off later.

I wanted his smell coating me.

My touchstone pulsed. Someone was attempting to reach me. I stared at the glowing blue stone, holding my mate tight in my embrace. I grabbed it, and Hallonnixmin's voice filled my ears. My fingers squeezed the stone, and I chucked it across the room. It hit the wall with a crack.

Vince snorted, eyes fluttering open. I smoothed a hand down his back and pressed a kiss to his hair. "I have you, Mate," I whispered. He burrowed his face into my chest, and his thoughts fell into a sleeping pattern.

NAID appeared. "Prince, Crown Prince Hallonnixmin would like to speak with you."

I held my mate tighter. I wanted to linger in this moment of isolation with him. Vince and me—no one else was welcome, not even my brothers. "I'm unavailable to everyone, no matter the reason. Disconnect now," I ordered before it could come back with Hallonnixmin's response.

NAID wouldn't bypass the privacy laws, which could be overridden for a true emergency, but Edith would. Hopefully, with Seth and Kalvoxrencol on the *Admiral Ven*, she wouldn't be in a mood to prod around in my system, but one could never tell with her.

I pushed the thoughts from my mind. All that mattered was Vince. Everything else could wait.

———

I grunted as the water sloshed around me. Vince chuckled, beads of water running over his pale skin, clinging to him. "It's your own fault, Sweetheart," he commented as he scrubbed my scales. "You refused to clean my cum off you, and now it's dried onto you."

He'd insisted on cleaning me. I couldn't say why, even though I could hear his thoughts on exactly why he liked washing me, but Vince took pleasure in simply caring for me, and I adored it.

Once he was satisfied, Vince settled on my lap as we soaked in the warm water. His head rested back against my shoulder as we simply remained silent. He was content, and so was I. Even the bathroom around us spoke of his comfort here. The stone shower and tub were the same, but I could see his products and new drying cloths and even more artwork in here.

Drakcol, in general, weren't a creative species. We didn't value art in basically any form, which was why all of our clothes were the same style, no artwork or decorations covered our walls, and we rarely wrote our own novels or created our own experiences.

But humans were different, and it pleased me to no end that Vince had placed his touch on our space in my absence. It spoke of his desire to stay. I swallowed as my tail curled around his ankle. He would stay, wouldn't he?

Vince didn't notice my tension. His mind was peaceful with little thought, basking in my warmth. He played with my hand and stared out the window, watching the curtains flutter in the never-ending breeze.

I trailed my fingers through his hair, adoring the way the black strands slid around my scales. My mate was here, and I could hardly believe it.

Vince kissed my palm, and I tensed even further as his thoughts began to change.

"Relax," he whispered. "Just relax, Sweetheart."

My breath rushed out. I was terrified of scaring him away. I knew what it was like to live without him, and I could never do it again. Never again.

"What's wrong?" he asked, and he wasn't meaning my current tension. Vince was thinking of my rough appearance. When I didn't say anything, he turned around to face me. "What if I promise not to get mad?"

His thoughts shifted to wondering if I cheated on him, then felt guilty for even assuming that. I growled and said, "I did not fuck anyone else."

Hooking his arms around my neck, Vince asked, "Then what? Something's wrong?" Before I could lie, he continued, "If you came home and saw me looking as bad as you do, wouldn't you want to know? Wouldn't you demand I tell you?"

I pushed my forehead against his. Vince was, of course, right. I would've insisted on knowing what was wrong with my mate. He loved me as much as I loved him. I'd promised myself that I would be honest with him about my needs, and now was the time, but I feared Vince would be angry, even if he promised not to be. I knew my mate well, and he would be furious.

"I won't ask you to not be angry, because that will not be possible," I said.

"Are you dying?" he asked, voice barely audible as a terror so visceral ripped through him that my soul spasmed in pain.

"No," I replied instantly, holding him close. "No, I promise."

Vince kissed my neck, tightening his hold. "Talk to me. Trust me."

Was that what this came down to? Trust? I'd worked so hard to gain his trust, but had ever given him mine? No. I'd hidden—afraid he would hurt me in the end. I cupped his cheeks so I could look into his blue eyes.

"I love you," I said.

He lifted his eyebrows. That wasn't an answer.

"When you left me to go to the station," I started, mouth dry and muscles tensing, "I thought that would be the last time I would see you."

"But I told you we were still together."

"I didn't think that meant you would wait for me. I thought you were going to return to Earth."

He closed his eyes. "Sweetheart, why didn't you tell me that all the times we talked?"

"I was afraid."

"Of what?" Vince asked.

"That you would only choose me because…" I couldn't get the words out.

"Because I'm your mate."

Pain stabbed my soul as a gasp escaped from my lips. "You knew?"

"Only afterwards. Kal informed me."

"I told him not to. I told them all not to," I growled.

Anger rolled through him like storm clouds. "What was your plan, Don? Are you telling me that you were going to let yourself die while I went home?"

"Yes."

"Are you fucking kidding me, Dontilvynsan?" Vince shouted, slapping the water. It splashed me, and I looked away, unable to hide from his thoughts like I could from his eyes. "You were going to let me travel all the way to Earth when you needed me here? Didn't you know I would stay for you? I love you, you… I don't even have a word, that's how frustrated I am!"

"Vince—"

"This is why your brothers hated me. They thought I was killing you. Did you think they would've held their peace? Let me get all the way to Earth, and not one of them would have told me? They would have, and then I would've come back, pissed. Fuck! I'm pissed now."

I was unable to stay a word.

He took a deep breath. "I'm so furious right now."

I kept my eyes down, so when he touched my chin, I started. Vince nudged my face up. Stars, I flinched from the heat in his gaze. "Tell me what was going through your thoughts, Don. Did you want to die? Is that it?"

"No," I whispered. I didn't.

"Then what?" Vince's fingers refused to let me go.

"My happiness doesn't matter. Yours does."

Something broke in Vince. I could feel it, but I didn't know what it was. Tears slid down his cheeks.

"I'm sorry," I whispered.

He shook my chin, gentle despite how angry he was. Vince snarled, settling on my lap and fisting my hair, "Listen to me, Dontilvynsan. Your happiness matters. Of course it fucking matters. You think only your gift matters, and that is a lie. You matter. *You*. Do you understand me? You matter. And so does your happiness."

Tears burned my eyes.

"You want me to be happy? Well, shocker, I want you to be happy too. Do not *ever* sacrifice yourself like this again. Talk to me. Do you understand?"

"I understand," I whispered, snuggling my mate, who in turn pressed against me like he was never going to leave my side again.

Vince

I held my mate close. Having Don tell me about his plan had made me so angry again, even though I already knew. It was... heartbreaking to realize how little he valued himself when I would literally give up everything for him. He was the most important person in my life.

Don nuzzled the top of my head in response.

God, I was furious still, but I held Don tight in my arms. We were lying on the rug I'd added to cover the wood floor in the living room, naked. After he'd confessed, part of me had wanted to leave so I could blow off steam, but that would've hurt Don more than my thoughts.

He had his arms and wings around me, his leg thrown over my hip, and his tail coiled around my calf. Don was trying to get as close as possible. I brushed my hand through his hair, and Don grunted. He knew how angry I was, and I was glad for once, he wasn't sharing his thoughts with me. I didn't want to feel his pain.

Taking a deep breath, I kissed his chest, so fucking relieved he was fine. What if he'd gotten worse while he was away from me? I couldn't imagine him leaving me behind.

Don kissed the top of my head. "My apologies."

"Stop," I said, unable to keep the snap out of my voice.

He fell silent, and I felt like shit, but I didn't need his apologies. I needed him to communicate with me so this never happened again.

Not all drakcol died when their mate passed or separated from them permanently, in the case of outside species, or when someone rejected the Crystal's choice, but a good portion did, and Don knew that. I gripped his hair. I could've lost him.

"Don't," I said when his mouth opened. I knew what he was planning on doing, and I wasn't going to let him. Don had apologized enough. I was just angry because he scared me.

I took a deep breath. "I am going to take care of you, and you will be fine. We'll be fine."

"Alright," he whispered.

God, I felt like a bastard, though my anger was perfectly rational. I closed my eyes and inhaled his scent, relaxing. "I love you, Sweetheart, and you scared me. I'll get over it and soon, I promise. You just... scared me. Though it is partly my fault. I assumed you knew I was staying."

Don kissed my forehead. "I didn't mean to scare you."

"I know." I tried to lean back, but Don held me too tight. "I'm not going to leave," I told him. I hated that he was afraid of that. That he didn't trust how much I loved him. Dontilvynsan was mine, and I was his. There was no alternative.

He loosened, and I leaned back to meet his gaze. I slid my hands up his body to cup his cheeks. "I love you."

"I love you so much. More than anything."

I smiled. "I know, but I need you to love *yourself* a bit more than you currently do."

He frowned.

"You need to be selfish sometimes. I can't read your mind, Sweetheart. You have to tell me what you need, and trust that I'm going to give it to you. Trust that I love you. Trust that I'm going to stay. I trust you, Don, and I need you to trust me."

"I know."

"Good." I planted my lips on his. "Now, this is either going to make you happy or upset."

His tail tightened on my leg as his breathing increased. I rubbed my thumbs over his cheekbones. "Breathe."

He shook his head. "Don't leave."

I swallowed a growl. This was going to take time. A lot of time, which he could have. I said, "I sought the Crystal."

Before I could speak, I was on my back and he was curled on top of me, surrounding me. "No," he snapped. "I will not give you to another."

I breathed deeply, holding him close as I fought the initial panic of him covering me. When I calmed, I intentionally started to think about when Don had played the harpsichord. The joy of hearing him play. The way I loved how his voice sounded. I grabbed his hand and placed it on my cheek, trying to calm him as he calmed me in the past.

Something unlocked in the back of my mind, and Don's panic swamped me, but I kissed him, ignoring it and continued to feed him the memory. Of how beautiful he'd looked. How much I enjoyed it. Don's own memories started to surface. How my eyes made him nervous and aroused. How much he loved me. How much he wanted to please me.

My lips skated over his, teasing him, then I pushed my tongue into his mouth, fucking him. Don moaned, relaxing further on top of me. I started to think of when I'd sought the Crystal. He tensed, but I kept kissing him, tasting him, thinking of the music, our music, our song. The memory played out, and when I got to where the priest had told me who my soulmate was, he ripped his mouth away from mine.

Shock radiated through him. I wanted to laugh. Don honestly didn't think he would be mine—even I hadn't been that surprised.

Of course, I wouldn't have accepted anyone else. No one besides him would ever hold my heart or hand.

"You're mine," he whispered, his voice full of wonder.

"Yes. And you're mine. I'm not going anywhere. You and me are stuck together whether you like it or not. So if you have a pro—"

Suddenly, I couldn't talk because my mouth was very busy. Don's joy flooded me. I couldn't understand Drakconese, but even I had no problem understanding the possessive happiness. We were bound. Him and me. Everything else would work itself out because if we were together, nothing was impossible.

I forced him onto his back, and Don didn't fight me. His cock was hard and dripping. With the connection between us, I easily felt his arousal and his desperate need to have me inside of him. I wanted that as well. I wanted to tunnel into his warm hole and claim him, so Don was finally assured of just how much I loved him.

Pulling back, I ordered, "Wait here for me like the good boy you are."

He whimpered.

When I broke the connection by standing, Don reached for me. I kissed his prominent knuckles before heading to the bedroom. I snagged the lube, then paused. There was something I wanted to give him. Something I needed. I went into the closet that was right off our bedroom and grabbed it, then went back to Don.

All of the tension in his body leaked out at the sight of me. He opened his legs in a clear invitation. Smiling, I settled between them. "I need something from you."

He smiled softly and his tail twitched. Don had to have heard what I wanted. "I did," he said, "but can you say it?"

I grabbed his left hand and asked, "Will you be my husband?"

"I would love nothing more in this world than for everyone to know I belong to you."

Carefully, I slid the gold band onto his ring finger. It wasn't the same one I'd made in the dispenser; rather I'd commissioned a ring with star carvings that matched my necklaces.

"You are mine, Dontilvynsan," I said, kissing his hand. "Never did I think I would get married. But you are so special and so perfect for me. I know we have to do the whole binding with the Crystal thing, though you haven't officially consented to be my mate, but I never want to be away from you. I want to spend my life with you."

"I love you," Don whispered. "I love you so much, Little Warrior. I never would have thought one as amazing as you would be mine."

I scoffed and claimed his mouth, laying on top of him. "I'm an asshole, Sweetheart. You're literally the only person who doesn't think so."

He shook his head and kissed me again. "You are strong, kind, gentle, and absolutely perfect for me."

I pressed the most gentle of kisses on his eyes, cheekbones, the tip of his nose, before molding my lips to his in a slow, claiming kiss. I fiercely thought, *You are mine, Dontilvynsan, and I will never let you go.*

Chapter 51

SIX MONTHS LATER.

Vince

"I do believe Seth will be very upset with you, my Mate," a warm voice said behind me before arms slid around my waist.

I leaned back into Don's wide chest and linked my hand with his. I played with the gold ring on his finger—his wedding ring. I'd never thought I would marry, but here I was: mated to Don and calling him my husband.

"It was Caleb's idea," I said. "And as the only drakcol in the know, I expect you to keep the secret."

He kissed my neck. "I don't divulge people's private thoughts."

We both stared at the fifteen foot monument of Lucy, Seth's black cat, in the middle of the first human settlement on the moon orbiting Tamkolvanloknol. We humans had voted to call the moon Terra. Caleb had suggested something wholly stupid—Dirtopia—but thank god, sense had prevailed. I'd been utterly terrified his name would win the vote for days.

But the drakcol, all besides Don, thought humans worshiped cats—the sheer amount of cat videos didn't help—and had erected a temple to our house gods. Caleb, being Caleb, had put in an order for a statue of Lucy in front of the temple. Seth had no idea.

Technically, I was in charge of Terra's development, but Caleb was helping, as were other humans. But I was going to have to turn over all of it to Caleb because Don had been ordered to the Immortal Planet again, and I refused to be left behind. Don and I would never be apart again. Also, the Crystal had genetically linked us in a private ceremony with his family, so we *couldn't* be apart again, which I very much liked, almost as much as I liked his thoughts and feelings always being in my brain.

Normally, you could still have privacy once you were connected by the Crystal, but because of Don's inner fire, our bond was so much stronger. We were connected all the time.

He kissed my neck, and I grinned.

The last six months had been magical, for the most part. I'd continued therapy, which was good, though man, it sucked and was hard work. I spent a lot of sessions crying, but like Camden had told me, it did help. Slowly but surely, I was working through what happened to me. Would it ever leave me? No. But I would survive and more importantly, thrive.

Don kissed me again, and I sighed, rubbing my hand over his arm. He'd started to trust me, talk to me, and finally, *finally* be selfish with what he needed. I fucking loved it when Don would ask for what he wanted, trusting me. It was sexy when he told me how much he needed me to hold him or fuck him or even when he needed a moment of space. I loved each request because it meant he was trusting me.

"I love you," he whispered against my neck.

I moaned. Why wasn't there a bed in one of the apartments? If there had been, I would have fucked him. Though the grass, while purple, looked rather soft. I bet Don wouldn't mind riding me. There was literally no one around. We could fuck in the middle of Lucyville with zero observers.

He took a deep inhale. "Mate, please."

I smirked. My husband was always desperate for me, and I loved it. "I'll take care of you at home, then."

"I would like that." He kissed my neck again. "I have a gift for you."

Turning around, I looked at him. "You do? Why?"

"Because I wanted to buy it for you."

That was a good enough reason, I guessed.

"It is," Don replied to my thoughts, though his smile was shy. It was a work in progress, but I loved his growing confidence with me.

I held out my hands, and he bent down to pick up a box. I frowned, expecting more jewelry, and opened the box. My mouth dropped open and tears burned my eyes. "You remembered."

"You said you couldn't have one because you couldn't give forever. Now you can."

I pulled out a small gray kitten with a smushed face. She was the crankiest looking kitten I'd ever seen, and I loved her already. I squished her close, earning an annoyed growl. "I love her."

"You deserve a house god, or goddess in this case, like any other human."

I looked up at my husband and fought tears. I'd always wanted someone to love me as much as I loved them, but I could never have planned for Dontilvynsan and how utterly perfect he was for me. He was everything I'd never known I'd needed.

Wyn

I stepped onto the *Admiral Ven* for the first time in three cycles. I couldn't believe I was back, and yet here I was. I looked at the familiar docking ring, and my tail twitched. There were things I loved about my tenure on the *Admiral Ven*—Seth, Urgg, and Edith to name a few.

The reason I'd dreaded coming back made himself known almost instantly—Commander Monqilcolnen.

Keeping my head down, I moved toward the lift that would take me to my bunk. Monqilcolnen didn't glance in my direction, which was a relief. I always said and did the wrong thing, tripping over my tongue when he was around. Monqilcolnen never, to my face at least, talked about my mistakes, but he would arch one of his eyebrows and it was enough to send my soul to my toes.

An elbow bumped me, and I started. Camden, another human who'd become my friend. "I'm excited to be going," he said.

"It should be a fun journey." I replied.

"You've been before, right? Some of the other scientists said that," Camden said.

"Yes. I was there when Prince Kalvoxrencol retrieved Seth."

"Retrieved," he repeated, chuckling. "I think you mean abducted."

As we turned to enter the lift, my eyes flicked back to Monqilcolnen, for some reason, and found him already looking at me. His golden eyes traced my face, and my breath slowed. Camden bumped his shoulder with mine, and Monqilcolnen arched one of his brows. My head instantly ducked, and I slipped inside, ready to escape his gaze.

This was going to be a very long journey.

Afterword

Back when I was writing *Cosmic Husband* and I wasn't sure if I'd ever do anything with the stories in my head, I wanted to write a book about Vince. The problem was that I couldn't picture who might be a good match for my eternally spiky baby. Then Dontilvynsan came in, and he oddly matched. My sweet, calm alien matched perfectly with my cranky, asshole human. It was so hard to picture their story, but I adored them so much that I had to try.

In so many ways, writing *Cosmic Captain* was the hardest thing I've ever done. Healing from trauma is not linear, so capturing that experience was difficult. But it was a necessary story to tell.

I wanted to listen to survivors' stories, to hear their words, and that's what I did. I watched so many videos of survivors speaking of their trauma and healing process. I read countless blogs. I read therapy journals regarding healing from sexual assault. I even spoke to my therapist friend about how someone with Vince's personality might react and heal. I spoke to multiple authors who had written about this topic and asked for advice as well as their opinion on several key scenes.

I did my absolute best to write this story as carefully and empathetically as possible. The last thing I wanted to do was harm survivors or do ill service to the horrific trauma they'd experienced. In light of that, I had the most wonderful sensitivity reader to make sure that I wasn't writing anything harmful. Rae Simmons, you were absolutely marvelous, and I want to say how much I appreciate you, your kind words, and your willingness to read my book!

People often say it takes a village, and I have a village to thank for this book!

Becca Neil, Logan Sage Adams, and Ally Avery: Thank you for giving me guidance, tips, advice, and encouragement. I wouldn't have been able to publish this book without you. All of you boosted my confidence and gave me so many things to think about. I can never thank you enough.

Jonathan Hawker: Thank you so much for answering my inane and sometimes awkward questions. I will always be eternally grateful that you and KJ adopted this baby trans dude who needed gay friends.

Lincoln Mercer: Thank you for helping me with my blurb and loving my guys as much as I do. And more than that, thank you for being my friend and my trans guru. You have been a light in my life, and that is something I'll never be able to repay you for.

Marra Moore, Christine Nolte, and Rae Laniley: Thank you so very much for beta reading for me! I couldn't have done this without you. The amount of typos, repetition, and issues you caught was amazing, and I'm beyond grateful to each of you for taking time out of your busy lives to help me.

Adie Hart: You are the best editor a person can ask for. You found typos, misplaced commas, and awkward sentences like no other. Thank you for working with me and being my friend.

Sam Northman: My British counterpart, the pot to my kettle, you know how much I love you, friend. But you not only read my book (and claimed Don as your husband), but you talked me off the ledge so many times. This book is here because you told me not to abandon it like I wanted to. I appreciate you more than I can express!

Adrienne Lothy: Babe, you're my sanity most days. Thank you for reading my book and loving it as much as I do. Your advice, kindness, and encouragement have meant the world to me. You're my ride or die, and I wouldn't be here without you.

RR friends: I love you all and appreciate your continued support.

Andra: Thank you for your never-ending support, loyalty, and love. Also, I appreciate you holding Monster when I needed to write and edit emotional scenes, and she was so very insistent that she *had* to protect me from my evil laptop.

Finally, thank *you* for reading my book. I'm so damn grateful for every one of you. It still shocks me when I see people reading, buying, and loving my books. Like, what? How is that possible? You're making my dream of being a full-time author more possible with every page you read. Thank you, Martians, for supporting this chaotic potato! I'll catch you in my next book or on my socials.

P.S. Yes, yes, *yes!* Wyn is the main character in my next book. Your wishes were heard, and you'll soon be able to read about his epic romance.

P.P.S. No, I couldn't put Lucy in this book more (she, like my Monster, is a shy creature), BUT you can see pictures of Monster on my socials. And for those of you who follow me, you've already met the inspiration for the cat who will be in Wyn's book.